FLEE

FLEET

RAYMOND HARDIE

Hodder & Stoughton
LONDON SYDNEY AUCKLAND TORONTO

British Library Cataloguing in Publication Data
Hardie, Raymond
  Fleet.
  I. Title
  823′.914[F]

ISBN 0-340-42349-8

· First published in Great Britain 1988

Published by Hodder and Stoughton,
a division of Hodder and Stoughton Ltd,
Mill Road, Dunton Green, Sevenoaks, Kent TN13 2YA.
Editorial Office: 47 Bedford Square, London WC1B 3DP.

Typeset by Hewer Text Composition Services, Edinburgh.
Printed in Great Britain by Biddles Ltd, Guildford and King's Lynn.

For Judith
with love and thanks

1

October 1936 was warm, not unseasonably so, but pleasant, in the gentle manner of an English autumn. Then on that Friday morning a cold wind started out of the east, coming from the vast, fertile plains of Poland and Germany. It blustered and squalled its way across Holland and Belgium until it reached the North Sea.

There, over that dark grey water, it gathered up a chill dampness and swept on towards the south-eastern corner of England. As it passed the Isle of Sheppey it seemed to taunt the massive hulks of the two China Fleet cruisers as they gently rolled at their new berths off the port of Sheerness. It spun around their gun turrets, rattled past their hatches, and then skimmed on out over the white-frothed surface of the River Medway.

On and on it careened, past the tugboats chugging to and from the wharves, through the elegant red-brick buildings at the Pembroke Naval Barracks, around the submarines being overhauled at the north-east corner of number-one basin. Finally it hurled its careless chill over the long brick wall and into the Royal Naval Dockyard of Chatham.

The man behind the long oak table sat perfectly still. The chill of that eastern wind did not penetrate the courtroom, and yet Lieutenant Commander Rupert Kingsland felt a series of shivers coursing through him. He quickly swept his arm up and ran his hand through his thinning brown hair. Normally he was vain enough to brush it to the side but now he didn't care. He sat up and stared straight ahead of him. He was a handsome man, with a long aquiline nose, high cheekbones and a broad, sensuous mouth. If there was any criticism of his looks, it was perhaps that he was too handsome.

He tried to steady his breathing and still his fears. As he did so, he recalled that morning two months ago, when the captain from Intelligence had stepped out of the car and followed him into number-seven slip. The captain had stopped him with a curt shout. "Lieutenant Commander Kingsland, a word please."

Kingsland gave a bitter smile now as he listened to the muffled sounds of the courtroom. What a wonderfully English understatement, "a word", for charges that would end a career. The captain had stopped him outside the open door of the painter's store and all through the long weeks of mulling over the charges, Kingsland was constantly reminded of that pungent smell. Now as he tried to suck in a calming breath he could smell that paint again.

He pressed his damp palms on his trousers and gently rubbed them backwards and forwards. At all costs he did not want to show them his fear, his unutterable sense of humiliation and shame. He looked up from the scarred surface of the oak table, and glanced towards the door at the back of the room. He could feel the beads of sweat gathering along his brow and deftly pulled out a handkerchief; he did not want them to run down his face like tears when the verdict came. He gave a small groan and tried to stop himself from thinking. He was certain there could only be one verdict, but he did not want to face that yet.

He looked up as the door opened. The officers stepped forward and took their seats behind the long table. It was all so simple and low-key, just a bare table with sparse furnishings. It was hard to believe that this was a court martial.

He glanced at the line of naval uniforms as they settled themselves in front of him. The whole process had a slow but awesome inevitability about it. He stared at the blue hats placed on the table, the gleaming brass buttons, the rings of gold braid on the sleeves. These were the Establishment, the senior officers, the powers that moved his world.

Vice Admiral Bennett-Clinton from Pembroke Barracks was the presiding officer. He stared at Kingsland for a moment, then leaned forward and cleared his throat.

Kingsland glanced back at him. He saw the rows of multicoloured ribbons across the vice admiral's dress uniform, the bluff, red sailor's face but, beyond all that, he saw the cold hostility in the deepset, steel-grey eyes and he felt his first thrust of real fear.

The muffled beat of the drums from the parade pounded through the window. The vice admiral gave a quick glance to an orderly and the window was shut with a resounding click, closing the court to the world beyond.

For a moment there was silence. It was agonising. Kingsland watched the vice admiral shuffling his notes. Everything was played out with such decorum and yet the final result was akin to a finely tuned torture.

Kingsland concentrated all his energy on remaining still. He felt like an actor aware that this was his moment in the spotlight. There was, however, nothing pretend about his circumstances, the shame was tangible.

"Lieutenant Commander Rupert Kingsland."

Everyone turned to look at the presiding officer. Kingsland pushed his chair back and stood to attention. The whole courtroom seemed to hold its breath.

"It is the verdict of this court martial that you have been found guilty of sodomy." Bennett-Clinton paused and settled his notes into a neat pile.

For a brief instant Kingsland sagged forward, and his hands grabbed at the lip of the table to try and steady himself. If the vice admiral had not been watching him closely he would have missed the momentary collapse of courage. Then with a forced intake of breath, Kingsland quickly gathered his strength, pulled back his head and once more stood erect.

The cool voice of dispassionate justice continued. "And it is our decision that you immediately relinquish the rights and privileges of an officer in His Majesty's Navy."

Kingsland felt sick. He maintained an outward-seeming calm but the lights, the table, the uniforms all started to drift disembodied before him. He thought of his father. Prize Days at school, when his father was housemaster. His mother lining up his cricket trophies . . .

9

". . . this judgment, being the unanimous verdict of the court, we declare these proceedings closed." The vice admiral looked up from his papers and there was a cold ringing silence. Slowly and with dignity, Kingsland sat down. Then the few other ranks present began to gather their papers and hats, the spell had been broken. And he felt nothing but a great and bitter numbness.

The wind whistled around the chimneys that topped the main dockyard entrance. A crowd had long since gathered and now they too could hear the insistent beat of the drum as the parade made its way from the Navy's Pembroke Barracks towards the main gate. Chatham was welcoming home its men. Those men who served their King and Empire at the other end of the world, the men of the China Fleet.

Captain James Kerr Hanley pushed his way through the throng. There were barmen and waitresses, apprentices and shop girls, squeezed together with gangs of scrawny, pasty-faced slum kids. Solid burghers stood side by side with the prostitutes who scoured the bars along the infamous Brook. All were united in their love of this rousing pageantry.

They turned to see Hanley as he passed. He was in all senses a man who suited a uniform. He was of only medium height, but his square shoulders and erect bearing made him seem taller. He had fair hair and a pale Saxon look. His light blue eyes had an intensity about them that alternately suggested a receptive intelligence and an iron will. It was a combination that sat easily with his position of authority.

The band turned the corner and the crowd surged forward to the line of "Crushers", the naval police. As they played, they followed the edge of the dockyard wall and marched down towards the main gates. It was a resplendent burst of colour and sound: shiny instruments and navy blue uniforms with one contingent shivering in the chill wind after months in the tropics.

Inside the high arch of the Georgian gate, Hanley stopped and glanced at his watch. They would be handing down the verdict any time now. He looked up towards the

10

small dockyard chapel with its simple white porticoed tower and for a brief moment considered stepping inside. A moment of peace on a bad day, a prayer for a friend. But then he shrugged. There was nothing that could change it now. Rupert Kingsland's future was to be decided in that court-room.

Instead Hanley turned right, down the path between the church and the dockyard wall and then continued along behind the garden of Medway House, Rear Admiral Walker's private residence.

The sound of drums rolled over the yards. The colour guard and colour party were now forming outside the admiral's offices, waiting to receive the flags from the China Fleet.

"Captain Hanley."

Hanley turned. Warrant Officer Campbell was standing behind him. He was a large bear of a man, with a bushy beard and a ruddy, amiable face. But now that amiability was gone. His eyes registered the news from the court. Hanley took one look and immediately knew the outcome. He turned away and glanced down towards the Old Pay Office and the river beyond. Somewhere in the distance the band was playing a solemn hymn.

"What is it?"

Hanley felt foolish asking the question. There could only be one verdict.

"Lieutenant Commander Kingsland's been drummed out."

Hanley raised an eyebrow and took a few steps towards the stone staircase that led down to the admiral's offices. Down along the riverfront he heard the band's sombre music reverberating amongst the covered slips.

"He was found guilty, sir." Campbell's voice was quiet but firm.

"Guilty." Hanley tried to absorb the word. He and Kings-land had met at Gallipoli. Twenty years ago. Twenty years of service all erased by a simple word, "guilty".

Campbell waited, then spoke again. "You have that meeting with the admiral, sir."

"Yes, yes." Hanley nodded, gave a bitter smile and then

11

started down the steps. Yes, careers might be ruined but, the work went on.

Rear Admiral Walker was not a patient man, even at the best of times. When he was particularly agitated his face would assume an icy stillness, betrayed only by the way he insistently tugged on his beard.

Immediately Hanley entered the office, he recognised the signs. Walker was standing by the window, holding the telephone receiver in his right hand and rhythmically tugging his beard with his left. In profile he looked like the late George V and there was a suspicion that it was a likeness he actively cultivated. He was not a tall man, and his years of deskwork had given him the suggestion of a paunch; however, there was the unmistakable iron of authority in his stance.

Hanley watched the hand tugging away at the grey and ginger streaked beard and noticed the eyes tighten with tension. "Yes sir. Yes." Walker spoke tersely into the phone. Hanley looked away; Walker was not one who enjoyed close scrutiny.

Walker's personal office was on the ground floor at the southern end of the building and had a magnificent bay window with a view of the Medway and Thunderbolt Pier. The walls were half-panelled up to about three feet and the upper portions were filled with blueprints of engines, drawings, charts, and noticeboards full of detailed schedules. Walker was a "hands on" admiral and Hanley admired his breadth of technical knowledge. Walker had his finger on the everyday pulse of the whole dockyard.

Hanley turned from the drawings and plans on the boards and once more glanced over at him. He heard the anger building behind Walker's clipped answers. "Yes sir, of course, any assistance we can give."

There was a moment's pause, then Walker put the phone down with a firm click. He turned away from Hanley and glared out of the window towards the pier, where the launches from the China Fleet cruisers were loading and unloading.

"Rear Admiral."

Walker's hand had fallen behind his back and he was now clicking his thumb and middle finger silently. After a moment he turned, stepped back to his desk and picked up a folder. "That was London."

Hanley watched Walker as he scanned the pages in the file. London? thought Hanley, then he nodded. Of course, Kingsland, it was about Kingsland.

Walker seemed distracted, lost in his thoughts. He picked up a pile of loose papers and settled them into a neat bundle.

"Take a seat, Hanley." As Hanley took a chair, Walker waited, and watched, as if he was assessing the situation, calculating what to say and what to leave unsaid. When Hanley had settled himself the rear admiral spoke again. "This Kingsland business has stirred up a hornet's nest."

"Perhaps," Hanley said with slow deliberation, "they should have given him the opportunity to resign quietly, sir."

Walker flashed him a dark, guarded look. "Hanley, the Admiralty don't give a damn about keeping this quiet. Perhaps it will serve as a lesson." There was an edge of venom in his voice. He paused and took a deep breath. "Anyway, with this new build-up of the fleet their main concern is security, everywhere, and what I care about is security in this yard."

Walker dropped the neat pile of papers on to the desk and once more started tugging at his beard. Hanley looked puzzled. "But there's been no breach of security." Then he paused, "Has there?"

Walker looked over at the large map of the dockyards on the wall behind the door. There was a momentary suggestion of evasiveness. He gave a brief sigh and continued, "It's the implication, Captain, when this kind of thing happens, then the whole yard suffers." He swung round and once more gazed at Hanley with that unwavering look of his. "If someone had kept a closer eye on your friend, then perhaps we could have dealt with it internally."

Hanley sat upright in his chair, bristling. "Someone, sir?"

The two men held their look steadfast, as if exploring

each other's motives. Hanley was not a man to bend in the wind. Finally Walker wavered. He gave a dismissive wave of his hand, stood up and walked to a filing cabinet. "Don't volunteer your head today, Captain, I'm not in the mood."

Hanley knew when silence was strength. He watched as Walker pulled a file from the cabinet, and glanced at it. "This Lieutenant Commander Crowe, when does he arrive to take over Kingsland's responsibilities?"

"He arrived this morning, sir. He sailed into Portsmouth a week ago, from Alexandria. He's just spent two days in London at the Admiralty and then . . ."

"Good, so he's here." Walker slapped the file down on his desk. He spoke softly but with great precision. "I want something understood, Captain. We cannot afford any delay, you understand, any delay, either in the launching of the *Graplin* or in its trials. This, this late change of command," here Walker paused as if he was stopping himself from saying any more. Then he took a breath and continued. "It mustn't be allowed to interrupt any of the scheduling, especially in the light of Kingsland's departure."

"Departure." Hanley winced at the euphemism and only half listened as Walker elaborated on the need for the *Graplin*'s prompt delivery. "The *Graplin* is to be commissioned into the China Flotilla . . . Japan's increasing threat to Indo-China . . . need to increase the number of mine-laying submarines so that we can isolate their ports . . ."

Finally, towards the end of the mini-lecture, Hanley interrupted. "Sir, I can assure you that the *Graplin* will be commissioned on schedule. I intend to work closely with Lieutenant Commander Crowe during all of the sea trials."

Walker stared at Hanley and saw by the firm set of his jaw that he was attempting to close the discussion. "Yes, well, perhaps you and I should lunch with Lieutenant Commander Crowe tomorrow, after you've briefed him."

"Yes, sir." Hanley quickly saluted, turned and left. The trick was not to give Walker time for another opening. It was only when he was halfway down the stairs that he realised the invitation was a conciliatory gesture. But conciliatory or not, it had come too late in the day. A throbbing headache had already settled in behind his eyes.

2

That morning while Chatham was feeling the first bitter blast of an easterly wind, the sun was shining down on Liverpool's grimy backstreets. It gave a breath of hope to an otherwise hopeless scene. Row upon row of high narrow tenements. Courtyards and alleyways with cracked pavements and puddles of dirty water, roads with unfilled potholes and missing paving stones. Worse than all of this, there were the smells, the unmistakable smells of poverty. The cracked sewage pipes, the sweet, sickening odour from the bone factory down by the docks, the acrid pall from the coke plant. But today, though the smells remained, the blue skies and sunshine lifted many a spirit.

As Kitty Cullen lay in bed she could see the bright sky behind the thin, patched net curtains. Her mother had tried to get her up over an hour ago but Kitty had managed to stay in bed until she left the flat. Then Kitty had drifted off into a light sleep thinking, One day, one day when I'm a film star they can all go and jump in the Mersey!

When she woke up, it took a few seconds for the reality of Culver Street to penetrate. As it did, she gave a curse and sat up. Then after rubbing her eyes, she swung her legs out and sat on the edge of the bed.

Kitty was not beautiful in the usual way. At times she could look positively drab, but at other times she could look stunning. Her attractiveness came from her surging energy. She had handsome rather than beautiful features, framed by thick, lustrous dark hair. She had a way of angling her head and tossing her hair aside that gave a taunting suggestion of a free spirit. But most of all it was her eyes, her dark eyes that either radiated a sparkling humour or drew men to her with their sultry, almost sexual languidness. One had to say "almost sexual" because men were continually confused by her demeanour. Always lurking behind those bedroom eyes there was a sharp bright intelligence and a cutting wit. She seemed at once a light-hearted girl and a calculating *femme fatale*.

At sixteen she had already learned to wear blouses and dresses that accentuated her better points. It caused many an argument between her and her mother. The words "I'll not have a daughter of mine going out like a tart" constantly rang in Kitty's ears. What right had her mother to talk to her like that? Was it being a tart to want to better herself, or to want to get out of a kip like this?

She had lived in this miserable bug-infested flat since she was six years of age. There were two bedrooms and a kitchen. They shared a bathroom with two other families on the same floor. The kitchen ceiling leaked over their dining table and almost every wall in the place had dark brown water stains running down the faded paper. Ten years they had lived here, ten years! Ever since her dad had left home. Not that she remembered much about her father. They still had a few photographs of him lying around in one of the drawers. From these, she could see that he looked like her eldest brother, Tom. A big, bulky, well-built, amiable Irishman.

She could not really remember him living with them. Not that he was forgotten, for her mother never let his memory die. It became so that every time Kitty heard the name "Billy" she knew she was going to hear something bad.

Kitty opened the door of her room and walked into the dark hallway. As she did, she caught that whiff of cabbage water and bacon grease and bad sewers. Kitty had come to think of it as the smell of poverty. It seemed to cling to her clothes no matter how far she went from Culver Street, or how much she scrubbed herself. It was one of the reasons she loved perfume because, for a few hours, she could forget that she was poor,

16

forget that she worked in that bloody dismal Glen Laundry, fingering other people's dirty clothes. She could imagine herself walking through one of the Beverly Hills mansions she saw in her film magazines. But not this morning. This morning the rancid smells of Culver Street were all-engulfing.

"No! No! No!"

She shouted out in a sudden surge of joy, grabbed a cup off the shelf above the sink, and poured herself some milk from the jug. Tonight they were all going to leave this dump! They were going to Chatham!

At the other end of the dim hall the ceiling sagged and dark brown rings in the paper showed where the damp was once more threatening to break through. The door directly beneath this bulge was ajar. She pushed it open and saw her brother, Ernie, sprawled out across the bed. His naked foot was sticking out from underneath the khaki-coloured army blanket. He was lying on his back and for a moment she stared at him. He had the careless, handsome looks of all the Cullen men. His dark curly hair had been flattened to one side by sweat, and his mouth lay open. She could smell the beer in the room.

"God but you're a louser!" she mumbled. Then she pushed aside the saxophone case that was lying by the door, picked up one of the shoes lying beneath it and threw it at the bed. It hit him on the thigh. Ernie jumped, opened his eyes and glared at her. "Wha' the hell!" he yelled.

"There's our mam out begging suitcases and here you are, lyin' on your fat arse," she paused and then continued in a louder voice, " . . . and we're only leaving because of you."

"I'm warning you, don't start that again!" he yelled. But Kitty was not to be silenced. She continued, "You gamble all your money, get into debt, and you've the nerve to lie there reeking of beer . . . you're just like our dad!"

Ernie simultaneously lurched forward, tossed his pillow at her and bellowed "Shurrup!!" Then he collapsed backwards and pulled the blankets over his head.

Kitty kicked the pillow then retreated out of the room, slamming the door behind her. She stood for a moment wondering at her own anger, then started along the hall. She was beginning to sound like her mother. Maybe it was just as well she was leaving! Maybe, when they got to Chatham, she should try and get away altogether.

Closing the front-room door behind her she crossed to the window, where her handbag was lying on an armchair. She opened it and pulled out the packet of Ballito silk stockings which Johnny McIvor had given her the night before. Carefully she opened it and slipped the stockings out. She had met Johnny at the Roxy dance-hall, down on Bridge Street, just over a month ago. He was a skinny, unprepossessing young man in his early twenties and when she caught the faint whiff of bad breath she'd almost refused him the dance. But Johnny worked for Flanagan, the bookie. While most of his mates were on the dole or scraping by as delivery boys Johnny could afford new clothes and even managed to run a battered Austin Seven.

There was however one small hitch in the relationship, and that was the fact that she actually didn't like Johnny. Every time he kissed her she was reminded of his clammy hands and his bad breath. And he was not content with kissing. Last night, there had been another wrestling match in the back of the car. They had driven down to the river and watched the Irish ferry sailing out. Underneath a flickering gaslamp, he had given her a bottle of Evening in Paris perfume and quickly told her that it had cost him "nearly thirty bob". He need not have bothered lying, she had memorised virtually every advertisement for perfume and knew that it cost only twenty-one shillings. However she said nothing. Getting the gift made her feel good. It reinforced what she had always thought, that she was worth more than a twopenny packet of chips and a pint of beer.

With the thought of the perfume, she had let him fumble around under her blouse for half an hour but God how she hated it.

"Creep!"

She leaned back on the bed now and slipped the silk stockings over her firm thighs. Then she smiled as she looked at them appraisingly. Not bad! Soon the Johnny McIvors of the world would be behind her! Soon she'd be sitting in a cocktail bar in Chatham, chatting to a group of naval officers, sipping a sophisticated glass of port and lemon.

Suddenly she heard the front door open and then slam again. It was her mother coming in! In a panic she pulled off the silk stockings and jammed them back in the package.

"Kitty, come on, get up . . . the maid's on strike this morning so you'll have to do."

Her mother half stumbled into the room carrying three empty battered cardboard suitcases and dropped them on the floor. She was panting, and used the cuff of her brown overcoat to wipe the sweat from her brow. When she had caught her breath she looked up at Kitty and registered fake surprise. "Where's the fire?"

Kitty glared at her, "What do you mean?"

"I mean you're up already," said Mary, taking off her overcoat.

Kitty tossed her hair back out of her eyes and pouted her lips like an impregnable movie star. It was her defence against her mother's wicked barbs. "Stop it, Mam, I'm looking forward to getting out of this slum, that's why."

"We'll have less of the slum business, thank you," said Mary. "When you're Lady Plusfours in your own castle you can afford to criticise. Where's Ernie?"

Kitty prodded one of the battered cardboard suitcases as though it was alive. "He's asleep, what else?" she said. Mary gave a look of disgust and threw one of the suitcases on to the bed. "This is for you," she said, "and I want all your packing done soon." Then she looked around the room and gave a sigh. "God but I'll be glad to get out of this place, I should've gone years ago. At least we'll be able to get work for all of us down there in Chatham. I know the Gillings'll help, especially since Albert's so well placed in the yards. And I bet you Tom'll have found us a lovely place."

Kitty listened to her mother ramble on, as she slipped off her nightgown and got dressed. She raised her eyebrows as she heard her mother mention Tom. It wasn't something Kitty would have done, bet on any of her brothers. The Gillings were another kettle of fish. It was hard to imagine someone in the family with money. She was just doing up the last button on her dress when she heard a loud banging on the front door.

Mary stopped talking and glanced around nervously. She was wondering who it could be. Her mind sped along as she tried to remember her debts. The rent man didn't come until tomorrow, and by then they'd all be gone. The man from Curry's had already repossessed their radio a month ago, because she couldn't keep up the repayments.

There was another loud knocking. Mary suddenly came alive. She grabbed two of the suitcases and shoved them under the bed, then she took the other one and thrust it on top of the wardrobe. "Here, go on and answer it now."

Kitty looked at her as if she was mad, then sauntered out and opened the door. There were two men standing in the stairwell. She instantly recognised one of them. Johnny had pointed him out to her in a pub one night. He was a "heavy" who worked for Olahan's, another bookie. Though Kitty was scared she didn't show it. Instead she produced a pert little smile. "Can I help you?" she asked.

The man who had been knocking at the door was heavyset and unsmiling. Still Kitty's charm was never completely lost. For a moment he fumbled for his words. "Well, yes. We're looking for Ernie Cullen." The smaller man who was standing back in the shadows at the top of the stairs moved forward. He was greasy looking, smooth talking. "Yes, luv, we're friends of his, you know."

Kitty gave them another lovely, innocent smile and replied, "Oh yes, well I'm sorry but he's not in at the moment, he's at work, but he'll be home by six." The smaller man watched her, a thin smile on his lips. She knew he was trying to gauge if she was lying or not.

Kitty turned her charm on him, smiled and continued, "My mam's in though, would you like to come in and join us for a cup of tea?" The one with the thin smile shook his head. "No, that's all right, luv, we'll see him later. It's nothing to bother your mum about."

They were just turning to go, when Ernie staggered out of his room, bleary eyed, and yelled out, "What's goin' on, Kitty? All

I want is a bit of sleep . . ." He barely had time to finish speaking before they pushed into the hall.

"Oh you're back home from work, isn't that nice?" said the one with the thin smile. Then he turned round on Kitty and saw Mary standing behind her. "We've just got to have a talk with your son there, Mrs Cullen."

Mary would have none of it. She pointed to the door. "Talk nothing, you can get out of here now."

But the big man had already pushed Ernie back into his room, where the latter was shouting his protests. "Who the hell're you? Let me go!" The door was slammed, and the man with the thin smile slipped in front of it.

Mary screamed at him, "You get outta my bloody place or I'll call the police."

The man nodded his head slowly. "I don't think any of us want to do that. A little talk, that's all we want and then we'll be back this evening, collecting, if you catch my drift."

The door opened and the big man walked out. He nodded to his companion and continued out into the stairwell. The little man flashed another of his cold, weasel-like smiles. "You see, nothing to it, a nice friendly visit."

He followed the other one, giving Kitty a wink as he passed. She slammed the door virtually on his heels and then collapsed back against it.

Mary ran into Ernie's room and saw him standing by the window, looking out. She noticed that his shoulders were slightly hunched and that he was holding his stomach. "Ernie."

He turned to her slightly and she saw that his face was ashen. "Mam, I'm scared." There were tears in his eyes.

He was almost a year older than Kitty, but she always saw him as the baby of the family. She walked over and put her arms around him. "It'll be all right," she said. "When they come back tonight all they'll find is the landlord's furniture, and they're welcome to it. But you learn a lesson, my lad, no more bloody gambling or I'll have your hide."

Kitty stood alone in the hallway, her back against the door. She heard her brother snivelling in his room. And though she loved him, she also felt a deep disdain. He seemed to stagger from one catastrophe to another, a weakling, not the kind of man she would ever marry! She gave a sigh and once more caught a whiff of the bacon grease and sewers. Oh Christ, she thought, I've got to get away from all of this, from all of them. Then she thought of the three railway tickets her mother had safely hidden in a pair of shoes in the wardrobe. Thank God for Tom. He might have complained but at least he had sent them the money. And please God, maybe Uncle Albert could find her a good job. Anyway tonight they would be in Chatham. It was a new world and she would start a new life!

3

Albert Gillings had heard the sound of the parade earlier as it left Pembroke Barracks and started up the public road towards the main dockyard gate. It floated over the yards, towards his office in the main dockyard offices between number-one and number-two basins. Altogether there were three large basins at the northern end of the yards, cutting across the large loop in the River Medway. They were vast expanses of water that could hold up to four hundred Navy ships, ranging from submarines to frigates.

Albert Gillings' full title was senior engineering foreman for submarines and small craft. But when his men saw his bowler hat bobbing into view, the snide title of "God" was more than occasionally applied. The nickname was not lightly used, for he held the lives and careers of over a thousand men in his hands.

On this day, however, he felt nothing but frustration. As he listened to the band music, he stood at his window and stared across the clutter of masts and funnels of the ships in dry dock.

One of the ships was HMS *Challenger*, a small eleven-hundred-ton naval survey ship, in to have its engine rebuilt. Gillings was supposed to have it out within a month. In another dry dock the submarine HMS *Starfish* was going through a major refit. Beyond that, at the northern edge of number-one basin, was "submarine corner", where two more submarines were in for electrical alterations and battery changes.

"Damn it." He glanced down at the report on his clipboard. This was not a time for new problems.

He had just returned from a four-day trip to Portsmouth and everything seemed to be in chaos. The latest submarine, the *Graplin*, was scheduled to be launched from number-seven covered slip in three weeks. Scheduled, that is, until he had returned to discover these strange delays on the engineering side.

He cleared his throat with an angry groan and then slammed the window shut, closing out the smooth, liquid tones of the brass. He stood for a moment looking out at the grey choppy water, tapping the clipboard against the sill. He was not a tall man, but he had a lean muscularity that gave him a commanding physical presence. He had short, dark, wavy hair streaked with white, and it framed pleasant, almost handsome features. His nose was strong and his broad mouth always seemed to harbour the suggestion of a smile. But it was his green and hazel eyes that held men's attention. In argument they flashed with a sharp, icy logic. They told his workers that here was a man who knew what he wanted and, what's more, would get it.

He knitted his brow as he watched a locomotive shunting along with its load of steel plate, then gave a grunt of disgust. The *Graplin* couldn't get behind. It couldn't. Or the damned brass'd have his guts for garters.

The submarine, *Graplin*, sat inside number-seven slip like a long, sleek, grey shark. With only three weeks to go before launching, the whole place pounded with sound. Shipwrights, boilermakers, electricians, riveters, carpenters all jostled with each other contributing to the cacophony. The workmen scrambled around the fat grey tube, moving backwards and forwards, in and out and up and down, like ants serving their queen.

Wallis, the electrical foreman, had no time for such metaphors. He hurriedly walked along the side of the slip and into the empty office. There he unrolled the blueprints for the *Graplin*'s electrical circuits and spread them out across the desk. Then he pulled out the report on work completed, and quickly scanned the complex pattern of blue lines.

Suddenly the door opened and Gillings strode in. He jabbed his finger at the plans and glared at Wallis. "How the hell did this happen?"

Wallis swallowed nervously and shrugged. "Gates is down there now, he says if he works with his electricians he can make it up by launching . . ."

Gillings swung away and pointed to the gigantic hull lying down in the slipway. "Gates is the electrical superintendent. How the hell's he going to "supervise" the electrical work on a three-hundred-foot submarine if he's working with a screwdriver in the engine bay?"

Wallis waited for a moment to see if the question was purely rhetorical. Then he cleared his throat. "Well, to be fair, Mr Gillings. He has had problems that are beyond . . ."

Gillings snatched the blueprint from the desk and thrust it at the other man. "He's paid to have bloody problems!" Then he turned and strode out of the office towards the submarine. Wallis quickly rolled up the blueprints and followed.

On the inside, the *Graplin* looked like a long dark tube. It had not yet been divided into its various compartments, but here and there a half-constructed metal wall broke the monotony.

Gillings followed a bundle of thick black electrical cables to where they disappeared into a gaping hole in the deck, then leaned over and shouted, "Mr Gates!" There was no reply. For a second he looked up and glanced along the boat. Strings of bare electric bulbs stretched into the distance lighting up the activities of the various workgangs. The whole place throbbed with the echoing sounds of work in progress.

He knelt down and shouted again, "Mr Gates!"

This time an irritated voice replied, "Yes, what the hell is it?" Then a balding head stuck out from under the deck. His scowl immediately disappeared as he recognised the senior engineering foreman. A visit down here did not bode well. "Oh, eh, Mr Gillings."

Gillings immediately stood up. Kneeling at this time was distinctly unsuitable. "I want to speak to you, Gates." His voice was cool and authoritative. Gates glanced back at the job left undone behind him. "I'll be up in a minute, Mr Gillings." As soon as he said it he could have bitten his tongue.

Gillings eyes flashed cold anger. "You'll be up bloody now!" Then he turned on his heel and walked to the other side of the hull.

Gates quickly climbed out of the battery bay and gave a quick glance over at Wallis. Christ, it was gonna be one of those days. He wiped his hands along the back of his overalls and then stumbled across the deck, kicking aside cables, screws, bolts and other debris.

"Well, Mr Gillings, I suppose you've just heard this morning . . ."

Gillings interrupted, "We've had enough of supposing, Mr Gates. I want some facts, you understand, facts." He spat the word out like a challenge to arms, then continued. "But you *are* right, this morning was the first, mark you, the *first* I'd heard of any delay."

Gates glanced over at Wallis who was studiously counting the bolts lying on the floor. Gates quickly gathered that he was on his own. He continued, "I thought I'd be able to catch up if I got down there with the men myself."

"Well, it doesn't seem that you have caught up, does it?" replied Gillings with scarcely concealed contempt. He had the pressure of knowing that the Admiralty were not tolerant of delays. There was now a panic over Mussolini's new navy in the Mediterranean and a long list of ships had been slotted in for modernisation. The last thing the Admiralty wanted to hear was that launchings were falling behind schedule. The clatter from that row of falling dominoes would resound all the way up Pall Mall.

Gates however had more immediate concerns. He burst out angrily, "I know all about the engine schedule but I can do no more. I've lost my chargehand Harry Daniels and two of my best electricians."

Gillings glared at him as though he was an idiot. "Lost? What the hell're you talking about?"

Gates and Wallis exchanged surprised looks. Then Gates continued in a quieter tone, "Well, you know, they've been taken over to that new research place or whatever it is behind the torpedo section."

Gillings looked genuinely puzzled. "No I don't know. What're you saying? I signed no one out of any of your gangs."

Gates shuffled from one foot to another. He sensed another storm gathering. "Captain Hanley did. I thought you knew. Two weeks ago."

Gillings made his way through the maze of low buildings near the torpedo shed. He was puzzled as to why his electricians were needed for torpedo work, especially when the *Graplin* was behind schedule. Some two months ago, Hanley had mentioned this research unit being set up. But Gillings had enough to do overseeing the engineering section of the yard without following every new device the torpedo section worked on. He turned a corner and noticed the small painted sign on the wall opposite him. It was written in neat black letters: *Dr Philip Grainger*. There was a metal door beside it with most of its grey paint blistered or peeling. Grainger, yes that was the name of the boffin in charge of the research. Gillings stepped over to the door and pushed it open.

Inside there was a small foyer, with doors leading off to either side. At the back there was a desk, and around the walls were a number of bulletin boards, cluttered with yellowing notices. As the outside door closed behind him, Gillings heard the short sharp ring of an electric bell. Then the door to the left swung open, and a young naval rating stepped out. For a brief moment, Gillings caught a glimpse of a darkened workshop and heard a strange high-pitched sound like a radio malfunctioning.

26

The rating slammed the door behind him and crossed to the desk. "Are you delivering something?" He had a gruff Scottish accent.

Gillings shook his head and answered, "No." The rating had pulled out a clipboard with a list of names on it. He looked up with a frown. "Well, you cannae come wandering in here, as you please."

Gillings bristled. "What did you say to me?" The rating pulled himself up straight. Gillings suddenly realised there was something about the cut of the man, it suggested naval police. The rating tossed the clipboard on the desk and glared at Gillings. "Listen mate, I dinnae want an argument."

That was the last straw. Gillings stepped forward and they were now eyeball to eyeball. No one, naval police, Admiralty brass, boffins, spoke to him like that. The cold cut of his anger was obvious in his tone. "My name is Mr Gillings, I am the senior engineering foreman in these yards. I am not addressed as mate, not by anyone! You understand?" The rating absorbed the information and then gave a quiet little smile. "Well I'm sorry, Mr Gillings sir, but you still can't go in. Not without a pass from Dr Grainger or Rear Admiral Walker."

Gillings stood for a moment and waited for the half-smile on the man's face to fade. Then Gillings gave his own cold smile, "Thank you for the information. I'll be back." With that he turned on his heel and walked out.

4

The crowd outside the main dockyard gates had not yet dispersed. The sounds of the Navy band were carried up from the parade ground and swirled round by the wind. It was a free

spectacle, to be enjoyed by all. Soon the sailors would be coming out. All around there was talk of Hong Kong, Singapore, Macao, Shanghai. England after two years! The bars would be booming, the clubs, the brothels. Chatham not only serviced the ships; through the centuries it had learned to service the fleet in many other ways.

Kingsland was one man who did not share this general mood of rejoicing. He slipped out of the door to the right of the main gate like a shadow. He looked grey and haggard. The collar of his trench coat was pulled up and he was clutching the front, as if closing it against the wind. For a brief second he stopped and sagged back against the wall, oblivious to the noisy crowd around him.

Kingsland had upheld a proud front all through the trial and now he could do it no more. He felt broken, drained of all energy. He knew there were a few more things to do, affairs to be settled, but just at this moment he felt that he did not have the stamina to go on. There was something about being outside the dockyard wall, amongst this raucous crowd, that emphasised the exposure and humiliation he had been through. His legs felt weak and for a second the crowd, the wall, the gates seemed to reel around him.

From this moment on the comradeship, the camaraderie was gone. Hanley, Campbell, Gillings, Walker, they would continue, focused on their work, feeling needed, a part of something greater. But now he was truly beyond the wall and there was no way back. He felt himself slipping and gasping for breath. He clutched at the wall and steeled himself, no, no, not here.

He dragged himself up and stared across the throng of hangers-on. Whatever way it ended, he would not allow himself to become one of that crowd. He would choose death before insignificance.

Yes, yes. He was still a Kingsland. He took one last quick look through the gate, straightened up, and skirting the crowd started down the long road, under the shadow of the dockyard wall.

Consumed in his own thoughts he did not notice the man who walked out of the crowd and started to follow him.

28

5

Eunice Hanley held tight to the strap of the taxi as it rattled across the roadworks. They were turning into Bayley Street from Tottenham Court Road, swinging out past mounds of dark clay.

"Sewage pipes," the cabbie volunteered. Then he waved his hand airily at the gang of navvies and continued, "See what I mean, this unemployment malarky's a load of old codswallop. I'm sick of hearing about Jarrow, there's work all over the place, but all these friggin' northerners wanna do is sit on their bums, instead of gettin' up and looking."

Eunice nodded distantly. She was absorbed in her own thoughts. She felt like a schoolgirl playing truant, yet she was sick of sitting at home alone. Hanley seemed to spend more and more time at the yards or out on sea trials. And in the last few weeks she had scarcely seen him at all. Last night when she had received the invitation from Olivia it was like a clarion call. One of Lady Olivia Brampton's fashionable soirées in London! She had told no one the truth, she had just said she was going shopping. Hanley did not like Olivia and had never made a secret of it. But then Hanley had never shown much liking for any of her old friends.

She had known Olivia since Roedean. They had both had their coming out in 1919. It was a crazed year. London was full of young men who seemed surprised to be still alive after the Great War, and desperate to enjoy something of life before it was snatched from them. Eunice had been "stepping out" with a friend of her brother's, Harry Cruikshank Rawlston. He was a shy, rather lanky young man who had just returned from an infantry brigade in northern France. Each night a group of them would go off to the theatre, or a party, or a restaurant, invariably ending up at some nightclub. One night a young naval lieutenant had joined them. He was handsome in that careless unposed manner and there was something different in his intense blue eyes. Unlike many of her friends, here was someone who knew where he was going, someone to whom the word ambition was not a bitter word. That was how she first met James Kerr Hanley.

The cab rolled to a halt. She paid the driver, got out, and then stood for a moment looking around her. She loved Bedford Square. There was a kind of subdued arrogance in Georgian architecture that proclaimed a certainty about the order of the universe. It was something to grasp at when there seemed to be only chaos in her own life.

"Darling, up here!"

Eunice looked up and saw Olivia leaning out of the second-floor window. Olivia smiled and continued, "Do come up, you look like a stray cat."

This was Olivia's *pied-à-terre*, as she called it, her "fashionable urban retreat". Eunice had never understood why anyone would want to retreat from the splendour of the estate in Gloucestershire. But then it was best not to enquire too closely into Olivia's life with Lord Brampton, her husband. He was often away on business in France and Egypt and occasionally Malaya and during those times Olivia, as she herself said quite openly, "enjoyed her freedom".

Olivia met her at the door, waving her maid aside. She took Eunice by the hands and slowly twirled her round. Eunice could see Olivia's languid, pale blue eyes taking her in and she suddenly felt self-conscious. She was dressed for a day's shopping, in a forest green, belted, cape jacket and a slim black skirt. But at the top of the stairs she could see women in evening dress.

"Oh, I don't think I'm dressed for a party."

Olivia leaned back and gave Eunice a quick appraisal. "Sweetie, you look slim and beautiful, what's more you look as though you're dressed for anything, let alone a party." It was true Eunice was still an attractive woman, with her lithe athletic figure and strong, prominent cheekbones. She gave a giggle and started to undo Eunice's thin black belt. "Take off your jacket; your blouse and skirt are simplicity itself."

Eunice gave a shy laugh and let her friend undo the silver buckle and help her out of the coat. She swept her long dark hair back from her forehead and as she did so, Olivia noticed a twinkle in her friend's brown eyes, a wayward energy that she had not seen for years.

Olivia finally pulled off the jacket and gave it to the maid, then she took Eunice by the wrist and gently tugged her up the stairs.

The languid sound of a Noël Coward tune from *Bitter Sweet* drifted down from the piano in the drawing room above. Eunice glanced through the railings of the banister and saw small groups of men and women talking and laughing. This was everything she had hoped and feared. She felt another wave of panic and glanced back at Olivia who was half turned towards her on the stairs above. "There's a young poet I want you to meet, à la Eliot, *très chic* if you like long greasy hair."

Olivia started up the stairs again and for the first time Eunice noticed her friend's daring backless evening gown. It was a Schiaparelli in wine-red satin jersey and it fell in long folds from her waist. It gave Olivia's small figure a strange mix of sexuality and fragility.

"So, darling, here we are, my monthly homage to bedlam." She flashed Eunice one of her bewitching, crooked smiles and gently pulled her into the crowded room. Eunice paused for a moment and felt submerged. The lilting voice of the young blond tenor at the piano, the blue haze of cigars and French cigarettes, the smell of cocktails and perfume.

Olivia sensed her discomfort and whisked her through the crowd to a small bar in the corner.

"Come on, what's your poison?"

"Whisky and soda."

Olivia first sent a maid off with another full tray of champagne and then set about making Eunice's drink. Meanwhile Eunice gazed around her, feeling like a hungry urchin with her face pressed against the bakery window. It had been a

31

long time since she had mixed with such glittering people. Her life was filled with weekly visits to the veterans in the naval hospital, bridge games with the other officers' wives, talk about the yards and its ships. Masts, prows, sterns, torpedoes. Navy, Navy, Navy . . .

"Brampton's up the Nile again, of course, in Sudan. He has some new partners in his ghastly cotton business, Egyptian Jews, educated in France."

Eunice was suddenly caught off guard. It was a sharp penetrating gaze. The man was tall and blond. He was talking to a rather effete young actor and his female companion. The woman, who must have been in her early fifties, was obviously rich. She had squeezed herself into a long winter green dress with rings of gold fringe from the waist to the ankles. Eunice gave a wicked smile and thought how much she resembled a long lampshade. The blond man returned her smile, thinking it was meant for him, and for a moment Eunice was flustered.

He was staring straight at her with intense steel-blue eyes. His gaze was nakedly appraising, and even his smile had a cool, almost arrogant edge to it.

"You're not listening, Eunice," Olivia said as she thrust the drink into her hand.

Eunice smiled, took the whisky and replied, "Of course I am."

But Olivia was too quick. She glanced across the room and saw the man. "Aaah, Herr Weichert! He is a handsome sod, isn't he?"

Eunice took a slow, delicate sip of her drink and gave a bored shrug. "I suppose."

Olivia leaned across the glass-topped bar and drooped her eyelids. "Well, sweetie," she said in a low throaty whisper, "if you get the trousers off him, you get the pot of gold. He has a reputation as a military machine."

Eunice caught the man's eye again and felt a strange schoolgirl shiver of excitement. No, Olivia was wrong. There was something else there, something dangerous, a coldness, like cracked ice, but also something enticing and yet elusive.

She quickly looked back at Olivia who was rattling on as she adjusted one of her diamond earrings.

"Anyway, dear Brampton won't be home for another month or so. So once again I'm a cotton widow!" Somehow Olivia did not seem too sad at the prospect.

"Olivia, I have not met your friend."

A young man, barely in his mid-twenties, had materialised beside them. He had jet-black hair and a well-groomed moustache. His eyes were dark and imperious and there was something too about his fine cheekbones and the curl of his lips that suggested privilege and wealth.

"Count Andrezzino, I would like you to meet a dear friend of mine, Eunice Hanley." The young man flashed an enigmatic smile, leaned forward and kissed her hand. He was gracious and polite, but barely, for he kept his eyes continually on Olivia. It was obvious that something was smouldering between them.

Andrezzino let go of Eunice's hand and smiled at Olivia. "I am not a count yet, Olivia. You must allow my father a few more years of life." Then he turned back to Eunice, "Please, call me Antonio."

Eunice nodded and gave a reserved smile. Olivia stepped forward and gently laid her hand on his arm. Though it was a simple gesture there was also something very intimate about it. "Antonio is an aide to Count Grandi, the Italian ambassador," she said. "We first met in Rome, earlier this year when Brampton and I were visiting."

"Eunice? Is that you?" She spun round immediately, recognising a voice from her past. Harry Rawlston was walking towards her. He still had that boyish smile and lean lanky figure, but his brown hair was thinning at the front and greying at the sides.

"Harry!" That was all Eunice could manage. They stopped and stared at one another, not knowing what to say next. It had been almost sixteen years. Harry had left to run a plantation in Malaya the year after she had married Hanley.

Eunice looked quite stunned and Olivia stepped forward apologetically. "I'm sorry, it's my fault, I was playing", Olivia was about to say "matchmaker" but decided against it, "silly buggers. I invited you both because Harry'd just returned. I . . ."

"That's all right, Olivia, it was just a surprise." Eunice turned to Harry and continued, "It's good to see you."

Olivia gave an arch smile. "Why don't you both go off and catch up on the 'lost decade'?"

And that was what they did. They drifted over to a quiet spot by one of the high Georgian windows and talked. They found that the years had mellowed any residue of bitterness and allowed the warmth and caring of their youth to flow back.

She heard about his marriage to the daughter of an English banker living in Singapore. Then about their subsequent divorce, his bouts of malaria, his successes in the rubber business, the death of his father and his inheritance of the title and estates.

"So that's why I came back," he continued. "In a way I'd have preferred to stay there. That's where I'd made my life, but then things change, don't they, and you suddenly find that you have to go with them." She nodded in reply and glanced past him across the room. Yes, Weichert was still there. The words rang in her head. "Things change and you have to go with them." She quickly turned away and glanced out of the window. The dusk was well advanced and the silhouetted trees swayed starkly in the tugging wind. She had a sudden feeling of foreboding. She had stayed here long enough, the family would be wondering where she was. She handed her glass to Harry and said, "I'll be back in a moment."

She walked through the room looking for Olivia and then went out into the hall. She suddenly wanted to find her friend and tell her that she had to go. She rationalised that she had had her day's release from Chatham, her "yearly excursion".

Suddenly he was beside her. His English was clear and crisp and there was a warmth in his voice that belied the coldness of his eyes. "Please excuse me, I hope I am not being forward. I wanted to introduce myself before I left. My name is Commander Hans Weichert. I am the German naval attaché here in

34

London." He gave a quick formal bow of his head and then a surprisingly warm smile. "And your name?"

"Eunice, Eunice Hanley."

"Aaah." It seemed that somewhere that name rang a bell, but he did not comment. He merely bowed again. "Well, I have to leave but I hope we will meet again perhaps at Lady Brampton's?"

"Perhaps." She gave him a nervous, fleeting smile. He turned away and disappeared down the stairs. For a moment she stood there not knowing what to think. Then she shook herself. She would find Olivia.

A claque of young people were standing around the stairs arguing the comparative merits of T. S. Eliot and Auden. Eunice looked around with no success and then glanced up to the next floor. Olivia was probably up in her studio.

Eunice caught the first whiff of oil paints and smiled. Everywhere Olivia had lived she had seemed to bring that smell with her. Eunice remembered the rambling set of rooms Olivia had shared with a group of young artists in Paris, but that was before she met Lord Brampton.

At the top of the stairs she opened the door into Olivia's studio. It was a large room, with massive skylights. The last fading light of the day filled the place with the long shadows of easels and canvases. Olivia was nowhere to be seen. Eunice looked past the easel with a large "work in progress" towards a long dividing curtain. She knew that beyond that there were two doors, one was a storeroom and the other a photography darkroom. Perhaps she was in there showing some of her plates.

Eunice crossed the studio, consumed with her own problems, then she stopped short. Somewhere she heard the sound of laboured breathing. She walked forward to a break in the curtains and looked through. The door to the darkroom was open. There was a dim red lamp on inside and in its lurid light she saw Olivia lying on the floor with the young Italian, Andrezzino.

Eunice was stunned. Her first impulse was to turn away, flee the room, and yet she didn't. Instead she continued to watch as the pace of their lovemaking quickened. She felt hypnotised.

35

There was her friend lying on the floor, breaking all the rules, abandoning herself to the careless passion of the moment. She watched transfixed as Antonio ripped aside the top of Olivia's dress and grabbed hungrily at her friend's breasts.

Eunice could barely swallow. She wanted to find some censure in her heart but she couldn't. She could only feel a strange thrill in her friend's debasement. She saw Antonio biting at Olivia's ear and then running his tongue along the side of her neck and on to her bare breast. He caught her erect nipple between his teeth and Olivia groaned, then she slipped her hand down and pulled greedily at his trousers. Her dress slipped up along her thigh and revealed the slash of white flesh at the top of the silk stockings.

Eunice fell back into the shadow of the studio and tried to steady her shaking hands. She felt that something had snapped inside her. A door had opened, both literally and figuratively, and there was a thrilling yet frightening darkness looming beyond it.

She took a deep breath, steadied herself and walked out of the darkened room. "I hope we will meet again." Weichert's words rang in her mind. But anyway there was more than just him. Harry Rawlston, her old love, was downstairs in a room full of exciting men. Why should she not resurrect her life? Why should she not resurrect past passions? She was not dead yet, and what had Hanley and Chatham to offer her but stultifying boredom?

She shut the door of the studio, closing in the rising sounds of their illicit passion. She stood for a moment in the shadows and caught her breath, then she started down the stairs towards the music and conversation.

6

"Captain Hanley."

Hanley glanced up from the papers on his desk. Warrant Officer Campbell was leaning in through the doorway. Hanley recognised the bemused look on his face. Campbell had a finely tuned sense of humour and also a well-developed sense of impending trouble.

"Mr Gillings is outside, sir . . . in my office." Campbell nodded as if to underline the implied note of caution.

"Ah, I see. Just give me a second or two, and bring him in."

"Yes, sir."

Hanley gave a sigh and then glanced out of the window into the twilight. The lamps around number-two dry dock had just been lighted. It was in this dock that HMS *Victory*, Nelson's flagship, was laid down in 1759. He found that sense of continuity in the yards reassuring.

He lifted the chart he was working on and took it to one of the many boards on the walls around his room. The walls were half-panelled and above the panelling they were crammed with charts, graphs and diagrams. He replaced a roll of blueprints in one of the pigeonholes above his angled drawing table and then opened the door.

"Come in, Mr Gillings."

As Gillings walked in, Hanley settled himself back behind his desk and slowly screwed on the cap of his fountain pen. He nodded towards one of the chairs by the wall. "You look worried, Mr Gillings, take a seat. Is there something wrong in number-seven?"

Gillings barely perched himself on the edge of the chair. He looked wary, tense, like a man waiting for combat. "No, Captain, no, there's nothing wrong with the *Graplin*, yet . . ."

37

Hanley leaned forward. It had been a difficult enough day without having to deal with any further problems. "Please, Mr Gillings, I am not in the mood for riddles."

"Neither am I, sir, that's why I came over here right away, to find out why my electricians have been moved to Dr Grainger's new research project without my knowledge."

Hanley stared at the other man, his brain slowly ticking over, taking in the moment. Then he opened the top drawer of his desk. "Ah yes, yes, Dr Grainger." He tapped the navy blue cover for a moment, then flicked through it and glanced up. "I believe we had a meeting about this project on the twentieth of August, seven weeks ago, just before Philip Grainger and his men moved in."

Gillings remembered that meeting but he was certain there had been no mention of men being moved from duties in the yards. He began to suspect that Hanley was being evasive. "I know about the Grainger project, Captain. At least as much as the Admiralty cared to tell me. What I'm concerned about is that my electricians have been pulled off the *Graplin* without my knowledge."

Hanley fished in his jacket pocket, then pulled out his pipe. He was obviously playing for time as he knocked it in the ashtray and then began to fill it with tobacco. "I think you should know, Mr Gillings, that the Admiralty have given top priority to this."

"I'd gathered that." Gillings let his sarcasm sink in and then continued. "However, I think it's obvious I should be told when any of my men are moved. Firstly it affects my authority and that's bad for discipline in the yards, and secondly there's a boat supposed to be launched in three weeks."

"What do you mean, supposed to be?" Hanley sat forward and slapped the bowl of his pipe against his open palm.

"I mean, that unless I start shifting men from work all over the yards to compensate, we're not going to have the bloody electrical work on the *Graplin* finished on time."

Hanley walked to the window and then swung round. "Mr Gillings," his speech was clipped, his tone forceful, "I have just come back from Rear Admiral Walker, he was most insistent

38

that we stick to the *Graplin*'s schedule. You will take your electricians from wherever you can. Do you understand me?"

Gillings waited, holding in his temper. "Yes, Captain, I understand, but I still resent my workers being pulled out of their gangs and hidden away inside some secret project in the middle of the yards."

Once again Hanley slapped the bowl of the pipe against his palm. "It's hardly secret."

Gillings raised a sceptical eyebrow. "If it isn't secret, then what's this about passes and being stopped at the door?"

Hanley gave a tired sigh as though he did not deserve this at the end of such a day. "Ah, you've been up there. Well, our scientist friends asked for restricted access, and that's what we gave them. I'll be honest with you, Mr Gillings, I know as much as you do about what's going on."

There was a silence and Gillings knew that there was no more to be said. He nodded at Hanley, obviously unconvinced. "Yes, Captain, I see. Well, we'll just have to make sure nothing else gets in the way of this launching." Gillings stood up.

Hanley gave a cool smile. "Fine. If that's all, Mr Gillings, we'll talk tomorrow."

Gillings turned and walked out. He was obviously not happy. Hanley crossed to his drawing table, pulled out the blueprints for the *Graplin*'s mine tubes, and clipped them on. He took down a ruler, a pencil and a pad and started on a series of calculations. They were not necessary, but then Hanley used his maths like some men play the piano, as a sanctuary, a release. Too much had happened today. He felt overloaded like a hot battery.

One set of specifications made no sense and he stepped over to a small mahogany bookcase containing a set of thick drawing books. Submarine officers were expected to be able to make detailed technical drawings of a boat's working parts. Hanley was proud of his manuals and continued to use them daily.

As he knelt and pulled one of them out, Campbell knocked and entered.

"I've made arrangements for Lieutenant Commander Crowe to go over the *Graplin* tomorrow, sir. Also, after he meets

Rear Admiral Walker, we should take him over to Mr Gillings." Campbell paused and waited for a response to his mention of Gillings' name, but Hanley merely grunted. He was not to be drawn. Campbell continued, "If you have nothing else, sir, I'll make my way back to Pembroke Barracks. I'm having a drink with Warrant Officer Greaves tonight. He's off to Liverpool tomorrow, Cammell Laird are starting another T-class submarine."

Hanley nodded. "Oh yes. No, that's fine, you go on. I've nothing else."

They stood for a moment, like runners catching their breath after a race. It had been a long, painful day. Neither of them had mentioned Kingsland since that brief meeting on the steps just after the sentencing, but now they could almost feel his presence. Many an evening the three of them had spent here in this office, going over the day's events.

Campbell cleared his throat awkwardly. "I saw the young rating today, sir. The one that was involved, the one that gave the evidence against the lieutenant commander."

"Oh, did you?" Hanley drifted back towards the window.

"Yes. He was going back to Belfast, he said."

"I see." Hanley stood beside his desk chair and ran his hand along the worn dark brown leather at the back. "Slim evidence in the end, wasn't it. One man's word against another's."

Campbell shifted uneasily. "No sir, not really. I had a friend in court. He told me that they'd had a lot of evidence from a Captain Marsh about other, well, others."

"Yes, I," Hanley gave an embarrassed cough, "I see." Then he turned and looked at the other man. Campbell really did have his finger on the pulse of the yard. Not much escaped his attention. He was like a rock of certainty in times of crisis. And yet he had problems of his own, problems that would have sunk a lesser man. As Hanley stared at him he noticed the tiredness around his eyes.

"How are the new quarters, Mr Campbell?"

"Fine, sir. I still keep the house. Got a teacher renting it, has a young family. And it's better being up in Pembroke Barracks now that, well," Campbell's voice faded out.

"How is your wife?"

"Oh, fine. As well as can be expected, sometimes she even recognises me when she's not hearing her voices." He gave a mirthless laugh, to cover his embarrassment, and then stepped back towards the door. "Well, sir, I should go."

"Yes. Have one for me, Mr Campbell. I think we deserve it after today."

After Campbell had gone, Hanley turned to his calculations again. But he quickly tossed his pencil aside. He glanced at the shelf between the windows where he kept photos of Eunice and his children, Nigel and Elizabeth. They stood in small gilt frames between photos of the crews with whom he had served.

He ought to be thinking about leaving, himself. The prospect of going home was not altogether inviting. For the last six months Eunice had oscillated between silent hostility and loud arguments, the latter often inspired by alcohol. He knew things were going wrong and he knew that he shared the blame but tonight he just couldn't face another blow-up. Then he thought of Campbell's troubles and his unstinting devotion to his wife, how he paid a fortune to keep her in the best asylums, and he felt a twinge of guilt. He should go home, he had scarcely spent an hour with Elizabeth and Nigel in the last month.

He unlocked his bottom drawer and pulled out three large files. He was about to put them into his briefcase when he stopped. He had spent hours with Kingsland talking over this material. All day long he had pushed his friend to the back of his mind but now the day's events started rushing back with a vengeance.

Hanley kicked the drawer shut with a bang. Sometimes the Admiralty had a way of making all the efforts of a career seem worthless. And yet what would he say to Kingsland, when he met him next? How would he treat him after this court martial? And then the thought came to his mind that perhaps he shouldn't meet him again. Kingsland was now for ever on the other side of that dockyard gate.

"Damn!" One of the files slipped from his grasp and spilled a series of photographs across his desk and on to the floor. They were photographs of submarines in various stages of construction. In one of them a large Swastika flag was draped over the prow. Hanley started to pick them up, then stopped and sat down.

This had become his fixation over the last year or two. He had got these photographs from friends, two Dutch engineers who worked in the Deutsche Werke shipyards in Kiel.

Under the terms of the Treaty of Versailles, the Germans were not allowed to have a submarine fleet. However, under the leadership of the 1914–18 U-boat hero, Commander Dönitz, they had started to build them secretly. Firstly a number of hangars were built in the German yards. These were surrounded by fences and heavily guarded. In these secret slips, the Germans started illegally building their new U-1 to U-6. These were two-hundred-and-fifty-ton boats that they had developed in the early thirties, with Finland.

Hanley had brought all of the information and the photographs that he had acquired to the attention of Naval Intelligence. It was the last he heard of it. Then, just over a year ago, in June 1935, a naval treaty was signed between Britain and Germany. Part of the treaty was that Germany was now allowed to build submarines. Hanley was disgusted. It was a sign of weakness to just accept these illegal acts, but there was nothing to be done. Obviously Baldwin's government was one that sought peace before principle. In Hanley's eyes, and the eyes of many of his fellow officers in the yards, that was a formula that could only lead to another war.

Hanley found the subsequent events laughable. One month after the signing of the naval treaty, the first U-boat of the new fleet was spotted on patrol. One month! It was virtually impossible to build a yacht in a month, let alone a submarine. The Germans had obviously been in flagrant violation of their international agreements for years. However, the Baldwin government sat meekly by and watched one U-boat after another slide down the slips and out into the North Sea.

Every two weeks from the end of July onwards, another submarine had joined the German fleet until they had six Type 2A U-boats in their first flotilla. Hanley heard the figures from his Dutch friends with a growing sense of doom.

He remembered too clearly the terror and havoc wreaked by the German U-boats in 1917 and 1918.

Hanley had taken his concerns to Rear Admiral Walker. Walker was of course interested that Hanley had such contacts within the Kiel shipyards. However, he pointed out that these submarines were only small, coastal, defensive vessels and as such would raise no hackles in the Admiralty.

But if that were true, the photographs that Hanley had now spread across his desk were in a different league. The photographs showed the keel and ribs of much larger vessels, in the area of six hundred tons. Hanley had learned that these had just been laid down that summer and they were known in the German yards as the Atlantic U-boats.

When Hanley had taken this new information to Walker a few weeks earlier, he had received a careful hearing. It was obvious that the only use such submarines could have would be against Britain. As such it was a shock to all those who thought Hitler only had eyes for Russia and *Lebensraum* in the east. Walker asked Hanley to write a report; surely this would help them with the next series of Navy estimates.

A report? Hanley stared at the photographs and the mountains of figures. Then he collected them all together and stuffed the files into his briefcase. There seemed to be no end to this day.

7

Kingsland gazed out of the window at the grey Thames below. He looked despondent and felt worse. He had chain-smoked all the way from Chatham and was finally reduced to nursing

43

his last two Players. He did not know where he was going, but he knew that he needed a refuge for a week, even for a day. He just wanted to lay his head down somewhere, sink into oblivion.

The young woman opposite eyed him again and then returned to her copy of *Woman and Home*. Kingsland stood up abruptly, pulled the case from the rack above him and walked into the corridor. They would be in Victoria Station in a few minutes. He couldn't wait to get off the train, lose himself in the crowds.

He walked along the corridor to one of the doors, then pulled the leather strap and let the window down. The acrid smell of the coal blew in, mixed with a cool damp breeze off the river. It was a painful reminder of all those days and nights he had spent on patrol. Those times when he was alone on the bridge watching the lonely yet comforting roll of the sea.

There was a long, low, screeching of brakes and the train pulled slowly to a halt. Kingsland jumped out and was soon swept along past the hissing bulk of the engine and through the barrier. He had no clear idea what he should do. He had thought about going down to his father in Torquay but dismissed that as impossible. His father would not understand, it was not within the parameters of his well-ordered headmaster's world.

In the main station concourse he drifted to the edge of the crowd and leaned back against a hoarding, advertising the nerve-soothing properties of Wincarnis wine. A newsboy stood beside him shouting out lurid headlines about Franco's advance on Madrid.

Through the hubbub, Kingsland tried to gather his thoughts. Ronnie, the performer at the Unicorn nightclub, had offered him his flat in London. That was all right for a few days. But he had to get away, go somewhere quiet, somewhere safe. He gave an involuntary shudder, pushed himself away from the hoarding and made for the exit.

He was looking behind him when he felt a touch on his arm. He spun round and confronted a middle-aged woman, neatly dressed in a dark overcoat trimmed with fox fur. She was so startled by his sudden movement that she dropped the pile of pamphlets she was carrying.

Kingsland gave her a quick nervous smile as if to reassure her that he was not a maniac. "I'm sorry, dreadfully sorry." He knelt down and quickly helped her pick up her papers. He gathered a pile and handed them back to her. "Ah, the Peace Pledge Union, well done; Canon Sheppard, well done." He thrust them into her hands and then started off towards the exit again, regretting his inane comments.

However, the incident had in a strange way calmed him. Life goes on. Little ladies take on the might of armed empires. He gave a smile and then noticed the phone boxes just beside the cab rank. He needed to speak to Hanley, he needed someone on the inside to know.

Kingsland's mouth dried as he listened to the shillings and pennies drop into the box. Even though he wasn't going to tell Hanley everything in a three-minute telephone call, he felt nervous. He heard the phone being answered and pushed button A. "Hello, Chatham 2551."

Meanwhile, just along from the phone boxes, a man was leaning against the wall reading a rather crumpled copy of the *Daily Express*. Over the top of his paper he observed a black car pulling up just beyond the cab rank. They had received his message. The man driving the car got out, looked around and spotted the newspaper reader. He gave a slight nod, then got back into the car.

Inside the phone box, Kingsland had replaced the receiver. He stood for a moment staring at the A and B buttons on the box, then he glanced at his watch. Hanley was not at home yet. He would phone him later.

He picked up his suitcase, walked outside and immediately hailed a cab.

The *Daily Express* reader suddenly ran forward and signalled to the waiting car. Within seconds he was in the front seat and they were speeding off into the evening traffic.

Kingsland walked quickly down the steps to the basement below the Hungarian restaurant. A few moments later the man with the *Daily Express* appeared at the railings above and glanced down, noting the shabby sign over the door: The Unicorn.

For a few seconds he contemplated waiting on the pavement but the rancid smell of the goulash slops in the dustbins drove him back to the car.

The Unicorn had a small, dimly lit foyer and every wall was plastered with old nightclub posters from Berlin and Paris. There were drawings of sensuous, long-necked chanteuses in bright Art-Deco surroundings, women with mauve hair and mauve eyelashes, women with bald heads and pursed scarlet lips. There was a poster of a Venus de Milo with genitals rising up out of a sea of blood-red butterflies. But now dust had settled on the frames and the posters themselves were curled and yellowed with age.

Kingsland came down the steps, quickly glanced around him and then crossed to the young man standing behind the tiny cloakroom counter. "Excuse me, is Ronnie in?"

The young man was leaning over the counter and peering through the curtains at the stage beyond. Inside, a raucous-voiced female impersonator was belting out an impression of Marlene Dietrich in *The Blue Angel*.

The youth let the curtain drop back into place. He was a thin-faced, ginger-haired young man with a sulky, bored expression, "Sorry, what did you say?"

Kingsland was edgy, his speech abrupt. "I'm looking for Ronnie." Beyond the purple curtain with the tattered fringe, he could hear the singer building to a sultry climax. The ginger-headed youth nodded his head towards the club and mumbled in his theatrically languid manner, "I'm sorry but you can't talk to the artistes during the show. And Ronnie, dear heart that he is, will be going on in about five minutes."

Kingsland leaned forward and very firmly took the young man by the arm. "I need to see him, now." There was something in Kingsland's eyes that did not invite argument.

The youth quickly pulled his arm away and tossed back his head as though reasserting his position. "Oh well all right," he huffed. "If you're a friend I suppose you may as well go back. It's that door over there."

Kingsland gave the youth a cool smile and then crossed to a door bearing a poster of Kurt Weill's *Mahagonny*. He pushed it open and found himself behind a rack of costumes. Down to his left he could see the the wings and the bright lights of the stage. He squeezed past the rack of clothes. The backstage area was a shambles. All around were skips full of costumes and props. Painted flats were stacked against the walls and furniture was heaped up in corners. There was a painted golden throne, a set of prison bars, a drinks counter with fake bottles, mirrors, a guillotine, chairs, drapes. All in all, it was a chaotic tangle of colour and shape.

At the rear, Kingsland noticed a small room with an open door. It was a ramshackle affair that looked as though it had been constructed out of hardboard. Kingsland walked over and glanced inside. There was a table cluttered with wigs and stage make-up. Over the table a long mirror was surrounded by a string of naked lightbulbs. A brassy-looking blonde in a long, glittering, silver evening gown was applying bright red lipstick.

"Ronnie?" Kingsland asked tentatively.

The blonde swung round towards him and the blue shadow of a beard was obvious under the make-up.

"Rupert, my God Rupert, what're you doing back here?" He spoke in a rasping Yorkshire accent that was in direct contrast to the image of the pouting blonde applying the lipstick.

Kingsland slumped back against the make-up table and dropped his suitcase on the floor. He looked tired and desolate. Ronnie quickly stood up and closed the door. Then he placed a hand on Kingsland's arm and squeezed. "So, it's over, eh?"

Kingsland barely nodded, "Yes."

Ronnie leaned down and pulled open a drawer in the make-up table. He reached to the back and took out a half-bottle of scotch. "Barbarians," he mumbled as he opened it and poured a hefty amount into a cup, "fucking barbarians, that's what they are." He pushed the cup into Kingsland's hands. "Come on, knock it back as my Auntie Edna would say." Kingsland took the cup and drank.

Ronnie looked at him and shook his head. Kingsland was ashen, his eyes glassy. Ronnie leaned forward and jabbed a finger into Kingsland's chest. "Here, come on, don't let them win. Remember 'prohibo illigitimo' or whatever it is, 'don't let the bastards get you down.' They'd be throwing us all to the fucking lions if they still had amphitheatres."

Kingsland gave a grudging laugh. "I'm sorry," he said, "I didn't mean to fall apart."

Ronnie pulled open the door, listened to the music and then quickly shut it again. "Look," he said as he hastily finished his lipstick, "I'm going to have to go on again right now. Do you want to hang around here or what?"

Kingsland looked him straight in the eye. It was a direct appeal for help. "Ronnie, I'm desperate, you once said if I needed a place . . ."

Ronnie held up his hand to silence him. He reached into the drawer once again, pulled out a set of keys. "There," he said, "you've no reason to say any more."

Kingsland caught the keys. "I, eh. Thank you."

Ronnie waved his thanks aside and quickly patted some powder on to his well-rouged cheeks. "Why don't you go back there now?" he continued. Then he tossed aside the powder puff and opened the door. "I'll be home later."

The last bars of the song blared out and filled the tiny room. Ronnie started to walk out but Kingsland grabbed him by the arm and pulled the door shut again.

"There's something else." He reached into his overcoat and pulled out a large envelope. "I'd like you to keep this for me . . . somewhere safe . . . not your flat."

Outside they could hear the sounds of the audience applauding. Then someone gave a quick knock on the dressing-room door and shouted, "Ronnie ducks, you're up!"

Ronnie turned the envelope over in his hands and nodded. "All right," he said, "if you need me to."

"Yes, please," replied Kingsland and there was a note of urgency in his voice.

Ronnie flashed him a reassuring smile, then tossed the envelope into the open drawer and shut it. "I'll stash it away later, it'll be as safe as Garbo's knickers." Then he opened the door and rushed out towards the lights.

Kingsland glanced at the envelope, put the key in his pocket and drained the last of the whisky.

Meanwhile just outside the Unicorn, about thirty yards along Frith Street, the man with the *Daily Express* and his "chauffeur" had been amusing themselves watching the prostitutes. They were just settling in for a long evening when they saw Kingsland come up the steps past the overripe dustbins.

He turned left towards them and they found themselves facing the wrong way. They waited until he had passed and then started the engine and did a U-turn.

Even though there were taxis and other vehicles along the street, Kingsland suddenly became aware of being followed. He glanced round in time to see the car making the final part of the turn. He saw it stop and a man get out and walk over to the pavement. The man stopped, looked around him as though he was trying to find the number of a building and then started to walk away in the opposite direction. But Kingsland was not fooled. He turned on his heel and walked quickly towards the corner. There he turned right and broke into a run, dodging the traffic as he crossed Dean Street. When he reached the other side, he glanced behind him again and saw that his pursuer was still there.

Kingsland zigzagged his way through pedestrians, bicycles and cars, then made a quick dash between a newspaper-van and a taxi. The taxi squealed to a halt. "Hey you stupid prick, you friggin' blind?" But without stopping to put his case, Kingsland quickly turned into a darker side street and sprinted along the pavement.

Then, over on the right, he saw an alleyway between a small tobacconist's and a cheap café. He gave a quick glance behind him and ran into the welcoming shadows. It was dark, but he could see the lights of Meard Street at the other end. About halfway along, he noticed a wooden door. He slammed against it and burst into a small yard. Then he quickly closed the door and lay back against the crumbling brick wall.

A few seconds later he heard someone running along the

49

alleyway. The footsteps stopped somewhere close to the door. Kingsland held his breath and leaned forward as he strained to pick up every sound. There was a shuffling movement, then the running steps started again, continuing in the direction of Meard Street. Then there was a squeal of tyres, the slamming of a door and the welcome sound of a car accelerating away.

They were gone. He heaved a sigh of relief and slumped back against the wall. Oh God, was this it, was this how it was going to be from now on? There was no answer to that, except that now he knew he needed help. And quickly.

8

Hanley yawned as the car crunched its way along the gravel driveway. Number 53 Cloister Avenue was a large, detached, mid-Victorian house. It had a long front garden shadowed by two giant chestnut trees and the driveway leading to the garage at the back was sheltered by a high evergreen hedge. Eunice loved the sense of space and privacy and, after years of Navy houses, she was thrilled to have something that was hers alone. That was why she had insisted on using the money from her father's will to buy it.

Maybe that was the beginning of their troubles. "Ah dammit!" Hanley shook his head and rubbed his eyes. It had been an exhausting day and he couldn't weave his way through that tangled mess again. As he got out of the car to open the garage door he gave a silent prayer that Eunice had not been drinking.

Inside, the light was on. A motorbike had been upended on the floor and its engine partly stripped. Hanley gave a sigh and then a laugh. A youth of seventeen stood up beside the bench at the back. He was a tall slender young man and as he turned round into the light it struck Hanley once again how much he resembled his mother. Eunice had the same rich dark hair, the same brown eyes flashing with intelligence and passion.

"I needn't ask what you're doing, Nigel." The young man had a basin of petrol in his hands. He looked at his father, gave a sheepish smile and then placed the basin on the bench.

"I'm just cleaning the engine, Father."

Hanley nodded. "Uh huh? Well, as long as you understand, I still haven't decided whether to give it to you."

Nigel pulled the carburettor out of the petrol and began rubbing it clean. "I know. I told you, I was just cleaning it."

Hanley stared at him, he had his mother's deviousness as well. "Nigel, even Elizabeth is more technically adept than you are. Your only interest is in riding the thing, you should admit it." As he spoke, Hanley could see the glint in his son's eye.

"All right, but it's only sitting here. I can't see you on it any more, or Mother clinging on behind you."

"Enough of this, it must be time for dinner." Hanley turned back towards the car. As he was taking his briefcase out, he wondered if there was anything in that last remark about Eunice no longer "clinging on behind" him. How much did the children know?

Olwen, the housekeeper, had heard the car pulling up the driveway. She was taking the pie out of the oven as Hanley walked into the kitchen. "Good evening, sir."

"I'm sorry I'm late, Olwen, we had meetings all day."

He walked on through the kitchen, into the hallway, past the dining room on his left and on towards the table near the front door. Both the living room to the left and the music room to the right were empty. As he placed his cap on a peg and glanced at the mail, he wondered where Eunice was.

He turned round and saw Olwen standing at the dining-room door. She was a small, rather dumpy woman with a round happy face but Hanley could see that something was now troubling her. "Is this all the mail?"

"Yes sir, but there was a phone call for you earlier, a gentleman, he seemed upset, he said he'd call back."

"I see." Hanley instantly thought of Kingsland and for some reason found himself deflecting the conversation. "Is Mrs Hanley upstairs?"

Hanley noticed that troubled look returning to her eyes. "Oh, the mistress isn't back yet, sir." Hanley looked at her, trying to show as little surprise as possible. "Isn't back?"

Olwen lifted her apron and nervously rubbed her hands on it. "No, sir, she went to London for the day, she said she'd be home by six thirty but . . ."

"Oh yes, yes, I see." Hanley interjected. He did not see, but he wanted to save her from bumbling on. She nodded and started back towards the kitchen.

"You didn't know Mummy was going to London, did you?" Hanley turned and saw his daughter Elizabeth standing on the stairs. She was home from boarding school for the weekend.

Hanley had noted the edge in her voice. "Elizabeth, sometimes you sound like a paperback sleuth."

Elizabeth skipped down the remaining steps. "She didn't tell me either," she said. She was handsome rather than pretty and took after Hanley with her fair looks and blue eyes. At sixteen she wavered between being a daddy's girl and treading her own individual path to adulthood. Somewhere in the middle fell her constant conflict with her mother.

She pushed back her long fair hair and gave her father a peck on the cheek. He returned her kiss warmly. "It's hardly very important, Elizabeth. Come on, wash your hands, we'll have dinner now."

"Not waiting, huh?" She turned and walked on down towards the kitchen yelling, "Wake up, Nigel, dinner!"

Hanley walked into the dark living room. Though he had told Elizabeth that it was "hardly important", he was disturbed that Eunice had gone to London without telling anyone. As he crossed to the drinks cabinet, he recalled that dreadful period in Portsmouth seven years before. The light went on automatically and he saw that the whisky decanter was almost empty. He gave a despairing sigh. It had only been filled about three days ago.

"Daddy! Dinner! We can't wait." Elizabeth was shouting in her best hockey captain's voice. Hanley closed the cabinet and left the room thinking that the day was not over yet.

9

Chichester Street was one long row of tenements with shops on the ground level. Number 41 was built over a butcher's shop called Brindley's and the smell of meat and blood permeated the hallway and stairs.

A hoarding about halfway along the street showed a slim young woman in a long fur coat advertising Bile Beans and asking the question, "How does she slim safely in winter?" In the gutter underneath the hoarding, a gang of street urchins was playing a game of marbles. They looked up as a lorry rumbled round the corner, past the Cricketers pub, and then quickly returned to their game.

The lorry jerked to a halt outside Brindley's, with its engine still running. Mary Cullen and her eldest son Tom were seated in the front and it was obvious even to the most casual eye that an argument was in full swing.

"I don't believe you, Tom." Mary Cullen had her coat tightly pulled around her. "I don't believe you! All I asked was a shelter over our heads."

Tom Cullen, like all the Cullen men, had a broad, well-sculpted face, with full lips and an easy, generous smile. But at this moment he looked more like a child who had just been scolded. He thumped the steering wheel and then glared out of the window.

"Look, Mam, I'm sorry, I told you I've been hunting for weeks for you and I've got you this place, you just can't move in till Sunday night."

There was a banging just behind his head and the muffled sound of Kitty's voice raised in anger. "Hey, d'you mind? Can we get out of here?" Tom slid back a small wooden door between the front and back of the truck, revealing Ernie and Kitty amongst a pile of luggage. Kitty lunged forward dramatically and gulped in a few breaths of air. "God, I can scarcely breathe in there, the reek of coffee and tea'd rot your lungs."

Tom spun round on Kitty, his eyes blazing. "Who the hell do you think you are, Miss Charabanc 1936? You're all lucky I had the lend of the lorry." Mary turned too, and waved her hand at her daughter. "Yes, be quiet, Kitty, we have enough trouble without you chipping in."

Kitty was ignoring them as she gazed round at the drab tenements and the ragged dirty children. Then she saw the plaster pig hanging in the window of the butcher's shop and grimaced. "What're we doing parked in the middle of these slums?"

"What the hell do you mean, slums?" shouted Tom.

Mary waved a threatening hand and turned to her daughter again. "Kitty, watch your mouth! You know fine well this is where we'll be living. It's no worse than where we came from."

Kitty sank back and gave a theatrical growl of disgust. "That's what I mean, it's a slum!"

Tom slammed the sliding door shut again and ignored the ensuing thumps. "I've had enough of you, Miss. Belt up." After about thirty seconds, Kitty's bangs and shouts subsided, leaving Mary and Tom sitting in the front in silence.

After a moment Mary clapped her hands together. "Well then, start up, there's nothing left for it. There's only one thing to do. Go on, get moving."

Tom rammed the lorry into gear and with a shudder it started off down the street, leaving the marble-playing boys and the smell of the butcher's shop behind.

Irene Gillings finished the Peace Pledge pamphlet, closed it and then sat back against the pillow. It all seemed to make such good sense. Surely there was a tremendous potential for good in economic sanctions, if only the League of Nations would use them properly. What an irony! she thought. Here she was supporting Canon Sheppard and the Peace Pledge Union in their opposition to the armaments industries and yet Albert was downstairs poring over submarine plans.

She got out of bed, took his old grey dressing-gown from the back of the door and slipped it over her white cotton nightgown.

As she walked past Terry's room she noticed the light under the door. She was about to knock but stopped herself. He would be working at his books. He never seemed to stop.

She started down the stairs and glanced at the blue and red patterned carpet. About three inches of the wooden steps showed on either side. It had been painted white but now looked scuffed and chipped. They would have to paint it again soon.

The door to the living room was open and she could hear the sound of the radio crackling out a version of the "Blue Danube Waltz". Irene walked in. The room was dark, except for the light that spilled out from the kitchen. She looked in and saw Gillings sitting at the kitchen table. His papers were spread across it and the smoke from his pipe hung like a thin, blue-grey mist above his head.

She watched him for a moment as he sucked at the pipe and then scribbled notes on one of the lists. He paused, then tapped his pencil on the tabletop, thinking. After a few seconds he sensed her presence and looked up.

"Irene! I thought you were a cat burglar!"

"No. Just looking at you."

She crossed to the sink and filled the kettle. "It's funny," she said, "I remember when I was a child, my Uncle Arthur – he was a policeman – he used to talk about cat burglars. I didn't know what they were and I imagined these men with bags, tiptoeing round stealing cats."

Gillings gave a distracted smile. He loved her. She was quiet but she was his rock. For a moment he simply stared at her face. Her hair was light brown, almost fair, and even now there were still streaks of the coppery red colour it had been when she was a girl. She had intelligent, soft grey eyes that somehow always melted his worst humour.

55

"And what has you down? I thought you'd be asleep by now."

"Oh I was reading and I thought you might fancy a cup of hot chocolate."

He held out his hand and gestured for her to come over to him.

"What is it you want?" she asked.

He gave her a broad boyish smile and she crossed to him, put her arm round his shoulder and planted a kiss on his forehead. "What has you working so late?"

He grimaced and started to collect up his papers. "Oh, arranging schedules, trying to make sure we get the *Graplin* launched on time."

She gently rubbed her hand across the back of his waistcoat. Then she crossed to one of the glass-fronted cabinets, opened it and took out a box of Fry's drinking chocolate. "Are you having trouble then?" she asked.

"Oh, let's not talk about it. I promised I'd never bring my work home and I won't start now." She took down two cups and the sugar bowl and then paused. "Wasn't that what you were doing at dinner?"

Earlier that night he and Terry had gone at it like hammer and tongs again. But she had suspected then that it had less to do with politics and more to do with pressure at the yards. For a moment Irene wondered if he had heard her, but then she could see, from the knitting of his brow, that she had hit home. Well, she thought, she was best to go all the way now. "Albert, you know, sometimes you're very hard on him."

"Listen, Irene, he . . ."

"No, wait a minute and let me finish," she dropped the teaspoon into one of the cups and sat down in the chair opposite him. "I remember Carlisle Street in Liverpool. You and your dad shouting at each other over the kitchen table, something about him wanting you to go and work as a paviour with him and your uncle. If Terry's got different ideas to you, just let him be. If you'd only step back you'd be proud he had the brains to stand up to you." She stopped and watched the effect of her words, half expecting another argument. But he just sat there and absent-mindedly stirred the dry mixture of sugar and chocolate in his cup. Then, after a while, he clinked the spoon against the side and looked up at her. "You're a tough woman, Irene."

She looked at him, puzzled. "Tough, that's a funny word to use."

He gave a smile. "No, tough, I mean tough. But I'm glad you are. You're right. I'll talk to him before I go to bed."

She was leaning over to take his hand when she heard the knocking at the front door. "What's that, this time of night?"

Gillings looked equally puzzled, but he quickly stood up and started for the hallway. "I have no idea. I just hope to God nothing's gone wrong at the yards."

He switched on the hall light and opened the front door. Mary Cullen was standing there with Tom. Gillings was surprised. He had helped Tom to get his job at Pulbrooke's, the dockyard's provisioners but he hadn't seen him much in the last few months.

"Tom . . ."

Gillings stared at Mary. He hadn't seen her in over ten years. She looked older, and worn. "Mary?"

"Mary!" Irene had come into the hall behind him. For a moment there was an awkward pause as if no one knew what was happening or what they should say. Then, from somewhere in the dark beyond the porch, came Kitty's voice. "Well, are we going in or not?"

Irene gave a laugh as she walked forward and gave her cousin a hug. "Of course you're coming in. I'm sorry, Mary. I just had a bit of a shock seeing you turn up at the door."

"I had a shock myself. You see, Tom here was supposed to get us a place, but we can't move in until Sunday. I was wondering if . . ."

Irene looked at Mary and then back at Gillings. "Listen, you'll stay with us, that's all right, isn't it Albert?"

Gillings stared at her and then realised there was nothing else they could do. "Of course, if you're stuck, you're family, where else would you go."

Mary visibly relaxed and Irene pulled her into the hallway.

"And who was that I heard in the garden? It couldn't be Kitty. Come in here . . . and Ernie . . . and Tom of course we've seen. We were just reading about him in the papers this week with his boxing . . ."

While Irene rattled on, smoothing over the awkwardness, Gillings walked outside with Tom. The van had been parked at an angle, with the front wheel on the pavement. Tom opened the doors with "Pulbrooke's Purveyors of Goods" written across them in faded gold script. The pungent odour of coffee and tea was overpowering. "So how do you like the job, Tom?"

"Oh, it's all right, Uncle Albert. I mean, thanks for the nod 'n' all, it's a wage, keeps me going while I'm in training."

Gillings stared at Tom as the young man pulled the suitcases and other packages towards the door. In the dim light from the streetlamp he could see the close resemblance between Tom and his father, Billy. Billy was a man of dreams too, a man who always had a scheme. Gillings shook his head, stepped forward, and picked up two of the battered cardboard suitcases. "Hmm. Well anyway, let's get you all unloaded."

Terry was working on a graph for his maths class at the dockyard school when he heard the rumpus downstairs. Putting down his slide rule, he looked out of the window and saw his father at the side of the road helping to unload something from an old van. Then he recognised Tom Cullen jumping out of the rear doors.

He let the curtain drop. The Cullens? He collected his work and set it neatly to one side of the desk, then walked out into the hallway.

"At the top of the stairs and second left . . ." he heard his mother shout. Someone was coming up. He watched as a figure climbed up from the light of the hall into the shadows of the landing. Stepping back towards his bedroom door he found the landing lightswitch and clicked it on.

"Oooh!" Kitty spun round and suddenly saw him. For a moment she looked like a startled fawn. Then another look came into her eyes. She saw a young man with wavy black hair, fine features and dark eyes. She was immediately intrigued. She stepped towards him and gave a tentative smile. "Hello, I'm your cousin, Kitty."

Terry immediately liked this new cousin. She had an almost tangible energy.

"I think we're going to stay with you for a day or two."

"Oh." He did not know what else to say. It was a bolt from the blue. He watched as she pushed her hair back behind her ear, and noticed the smooth alabaster skin of her shapely neck as she ran her finger around the top of her dress. Then Irene shouted up the stairs again.

"Kitty, have you found it yet?"

"It's all right, Mum, I'll show her." Terry crossed to the bathroom door. "It's in here."

Kitty walked past him and quickly took it all in. "Oh, this is lovely, lovely."

Terry stood for a moment, intrigued. He had never thought of their bathroom as "lovely". He watched her, fascinated, as she turned to him. Her eyes were wide and dark. "You're lucky living in a house like this," she said, turning on the hot tap in the handbasin and letting the water run through her fingers, "very lucky."

"I'd better get down and meet your mum."

Kitty gave him another of her sparkling smiles. "Yes." Then she slowly closed the door.

Terry turned away and walked to the top of the stairs. There he stopped and took a breath. Something new had entered into the Gillings household.

10

Hanley's desk was spread with papers. He had almost completed his report and was looking over the photographs of the new U-boats being built in the Germania yards in Kiel, when he heard a car pull into the gravel driveway. Eunice must have taken a taxi from the station.

As he waited to hear the front door open, he collected his photos together and put them into a file. Then he leaned forward and re-angled the green shade on the desklamp, so that it threw light on the rest of the room.

Still no one had come in. He stood up, listened again and then walked into the hallway. Everything was quiet. Nigel had a Rugby match in Canterbury next morning and so he had gone to bed early. Elizabeth was up in her room, lost in one of her books as usual.

Hanley turned left into the living room. The room was in darkness and the curtains were open. Through the front windows he could see a car parked in the driveway and a chauffeur opening one of the back doors. Eunice got out, stood for a second, seemed to sway slightly and then, with a flourish, held out her hand towards the car door. The silhouette of a man's head appeared and Hanley saw him kiss her hand. Then with another dramatic sweep of her arm she started unsteadily across the lawn.

The chauffeur moved to help her but she waved him aside, laughing, and strode on towards the front door. A few seconds later, the car reversed out of the drive and drove off along Cloister Avenue.

Hanley barely had time to register all this before he heard the front door open. After a moment he saw her walk past the living-room door towards the foot of the stairs. He moved quickly towards the hallway. "Eunice!"

She spun round and saw him standing in the doorway of the darkened living room. "My God, James," she said, looking completely surprised, "you scared me. What are you doing?"

Hanley stepped into the light of the hall, uncomfortable at being caught in the shadows. "I heard a car, and came out to see who . . ." He stumbled to a halt.

Eunice raised her eyebrows and then waved her hand towards the front door. "Oh, I see. Standing guard now, are we?" Then she gave a giggle and walked past him into the living room.

He stood for a moment, feeling an instant anger at her innuendo. Then he forced himself to calm down, turned, and followed her inside. She had opened the drinks cabinet and stood in the glow of its light. "I just glanced out," he said, as he watched her lift the whisky decanter and open it. "You're late."

"Oh, am I?" she replied airily. "And what are you doing then, enforcing the curfew? Damn!" Eunice had upended the whisky decanter and found only a dribble. She banged it down on the mirrored surface and spun round to glare at Hanley.

"Eunice, do you mind telling me where you were today?"

"No, not at all," she said, as she pulled out a cigarette and lit it. For a moment the flame from her lighter played around her handsome face and showed the determined curl of her lips. "I got depressed, again, and I decided to cure it. I went up to London for the day."

She reached back to close the cabinet, but slipped and knocked over the empty decanter. It fell to the side, smashing one of the glasses.

Hanley walked forward, picked up the decanter and then firmly closed the cabinet door. They were now standing close together with the only light in the room spilling in from the hallway. He could smell the alcohol on her breath. "You've been drinking again."

She looked up at him, a glitter of anger in her eyes. "I don't have a problem with my drinking," she said loudly. "*You*, you have the problem." She turned away from him and made her way towards the hall.

"There's no need to raise your voice, Eunice."

She spun round again, silhouetted in the doorway. "Why?" she said, in sharp, clearly enunciated tones. "I have nothing to hide. I went up to London, yes. I was *invited*. I went to see my old school chum, Olivia, Lady Brampton." She lingered over the word "Lady".

But Hanley was not to be drawn, his response was quiet and rational "I know who she is. And the car?"

"Oh, of course," she said with a snorting laugh, "we were at the window watching, weren't we?"

That was it. Hanley felt himself swept by a wave of icy cold anger. "It doesn't matter," he said, as he brushed past her into the hall.

"But it obviously does –" He stopped about halfway down to his study, but kept his back to her. "Olivia, an old friend, calls me up. I go to one of her intellectual soirées. I meet another old friend. *He* drives me home and suddenly I'm a loose woman!"

Hanley gave a barely audible sigh. "Just go to bed, Eunice!"

But she was in full flight now and not to be stopped. "It was Harry." She took a few steps towards him and steadied herself by grasping the bottom post of the banister. "You remember Harry Cruikshank Rawlston, don't you? Back from Malaya, just inherited his father's estate . . ."

Hanley spun round to face her. "That's enough, Eunice. I'm delighted you've had a good day, but we're all tired."

She slowly swung herself back, still holding the banister, and sank on to the stairs. "Sir Harry now. Has it all, manor house, money, title . . ."

That was it, thought Hanley, it always came out when she drank. All of the resentment, the thought that she'd missed out on the privileges of her class. As he watched her sitting on the stairs, he felt no anger, only a great sympathy. "We can talk tomorrow," he said, as he turned and started towards his study.

She looked up at him. "When I'm sober?"

"Good night, Eunice." He shut his study door with a firm click.

She kicked her shoes across the hall. What was the point of coming home! She should have stayed at the party. She could have laughed and joked with Harry all evening. What the hell did Hanley care about her? All he thought about were his damned submarines!

Then a dark thought shuddered into her mind through the haze of resentment. She saw the handsome German, Weichert, his blue eyes boring into her. Felt that thrill of danger and novelty. Olivia on the floor of the darkroom, the flash of her naked thighs, the moans of passion. She caught her breath. Once again she saw Weichert with that alluring smile, standing close to her in the hall. "I hope we will meet again." Hadn't he said something like that?

Suddenly she pushed herself up from the stairs and staggered across the hall to the mirror. She leaned on the small half-table, steadied herself and gazed at her reflection. Her eyes looked tired and her dark hair had fallen across her brow in bedraggled strands. She brushed it aside and ran her forefinger over the fine lines around her eyes. Oh damn it, damn it, she thought, where am I going? Then she sank forward and rested her forehead on the cold glass. It felt good.

Kingsland took the stairs two at a time. He dropped his bag outside the red-painted door on the third floor and quickly put the key into the lock.

Inside, the flat was dark and stuffy. There was a coat-rack behind the door, bulging with overcoats, dressing-gowns, hats and umbrellas. Kingsland pushed his hand deep into the pile, found the lightswitch, and clicked it on. It revealed a small hallway filled with clutter, boxes of theatrical props, an old pair of golfclubs, two scarred old leather suitcases. He quickly slammed the door behind him and slumped against it, trying to catch his breath.

Ronnie's flat was in a quiet side street in Chelsea. It was at the top of a tall but rather narrow Georgian house, not far from the river. As he stood now in the hall, he finally began to feel safe again. Surely no one had followed him here. He dumped his suitcase on the floor, walked past the coats and glanced through the open door to the right. The bedroom was almost as cluttered as the hall, with boxes, costumes, suitcases and books. Kingsland smiled at the mess and then glanced over at the bed. There was a large, black lace Spanish shawl draped on the wall behind it and a gallery of family photos in brass frames on a small side-table. The heavy red curtains were pulled open. Kingsland stared at the top of the trees beyond and then past them to the dark sky. Suddenly he was startled by the plaintive sound of a horn blasting out from a distant tug. In some peculiar way it made him feel uneasy. He hurried out of the bedroom and slammed the door.

63

Back in the hallway he reached behind the coats again and clicked off the light. Then he quietly edged his way towards the other end of the hall and opened the door into the living room. There was a dim light from one of the streetlamps and he was able to avoid the furniture. He stopped at the window and carefully peered down along the street. It seemed empty. He pulled the curtains shut and then made his way, half feeling, half seeing, to the lamp beside the sofa. He clicked it on and stood for a moment looking at the telephone on the table. He took out a handkerchief and wiped the sweat off his face, then suddenly looked towards the door as if a thought had just struck him.

He rushed out of the room, down the hall, and wrenched open the last door on the right. In the light that spilled in, he could make out the faded stained enamel of the bath, the sink and the toilet. He stepped on to the toilet bowl and lifted the top of the cistern. Then he pulled up the sleeve of his jacket and fished around inside. After a moment he gave a gasp of relief and pulled out a parcel wrapped in dark brown waterproof paper.

As he sank down on the edge of the bath, he ripped off the paper. The touch of the cold hard metal in his hands gave him a renewed feeling of security. He slipped his index finger around the trigger and held the .38 in front of him as though he was aiming. Yes, that felt better. Now he would phone Hanley. The time had come to tell all.

Hanley woke with a jerk. His hand knocked the half-filled glass of gin off the arm of the chair and on to the carpet. "Damn!" He quickly slipped out of the chair, knelt down and mopped it up with his handkerchief. Then he sat there for a moment slightly disorientated. He could hear the last aria from *La Traviata* trilling out on Radio Toulouse. He staggered to his feet and glanced at his watch. It was one fifteen! "God!" he mumbled.

"Yes, it's really that late."

Hanley swung round. Eunice was standing in the doorway. She was wearing the long, rose-coloured silk negligée with the intricate lacework around the collar. He had bought it for her in

Alexandria almost ten years ago, and he noted that she still had the figure to wear it. Her dark hair fell down across her shoulders and made her look vulnerable. "I fell asleep. I just woke up. Thought you must've left me." She gave a rueful smile.

"No, I fell asleep myself."

She walked on into the living room and perched on the arm of one of the chairs. "Well anyway, I knew you'd be down here and I thought I'd make a stab at my entrance again. That earlier one wasn't too good, I thought."

He gave her another tentative smile and then gestured with his empty glass. "Can I get you a drink?"

She pulled back her long dark hair with her left hand and raised an ironic eyebrow. "I think we both think I've had enough."

Hanley placed his glass on the open drinks cabinet, hoping that there wouldn't be another row. "Eunice, I'm sorry, I shouldn't have said what I did about you drinking."

"Of course you should," she said, "and I'm apologising. It was wrong to just disappear off to London like that. It's only that . . ." She stopped and gave a deep sigh.

Hanley saw her head sink forward and he instantly felt a wave of sympathy. "Eunice, it's all right, there's no need to say any more. I do understand, you know. I know how hellishly boring it must be here in this town with nothing but naval talk and naval wives."

She looked up, interrupting him. "Please don't go on, James, you make me sound like a restless schoolgirl complaining to her father."

Hanley picked up his glass again and twirled it nervously. "I promise you I didn't mean it like that, I just meant that you don't have to say anything, I already know and I sympathise."

Eunice sat forward on the arm of the chair and tugged gently at the long sleeves of her negligée. It was a sign that she was waking up. "But James, don't you see that I should say it. I mean, we have to talk this out, we just can't coast along any longer. Week after week, month after month things are left unsaid until one day, it all explodes!"

65

Hanley turned from her and placed his glass on the mirrored surface inside the drinks cabinet. He didn't want another blazing row. He poured himself a full measure of gin and added some tonic. "I don't believe there's anything to be gained in arguing," he said, and then he turned back to look at her. To his surprise he saw only warmth and sympathy in her eyes.

She flashed him a childlike smile. "James, sitting down and talking to each other isn't arguing!"

Hanley sat in his chair and watched the bubbles breaking in his drink. "I'm not particularly good at that kind of 'talking' either." He took a sip and looked up at her. "But I know that I don't say this enough. I do love you, Eunice." Even as he said it, he hated his awkwardness. His inability to say anything except in a blunt, straightforward manner.

Eunice flashed him a sympathetic smile and then shrugged her shoulders. "That's nice to hear but I need more than words, we both need more than words, James, we need to share things. In the last two years we've hardly spent a full day together."

Hanley nodded and waved his hand as if asking her to stop. "I know, I know."

But Eunice was not to be put off this time. She slipped from the arm of the chair on to the seat, and sat forward. "Knowing doesn't help if we don't do anything about it. It doesn't help me when I'm sitting here alone at nights, yawning over my historical romances or trying to keep my temper with Elizabeth." She stopped and looked at Hanley but he simply stared down at his glass, looking like a schoolboy waiting outside the headmaster's office.

After a moment's silence he glanced up at her. "You're right, of course." He swirled his drink around in his glass and took another sip. "Look, why don't we all go down to your mother's this weekend? She's been asking us for months."

Eunice laughed and yet somewhere inside her a note of warning sounded. Had he really understood or was he just palming her off with another quick fix? "Come on now, James, let's not get reckless."

"What do you mean?"

"Oh nothing, it's just that it seems to be taking a bit of a chance. You and Mother don't always strike it off."

He shrugged and gave a smile. "I promise not to talk about Mr Baldwin or brandish Churchill's name around."

Eunice thought for a while and then nodded. "Well, why not? It is a good idea and she hasn't seen Nigel since his last birthday." Then she pulled her legs up and hugged them, like a small girl waiting for a story. "Well, that's settled, that's the family, now what about me?"

The sound of the telephone bell rang sharp and clear along the hallway. Eunice saw Hanley's eyes suddenly narrow but he did not move. She leaned forward and touched his hand. "Can't we leave it and go upstairs?"

The ringing continued, harsh and demanding. Hanley looked towards the hall and then got up. "I can't."

As he reached for the receiver on the hall table, he heard Eunice walking to the door behind him. He paused, his hand hovering over the phone. It was like an image for his life. The call was either from Kingsland or from the yards but, whichever, it concerned his career. Behind him he heard Eunice's soft breathing.

The phone rang again and he quickly snatched up the receiver. "Hello." There was a pause at the other end of the line, long enough for him to feel a pang of guilt. He had once again chosen his career over his home.

When Kingsland spoke, he sounded tired and despondent. "Jimmy, I'm sorry to call you this late. It's Rupert."

"Yes, I've been expecting you." Hanley turned to Eunice. His manner was brusque. "Eunice, I'll be up later."

She walked past him and up the stairs. It wasn't worth another argument, those years were all gone. Every time she saw that look in his eyes she knew that his career had won.

Hanley waited until he saw her disappearing into the shadows of the landing above. "I'm sorry about what happened today . . ."

Kingsland cut across him. "Stop, Jimmy, please. I didn't call you for sympathy." He paused and Hanley could hear him take a deep breath before he continued. "Look, Jimmy, I need to see you, it's important and it's not personal."

Hanley paused. Something in him wanted to simply replace the receiver and walk away. It was a strange feeling of foreboding. "Well, I really don't have much time in the next few weeks what with the *Graplin* . . ."

Kingsland interrupted. He sounded desperate. "Please, Jimmy, I need to see you as soon as I can. I don't have much time."

"What do you mean?" said Hanley.

Kingsland hesitated for a second. "Just that . . ." Hanley heard the note of subdued panic in Kingsland's voice and he knew that he really had no choice. "All right, all right, call me here tomorrow. I'll arrange some time at the weekend."

Hanley put the phone down and then stood looking at the black-and-white chequered tiles along the hall. It seemed that no matter how much one tried to organise life, it had its own surprises. Chaos was never far away. It was not a pleasant thought.

11

It was Saturday morning. Irene was at the kitchen table sipping a cup of tea and nibbling a piece of toasted Hovis. Albert and Terry had gone off to the yards, Terry to the dockyard school. Irene had a few minutes alone to glance over an open Peace Pledge letter to the Italian ambassador. She was busy scribbling out notes about bombs over Addis Ababa when Mary walked in. "Mary, I didn't hear you."

Mary gave a self-conscious smile, she looked much calmer than she had last night, more rested, younger. "I'm ashamed sleeping in so late. I'm usually up at six." Irene pushed her papers aside and crossed to the sink where she started filling the kettle. "Ashamed nothing. You needed the sleep after that journey. You should still be in bed."

Mary lingered by the door, not knowing whether to sit down or help. "Oh, I heard Albert and Terry going out, so I thought I'd come down. I thought you and I might catch up on our own."

Irene turned and smiled. She knew what Mary meant. They had grown up together as children, living only streets away from each other. Their fathers were brothers and had worked on the docks for years. Now their lives had taken completely different paths. They hadn't seen each other for some ten years and there were things that couldn't be conveyed on Christmas cards and scribbled notes.

As they talked Irene made breakfast and Mary watched her with a growing sense of unease. She looked at the almost new gas cooker, the small refrigerator, and realised how far these "luxuries" were beyond her grasp. As Irene was pushing the bacon aside and cracking two eggs into the pan, she asked Mary to go into the pantry and bring out a new jar of marmalade. The pantry was no bigger than a walk-in cupboard but Mary stood there in the dark coolness, overawed. She gazed around at the laden shelves and then picked up the jar of marmalade. It was in a corner with two tins of Tate & Lyle syrup, three jars of mincemeat and two jars of honey. She herself could scarcely afford to buy these things let alone store them. She stood for a moment and took a deep breath. And as she did, it all flashed before her. Billy was the cause! She could have had some of these comforts if it hadn't been for him. He had broken up their lives, split the family.

She gave a sigh as she remembered the time, years before, when all four of them had walked out together. They were in their late teens then. Billy had a good job on one of the pilot ships in the Mersey and Albert was just starting at the Cammell Laird shipyards at Birkenhead. Billy was a handsome lad in those days and he turned many a young girl's head. But Albert was always the salt of the earth. As the years went by the differences between the two men became more and more obvious. They were both hard workers but Albert was always singled out as a young man with a future. Billy earned just as much money but somehow very little of it found its way home.

Mary had blamed their separation during the Great War for the beginning of their troubles. For the first time, Billy became a deep-water sailor. He joined the merchant navy and sailed the convoys to the States. He never settled after that. His drinking became worse and there were always rumours of other women. One day he just sailed off and never came back.

Mary looked at the long shelves filled with provisions then down at the marmalade in her hands. Now she was dependent on her cousin's charity. After a moment she settled herself and took the marmalade into the kitchen. After all, whatever Billy had done, it wasn't Irene's fault.

Kitty's fascination was with the world beyond the house but Mary would not let her "wander off" on her own. Tom came round and took Ernie off to a football match. At first Kitty huffed at being left alone, then she buried herself in her film magazines.

When Terry returned home from the dockyard school she saw him disappear into the shed out at the back and quickly followed. The shed was really a small workshop. In earlier years it had been Albert's, but with his increasing workload at the yards, Terry had taken it over. The dark brown, wooden structure with its tar-papered roof patched around the edges, stood on its own at the other side of the yard.

Kitty stepped inside and caught the strange mix of smells, creosote and tar, oil and turps. There were tools everywhere competing for space with piles of magazines and mechanical manuals. She stared around in amazement at all the electrical equipment packed on to the shelves: valves, condensers, transformers and wires.

"What's all this stuff?"

"Oh, electrical gadgets . . ." She looked at him blankly and he continued, "things for fixing old radios." Terry leaned along the bench as he was talking and pulled a radio towards him. It was cathedral-shaped and the dark lacquer on its wooden top was cracking and flaking. He switched it on and soon it was booming out the Saturday afternoon football match. Everton and Spurs. "I put this one together out of spare parts."

Kitty was impressed. "You built it?"

Terry laughed and turned the dial to some waltz music. He gave her a smile. "That's the best I can get, it's Hilversum or Leipzig I think. This one hasn't got a plate with the stations on it."

"Well, anything's better than football. Ernie went off with Tom earlier this afternoon to see Gillingham playing. My mam says I have to learn my way around first, before I go out. That's real Irish for you, isn't it?"

Kitty walked over to the shelves on the other wall and stared at the boxes of valves and bits of electric motors, the coils of wire and the rows of tools.

"What're you doing tonight?"

Kitty's question came out of the blue. Terry spun round and looked at her, but she had her back turned to him and was scrutinising a voltameter.

"Nothing really."

She cocked her head to one side. "Well, why don't we both go out together somewhere? I mean we could go for a walk and I could have a look at Chatham, without my mum having a fit."

Terry stared at her and then gave a half-smile. She had a real "brass neck", as his mother would say. And yet, he had the suspicion that he liked it.

After tea, Kitty got her way. She and Terry went out for their walk and ended up at the top of Brompton Hill. There was a cool breeze from the river and they both enjoyed the view as they stood gazing out over the Medway estuary.

Between them and the river the dockyards stretched out along the bank. The oldest part, the centre, was at the southern end. This had been the Chatham of Charles II and Pepys. The Georgians had rebuilt the yard and its graceful buildings reflected that rational period, with high ceilings and tall elegant windows. Later, as the shipyard expanded, it crept eastwards towards the sea. Each successive generation simply added on, giving a final result that was a hotchpotch of buildings, a mishmash of styles, underlining the yard as a vibrant and creative workplace.

"What's that down there?"

Kitty pointed down the hill towards the town. She could see a long narrow street with low houses and shops. The distant noise of bar-room pianos and raucous voices drifted up.

"The Brook."

"It sounds lively, let's go down."

"Well, it's not really the 'nicest' place in Chatham, if you know what I mean."

Kitty gave a mischievous smile. "No, tell me." She turned halfway towards him so that her arm tightened on his.

"It's eh . . . what you call a red light district."

"Well, so what. Let's go down."

Terry gave a grudging laugh. "Oh all right but don't tell your mum. I really shouldn't be taking you down there at night."

The Brook was nothing special to look at. In fact by day it was just a squalid urban scar of squat, ugly buildings. But dusk was falling and the lights in the pubs and clubs and dingy little cafés gave the drab side streets and the winding Brook itself a new face, a bright but brittle cheeriness, like a tired chorus girl grinding her way through the last, late show.

As Kitty and Terry walked down the hill into the crowds, they saw uniforms everywhere. There were the Navy blues and whites of the sailors, the khakis of the Royal Engineers and the occasional dress uniform of the Marines. At night the Brook pulsed with a life and a spirit common to a dozen other "sailor towns". The Empire was dotted with such sanctuaries. Along their crowded narrow streets, in the small tattoo shops, in the pubs smelling of vinegary beer-slops and spittle-sodden sawdust, these men who manned the Empire's fleet would meet.

There, the stories and memories were exchanged and refined. Tales about Shanghai and Singapore, Alexandria and Malta. On such nights, drink and women made strangers friends and friends strangers.

Kitty took it all in. Her eyes sparkled with the excitement of the street, with its bars, its lights and its music. But she clung tightly to Terry like a bodyguard. They turned right and wove through the crowds blocking the pavement. Beside them, cars, taxis, buses and bicycles slowly pushed their way through the throng.

A group of sailors had spilled out on to the streets and were holding their pints and glasses as they watched an old man with a barrel organ. He had a monkey dressed in a rough approximation of a sailor's suit, with a small hat perched on the top of his head. The hatband read "HMS *Pembroke*", the naval barracks.

The old man turned the handle and the organ boomed out a very passable version of a hornpipe. The monkey danced, not well at first, but he soon found his stride and the crowd began to join in with a rhythmic clapping.

Terry was just beginning to enjoy it when Kitty pulled him out into the road behind a passing Maidstone and District double-decker bus. "Come on, Tom's over there. Hey Tom!"

Tom was standing in the middle of the road talking to someone in the front passenger seat of a sleek, well-polished, black Wolseley car. His face dropped when he saw Kitty.

As Kitty approached, the man in the car looked round. He was wearing a navy blue snap-brim fedora, pushed back on his head. His small eyes quickly settled on Kitty. His glance was penetrating, and he seemed to take her in with a disconcerting thoroughness. He gave a thin-lipped smile and then patted Tom on the arm. "Just go on into the Parrot and have a drink on me, Tom." He turned to the driver, a large thug of a man with massive hands. "We're late, Charlie." The other man revved the car and they both sped off.

Kitty sidled up beside her brother. "So who's Mister Big then?"

Tom looked annoyed. "You should watch your mouth, Kitty. He's the man that's got you the place on Chichester Street. He owns it."

"Oh, that slum. I suppose we should feel privileged."

Tom gave an exasperated groan. "Great. I suppose the last thing I can expect is thanks. How are you, Terry?"

"Tom."

"And what brings you both down here?"

"We're out for a walk. Why are *you* down here?"

"If it's any of your business, I'm down here training. My gymnasium's round the corner. But you shouldn't be down in this part of the town."

Terry shifted uneasily. Kitty saw this and turned on her brother. "I asked Terry to bring me here and what's wrong with it? You're here, aren't you? It's just a street."

Tom sighed. "Christ, Kitty, does everything have to be an argument?"

"Tom, Tom, over here!" Kitty glanced over his shoulder and saw a blonde-haired girl standing under a small red and white striped awning. The sign over the top read: The Chinese Parrot. Tom turned round and nodded. "It's all right, Flora, I'll be over in a minute." The girl nodded and then sauntered into the nightclub.

Kitty tossed her hair back and then gave a cheeky grin. "I suppose that's the training you're up to, is it?"

Tom was not amused. He turned to Terry, pointedly ignoring his sister. "You'll come and see my next fight, will you, Terry?"

Terry grinned, happy to be asked. "Yeah, sure."

"Great. Listen, don't stay around here too late." Tom gave Terry a playful slap on the back then turned away and quickly walked across the road to the nightclub.

Kitty watched him for a moment. The place looked exotic, all the more so because it was prohibited to her. She turned back and grabbed Terry by the arm again. "Oh poor Terry, he probably wonders what kind of a family he's got for cousins."

12

As Hanley's train started across the River Medway, he gazed down at Rochester with its cathedral and narrow cobbled streets. It looked particularly Dickensian in the depressing Sunday rain and the sight did not help his mood. He felt guilty enough about having to cancel family plans but, on top of this, he found himself completely distracted by the events of the last few days. Kingsland was obviously in trouble, deep trouble.

At Victoria Station Hanley had to make his way through a rowdy but cheerful group of young men who were gathered under the clock. At first he mistook them for a Rugby club, still lingering in London after a game, but overhearing fragments of their conversation as they jostled and joked with one another he realised that they were a group of young cadets from Sandhurst.

Hanley crossed to a newspaper kiosk where a squat, jowly man with greased curly hair was slurping tea out of a large tin mug. Sunday papers were piled everywhere. He glanced at the *Sunday Express*, "Heavy losses in rebel fight for Madrid", then picked up a plug of Players tobacco and a box of matches, giving the man half-a-crown. As he waited for the change he watched the cadets, and a long-forgotten memory leapt into his mind. A day in February 1915, waiting for the train to Portsmouth with a group of other young midshipmen, a journey that would in a few short weeks bring them face to face with the horror of the Dardanelles. He and Kingsland had nearly missed that train. They had gone to the station buffet and were chatting to two young Scottish nurses when they heard the whistle blow. They had barely managed to jump on board the last carriage as it left the platform.

Hanley took his money and walked towards the exit. They

could both have faced disciplinary measures because of two rosy-cheeked girls and yet, twenty years later, Rupert's career was terminated because of . . . He couldn't bear to think about it. He stopped just under the arch and looked back at the young men jostling one another. It seemed so long ago.

The cab drew to a halt outside a tall, narrow Georgian house. The wind was whipping the icy rain along the pavements and Hanley quickly paid off the cabbie. He ran up the steps and, finding the front door ajar, pushed it open and walked into a dark hallway that smelled of damp, and stale cooked onions. "Jimmy." His name echoed down the stairwell. He glanced up and saw Kingsland looking over the banister. "Up here, top floor."

Hanley started up the stairs. The smells got no better, but at least there was a dim yellow light on each of the landings. When he reached the third floor he found a red-painted door standing open. He walked inside and discovered a small, cluttered hallway. "Rupert?"

"I'm in here. In the front room." Hanley noted the slightly slurred tone that told him Kingsland had been drinking.

The front room was a wreck. The curtains were drawn and a small side lamp provided the only light. Newspapers and magazines were everywhere. There was a dining table with the remains of various meals strewn across it: two soup bowls, a plate with half-eaten sandwiches, innumerable cups of coffee and tea in various stages of emptiness.

The sofa was being used as a bed and two blankets were carelessly shoved to one end. A small suitcase lay open and shirts and underwear lay in disarray.

Kingsland sat in the midst of all this chaos like a man at a wake. He had not shaved for days and his hair was greasy and unbrushed. He was slumped down at the table staring straight ahead of him as if presiding over this feast of crusts and tea-dregs.

Hanley sat down and pushed a butter dish and a half-eaten tin of sardines into the centre of the table. He was noting the first tiny blue fuzz growing on the sardines when he looked up and saw his friend pulling a bottle of whisky out from under his chair. Kingsland carefully placed the bottle on the table in front of him. His eyes had dark rings from the many sleepless nights. "Would you like a drink, Jimmy?"

"No, no thanks."

Kingsland stared at him, then pulled over a cup and poured a large measure. "Cheers." He lifted the cup and Hanley noticed the violent shake in his hand. Then he watched as his friend gulped down half the whisky at one go. After the first shock it seemed to steady Kingsland. He grasped the cup with both hands, held it out before him and gave a bitter smile. "To the Navy. God bless us, God bless you all."

In the silence that followed, Hanley cleared his throat. "That bottle won't help. You have to pull yourself together."

Kingsland rubbed his hand over his unshaven chin and took another swig of the whisky. He gave a bitter smile. "Please Jimmy, no, I couldn't take your sympathy."

Hanley bristled. "Well, you're not damned well getting any. You have my friendship and my help if you want it."

"We'll see." Kingsland put down the cup with a clunk then placed his hands neatly in front of him and stared deep into Hanley's eyes. "I didn't ask you here today to be stroked or soothed, far from it. I fully expect you to walk out on me." Kingsland paused as if waiting for a response, but Hanley was silent. He continued, "I've been spying for the Germans."

The words died away in the dusty, disordered corners of the room. For a moment Hanley thought he had heard Kingsland say something else. He looked at him, puzzled, as though his friend had just made a very bad joke.

Kingsland pushed himself back in the chair and took a deep breath. "I've been passing on plans and specifications to the Germans."

Hanley glared down at the table and tapped his forefinger along the edge. He felt lost. He tried to fit this information into some kind of pattern but nothing made sense. This couldn't be his friend Kingsland, the man who had saved his life off the shores of Gallipoli, during the Dardanelles campaign of 1915. This couldn't be the Kingsland he had known since schooldays.

Hanley took out his pipe and pressed down the ash in the bowl, rubbing and rubbing as though the fire-hardened tobacco would provide some answers.

"James, would you say something. Something."

Hanley took a breath. He was stunned. "Why, why?"

Kingsland stood up and started to pace the room. As he did, he squeezed his hands together so that Hanley could hear the knuckle-joints cracking. Then he stopped and starcd at Hanley, wide-eyed. "They, they blackmailed me." He slumped down on the arm of the sofa and pushed his hands through his hair. "It was a Dutch boy, at least I thought he was Dutch. He said his father was in the diamond trade in Amsterdam. We used to meet," Kingsland stopped and for a moment covered his face with his hand and pressed hard on his temples, then he looked up again. "He said they had a flat here for business. It was in Mayfair. Well, we would go there and eh . . ."

Hanley rapped the pipe bowl against the table. "Please, no more. I really find this difficult."

"You! You find it difficult. You don't know what it's like. For years, for all your life hiding who you are even from your friends. Sneaking off like a criminal just to find some love . . ."

Hanley suddenly interrupted. "For God's sake man, what is this? Some kind of apologia for homosexuality? Get on with it. Give me the facts. Tell me what you want."

Kingsland visibly tensed. "All right. They took photographs of me and him. They blackmailed me. They wanted information on submarines. Apparently they needed all the technical information they could get. They've just started rebuilding their fleet."

"Yes, yes I know all about the new U-boats." Hanley slowly shook his head, then sucked at the cold pipe and looked deep into Kingsland's eyes. "You realise I'll have to go to the Admiralty?"

"Yes, I know that." Kingsland crossed to the table. He picked up the cup of whisky, took a gulp, then slowly sank into the chair. "I'm afraid, Jimmy. Afraid. I know a lot about what they're doing here, the Germans, that is, their contacts, their fellow travellers. Now I've been court-martialled, they'll know I have nothing to lose."

He stopped and glanced towards the curtained window. His right hand seemed to drift up and flutter in the dim light as he indicated outside. He paused, deep in thought. "I want you to arrange a meeting with the Admiralty. I have all this information about the Germans, their activities, the details of everything I've traded. I want to, to do a deal."

Hanley frowned and then raised a questioning eyebrow. "What do you mean?"

Kingsland swirled the whisky round in the cup and drained it. Then he looked up at Hanley. There was fear in his eyes but something else. A cold, hard, unsettling determination. "I don't want to go to prison, James, and I won't. Do you know what they do to people like me there? They break us. They use us. I want you to arrange a meeting and I want a promise before I go."

"Christ in heaven, man, they'll hunt you down. You're not in a position to negotiate with anyone."

Kingsland suddenly snapped. "Just deliver the message. I'm not asking for anything else, just one favour, for Chrissake, one favour!"

Hanley looked as if he was going to break his pipe in two. His fists were tightly clenched around the bowl and stem. Then he seemed to make a resolve and carefully put the pipe back in his pocket. "All right, I'll do it." He pushed the chair back and stood up.

Kingsland let out a long slow sigh, then slumped forward. "Thank you. I'm sorry. It's just that I'm near the edge . . ."

Hanley cut him off in mid-sentence. "It's all right." He still felt a sympathy for his friend, but he did not want to open up the doors of emotion. He also felt a growing impatience at having been put in the middle of this unsavoury mess. As he reached the living-room door he turned round. Kingsland was already pouring some more whisky. "I'll phone you after I talk to the Admiralty."

"Yes, yes, but it's probably best if I phone you, I'll be, well, moving around." Hanley watched as Kingsland sipped the drink. The message was plain. He trusted no one.

Hanley nodded and turned to the door. "I'll find my own way out." As he walked out he heard the cup clattering down on the table behind him.

Outside the street was dark and cold. There was a raw dampness in the air and it quickly settled around him. He pulled his coat tightly round his neck and started to walk down towards the river. But somehow he couldn't shake off the effect of the frigid air and soon the deep shivers had penetrated to his bone.

13

Hanley was in the middle of a meeting with the draughtsmen when he heard about the accident. It had happened at the north-west end of number-one basin, known as Submarine Corner. HMS *Shark* was at the dock getting her batteries changed. The electricians were slowly swinging one of the replacements on board when the winch on the crane snapped. The large battery, almost the height of a man, crashed on to the dock and cracked near the base. A jet of acid sprayed out and covered the neck, face and forearms of one of the young electricians, leaving him writhing in agony.

Hanley had been up in the main dockyard offices close to number-two basin. He rushed over, saw the state of the man, and ordered the ambulance driver to take him to the naval hospital in Pembroke Barracks instead of to the dispensary in the yards.

After the ambulance had accelerated away, a group of workers gathered on the dock in a wide circle around the smashed battery. A half-empty drum of electrical wire lay in the path of the spillage. The wooden drum had started to smoke as the acid ate into it. The men stood watching, shaken. Hanley slowly looked around him. It was a strange moment of despair, an insight into the bleak chaos that lay just beyond the boundaries of discipline. He quickly turned to the electrical superintendent. "Get these men back to work and clean up that spillage. We're behind enough in electrical."

As Hanley started back to the main dockyard offices, he heard mumbling behind him. Well, so what if they thought he was a bastard. There was only one way to keep the system going – work, discipline!

It turned out to be one of those very long Mondays. All day he had been trying to make an appointment with Rear Admiral Walker's office but had received only evasive replies. After he had finished with the draughtsmen in the main offices, he had a meeting with James Pollock, a Vickers-Armstrong engineer down from Barrow-in-Furness, going over new specifications for the submarine telemotors.

When Hanley finally arrived back in his office it was late afternoon. He slumped down behind his desk, pulled out his pipe and then turned to stare out of the window. He looked past number-two dry dock towards the river, wishing he was back at sea, smelling the tang of salt on the wind.

He had just lit his pipe when Campbell walked in carrying a bundle of blueprints. "The new T-class specifications are in, sir, and eh . . ." Campbell put the bundle of blueprints on Hanley's desk and pulled a note from his pocket. "A message from Mrs Wilcox, the rear admiral can see you tonight. Medway House at twenty-thirty hours."

Tonight? Hanley looked puzzled. It was rare for the admiral to call business meetings at his home.

"Must be something special, sir, eh?"

"Hmm?" Hanley glanced up. Campbell was staring at him intently, inviting him to continue. It was unusual for Campbell to be so inquisitive, and something about it upset Hanley's sense of etiquette.

Campbell smiled. "It's a strange time for a meeting, must be important."

81

Hanley slowly nodded as he put the matches into his pocket. "Well, everything's been a little strange lately, hasn't it."

There was a moment of silence as the two men faced each other across the desk. Then the shrill whistle on one of the steam engines echoed along from the covered slips.

"Yes, sir, I know what you mean." Campbell turned away, obviously feeling that he had been snubbed. He stopped at the door, "If that's all then, sir, I'll see you tomorrow."

Hanley nodded. "Yes, yes."

When Campbell left, Hanley felt a moment of regret. All he needed now was for Campbell to turn bolshy. It was probably the worry over his wife in the sanatorium.

He gave a sigh and glanced down at the blueprints. Well, at least he could use the time to go over these in peace.

They were the blueprints for the hull of the new T-class submarine, the *Thor*. It was planned that the keel of the *Thor* would be laid down within weeks of the *Graplin*'s launch. This new submarine was to be over a thousand tons, two hundred and sixty-five feet in length with ten twenty-one-inch torpedo tubes.

Even before the *Graplin* slid down into the Medway the ribs of the *Thor* would have been cast in the smithery. Hanley laid the blueprints for these ribs on his drawing-board and scrutinised every measurement. He always insisted on a final inspection of plans before they were sent to the mould loft. There, the ribs would be traced out full-size on the wooden floors. The smallest rib became a circle scratched into the wood. Then another circle was drawn outside the first until the whole thing grew, from the smallest to the largest, like a strange multilayered hieroglyph. Out of each of these tracings a mould or a template was made. These templates were finally taken over to the smithery where the ribs were cast in steel.

Hanley went over each measurement methodically. It was a tedious task, involving dividers and ruler, but he regarded it as essential.

Outside, the autumn light was fading, but he did not really notice it until the phone rang. Then he clicked on the drawing-table light, crossed to his desk and picked up the phone.

"Hello. Captain Hanley speaking."

"Jimmy." He knew instantly that it was Kingsland. "Jimmy, I had to talk to you." Hanley could hear that note of desperation in his voice again.

"Look, I haven't had a chance to talk to the admiral yet. I've just managed to arrange a meeting with him."

"Listen, Jimmy, I'm sorry, I can't do it."

"Can't do it! What the hell do you mean?"

Kingsland's voice began to crack. "The Admiralty won't make a deal. Who in the name of God am I fooling? They're going to put me away for life."

"The wheels are already in motion, Rupert. It's too late." Hanley's voice was cool and logical.

There was another pause, punctuated only by Kingsland's troubled breathing. When he spoke again it was in a quiet, considered tone. "I'm sorry, Jimmy, I won't be here. I've got to go away and think. I've got to go. I'm scared, scared . . ."

Hanley cut across him, "For Chrissake man, pull yourself together." But the phone suddenly went dead. "Hello, hello? Damn!" Hanley was furious. He slammed the receiver back into its cradle and glared out of the window at the lamps flickering along the docks.

He was angry that he was being pulled into the middle of Kingsland's mess. He had already made the appointment with Rear Admiral Walker for that evening. Now he would have to tell him that Kingsland had disappeared. He smashed his fist on the desk and gave a curse.

"Can I take your hat, sir." The maid at Medway House, the rear admiral's residence, gave him her usual pleasant smile and then led him through the house to the back door. "The admiral's up in the summerhouse, taking a cigar. He asked if you'd join him there."

Hanley was surprised. It was a damp evening to be outside. A chill mist had drifted in from the Medway giving the streetlamps an eerie glow. The maid opened the back door for him and he walked out under the verandah with its elegantly carved wooden pillars. He glanced out over the well-manicured lawn. There was smell of lavender in the damp air and also the hint of cigar smoke. Hanley looked up to the left where the white summerhouse stood on top of a small grass embankment. He could hear the murmur of voices and as he started up the stone steps he saw two dim figures moving behind the white slatted boards.

A small dull yellow electric light burned in the middle of the circular wooden building. As Hanley reached the top of the steps he saw the rear admiral in profile. He was tugging his beard in a characteristic gesture and pointing across the garden towards the back wall where a tall streetlamp was casting its hazy glow on two of the oak trees in the garden. ". . . So they offered to shorten the lamp, but I rather liked the play of light and shade through the leaves."

"It must be rather bleak in the winter though." The other man's voice sounded clipped, as though the speaker was impatient with small talk. He stepped forward and Hanley saw an officer of about his own age, with a thin face and deep creases in the cheeks. His fair hair was thinning and pulled tightly back from his forehead, and this seemed to bring his grey-blue eyes into sharper focus.

"I must say I find it all rather bleak in the . . ." the rear admiral was about to continue when he saw Hanley. "Ah Hanley, come in. Take a seat, we're just having a breath of fresh evening air but I can't persuade Captain Marsh here to join me in a cigar."

"Captain Hanley." Marsh nodded, gave a cool businesslike smile and stepped forward. They shook hands and Walker pulled out his cigar case and offered one to Hanley.

"No sir, thank you, I'll stick to this." Hanley sat down on one of the white-painted iron chairs and pulled out his pipe. Surely he would have the chance to talk to Walker alone.

"Well, Hanley, I believe we've been missing each other all day. What's on the agenda?"

Hanley was taken aback. He found it hard to believe that Walker was bringing up unknown dockyard business in front of a visiting officer. "Sir, I had hoped that I could speak to you alone."

"Oh, that's all right, Hanley, go on."

Hanley had never experienced such carelessness from Walker before. "Sir, this is about Lieutenant Commander Kingsland. I really need to talk to you alone."

Marsh stepped forward, glancing first at Hanley and then at Walker. "If you don't mind, sir." Hanley watched him and noted Marsh's cold, businesslike manner. He seemed like a man who was used to taking command of the situation no matter what other rank was present.

"Captain Hanley, I could tiptoe around this all night, but it's much quicker to get to the point. We've known about Kingsland for a long time or to be more precise, we've suspected. We also know that he contacted you."

Hanley felt winded. For a moment he couldn't think, then he began to feel angry. It was suddenly very clear to him that he had been used. When he spoke his voice was strained. "I don't think I fully understand this."

Walker took a puff of his cigar and then cleared his throat. He was obviously uncomfortable. "Hanley, Captain Marsh is in Intelligence." Walker let the information settle into the damp evening air and then continued. "I'm sorry that we couldn't tell you about all this but it was decided that all suspicions about Kingsland should be kept, well, restricted."

"Suspicions?"

Marsh ignored the question. "Captain Hanley, why did you arrange this meeting with us, with the rear admiral?"

"Kingsland phoned me. He told me that he'd been spying for the Germans and he asked me to meet him."

"Aaah!" Marsh's retort was like a rifleshot. "So, he's out in the open."

"You already know this!" Hanley gazed at each of them in turn. "Let me understand this. Was I being tested?"

Marsh put his hand into his trouser pocket and jingled some change. "No, Hanley, you were not being tested." He walked over to the edge of the summerhouse and sat on the white railing. "And we did not know about Kingsland, we suspected.

85

You see, about ten months ago we found out that the Germans were receiving submarine specifications from this yard. It was at that time that I started enquiries into everyone's background."

"Everyone." Hanley knew what that meant and it gave him a strange feeling.

Marsh pulled out a silver cigarette case and took a cigarette. He played with it for a moment and then looked over at Hanley. "It's not a pleasant kind of business but it has to be done. We found out that he was being blackmailed. We needed to stop the leak of information as soon as possible without alerting the Germans."

Hanley interrupted, "So you court-martialled him on the sodomy charges and hoped that would flush him out."

Marsh lit his cigarette. "Exactly." He inhaled and then blew a long thin plume of smoke out across the summerhouse. "And it seems to have worked."

"Only partly, I'm afraid. Kingsland called me late this afternoon. He had wanted me to arrange a meeting so that in some way he could, as he put it, 'make a deal'. Well, when he called, he told me that he'd changed his mind . . . that he wanted to go away and think . . . "

Marsh looked startled. "Do you know where he went?"

Hanley shook his head. "No, I have no idea."

"But you're sure he isn't in that flat?"

Hanley raised a questioning eyebrow. "You followed him?"

"We followed you."

Hanley flashed Marsh a cold look but he knew there was no point in saying anything. "As far as I know he said he'd left the flat."

"I see." Marsh slowly twirled the cigarette around in his fingers, then dropped it to the floor and stubbed it out. "Kingsland is in a dangerous position, we need to find him before his German friends do."

"Well, you seem to be quite expert at that kind of thing, Captain Marsh."

"Correction, Captain Hanley, no one is an expert at this. In matters of national security we take all the help we can."

The rear admiral broke his long silence. "What Captain Marsh is saying, Hanley, is that Intelligence wants you to work with them."

"What exactly does that mean?" Hanley's tone was brittle.

Marsh stood up and started his prowling movement again. "We need someone close to Kingsland. We believe that he's unstable and that he, well, that he could take his own life if we go after him." Marsh paused and then stared at Hanley. "Does any of that ring true, Captain Hanley?"

Hanley gazed into the deepening night as he thought of his friend slumped over the whisky bottle. "Yes, yes, you're probably right."

Marsh continued, "And we need to talk to him, now, before German Intelligence get to him."

Hanley watched the light casting its speckled shadowplay through the slowly stirring autumn leaves. It all seemed so desolate. "So," he mumbled, "I'm to track him down."

14

Tom Cullen felt good. He had won two fights in almost as many days and he had just been told that his professional licence would finally be through at the end of the week.

When he stepped outside the Golden Gloves gymnasium he felt as if the world was starting to open up as his personal oyster. He could tell that even Danny Brockway was pleased. "That was all right tonight, Tom, all right. Now if you could just keep the women and booze at the same distance as you kept that bruiser in there, you could do us all proud." As Danny spoke, his hand-rolled cigarette wagged up and down like a sparrow's beak pecking at crumbs.

Tom glanced along the street towards the Brook and saw a

crowd of sailors hanging around at the corner. In the midst of all the uniforms, Tom could see his brother Ernie, with Terry Gillings. Ernie was pushing his way over to him, grinning proudly. "Hey, Tom lar, that was great! Great! Another friggin' champ." Tom laughed. "Hey, watch your mouth, our mam'll flay you alive." Terry Gillings stepped shyly forward. "Tom, you were great, really." Tom grinned. Danny stepped back and watched. He saw how much Tom enjoyed basking in the limelight and gave a little groan of resignation. That was a two-edged sword. It could push Tom on to greater things or make him rest on his laurels.

Nearby, a car honked its horn and then someone called out, "Tom, hey Tom." They all turned round and saw Eddie Brent leaning out of a car window. "Over 'ere, my old sparrow, I'd like a word." Ernie gave his brother a playful tap on the arm. "It's tough being at the top eh? You get popular with the nobs." Tom gave a strained smile, and caught the look on Danny's face. Danny made no secret of what he thought of Eddie Brent.

Tom fumbled for words. "I ought to go over." Danny stared at him, his eyes blank, unyielding. "Ought you?" There was an awkward moment, then Danny seemed to relent. "Well go on, don't stand there like a prune. I'll meet you over in the Anchor. Your mum's there, isn't she?"

"Yeah, thanks," mumbled Tom.

Danny started off along the pavement with his jaunty step. "Come on, lads, see if you can squeeze a couple of pints outta me." Tom watched them turn the corner and then strode across to where Eddie Brent had parked his car.

It was a gleaming new silver-grey Jaguar. All around people were stopping to stare, or glancing over enviously. Brent got out of the car, leaving the engine on. It purred away beside him like some tame beast as he leaned over the open door. He had an antique silver cigar case in his hand. He opened it and took out a cheroot. "Still off them, eh?" Tom nodded. "Good lad. One of my ladies tells me they'll ruin my teeth. Still, just buy another set, huh?"

Tom laughed, then gestured towards the car. "This is a beaut. Is it yours? I thought the other . . ."

"I keep the other for business, Charlie drives me. This one's mine, strictly for pleasure. And watching you's pleasure too, let me tell you, pure pleasure."

Tom grinned and nervously tossed back his hair. "Thanks."

Brent pulled out a gold cigarette lighter and lit up. "No thanks needed. That was a nice fight Tom, very nice. I tell you, you've got real quality."

Tom shifted from one foot to the other like an awkward schoolboy. "Thanks." Brent took a deep drag of the cheroot and watched him. Then he leaned forward over the open door of the car and said in a quiet voice, "I tell you, Tom, you play your cards right and I can see big money in your future, and that ain't from reading your tea-leaves neither."

Tom gave a loud laugh and then nervously ran his fingers through his dark, curly hair. "Yeah thanks, but I could do with some of the money now though, not in the future."

Two young women strolled past arm in arm. Tom glanced round and one of them turned and gave him a cheeky smile. She was a thin-faced young woman, with bright red lipstick and her light brown hair swept back behind one of her ears. The other girl pulled her by the arm. "Come on, Vera, he's one of them boxers." Vera's smile broadened and Tom gave her a wink before she disappeared into the crowd at the corner. When Tom looked back at Brent, the latter gave him a cool smile. "You and the women, eh!"

Tom gave an embarrassed shrug. "Oh I enjoy a bit of you know . . ." He stopped in mid-sentence. Brent had pulled his wallet out of his pocket and was taking out two five-pound-notes.

"Tom, I don't give a fiddler's shit who you do a twinkle with. It's just bloody healthy as far as I can see. Here, take this." Brent pressed the two fivers into Tom's hand. Tom stared at the notes for a few seconds and then looked up, shocked. "What's this?"

Brent gave a sly grin and took another long drag on his cigarette. "What's wrong then, not the right colour for money, eh? It's a little gift for you, that's what it is."

Tom frowned. "I don't understand." Brent leaned forward

over the door again. His voice was low, almost conspiratorial. "Stick it in your pocket for Chrissake. Listen, Tom, I made a nice little bundle of money on you tonight. The whole of the China Fleet was in there betting on their friggin' stoker, Bruiser whadymacallim. So I reckon I owe you a piece of the action."

Tom stared down at the crisp new notes and then tentatively offered them back to Brent. "Listen, Mr Brent, I don't think I can take them, I don't think it would be right." Brent snatched the notes from Tom's hands and gave a wicked chortle. He quickly shoved them into the top pocket of Tom's crumpled jacket. "Bollocks! Sleep on it, then post them back if you still think it's wrong."

Tom gave a sheepish smile as he patted his pocket. All he could think was, ten quid, nearly a month's wages.

Brent jumped into the car and slammed the door shut. He revved the engine as he rolled down the window. There was a cold, calculating glint in his eye. "Tom, I know you're going professional soon." Tom registered his surprise. Brent saw this and continued with a thin-lipped smile, "You need a manager with contacts in London and you need someone who'll make you money. Money, remember it's not a dirty word. Just think of Eddie Brent before you sign on any dotted line – you know where I am. You're welcome any time at the Chinese Parrot, my guest. Think it over."

Tom stood at the kerb and watched the sleek Jaguar accelerating away and then turning right into the High Street. He had heard that Brent had a house somewhere out towards Maidstone, a mansion where he lived with his mother and cultivated orchids in a specially heated greenhouse. Of such stuff were legends made, and Eddie Brent did nothing to discourage them.

The Anchor was packed. It was always the same when the fleet came in, every night was a Saturday night. When Tom saw the crowd pushing around the bar he regretted that he'd asked his mother to meet him there. Still, it was close to the gym and the saloon was usually a quiet oasis.

Tom glanced around him just to make sure that they weren't at one of the tables. He looked along the line of heavy wooden cubicles. Every one was filled with sailors and girls. Tom gave a laugh, it was always the same. The unattached hung around the bar; bunches of blue-suited sailors, some awkwardly shy, others vulgarly forward. The women hovered around them in smaller groups like flies round meat in summer. There was nothing subtle about what went on here. When the first brief contact had been made, a couple would walk over towards the cubicles, squeeze in behind the polished dark mahogany tables and continue the "chatting up".

Towards the back of the bar there was an old upright piano under a large mirror advertising Dewar's Fine Scotch Whis. . . the final gold lettering on the last word having been erased over the years. A crowd of sailors had gathered around the piano and were banging their pints rhythmically on the top, singing their raucous version of a sea-shanty.

> When you came to port you'd see our Meg
> For she'd heave to with any sailor's peg.

A couple of young women sitting nearby were giving their coy version of embarrassed smiles. They were obviously not professionals. Tom gave a grunting laugh, the nightly pageant of sexual innuendo was in full swing.

The dusty multitiered chandelier overhead tinkled with the vibrations and as Tom gazed up into its mass of glittering beads he heard someone call his name. "Hey Tom." He glanced over to the bar and saw Joe the barman waving at him from behind a line of sudsy pints. Joe was a big beefy man with sloping shoulders, a large curly brown beard peppered with grey and a balding pate. He gave Tom one of his broad toothy grins and then boomed over the noise of the singing, "I heard you won tonight. You'll have one on me? Danny and your mother are in here." Joe pointed towards the wood-panelled partition with its frosted glass insets of sailing ships.

Tom gave Joe a cheery wave and then started towards the saloon. He turned the shiny brass handle, opened the door and stepped inside. The saloon was much smaller than the public bar but it had the same dark wooden booths along the walls. He saw his mother sitting with Danny, Kitty, Ernie and Terry, below a row of faded photos of ships built in the Chatham dockyards.

"Over 'ere, Tom." Danny, his manager, waved at him. "We've been telling your mum about your great win."

Mary looked up. "I'm just glad he's not hurt, that's all."

Tom sank down on the chair beside her, beaming like an eleven-year-old who had just scored for the school football team. "I'm all right, Mam, really. I'm a big boy now, you know."

Danny leaned over the table and squashed his hand-rolled cigarette into the ashtray, then scooped up some of the empties. "So, what can I get you? Come on, Tom, you're allowed at least one drink when you win." Tom looked up and wondered briefly if he was being sarcastic, but Danny had a broad smile on his face. "Well, thanks Danny, I'll have a pint of best." Danny nodded, "And two halves for the lads, a lemonade for Kitty, and, another sherry Mrs C?"

Mary flushed and automatically pulled her hair back from her forehead. "Yes, well, that'd be nice." She was enjoying the attention.

Danny took her glass and was reaching for Kitty's when she pulled it back. She gazed up at him and gave a plaintive smile. "I'd really like a sherry too, Mr Brockway."

Danny glanced over at her mother. "I think you'd better ask your mam."

Kitty gave Mary a winsome look. "Oh come on, Mam."

Mary paused for a moment and then raised an eyebrow. "Oh well, all right."

Danny gave Kitty a cheery wink. "Right, we're all set then, are we?"

Kitty responded with a broad smile. "Can I come up and help you with them?"

"Why not, I won't say no to a beautiful young woman elbowing me at the bar."

Kitty lifted the remaining glasses and followed Danny. Mary watched her for a moment and then turned to Tom. "Did you hear our Ernie's started working in the yards with Terry? His Uncle Albert got him a start."

Tom slapped Ernie on the shoulders. "Hey lar, that's great." Ernie looked less than thrilled. "Yeah well, I'm just a cleaner," Tom quickly cut him off. "It's a start, you should think yourself lucky." Then he turned to his mother. "Listen, Mam, a word with you." He turned his back on the boys and spoke in a low voice. "I'm going to go professional, quit my job."

Ernie turned to Terry and mumbled, "You can see how interested they are in me, they don't give a fiddler's fuck. I don't want to be spending my days cleaning up a load of crud. You haven't heard me play my saxophone yet, but you know I could be in a great swing band. Up in Liverpool I used to go to the Roxy and I . . ."

Slowly Terry's concentration faded. He didn't really want to hear about dance music or Ernie's dreams, but he nodded politely. As Ernie rambled on he glanced beyond him towards the door.

A couple of men had just walked in, each carrying a pile of pamphlets. He recognised one of them from the yards, Reggie Dickson. He was a tall slender young man with dark wavy Brylcreemed hair. As he glanced around, Terry caught his eye and waved to him.

"Sorry, Ernie," he had just cut across Ernie's description of how he would like to create a "Dorsey kind of band, you know" in London, "that's an electrician from the yards. I think he's handing out some political stuff."

Ernie looked instantly bored and Terry got up and pushed past the crowded tables. He caught Reggie sorting out his pamphlets and tapped him on the shoulder. "Hello, d'you remember me? You gave us that talk about wiring telemotors."

Reggie looked up and gave a cheeky grin. "Yeah, you're the Gillings lad, aren't you?"

Terry nodded, and then wondered about being identified as Albert Gillings' lad. But Reggie continued, "You're the one who had all the questions. I thought they'd find out I was a fraud."

Terry laughed with relief at being remembered for himself, then pointed to Reggie's pamphlets. "So what're you selling?"

"This? Trying to spread a little light about the war in Spain. But if you want to find out more, read one of them." He handed Terry one of the pamphlets. "This'll explain a lot and anything you don't understand give me a nod at work, in a tea-break preferably, so your dad or Wallis or Gates don't throw a fit."

Terry gave a tentative smile, pleased to be accepted by someone he respected. "Yeah, yeah, I will." As Reggie walked away, Terry glanced down and saw that it was published by the Communist Party. Surely Reggie wasn't in the party. Terry looked up.

Reggie had crossed to his mate who was waiting at the door. He glanced back, gave Terry a last nod and then left. Terry felt a twinge. That's all his dad needed to know, that he was friends with a communist, and there would be a first-class bust-up. Still that wasn't going to stop him supporting something if it was right.

Kitty peered through the heavy cigarette smoke, and past the jostling crowd. At one of the booths along the side she saw a woman sitting with a glowering gorilla of a man in naval uniform. He had drooping bulldog eyes and large dark nostrils that gave him the look of a pig. But it was not his ugly looks that fascinated Kitty. It was something about their isolation, the man's sultry silence, the woman's servile but desperate demeanour, that drew her attention.

The woman looked older than the others in the bar. She had made a brave attempt to cover the wrinkles with make-up but it had failed. She was like a gaudily painted doll with its cloth skin sagging and bulging beneath. Her face was framed by bright red, almost orange, hair and her lips stood out like a slash of wine-red paint.

As Kitty stared, she noticed that the refracted light from one of the tiers of glass beads in the chandelier fell across the woman's face like a multi-coloured wound. For a moment Kitty actually thought that it was a real scar. But then she saw it move and gave a shiver. It was like a badge, an omen.

The redhead had a large gin in one hand, and Kitty gazed at her completely engrossed. She watched her swaying drunkenly to the music of the piano and saw the potent liquor slopping over the edge of the glass and on to her already stained dress. The woman barely seemed to notice the wetness soaking into her thighs. Instead she made a fumbling effort like someone sleepily swatting a fly and then tried to regain her composure by pushing strands of her bright red hair back out of her eyes.

"There you are, love. I said there you are, all paid for." Kitty turned to Joe, a distracted, faraway look in her eyes. "We've caught you dreaming, haven't we?"

"Yes, yes," she mumbled. Then she picked up the two glasses of sherry and brought them back to the table.

Tom gave a satisfied grin. "Cheers. Ah there you are, girl, and now where's Ernie to give us a toast?"

They all glanced towards the public bar where the piano was now crashing out some jaunty ragtime tunes. Mary raised her eyebrows. "He's probably glued to that piano."

Kitty jumped up again. "I'll get him!"

Mary spun round "No you don't, my young lady. I don't want you in there . . ." But Kitty was already halfway towards the door.

Kitty pushed her way through the crowd towards the piano. For a few seconds she felt her heart throbbing as though she was in some forbidden sanctuary. She knew that all the women were here for only one purpose. These were the "bad women", like the ones she had seen hanging around the pierhead in Liverpool, waiting for the sailors.

The mixed smells of cheap perfume and gin engulfed her, and the jangling notes of the piano added to the exotic strangeness of it all. She continued edging her way through the crowd and saw Ernie standing there listening to the music. About half a dozen sailors and three or four sappers from the Royal Engineers barracks were drunkenly slurring the words of the new hit song "Moon Over Miami".

Kitty looked past the singers and saw that the pianist was a pretty young girl not much older than herself. Kitty was caught by something in her expression. She had pulled her fair hair back, and it was held by a large ivory comb carved in the shape of a schooner. It showed the baby roundness of her face, the smooth clearness of her skin.

The girl turned, and Kitty saw her languid green eyes and insinuating smile.

Kitty instantly liked her. She returned the smile then stepped forward and touched her brother on the arm. "Ernie, our mam wants you. Mr Brockway's got you a drink."

Ernie nodded. "Yeah, I'll be back in a minute." Then he indicated the piano.

Kitty stepped back, and as she did she stood on someone's toe. "Oh sorry." She spun round and bumped into a tall, skinny sailor.

"Hey darlin', so what brings you here?"

Kitty ignored him and turned back to the piano. After a few seconds she felt him shuffling around her and looked up to see a long, acned face partly covered by a scrawny ginger beard. "Yes?"

The sailor stared at her, puzzled. "What's wrong with you then, too good for us?"

Kitty gave a sigh and flashed a noncommittal smile. "I'm just listening to the piano."

He stared, as if trying to absorb her answer. "You wouldn't turn down a drink, would you?"

Kitty gave a weary shrug. "Thanks but I'm not really thirsty."

The sailor moved a little closer and dropped his voice to a conspiratorial semiwhisper. Kitty could smell the mix of sour beer, chips and cigarette smoke on his breath and she recoiled. "We could have a little chat," he continued unabashed. "I'm just back from the Far East, you know I've seen it all there. Hong Kong with the chinks living on their boats, Macao with those friggin' cunning Portuguese and the Japs everywhere o'course, kicking the shit outta Manchuria . . ."

Kitty glared at him. She had to get away. "Excuse me but I don't like language like that."

He gave a snickering laugh. "Aw come on now, love, give us a break." The sailor laid his hand on her shoulder. It was the wrong thing to do. Kitty rounded on him, sucking in her breath with an angry hiss. "Don't you *dare* touch me. Who the hell do you think you are!"

The piano stopped and the sailor realised that his mates were listening. He furrowed his brow and leered at Kitty through narrowing eyelids. He was teetering somewhere between surprise and anger. Then he swayed drunkenly forward. "You little slut, what are you coming in flogging your wares for if you're so snotty?"

The young girl at the piano suddenly banged her fist down on the ivories and the dissonant notes clanged across the noisy bar. Other people began to turn and watch the commotion.

Kitty spun round and caught the look of sympathy in the young pianist's eyes. The pretty fair-haired girl gave her a fleeting smile and then turned to the sailor. "You watch your mouth!"

But the sailor was now too far gone to watch anybody's mouth. Anger or sex, it didn't really matter to him now, it all felt like the same steam valve. "Shut up, you little tart! All this fucking place is, is a fucking kip joint for a lot of whores." He was stopped in mid-sentence by a deluge of beer pouring over face and clothes. Kitty had taken the opportunity, and tossed his pint all over him.

There was a moment of stunned silence. Then, before he could recover his senses, Kitty sidestepped and ducked between two of his friends. She was just in time. He swung round in a vicious attempt to hit her but found only thin air. The force of his blow caused him to lurch sideways and his feet slipped from under him. He fell with a crash to the floor and brought a table with him. Now he was seething. "Come here, you little fucking whore." He tried to scramble to his feet, half tumbling, half falling after Kitty in the attempt. Chairs, beer glasses and other tables crashed into his path.

Ernie had at first stood dumbfounded at Kitty's audacity. Then he quickly saw that she was in danger. The other sailors were not prepared to help and stood back laughing at their mate drunkenly scrambling after her. Ernie was scared, the sailor was lean and tough-looking, but he had to do something

97

to stop the bastard getting at his sister! He jumped over the debris of chairs and broken glass and slammed the man hard in the back. The sailor fell to the floor, winded. Then, as he tried to scramble to his feet again, Ernie wrestled to lock his arm behind his back.

In the struggle that followed another sailor rushed forward and grabbed Ernie round the neck. Suddenly the large figure of Joe the barman loomed over all of them. "That's it! Out! All of you!" Joe grabbed the man behind Ernie by the scruff of the neck and yanked him off. For a moment the other sailors looked uncertain.

Joe drew a deep breath and tensed as if preparing to spring. He flashed a cold smile. "I said I would like you to leave, gentlemen." One by one the sailors shrugged, mumbled to each other, and then slowly edged their way towards the door.

Ernie sidled over, caught Kitty by the arm and said in a low voice, "I can't believe you."

Kitty was taken by surprise. "What?"

"What d'you want to go starting a row for?"

She glared at him "Me? Did you hear what he called me?"

Ernie clenched his teeth, he did not want another argument to erupt. "Look, you should just've skipped out, you shouldn't have been in this bar anyway."

Kitty gazed at him in disbelief. "I came to get you."

"Yeah, well, in future you can leave me alone."

Kitty yanked her arm away and gave him a cold contemptuous look. "Ernie! You're a wanker! Did I ever tell you before – a top-class wanker!"

Ernie quickly stepped back, crunching a piece of broken glass under his foot. "Christ you," he was about to give vent to his feelings but he saw the determined glint in her eye and gave a shuddering sigh. "You're not worth it." He shook his head in angry frustration and then stormed off through the crowd.

Kitty stood for a moment catching her breath, then she tossed back her hair and brushed a band of tiny sweat beads from her forehead.

"Hello." Kitty turned. The pretty young pianist was standing beside her. "Thanks. I'm glad you did that, they think they can call you anything in here."

Kitty laughed, "We were a good team." Then she peered into the other girl's clear green eyes. There was a sharpness there, a translucent intelligence. "My name's Kitty, what's yours?"

"Susie, Susie Popham. I play the piano here and in the Chinese Parrot sometimes."

"Ooh." The name rang a bell and Kitty had an image of Tom's smooth friend Eddie Brent, driving off in his flash car.

"Hey, Susie, liven this place up a bit, would you." Joe ambled by, carrying a dustpan full of broken glasses.

Susie gave Kitty a bright smile. "Gotta go, gotta earn the pennies. Maybe see you again, eh?"

Kitty nodded. "Yes, I'd like that." Then she started back towards the saloon bar as the piano launched into another popular tune. She felt good. She was learning to cope, learning to deal with Chatham. She braced her shoulders and elbowed her way through the crowd.

15

Eunice had just returned from her charity rounds at the naval hospital when Olwen gave her Hanley's phone message. "Sorry, I'll be late. Have an important meeting." She restrained herself, but Olwen could tell by the tight cast of her mouth that she was angry.

Later, after dinner, Eunice sat alone in the music room and tried to plough her way through a Dorothy L. Sayers mystery. Usually she enjoyed Lord Peter Wimsey stories, but tonight she could not relax, even after two glasses of brandy.

At ten o'clock, Nigel came in and said goodnight. Soon afterwards, Eunice poured herself another glass of brandy and started up towards her bedroom. Obviously Hanley was going to be really late.

For a long time she sat in front of her dressing-table mirror, simply sipping the drink and staring. She gazed appraisingly at the delicate lines on her face, the crow's-feet, the laugh-lines as her mother loved to call them. Laugh-lines or not, it was obvious that she was getting older. She gave a sigh and wondered how life was managing to slip away so fast. Perhaps that was why she was so angry with Hanley. Time was ticking away relentlessly and yet she seemed to be condemned to a life of solitary evenings.

She thought of Olivia Brampton and the afternoon at her soirée. She had met such fascinating people and a number of men had seemed to find her interesting. She allowed her mind to drift and saw herself wandering through Olivia's drawing room. There was the small, dark-haired professor from the Sorbonne, talking excitedly about communism and art, the tall American who wrote the musicals and, of course, the German, Weichert. For the last few days she had been trying not to think of him. After all, she was being adolescent. They had hardly spoken except for those final words of parting, but she kept thinking of those ice-blue eyes nakedly appraising her.

She held the stem of the brandy glass between her forefinger and thumb and twirled it so that it glittered in the light and as she did so she thought of Olivia and her Italian in the darkroom at the end of the studio. She saw the door partly open, and in the dim red lamplight the two of them lying on the floor oblivious to all but their passion. The memory excited her. She saw Olivia's dress pulled off the shoulders, her bare breast and the Italian sucking greedily, saw his hand fluttering up along the length of Olivia's thigh, pushing the dress aside, revealing the slash of white flesh at the top of her silk stockings.

She stared deep into the mirror, deep into her dark eyes. Why was it a memory that would not leave her? Why was she so fascinated and repelled at the same time? She banged the glass down on top of the dressing-table. She knew the answer, she just did not want to face it.

She heard someone on the stairs and it jolted her out of her disturbing daydream. She shook her head, tossing her hair aside, as though in some way that would shake the thoughts of Olivia and her lover and Weichert out of her mind. But of course it wouldn't.

"Oh hello, I wondered where you were." Hanley walked in and immediately took off his uniform jacket and tie.

She glanced up at him in the mirror. "It was late, I was tired."

He heard the hint of an argument in her voice and sank down on the end of the bed. "Yes, yes, I'm sorry, Eunice. Is the bathroom free?"

Eunice dipped her fingers into the jar of cold cream and gently stroked it into her cheeks and neck. "Yes, Nigel's in his room studying. Have you had anything to eat?"

"I grabbed a bite up at the wardroom."

She saw him lean forward and press his fingers into his temples. "Is there some kind of crisis?" she asked.

"Hmm? Oh not really."

Suddenly she spun round on him. She knew he was under pressure, but it angered her that he would never share his problems. "Oh James, for God's sake how can we go on like this?"

He looked up, surprised. "What do you mean?"

"I mean, James, you never talk; we never talk."

He watched her gently rubbing the last of the cream down her neck and on to the top of her cleavage. She looked beautiful, inviting, with her hair up and the negligée pushed off her shoulders. "I'm sorry, Eunice, I'm sorry, I'm just distracted." Once again he put his fingers up to his temples and pressed hard.

"Oh really, I hadn't noticed." Hanley heard the gently teasing tone in her voice and gave a reluctant smile. She got up, crossed to the bed and put her hands on his shoulders. For a moment he seemed to stiffen, then he slowly relaxed and let his head hang forward.

101

"Massage?" she asked. He nodded and she stroked her hand along his shirt, feeling the shoulder muscles taut underneath. Then she pushed her thumbs deep into the flesh, making small circles.

"I'm sorry, Eunice."

"It's all right, you know, I'll do this anyway."

Hanley laughed. "Yes, but I am. I get caught up in the dockyards in all of this and . . ." He stopped. He didn't want to tell her that he might be away for the next week searching for Kingsland. For the time being he just wanted to enjoy the sensation of her fingers working into his shoulders. Then he continued, "I really am sorry about not getting to your mother's this weekend."

Eunice eased forward and leaned over his shoulders. Then she slid her hand down the front of his shirt and unbuttoned it. Her mouth was at his ear. "It's all right, James," she said quietly.

He felt her warm breath on his cheek and the softness of her breasts pressing into his back. She pulled the shirt back off his shoulders and gently ran her hands along his skin, then once again started to press her fingers into the tightened muscles. He gave a groan and momentarily tensed up as she pressed a painful knot. Then he relaxed again and as he did, he felt the first stirrings of desire. Her fingers moved up from the pain points and slowly caressed his neck and up behind his ear. Then he felt her fingernails gently scratching into his hairline.

She leaned in close again and said quietly, "Does it feel better?"

"Yes, yes, it does."

Slowly her fingers started to rub away his aches. "James, remember that holiday on the island of Sark, when we first got married." She stopped for a moment and pulled the comb from her hair so that it fell loosely over her shoulders. "I was thinking, it would be nice if we could take a couple of days, go away together."

As she massaged, he thought of the room they had had in the small hotel, Le Petit Pêcheur. The iron bed, the white walls and the simple, rough-hewn furniture. "Do you remember the old bicycles we hired from Madame Bonte?"

She laughed. "Yes. They rattled so badly, the locals could hear us coming a mile away."

"Thank God they didn't always hear us," he said.

She stopped massaging and leaned forward. Her long loose hair brushed lightly across his shoulders and fell against his cheek. "That's a very frivolous comment from you. I didn't think that a busy captain in the Navy thought of such things."

He gave her an almost boyish smile. "You're wrong then. I was just remembering how I would sit on the edge of that iron bed and you would massage my neck."

Eunice sank down beside him and her negligée slipped off her left shoulder. He turned to her and saw the smooth curve of her breast above the top of the fallen negligée. The silk was pulled tight and he could see her nipple pushing firmly against the shiny cloth. God but she was still a startlingly beautiful woman.

She watched him, and saw the desire growing in his eyes. She felt a tightening in her stomach and a dull glow in her loins. "Yes, James, but somehow those massage sessions in Sark always got interrupted."

He nodded slowly, then reached up and gently touched her breast. For a moment they sat like that, quiet and unmoving. Then she swung her legs around and stood up.

"Where are you going?"

She crossed to the door, closed it and turned to him. "Nowhere, I just want to make sure our interruption isn't interrupted." Then she sauntered back and smiled mischievously as she knelt on the bed, and slipped her arms around his neck. Slowly he sank backwards and she fell on top of him.

Hanley kissed her, gently at first and then with increasing passion. He ran his fingers over the curves of her shoulders and then down on to the firm smoothness of her breasts. He pulled at the edge of the silken negligée and finally tugged it off. As he caressed her fullness he caught her nipple between his finger and thumb. Eunice gave a sigh and slowly slipped on to the bed beside him, then she snaked her legs around his and squeezed him towards her. As the smooth silk edged up along her thighs,

103

a memory flashed into her mind. It was of Hans Weichert, his ice-cold eyes coolly assessing her across the room at Olivia's party, as if he was waiting for his chance. But it was just a flash and then it was gone.

16

Ernie Cullen glared at the pile of oil-soaked rags under the bench and cursed. He loathed his job, loathed every minute of it. He sank to his knees on the slatted wooden walkway and then crawled underneath. He could feel the sweat pouring down his temples. His back was aching and his eyes were stinging from the acrid smell of molten metal. His hands looked like swollen black gloves. They were covered in oil and full of small painful cuts from the tiny metal shavings. He tried to wipe them clean on his overalls but it made no difference. Then he clenched and unclenched his fingers. This was Ernie Cullen, the great jazz saxophonist, and his fingers felt like sausages. He hadn't touched his saxophone in over a week.

"Hey Ernie, what you doin' skulking in there?"

Ernie looked up and saw Jimmy Sawyer, one of the other cleaners. Jimmy was wheeling his dustbin down between the metal-cutting machines. "I'm friggin' working, you prick," said Ernie angrily. Jimmy gave an inane laugh and then leaned in under the bench flashing a cocky, smiling sneer.

"Hey, we're all going up to the dogtrack tonight, you coming?"

Ernie gave a groan. "Oh God! I can't. I've lost a fortune on the horses."

Jimmy looked at him as if he was stupid. "Well, you're getting paid today, aren't you?" Jimmy crossed to his cart and started down towards the engine test-beds.

Ernie pulled himself out from under the bench and gazed up at the latticed steel rafters on the ceiling of the factory. Beyond that, the long glass skylights opened on to the blue sky and clouds above. Christ, if he could only fly away from all this shit!

"Hey young 'un, I'm buried in filings over 'ere." A fitter was calling to him from one of the large drills. Parts of a metal gear-casing lay stacked on the bench around him. "I'll be back in a jiffy. Have it cleared up." As Ernie was picking up his broom, he saw Terry Gillings walking down towards the offices with some of the other young apprentices.

"Terry, over here lar." Terry swung round and for a brief moment Ernie thought he saw a look of embarrassment on his face.

However Terry left the others and jogged over. "Ernie, how are you?"

"I'm okay." Ernie glanced jealously over his shoulder at the other apprentices as they sauntered on through the factory. "No, I'm not okay, I feel friggin' clapped out cleaning up this shit."

Terry shrugged his shoulders and attempted a sympathetic grimace. "Well, sorry to hear that. Look, I must push on." Terry's eyes brightened. "I've got a couple of hours' work on the *Graplin* this evening, I'm to go on an inspection of the wiring with the foreman down in the battery bay." Ernie eyes glazed over in boredom. But Terry had already started towards the factory door. He shouted over his shoulder. "We can catch up some other time."

Ernie watched him walking away and felt as if he had been snubbed. Then he turned to the sludgy mixture of oil, dirt and filings on the floor and gave a groan of despair. He grabbed his broom and started to sweep. As he did so he glanced towards the foremen's offices and saw Terry talking to Reggie Dickson, the fellow they had met in the pub.

Probably talking about politics, thinking how friggin' clever they are. Who am I kidding? Terry's just as snotty a fart as the rest of them. Ernie flung his broom on to the floor, then started down the aisle after Jimmy. He was going to go to the dogtrack

105

tonight, no matter what. He deserved it. He deserved something out of life. He *earned* his damned money sweeping up in this greasy pigsty, surely he had the right to spend some of it for a bit of fun.

Ernie was not the only person to see Terry talking with Reggie Dickson. The electrical foreman's office was in the middle of the factory, up the stairs overlooking the long aisles of machinery. Albert Gillings was at the window with Wallis scanning a large blueprint of the *Graplin*'s telemotor when he looked down and saw Terry and Reggie laughing and joking together. He quickly turned from the blueprints, snatched his bowler hat from the rack and opened the door. The air was suddenly filled with the noises of the factory, the whirring of machines, the screech of metal on metal, the banging of hammers and chisels, the grinding clatter of chains on pulleys, the high-pitched whine of engines on the test beds.

"I'll finish this later."

Wallis was surprised at his quick exit.

"Mr Gillings . . ."

Gillings looked back, his face stern. "I've got to go, Wallis. I want to catch my son."

Wallis glanced down and saw Terry on the factory floor below. He nervously brushed his unruly mop of ginger hair out of his eyes. "Just one thing, I wondered if I could get two more tickets for the launching next Friday, my wife's mother and father are in town."

"Yes, of course," Gillings interrupted. He was already out of the door and clattering down the black metal steps. He shouted back, "Call at the main offices, they'll be there."

"Thanks, Mr Gillings, thanks." Wallis walked over to the door but Gillings had already disappeared.

Gillings had doubled back under the stairway to a small storeroom, used to make the tea and keep general office supplies. He saw that the place was empty and walked in. A large brown enamel teapot sat on an electric heating pad. He lifted a chipped mug from one of the shelves and poured himself some dark brown tea and took a sip. It tasted strong and bitter.

106

He stepped over to a small table, took two heaped teaspoons of sugar from a half-empty bag and quickly stirred them into the dark liquid.

When he glanced back towards the window, Terry was just walking past. Gillings stepped to the door and called out to him.

Terry spun round, surprised. "Dad, eh, Mr Gillings."

Gillings stepped back into the storeroom and gestured to his son to follow. Terry knew immediately that something was wrong. He walked inside and glanced around. They were alone. He took in the grey metal shelves, filled with rolls of blueprint paper, boxes of writing pads and envelopes, tins of pencils and bottles of ink. Then he crossed to the window and turned to face his father. Gillings was standing over by the gently steaming teapot adding some milk to his tea.

"Terry, I won't beat about the bush, what were you talking to that lad Dickson about?"

Terry was taken aback by his father's harsh tone. "I don't understand. What do you mean? Why shouldn't I talk to him?"

Gillings stared at his son's open face. "I asked you what you were talking about, Terry?"

Terry felt immediately defensive. "The war in Spain, there's a meeting about it next week and I'd like to go." He paused and then said quietly, "Though I don't see how it's any of your business."

"Lad, everything in this yard is my business, and don't you forget it." Gillings' voice had a sharp edge of anger. "Spain eh? Last week it was the Jarrow hunger crusade, then the month before that, Mussolini murdering the soddin' blackies in Ethiopia . . ."

Terry broke in. "Dad, please, what are you saying? I don't know what you're saying!"

Gillings slammed his mug on to one of the metal shelves. The tea slopped over the edge and dribbled down on to a stack of graph paper. "I'm saying he's a communist, Terry, he doesn't give a damn about other people's misery, it's just an excuse for creating trouble."

107

Terry slowly shook his head, keeping his eyes firmly fixed on his father's white, strained face. "I don't understand."

"You didn't know he was a member of the Communist Party?"

For Terry the next moment seemed like an hour. Then he shook his head again. "We never talked about it."

Gillings stared at him, and raised a quizzical eyebrow. "No, of course not, they're a damned sly lot, they'll work behind every front organisation they can get their hands on. They'll be out collecting for all the dispossessed wankie-wankie tribes of Africa . . . and then suddenly you'll turn round and see they've organised a strike." Terry laughed but Gillings was not in the mood, even for his own bitter humour. "Terry, I don't want you mixing with him, d'you hear me?"

"Oh come on, Dad, even if you're right, I mean communism's not a disease, you don't get it by breathing the same air . . ."

Gillings wheeled round on him, his eyes gleaming, his face flushed. His voice came out as half whisper, half hiss. "You do what you're told! I'm not having you, nor me either, dragged down by a load of communist bastards. Understand!"

Terry remained silent for a moment, then replied in a muted tone, "Yes, yes." There was nothing more to say. He had rarely seen his father so angry. "I better get on, I've got to get up to the *Graplin*."

Gillings picked up the rest of the tea and took a gulp. He attempted a grim smile. "And we won't bring any of this home, right?"

"No, of course not." Terry nodded and walked out of the storeroom.

Over to the left they were grinding engine pistons, and the high-pitched screech of metal on stone pierced his ears like a needle. In the same way, he could feel his father's eyes burrowing into his back. He had of course known about Reggie being a communist, but it just wasn't important to him.

He walked quickly towards the massive grey metal doors of the factory, past the pounding of the steam hammer pulverising the metal sheets into shape, and on out into the grey damp afternoon.

He held out his hands and saw that they were shaking. Whatever had happened in that room, he knew that he had told his first lie about politics. He also knew that it would probably not be his last.

17

Kitty was tired and disgruntled. It was almost nine-thirty and she had just got home. She had only started the job two days ago and already she was sick of it. The Johnsons' small newsagents shop was in Pringle Street at the Gillingham end of the dockyards. They attended the same church as her Aunt Irene and Uncle Albert and that was how she had found out about the job. But now as she felt her aching feet and legs she wished she had never heard of the *Daily Express*, the *Mirror*, *Herald* or *Mail*, and could happily have drowned every packet of Players cigarettes at the bottom of the Medway.

She pushed the half-eaten bag of chips to one side then dropped her head into her hands. In the dull yellow light she gazed up at the begrimed, grease-splattered walls. She might just as well be back in Culver Street in Liverpool!

"Holy Christ, what a way to spend a Friday night!" She quickly wrapped up the remains of her fish supper and tossed it into the bucket by the sink, then turned on the tap and filled a cup with water. As she did so, she thought of her new boss, Mr Johnson, slurping his tea out of a saucer. It was one of his many habits that set her teeth on edge. He was a small man but very fat, and as he squeezed by her, behind the narrow counter, she could feel his massive stomach. He always gave her a smile. "Sorry, Kitty, we'll have to widen this."

She took a sip of the water and then tossed the rest in the sink. "Dirty ol' bugger!" He was so repulsive with his small piggy eyes and grey greasy hair. What she hated most was his hypocrisy. He railed about the "lowering of moral standards" when he skimmed the headlines in the papers, but she noticed how he looked up her legs when she had to climb the stepladder and how his elbow would brush against her breast when he reached across to open the till. Well damn him! If the greasy old fart squeezed any closer to her, she would give him a Mersey kneecap in the balls!

Kitty turned from the sink and strutted out of the kitchen into the hallway. Friday night and she was alone eating fish and chips! It didn't fit her image of Chatham. Where were the fancy nightclubs, the handsome young officers? She stopped for a moment and looked along the dim hall. The place seemed so quiet. Her mother had just got an evening job cleaning some doctors' offices in Rochester, so she had to fend for herself. As for Ernie, he was probably in some pub or club now, living it up.

She switched on the living-room light, crossed to the window and stared out along the street. Then she banged on the chipped frame. She was fed up sleeping in here on the sofa. The window was open and the raw smell of the butcher's shop drifted up. A gang of young boys had tied a ragged rope from one of the lamps and were doing Tarzan swings out into the street. Further along, next to the Cricketers pub, the fur-coated woman in the large Bile Beans advertisement appeared to gaze at her in disdain.

Kitty slumped back on to the arm of the sofa and imagined the coat on her. She pursed her lips and leaned her elbow on her knee. "I'll have a gin and tonic." She could feel everyone around her being impressed. She was Joan Crawford or Greta Garbo or Claudette Colbert, by turn elegant, mysterious and playful.

The front door slammed and she jumped up from the arm of the sofa. "Mam?" There was no reply. She heard someone rumbling around in the kitchen and crossed to the hall door. As she opened it she saw Ernie disappearing into his room holding a couple of slices of bread in one hand and a bottle in the other.

"Ernie."

He did not even look round but quickly kicked the door shut behind him. Kitty strutted down the hall and threw it open. Ernie was seated at the end of his bed staring at the empty iron fireplace.

"Hey what the frig're you doin' busting into my room? Is there no friggin' privacy here?"

Kitty folded her arms and leaned against the doorpost. "No, not for me there's not. Remember, I live in the front room."

Ernie grunted, lifted the beer bottle, took a swig and then glared at her. "Well? Do you mind leaving me alone."

Kitty could feel her temper starting to fray. "What the hell's wrong with you? Didn't you hear me calling you when you came in?"

"Yes! But I just want to be left alone."

Kitty bristled. Her nails did a gentle drumroll on the cracked, white porcelain door-handle. She knew something was wrong and she wanted to wheedle it out of him, but she saw from the set of his jaw and his fixed stare that it would be no use. The door creaked as she started to pull it shut.

"Kitty, eh, wait . . ." His eyes were firmly fixed on the neck of the bottle. "Eh, well, I'm sorry."

There was something in his tone, the slump of his shoulders, that told her he was going to crack, going to ask for help. Sometimes men made her sick. They were all the same, tough as frozen shit on the outside, and whining mummy's boys on the inside.

He slowly turned and fixed her with his hangdog puppy eyes. "Listen, Kitty, I was wondering if you wouldn't have a few extra bob."

"You little weasel." She stared at him, her eyes dark and dangerous. "Where the hell were you tonight?"

He jumped forward, tightening like an elastic band. Kitty saw this and suddenly everything fell into place. Her eyes flashed with anger and she jabbed her finger at him. "You stupid friggin' bugger. You were out gambling, weren't you?" She strode over, grabbed him by the shoulder and yanked him round. "Look at me!"

111

He tried a last retreat, pulling away from her and shifting along the bed. "Leave me alone. It's no business of yours what I do at night . . ."

"What do you mean it's none of my business? Oh you can ask me for money, but it's none of my business! What a load of bollocks. You've spent your wages, haven't you?"

He stalked over to the window. The curtains were open and he glared out over the back yard filled with the butcher's dustbins. "Leave me alone!"

Kitty bared her teeth. "Oh I'll leave you alone, it'd give me no greater pleasure, let me tell you, I'd give a fortune to get shot of you, you feckless git. Come on! Where's your money? *Where's your money?*" She walked slowly towards him, her voice getting louder and louder.

Suddenly he swung round. His face was flour-white and tiny beads of sweat glistened on his brow. "All right, I lost the fucking lot, right. Those scummy yards drive me nuts, I've been betting on the horses and tonight I went to the dogtrack and I . . ."

"What did you say?" Kitty was furious, but her voice had an icy restraint.

"I lost the lot, fuck you, the fucking lot. Are you happy now . . . are you happy you know?"

She hit him across the face and the crack resounded through the room. There was a stunned silence, then for a brief second a murderous anger flared in his eyes. Kitty held his look and he slowly subsided on to the windowsill.

"Don't blame anyone else but yourself. I didn't hold your hand when you were chucking away my mam's money."

The mention of his mother was the last straw. He brought his hands up to his face and started to sob.

Kitty gave a sigh through gritted teeth and looked away but now there was no stopping him. "And I pawned my fucking saxophone tonight, I pawned my sax. I can't believe it, I've never done that. I love it. I love it. What'll I do now?"

"Shurrup." She did not want to crush him, just to stop him becoming hysterical. And yet she was stunned. He loved that stupid instrument as if it was his life and yet, he'd finally

112

chucked it in to get a few hours of pleasure. She stared at him wide-eyed. He was a weakling, a complete weakling. She felt a strange shiver coursing through her as if she had all at once seen his future written in his tears.

Well, damn him! He could do whatever he wanted, he wasn't gonna break their mam's heart. She suddenly realised she would have to take charge again.

"Hey stop it. Stop that pissing. We're going down to that club, we're gonna see Tom. You'll borrow money from him, money for my mam and money to get that damned trumpet outta hock and so help me God, if you ever do this again, I'll kill you with my bare hands."

Kitty strode across the pavement towards the door of the nightclub.

"Yes, can I help you, young lady?"

She turned and glared up at the bouncer, fixing him with her dark eyes. Then she cleverly let her fierce look melt into a full smile. There was something bewitchingly vixenish about her, and the bouncer found himself smiling against his will.

"I'm Tom Cullen's sister, the boxer."

The bouncer nodded and seemed to relax. "Yeah, I know Tom."

Kitty tossed back her hair and then turned towards the kerb where Ernie was skulking beside a lamppost. "This is my brother, Ernie. Ernie!" Ernie shuffled forward into the light and gave a pained nod. Kitty pursed her lips in exasperation and continued, "We're looking for him, it's very important and I know this is his home away from home."

The bouncer smiled, "Yeah you could say that. Wait here."

The bouncer opened the heavy black doors and disappeared inside. For a few brief seconds Kitty got a glimpse of dim red lights, black-edged mirrors and long velvet curtains. The whiff of cocktails and cigar smoke wafted out with the sound of a small jazz combo.

Ernie darted across the pavement. He caught the door with his foot and listened. Kitty pulled him by the shoulder. "What are you doing?"

113

"I'm just listening, this lot's not bad." Ernie seemed to have come to life. He leaned forward again and put his ear up to the crack.

"Excuse me, laddie." Two naval officers and their girlfriends had walked up behind them. Ernie stood aside. Kitty gave the girls a piercing look as though she were a botanist and they were under her microscope. They were both in their early twenties and she felt that she should have been in their place, with their smooth make-up, their jewellery and their smart clothes. One of them glanced back as her boyfriend opened the door. It was a simple look of interest but Kitty felt suddenly embarrassed. She looked down at her cotton dress and the shabby light blue jacket and felt a shudder of resentment.

The black doors closed behind them and Ernie drifted over to listen at the crack again. Suddenly all of the anger and envy welled up in Kitty. She pushed him aside and yanked open the doors.

"Come on."

Ernie's face fell. "Where the hell're you going?"

Kitty spun round and glared at him. "I'm not being stood around here like some snot rag from Dr Barnardo's."

At one side of the lobby there was a small cloakroom and on either side, toilets. One of the naval officers was standing at the counter, handing over a pile of coats to the cloakroom attendant.

The inner doors were made of coloured glass and showed bright green palm trees against a turquoise sky. Kitty pushed the doors open and was suddenly engulfed in sound. The small jazz combo was blasting out from the tiny stage at the front, and the dance-floor was crowded.

The Chinese Parrot catered for a classier clientele than the rest of the Brook, and yet there was still an edge of raw danger about the place. It was a combination that turned out to be very profitable.

As Kitty walked in she felt excited by that throbbing energy. The floor was full of dancing couples and around the edges other groups sat drinking, laughing, talking. This was where she should have been tonight, she thought. Here, sipping a drink with some handsome young officer instead of staring out along Chichester Street at an advertisement for Bile Beans.

"We shouldn't be in here." Ernie slouched beside her like a beaten dog.

Kitty's answer was to grab Ernie by the arm and pull him after her. The bouncer had just started talking to Tom when Kitty came up behind them. "There's a young girl outside says she's your sister . . ."

Kitty could hear the suggestive laugh in his voice. She stepped forward. "I *am* his sister!"

The bouncer swung round. "Hey you're not supposed to be . . ."

Tom nearly choked on his beer. "Kitty!"

"'ello then, what's this, a family gathering?" They all swung round. Eddie Brent had walked over from behind the bar with a drink in either hand. He nodded at the bouncer. "It's all right, Charlie."

The bouncer quickly left. Kitty glanced at Brent. She noted the expensive suit, the gold ring glittering on the small finger, and the thought occurred to her that he owned this place. The bouncer, the barmen, the musicians, the cloakroom attendant, they all did his bidding. She looked up and saw that he was smiling at her, a crooked smile that seemed to leave one side of his face untouched. "So why don't you join us then? Tom and I were just about to partake of a little beverage."

As they sat down, Kitty looked over at Tom and saw that he was not happy. Brent caught the look. "Right then, shipmates, I'll pretend I'm barman. What'll you both have?"

Ernie had caught Tom's look too, and squirmed uncomfortably in his chair. "Well, no, that's all right."

"No, come on, you're my guests, stop nancying around."

"He'll have a beer, thanks." Kitty's sharp decisive tone cut across the the table.

Brent glanced at her again. "And what about you, young lady?" The girl's dark eyes held him, fascinated. There was something there that he had not met before, something between a promise and a threat.

"I'll have a gin and tonic." Ernie gave her a furtive sideways glance. Brent broadened his smile. "Yeah, I think we could just about manage that. Keep that beer of mine warm, Tom."

Brent had hardly stepped away from the table before Tom swung round on them. "What the bleedin' hell are you lot doin' here? It seems I can't even fart without the family turning up."

Kitty bristled, and leaned across the table. "Lay off, Tom. We wouldn't be down here if there wasn't trouble."

Tom suddenly looked worried. "Oh Christ! What's wrong now? Is my mam all right?"

Kitty cast a dirty look at Ernie who was fidgeting with an empty glass on the table. "She is now, she won't be when she hears about Prince Charming here."

Kitty suddenly thrust herself forward and continued in a loud, exaggerated whisper, "He's just bloody well gone and lost all his wages on the horses and the dogs, that's all! And then gone and hocked his saxophone and lost that too."

Ernie's head sank into his hands. Tom looked thunderstruck. "What! You stupid little prick! *Stupid prick.*"

Kitty reached over and grabbed Tom by the wrist. "All right, all right. We know that! But we came here because we need some money to get through the week. It'll kill our mam if she finds out he's been at it again."

Tom threw his arms wide open in a gesture of despair. "But I've got no money. I'm skint."

"A beer. And a gin and tonic." Brent appeared beside them before they knew it. He slid the drinks across the table and then took his seat. "I hope I haven't interrupted a family argy-bargy."

Tom sat back and took a sip of his beer as if to reassure him that all was well. "No, no, everything's fine like, just fine."

Kitty's eyes flashed. "Everything's not fine."

Tom gave her a black look. "Kitty, we don't wash our dirty linen in public."

"What're you talking about? You'd think we were the Royal Family to hear you." She turned to Brent and once again he caught a flash in those dark eyes. "Our Ernie's lost all his wages at the track and he's gone and pawned his saxophone as well. It'll kill our mam if she . . ."

116

She was about to rattle on but Brent held up his hand. "Wait, wait, wait. I get the message." He looked over at Ernie who was slumped down behind his beer. Then he ran his finger along his thin moustache, first one side and then another. "So, young Ernie's a musician, eh?"

Ernie looked up. Brent saw a handsome but weak face. The eyes of a dreamer, either an artist or a ne'er-do-well.

Ernie gave a different nod. "Yeah, kinda way."

But Kitty had already got the drift of the conversation and she moved in like a shark after blood. "Kind of – nothing! He's great, but he's a bloody idiot!"

"Maybe he'd think of playing for me at the Parrot."

"He'd need to get his saxophone outta hock first. He'd look funny playing it in the shop window."

Brent gave another laugh, he liked this girl. Then he turned to Tom. "Come on, champ, let's have a little confab, eh?"

Brent took Tom to one end of the bar and then turned to him. "I think we could help your brother out there, Tom, whaddya think?" He reached into his inside pocket and pulled out his wallet.

Tom flinched and his hand fluttered out in an attempt to stop him. At the same time he leaned forward and mumbled, "I can't, Eddie . . . I mean I can't take any more from you."

Brent brushed his hand aside and gave a wide smile. "Take it, you can pay me back when you're a pro." He pulled three brand-new five-pound-notes from his wallet and pressed them into Tom's hand. "See if that covers it."

Tom stared at the money for a long time, then finally gave a sigh and slipped it into his trouser pocket. "Thanks, I mean like you know thanks."

Brent gave him a gentle poke on the upper arm. "And listen, if you let me manage you, arrange your fights, you needn't bother with paying me back. I'd get you set up with London venues, title shots, we'd all make money."

Kitty had sat at the table watching. She had seen the fivers slipped into Tom's pocket and she knew she had made the right move coming here. Now Brent, Mr Eddie Brent, there was a man who could hold her attention. As he walked back towards

117

the table, he gave her a smile. She looked at him for the longest time and then very coolly turned away. Mr Brent was a fish you played with a lot of tickling.

18

Hanley glanced north towards the high, dark banks of cloud forming over the Cotswolds and gave an irritated sigh. He was tired and the last thing he wanted to do was drive through a rainstorm. He felt he had already been away too long, travelling to London and Cambridge and Torquay. He was fed up with hotel food and the tedious hours of driving.

He was passing through the town of Burford when he saw the sign for the tearoom. It was too early for a drink, but he needed to stop, get out of the car for a while.

Burford was a picturesque little town with thatched roofs and dark grey Cotswold stone. A shepherd was driving a flock of sheep towards him, and beyond, two plodding carthorses were pulling loads of newly mown hay up the long hill. There were two cars and a small lorry parked near the Golden Lion hotel. Apart from that there was only an old cyclist with spade and fork jutting from his handlebars weaving his way unsteadily after the haycarts.

The little teahouse was in a long, low, two-storeyed building. Its thatch was old and grey and along the eaves he could see the small nest holes from generations of habitation. The cracked oak lintel was low and he had to bend his head to enter.

The place was half empty but in the corner beside a smouldering fire, a small group of ladies sat nattering. They paused as he entered, and glanced in his direction. One of them reminded him of a parson's wife, a large matronly lady with a dark brown dress set off by a long string of pearls. She had a wide-brimmed hat with a cluster of fruit at one side and a pair of horn rimmed, pince-nez glasses. For a moment she peered at him through her thick lenses. Then, when he looked over at her, she quickly adjusted her pearls and continued her conversation.

Hanley was dressed in civvies and felt somewhat uncomfortable. With his Fair Isle sweater and his tweed jacket he could easily have passed for an Oxford don out for an afternoon drive.

He took a table by the window. As he sat down he nervously adjusted his blue-striped tie and glanced out through the small, leaded, windowpanes. Along the main street he saw the sheep disappearing round the corner. Just above them a sign for the Wheatsheaf pub was gently swinging in the breeze.

Sitting back, he felt another wave of tiredness sweep over him. He hadn't been home for over a week. He had telephoned Eunice every other day but her voice had sounded noticeably chillier on each occasion. He had spent two days at the Admiralty in London, going over Kingsland's files with Marsh, then some time in Cambridge, seeking out Kingsland's "old friends", then, down to Torquay to see Kingsland's father. In frustration he gently banged the top of the table with the palm of his hand. He was tired of the constant travelling, tired of prodding around in other people's lives.

"Afternoon tea, sir?" The waitress was a plump, rather sleepy-looking country girl.

He gave her a curt smile, "Yes, please."

He felt angry with Marsh for dispatching him to do his dirty work and at the same time angry with Kingsland himself for disappearing. Going to see Kingsland's father was the most difficult thing he had had to do.

He had made the long drive to Torquay only last night. His first impression was that the town had a sad, desolate, end-of-season look. A slight squall had moved in from the sea and the wind was blowing the rain almost horizontally against the windscreen. High overhead, the clouds were scudding quickly across the sky, alternately covering and uncovering a brilliant autumn moon. It all felt wild and dangerous and sad.

119

But then perhaps that was just his mood. He was not looking forward to seeing the old man.

Kingsland and Hanley had gone to the same small boarding school, Bucksford, in east Sussex. Kingsland's father had been their housemaster, and then, after they left, he had become headmaster. He was a severe disciplinarian and yet a kindly man who was constantly aware of all his wards. Even after all these years Hanley could still see him standing at the side of the classroom gazing out of the window across the quadrangle. Woe to the boy who mistook that thoughtful look for dreaming. A mistranslation of Caesar or Cicero would provoke an acerbic comment. He did not suffer fools gladly.

Hanley found the house out along the Paignton road – a neat little bungalow facing the sea. The garden was impeccable, too impeccable, suggesting that its owner kept it tidy out of duty not out of love. Hanley stepped under the arch of climbing roses and quickly walked up the path.

He pressed the bell and almost instantly the front door opened. The old man was just as he remembered him, a little greyer, a little more stooped, but still lean and fit-looking. He gave a crisp nod of his head.

"I heard the footsteps on the path."

"Pardon?" said Hanley.

"People wonder how I get to the door so quick, I hear the footsteps." The old man ground to a halt and gazed at Hanley intently. "You're Hanley, aren't you, James Kerr Hanley, captain of house cricket. Rupert's friend?"

There was an awkward silence. Hanley was unsure how he would be received. "Yes sir, I am." But the old man simply gave a sad smile, pulled open the door and stepped aside.

"Come in, Hanley, I'm glad it's you they sent."

The small living room was kept cosy by a coal fire. A large comfortable armchair had been pulled up to the fender and a book lay open on its sagging well-worn cushion. Beside the chair, a small coffee table held a cup and saucer and a plate of digestive biscuits. The whole place looked neat, almost un-lived-in. Kingsland senior was as meticulous a housekeeper as he had been a classics teacher.

"You look fatigued, Hanley. I've just made a pot of tea, let me get another cup." As he spoke he crossed to the other armchair and pulled it towards the fire. "Sit down, warm yourself. I'll take your coat." He held out his arm and Hanley took off his overcoat and handed it to him.

"Excuse me, sir, but why did you think that someone would be sent?"

The old man fixed him with that penetrating housemaster's look. "Rupert wrote to me, before his trial, and told me why he was going to be court-martialled." As he continued, Hanley was struck by the strangely flat quality in his voice. "That kind of thing doesn't lightly fade into the night." Before Hanley could properly decipher his attitude the old man turned away and walked into the kitchen. Did he know about the espionage or even suspect it?

Hanley glanced around the room. It was like a college library with books piled high from floor to ceiling. In a large bookcase near the window, there were two shelves that had been cleared of volumes. They contained photos, and a couple of trophies. Hanley heard the clinking of china in the kitchen behind him and strolled over to glance at the photos.

They were pictures that rambled through the years. Family portraits of stern-faced Victorians, the old man in his Cambridge days on the river, his wife as a young woman, their wedding photograph. There were school photographs too, a Prize Day at Bucksford with the unmistakable Norman church tower in the background. Hanley spotted himself too, front row centre, with the First Eleven cricket team. He was beaming ear to ear with a large trophy firmly wedged between his legs. And behind him stood Rupert, with that shy, handsome smile of his. The last picture was turned on its face. He picked it up and looked. It was of the old man presenting Rupert with a small cup, the Houghton classics prize. He could see them both mastering cool, proud smiles.

Hanley looked at the inscription on the back: "Obscurior etiam via ad coelum videbatur quando tam pauci regnum coelorum quaerere curabant." As he stared at the confident elegance of the writing, the translation rang loud and clear

121

through all the rusty years. It would have been difficult to forget; it was one of the old man's favourite aphorisms, one he used to prod his students on to greater efforts: "The fewer there are who follow the way to perfection, the harder that way is to find." The words sent shivers along his spine as another image flashed into his mind. He saw Rupert slumped drunkenly at the table in that flat in Chelsea, his face gaunt, his eyes desolate; heard once again the slurred, drunken desperation in his voice.

The old man shuffled up behind him. "I found a tin of gingersnaps." He had noticed the picture in Hanley's hand and for a split second a spasm of pain flickered across his face. Then it was quickly replaced by that stoic mask, the schoolmaster's smile, the impenetrable eyes.

He crossed to Hanley and gestured to the photograph. "A long time ago." He lifted the photograph from Hanley's hands and peered at it. "I think that Rupert found it difficult having his father as housemaster." He traced a white, bony finger along one side of the gilded frame. His voice sounded reflective, distant. "I don't think he realised how difficult it was for me. He was so damned good at everything, but I couldn't show how proud I was, no matter how many prizes he . . ." The mask of restraint dropped and Hanley saw the hurt. There was a slight quivering of his lips, the suggestion of a rheumy glaze in his eyes.

Hanley turned away to gaze blankly at the shelf of mementos. He could not bear to witness the raw emotional pain on the old man's face. He heard him clearing his throat and saw him replace the photograph. "I'm just glad that his mother isn't alive." His voice was clouded, dark.

He crossed back to the coffee table and poured a cup of tea. "Milk, sugar?"

Hanley followed him over. "Yes, a little milk, and one teaspoon please."

The old man handed him the cup and saucer. His hand was eerily steady, his eyes were bright, clear, almost shining. "You're looking for him, aren't you?"

Hanley nodded. "Yes, yes, I am. We are."

They both sat and sipped their tea. Then the old man placed

his cup back on the coffee table and glared into the glowing fire. "I'll help you in any way I can. He's dead to me now, dead. You understand?" His voice was no more than a whisper and its cold purposeful edge cut through the air like cracked ice.

There was a long pause filled only by the sound of the flickering flames. Hanley searched desperately but could find nothing to say. The old man's pain was something he could not reach. He watched him staring morosely at the fire, slowly pressing his fingertips together as though he would snap them. Then in an instant, the old man turned and stared straight at him. It was the cold logical look of the old classics scholar. He cleared his throat. "I have the name of one of his . . . his friends. He once told me if ever I needed to find him . . . it's a cottage somewhere near Oxford."

That was last night. Now Hanley sat at the window of the tearoom in Burford, staring out into the gathering dusk. He ate the last of the scones and then pulled a piece of paper from his inside pocket. He scanned the old man's clear, firm script: "Locke Cottage, Wolvercote Road, Wytham, Oxon."

There was a low mist over the Thames Valley. A kind of sleepy dampness that made Hanley feel uncomfortably sticky. Thin ghostly wisps played in the headlights of the car and then sped past. The mist slowed his speed and gave an eerie quality to the evening, almost as though he was suspended in time.

To add to his difficulties, Locke Cottage was set back from the road at the edge of the woods. Hanley drove past it at first, keeping his eyes on his mist-dimmed headlights, then he noticed the light out of the corner of his eye. He stopped the car and glanced back. Over the hedge, he could see the tops of the windows, the thatched roof and the chimney with smoke coming out.

He turned off the engine and sat staring out of the front window. After a long pause he made his decision. He leaned over, opened the dashboard and pulled out a service revolver. Hanley had not carried one of these since the Gallipoli campaign and it felt strangely cold and heavy in his hand. Marsh had insisted on his having it, and perhaps he was right.

Kingsland was not the same man that he had known two months ago.

He got out of the car and put on his trench coat. Then he slipped the bulky revolver into the pocket of his jacket and pulled the coat loosely round him. He quietly closed the door and started back along the road towards the front path.

It had been drizzling lightly and the road and the hedge glistened in the moonlight. There was a smell of damp leaves and woodsmoke. Hanley stopped at the open gate and gazed towards the light in one of the ground-floor windows. The window was open a crack and the sounds of a Mahler symphony leaked out into the cool, damp night air. The trees behind rustled and creaked gently in the wind. They seemed to glower over the cottage, making it appear even more inviting and homely. For a moment he felt ashamed of the revolver in his pocket. Then he drew a deep breath and started towards the front door.

The path was paved with small flints and here and there, broken edges gleamed sharply in the pale moonlight. The front door was glass panelled and Hanley could see the light from the inner room spilling into the dark hallway. There was a brass knocker just above the letter box. Hanley lifted the knocker and the door swung open a crack. He tensed, then took a tight grip of the revolver in his pocket and pushed the door further open.

"Rupert? Hello Rupert, it's James. James Hanley."

The music in the other room rolled on. The light stayed constant. Along the hall a clock whirred and then chimed out the half-hour. Hanley felt his throat going dry. He took a step on to the polished wood floor of the hallway and called out again, "Rupert? It's James."

Still there was silence. He could feel the palm of his hand sweating as it clutched the hard metal of the gun. He stepped towards the door of the lighted room and slowly opened it. A quick glance showed that the place was empty. The logs in the fireplace had burned down so that they were rimmed with white ash. On either side of the fireplace there were bookshelves and from the middle of one of these a baby grand Philco boomed out the Mahler concert.

Hanley stepped carefully into the room, then crossed to the radio and turned it down. He looked around. Along the wall closest to him there was a table. It had a bottle of white wine with a glass beside it. A loaf of crusty country bread shared a wooden board with a wedge of blue Stilton. Hanley's first thought was that at least Kingsland was treating himself better. He glanced around again. Perhaps he was out the back. These old cottages often had outside toilets. At the other end of the room there were a number of small watercolours: Oxford scenes, colleges, churches, village markets.

Hanley's eyes were drawn to a door in the far corner of the room. It was open a crack and he could just make out the shape of a cooker in the darkness beyond. He walked past the armchair with a book lying open on it, and a memory of the elder Kingsland flashed into his mind. Father and son, both lonely, forever cut off from one another.

Then, for the first time, he heard the creaking. It sounded like floorboards, perhaps in one of the rooms above. He held his breath and listened, glancing up at the low-beamed ceiling. But no, that was not it. He heard the noise again and swung round to face the hall door, perhaps there was someone out there.

"Rupert, Rupert, where the hell are you?" But again there was only the low sound of the Mahler building to a crescendo, and the sound of dead leaves rustling around the house.

He spun round. The noise was definitely coming from the rear of the place. He could feel his muscles tense. Perhaps walking into the house so openly had been foolish. Now he was in the light and somebody or something was in the dark beyond. He quickly slipped the revolver out of his pocket and as quietly as possible moved to the back door. He flattened himself against the wall and felt the edge of one of the watercolours pressing into his back.

He heard the creaking again, a small noise but enough to grate on his nerves. He sidestepped, kicked the door and backed up behind the wall again. The door swung open and banged against a sideboard. There was a violent clanging as a saucepan clattered to the floor. Then silence.

"Rupert, God damn it man. Speak up." Hanley could feel a

bead of sweat trickling along his eyebrow and then down his cheek. This was all too much. His temper was beginning to break. Very tentatively he reached around the edge of the door and found a lightswitch. He clicked it, once, twice, three times, then gave a frustrated curse. Disregarding all the rules of safety he moved forward, his gun clutched in the firing position.

Standing in the lighted doorway he peered into the darkness. As his eyes adjusted he could make out a large country kitchen. The cooker had a black frying pan and a kettle sitting on it and above, a rack with three dishes. There was a large sink, shelves full of groceries, and two kitchen cabinets with serving dishes and plates.

He pushed the door open wider and stepped into the dark room. His eye swiftly took in the open beams, and the onions, garlic and bunches of herbs hanging from them. When he saw the rope, a sense of panic cascaded over him and everything clicked into place.

He rushed forward kicking the fallen chair aside and grabbed at the body. It swung round, creaking as it did so, and Hanley saw Kingsland's face, the eyes bulging, the mouth agape, the tongue swollen. He stopped for a split second and felt a paralysing sense of horror. The blood pounded in his head. He dropped the gun and staggered backwards fighting for breath, then turned and ran to the cabinets, crashing open the drawers. Finally he found a kitchen knife and jumped on to the chair beside Kingsland's slowly twirling body.

He slipped his arm around Kingsland's chest, taking his friend's weight, and then lunged at the rope with the knife. After a few slashing thrusts, it began to unravel. He sawed desperately at the last few strands, then tossed the knife aside and staggered to the floor. As he stepped off the chair his legs went from under him. He collapsed backwards under the dead weight of the body, and slammed into the side of the table.

When he had caught his breath he pulled Kingsland towards the swathe of light, spilling in from the open door, and gently lowered him to the floor. Hanley knelt beside him and cradled the body in his arms. He tugged desperately at the knot and finally opened the noose and pushed the rope aside.

126

The eyes were still open and they glared white and unseeing as if at some final horror. Hanley clenched his teeth as he tried to hold back his grief. He swept his hand up and closed the eyelids, then stared down unbelieving at the rigid face of death. He saw the photographs again on old Kingsland's shelf, the handsome boy full of hope and confidence, and he suddenly felt the tears coming. He closed his eyes and shook his head as if refusing to acknowledge the emotion. Suicide! Suicide! How could it end like this?

He was no longer able to choke back his grief. It burst from him in deep sobs that reverberated through the kitchen and living room, and spiralled out into the dark night beyond.

19

Hanley heard the marine band strike up and then, a few seconds later, the dockyard choir joining in with a hymn. He closed the window and gazed down at the crowds streaming past the admiral's offices. This was a day out for the dockyard workers and their families: the men in their Sunday suits, the wives in their best dresses, the children with their shoes shined and wayward hair oiled down. It was a day for a man to take a pride in his work.

Hanley watched for a while and then slammed his fist against the wooden shutters at the side of the window. Pride in his work? He could not get Kingsland out of his mind. The funeral had disturbed him almost as much as his discovery of the body. It was the bleakness of it all. Kingsland's father had arranged for him to be buried at the school church in Bucksford. The old Norman church was virtually empty and the older Kingsland had barely acknowledged Hanley's presence. He had called in many old favours to get his son a Christian burial and, in going through the motions of the funeral service, he seemed to be merely carrying his duties through to the painful end.

Hanley had pulled out his pipe and was lighting it when Campbell knocked and then entered. "Sir, they're going up to the *Graplin* now."

Hanley turned. There was something about Campbell, something that he had only begun to notice since his return. In retrospect Hanley recognised that the warrant officer's drinking had been getting worse over the last year, but somehow since coming back Hanley found himself all the more aware of it. There was just the hint of a slur in the voice, a rheumy redness in the eyes. "Sir Samuel Hoare arrived a few minutes ago, sir."

"Yes, thank you, Mr Campbell. I'll be down in a few minutes." Campbell paused for a moment as though he wanted to say something else, then seemed to think better of it and turned towards the door.

"Mr Campbell." Campbell glanced over his shoulder. Hanley took a puff of the pipe and then knocked the stem against his palm. "Anything wrong?"

Campbell's whole body almost imperceptibly sagged and, for a moment, Hanley regretted asking the question. So little of their personal lives ever entered into the office. Then he slowly turned and Hanley could see the exhaustion etched in the lines of his face. "Not really, sir, just the wife."

Hanley would have let it go at that but Campbell seemed to want to linger. "Have you been down to see her recently?"

"Yes. Yes sir."

"And how was she?"

"It's hard to say, sir." Campbell's voice was flat, almost dead. "She seems to drift further and further away . . . she seemed to know me for a few minutes, but mainly I needn't have bothered being there . . ." He stopped in mid-sentence as if his mind had suddenly focused on a painful memory. He stared blankly at the window and the sky beyond. "She's hearing more and more of her voices as she calls them. I'm just glad Dennis is stationed in Malta." Campbell scratched at his beard distractedly. "At least he won't see her getting worse."

128

Hanley had an image of Campbell's lively and pretty wife when he had first met her. A hearty, West Country girl, with a ready smile and sparkling turquoise eyes. He had seen her only rarely after her illness had started. The last time was some three years ago. She had been home for a weekend. The sparkle was gone from her eyes and only a dull and vacant bleakness remained.

Hanley puffed at his pipe and attempted a hearty tone. "Well, at least you have her at a good place." Somehow the word "asylum" stuck in his throat. Mental illness was still an embarrassment, no matter how openly Campbell spoke about his wife's affliction.

Campbell gave a gruff, cynical laugh. "Oh yes sir, a good place and bloody expensive. But by God I'll keep her there as long as I can. As long as I can."

Outside, there was a crashing of drums and a triumphant explosion of brass, then a cheer as the marine band burst into a magnificent rendering of "Hearts of Oak". Hanley gave a quick glance out of the window and saw Rear Admiral Walker's party walking from Medway House towards number-seven slip.

"Well I hope it continues to work out for you, Mr Campbell." Hanley's words were vaguely dismissive.

Campbell pulled himself to attention. He knew the moment of personal contact was over. "Yes sir, thank you. You should be leaving soon. I must get down and see that the various foreign attachés get their seats."

"Yes. I'll be along."

Hanley heard the door close behind him. Through the window he could see the launching party, with Sir Samuel Hoare sandwiched between Walker and Vice Admiral Bennett-Clinton from Pembroke Barracks. He was also pleased to see Eunice. When he had left home this morning it was not certain she would come. But there she was, looking radiant in a black velveteen cardigan suit, talking animatedly to Mrs Skipley, the widow of the former admiral in charge of the yards, and the woman who was to launch the *Graplin*.

The phone started ringing on the desk behind him and he quickly snatched the receiver from the cradle.

129

"Yes, Captain Hanley speaking."

There was silence along the wires, then the distant sound of a piano playing.

"Hello, hello. Who is this?"

The man at the other end of the line cleared his throat. "You, you don't know me, Captain . . ." the speaker paused again, he had a gruff Yorkshire accent and yet Hanley thought he heard something else there, a suggestion of the effeminate. ". . . I'm a friend of Rupert's, Mr Kingsland's."

There was another pause. Hanley heard the piano jangling in the background. He felt irritated. The last people he wanted to hear from were Kingsland's effeminate friends.

He wanted to bury Rupert with some decent memories. "Look, I don't care to know who you are, but what do you want with me?"

"I only heard about his death the other day and I . . ." For a moment Hanley had the dreadful feeling that the man was going to break down and cry. Then he seemed to recover, though his voice remained strained. "I've been meaning to phone you since then. You see, I think we should meet up. I have something. A package that he left with me. It was for you."

"A package, what do you mean a package?"

"That's all I know. He wanted me to keep it safe for him, in case something. Well, you know."

Hanley thought for a moment. "I see. Well, you can send it to me here. Do you know where I . . . ?"

"No, I'm sorry, I'm not sending it to you." There was a quiet but determined stubbornness in his voice. "I owe him more than that . . ." he continued, "he wouldn't want that. He told me to be sure and put it into your hands."

"All right, all right, I understand! Then bring it here. I'll arrange for a pass into the yards."

"No, I can't come there. I just can't. And I want you to take this as soon as you can . . ."

Hanley exploded. "Oh for God's sake, man, I don't even know what we're talking about. Rupert's dead and that's the end of it for me. I don't want to hear any more, do you hear me . . . any more!"

130

"Please don't hang up. Look, my name's Ronnie. I'm a singer at the Unicorn Club, Frith Street in Soho. Please come and take this. Or I'll just dump it. I'm beginning to feel as scared as he was." And with that enigmatic threat the phone went dead. Hanley stood for a few seconds holding the black receiver, then slammed it into the cradle.

"God damn it!" He quickly scribbled down the name and the address on a piece of scrap paper. He gazed at it for a moment and then almost reluctantly slipped it into his pocket. Apparently the past was not going to die as easily as he thought.

Kitty felt very pleased with herself. She clutched tightly at Terry Gillings' arm and glanced over at her Uncle Albert and Aunt Irene. They looked a handsome couple and she prided herself that everyone they met took her as part of their family.

Uncle Albert was in his best suit, a blue pinstripe and, with his bowler hat and starched white collar and cuffs, he looked to Kitty like a proper city gent. Even her Aunt Irene had been persuaded to dress for the occasion and was wearing her new, fawn-coloured "Sunday" suit.

Kitty beamed as she walked through the crowd with them. She was feeling good about herself as well. She still felt the job at the Johnsons' was "a pain in the arse", but at least they had let her off for the afternoon. And there was something to be said for earning money. She glanced down at the new wine-red waisted suit she had bought on the never-never from the fancy haberdasher's, Brigham's, in the High Street. There were some benefits to getting up every morning at five o'clock!

She looked around at the crowds. Chatham wasn't too bad after all. All right, she hadn't yet been taken out by some handsome young officer, but she had been drinking a "gin and tonic" in the Chinese Parrot and she had also met Eddie Brent.

As well as that, Tom had cleared up the mess with Ernie. Her mam hadn't found out what a wanker Ernie had been and that was important. She had had too much of that with their dad, Billy. Of course Ernie should have been there this afternoon but that was too much to expect from his Royal Highness, especially now that he had to practise every spare hour on his newly recovered saxophone. Two nights tooting away at the Chinese Parrot and he thought he was some Flash Harry playing with the Ray Noble or Lew Stone band.

Kitty had never been in the yards before and truth to tell she was not overly impressed. They looked to her like a pile of rusting, grey metal buildings. What did impress her, however, was the number of men who nodded or touched their caps as Albert Gillings walked by. For a brief while, she got a vague sense of what it must be like to be a film star. To have the crowds staring at her, hoping for a smile, a look.

"Hello, you're the lad who helped me with my motorbike, Terry isn't it?"

The stranger's voice was rich and fruity, what Kitty's mother would call "real toff". Kitty turned and saw the young man who was addressing her cousin. She was immediately caught by his dark eyes. They seemed to flash with an errant energy, as though something was boiling within him, and she felt an immediate attraction, a kinship. She had the strong sense that here was someone like herself.

"Yeah, I'm the 'lad'." Terry gave a good-natured laugh. "Have you bought that new carburettor yet?"

"Not yet, but that fix-up job of yours still seems to be working."

Kitty pushed herself forward. "Have you got a motorbike then?"

Terry laughed. "He's got an antique. That's why I found him stranded along Langley Road last Tuesday night. By the way, this is my cousin, Kitty, Kitty Cullen, and you're? Sorry, I forgot."

"Nigel, Nigel Hanley."

"Oh. Is Captain Hanley your dad?" The name had instantly rung a bell.

Nigel flashed an awkward, diffident smile. "Well yes, yes he is."

"Terry's dad is the engineering foreman here. Mr Albert Gillings." Kitty almost pushed Terry aside as she gestured towards her Uncle Albert in the crowd.

"Oh right. I've heard my father talking about him."

132

Even though he addressed himself to Terry his dark eyes flickered to the side to rest on Kitty. His gaze was intense. He seemed to stare through her and she felt a strange shiver, like a premonition. Then it was quickly gone and she was left with that lingering, first thrill of attraction.

Nigel too felt shaken. He covered his discomfort by turning back towards Terry and gave an awkward chuckle. "So, since our dads work together, you should give me your address so I can hop round and get a bit of advice on this bike."

"Sure, why not?"

Kitty stared at him, fascinated. Oh yes, he was handsome, and dangerous in an indefinable way, but from now on she would not let him see that. She grabbed Terry by the arm and pulled him away. "Come on, they're going in."

The marine band started marching in through the massive entranceway towards their position and Kitty followed. For a while Nigel continued to watch her. Even in her walk he found something seductively taunting. This girl was not like any of his sister's friends from boarding school, or the girls from the badminton club.

As she reached the shadows of the covered slip she suddenly turned and looked at him. There was the hint of a smile in her eyes. Oh yes, this was a quite different kind of girl from those he had known before and he quickly resolved that he would meet her again.

Hanley caught up with Eunice near the bottom of the steps. The marine band had launched into another hymn and was marching into the massive hangar-like, covered slip behind them. She was still talking to Mrs Skipley, the widow of Vice Admiral Skipley. "I believe the trick is to turn aside as quickly as possible." When she saw Hanley she turned and gave him a full, warm smile. Anyone else would have been fooled but Hanley recognised that there was something theatrical about her manner.

"You know James, of course, don't you, Mrs Skipley?"

The older lady gave a pleasant but nervous smile. "Oh yes, of course I do." She had a small birdlike face and pure white hair, tightly curled in the fashion of Queen Mary. She patted her hand over some rebellious curls with a distracted air.

Eunice gave another full smile. "Mrs Skipley is rather nervous about the bottle breaking but I told her it always goes well." Hanley heard the solicitous tone in Eunice's voice and thought how her breeding showed. Eunice was born to be lady of the manor, a social diplomat, and in a way it was her tragedy that she had left all of that life behind.

"Mrs Skipley, we should go up now." Rear Admiral Walker came up from behind, took her by the arm and quickly swept her towards the steps. Hanley and Eunice were left staring at each other.

"Thank you for coming. After this morning I didn't think you would."

Eunice leaned towards him. She had an icy look in her eyes. "I didn't think I would either, but then I reminded myself that I have a duty towards my family. One of us has to remember that."

She quickly turned and walked towards the steps. Hanley stood for a while and let the sound of the marine band wash over him. He had smelled the whisky on her breath and he felt a twinge of apprehension. If she was like this now, what would she be like afterwards, during the reception?

Sir Samuel Hoare, the First Lord of the Admiralty, did not stay long, but he did give an impromptu private speech to a small group of senior officers in one of the upper rooms. He spoke about meeting the Italian threat in the Mediterranean and Hanley was glad to hear someone in the government taking rearmament seriously.

Afterwards, Walker pulled Hanley aside and introduced him to Sir Samuel. He brought up Hanley's concerns about the construction of the new German submarine fleet, then left Hanley to develop his theme.

Hanley was not blind to the boredom threshold in politicians. All he wanted was a promise that if he presented a paper, it would be read. Sir Samuel was quick to pick up the main drift of Hanley's argument and he promised that Hanley's paper would receive consideration at the highest level. It was as much as Hanley could hope for. But then, just as Sir Samuel was turning to leave, he made a rather enigmatic statement, ". . . and anyway I hope that very soon we will have that other powerful eye on the horizon to protect our shores . . ."

Hanley registered the look of shock on Walker's face and for a brief second Sir Samuel seemed as if he was going to reconsider what he had just said. But then he turned and made his cheery farewells, sailing out of the room and down the stairs to the ground floor.

Hanley tried to catch up with Walker but Lieutenant Commander Crowe, Kingsland's replacement as captain of the *Graplin*, cornered him. "The rear admiral's just told me I have a meeting with a Dr Grainger, next week. Do you know what that's about? I know he works in the yards, but I don't know what department."

"I think it's best to wait for the meeting," Hanley replied noncommittally.

"I understand," said Crowe.

Hanley turned away and quickly left the room. He was glad that someone understood! When he got to the sweeping stairwell he glanced down and saw Walker talking to Commander Robinson, the torpedo engineering officer. Robinson moved off as he approached and Walker turned and gave Hanley a cool, businesslike smile.

"I know what you're going to ask, Hanley. Unfortunately you can't trust politicians to be discreet . . . but I promise that everything will be revealed in good time."

"This is connected with Grainger, isn't it, sir?"

Walker stared at him for a long time, then his eyes narrowed. "In good time, Hanley . . . let's get back to our guests."

The rear admiral followed Robinson through the open doors into the reception. Hanley leaned back against the bottom of the banister and glanced up at the rich dark colours of the massive oval painting in the ceiling at the top of stairs. Then he gave a grunt of despair and made his way towards the reception room.

Inside, Hanley glanced around. It was the usual mix for these occasions: dockyard engineers and officers and visiting Admiralty top brass; blue suits and naval dress uniforms. Hanley had not had a drink all day. Now, however, confronted by this crowd, he felt weary and very deserving of a little alcoholic relaxant. He stepped over to the drinks table and took a glass of Chardonnay from one of the waiters, then he made for the food. The rear admiral's cook produced the world's best poached salmon.

"Captain Hanley, excuse me, I seem to have caught you with your hands full but I would like to introduce myself." Hanley turned and found himself facing a handsome, flaxen-haired man in his mid-thirties. He wore a German naval uniform. "I am Commander Hans Weichert, German naval attaché in London."

Hanley gave a curt smile and lifted the plate and the glass of wine as if to indictate that he was burdened. "Ah yes, I know your name, Commander Weichert. Please excuse me for not shaking hands. I'm pleased to meet you."

Hanley saw a flicker in the other man's eye and turned. Eunice had walked up beside them.

"Commander Weichert, I'd like to introduce my wife Eunice."

"Yes, but I've met your charming wife before, all too briefly, I'm afraid, at a gathering at Lady Brampton's."

Hanley quickly looked up from the pink flesh of the salmon. "Ah yes, Lady Brampton. So, Commander Weichert, did you enjoy our launching?"

"Yes indeed. I would have liked to take a tour of the yards, like my predecessor, but apparently it's now deemed, how can I put it, a sensitive request."

"I must say I wish I'd had the opportunity two years ago to take a tour of your Germania yards in Kiel. You kept those covered slips well guarded, didn't you?"

"Commander Weichert, I see you finally met Captain Hanley." Walker had quietly moved up behind them. He continued, "He's my right-hand man on the engineering side." Weichert's eyes registered the information, something that Walker noted before he turned to Eunice. "Mrs Hanley,

Eunice, I'm delighted to see you again, my dear. I hope these old sea dogs haven't been boring you with naval chat."

"Not at all. I've been finding it all fascinating. Poor Commander Weichert's been complaining about restrictions on his visiting the yards."

Walker's smile stiffened but he maintained his poise. "Ah, those are things that are out of my hands . . . government policy. It seems that with Germany now rearming so fast we have to regard them as competitors, technically speaking, of course." Here, Walker gave his imitation of a hearty laugh and watched the effect of his speech on Weichert.

Weichert, however, looked mildly amused though he was eager to change the subject. "I've been hearing some strange rumours recently in London about the King." Both Hanley and Walker looked genuinely blank. There was silence.

Eunice leaned forward and gave a knowing smile. "Commander Weichert, these scandals don't get as far as Chatham." She turned to Walker. "You see, Admiral Walker, the rumour is that Mrs Simpson is getting her divorce in the next few weeks, her second divorce, I should add, and that then they are planning to marry."

Walker shook his head. "Rumour, just as you say, that's all. He couldn't marry the lady and keep the Crown. How could the head of the Church of England be married to a divorced woman?"

Hanley had turned away. Social chitchat of this kind bored him. And anyway, he had never had much time for Edward as King, the man seemed too emotional. As he looked around he noticed Marsh, the captain from Intelligence, signalling to him from the hallway door.

Eunice was arguing some free-thinking notion about a king having as much right as anyone else to "experience true love". Hanley broke in, "Excuse me, sir, I must speak with someone." Walker gave a cursory nod and Hanley turned to make his way through the crowd.

Marsh was waiting in the hallway, slowly pacing the polished marble floor. His face looked drawn and gaunt, his eyes troubled. "Hanley, good to see you. We need to talk."

Waiters had started scurrying back and forth from the kitchens returning empty savoury dishes and bringing out bowls of desserts and tiered plates of cakes and pastries. Hanley stopped one of them and handed over the remains of his salmon and his empty wineglass, then he followed Marsh out on to the covered porch.

Outside, it was getting cool, but it was still pleasant. The afternoon sun was leaking in under the clouds, tingeing them with a fiery orange. Marsh crossed to one of the thin, elegantly carved wooden pillars, leaned back against it and gazed up at the sky. Then he pulled out his silver cigarette case. "Cigarette?"

Hanley had already taken out his pipe. "No, I'll smoke this."

Marsh pulled out a cigarette, lit it and continued to stare off into the distance.

Hanley had never seen the man so indirect and vague. "You need to speak to me?" Hanley struck a match and then covered the bowl of his pipe and puffed it into life.

Marsh suddenly wheeled round on him. "Yes, yes I do. It's about Kingsland. I didn't want to drag you back into the middle of this again but I'm afraid we need your help. You see, I've been sitting on the autopsy report for the last week."

"An autopsy report? Why? There's no damned mystery about his death. He hanged himself. I pulled him down, remember."

Marsh slowly shook his head and took another deep drag at his cigarette. "Kingsland was murdered. His neck was broken and then he was strung up."

Marsh watched Hanley's face. It had turned a waxy grey-white. Marsh turned away and glanced at the white gazebo at the top of the small slope. They were both quiet. Inside they could hear the sounds of the reception, the clinking of glasses and plates, the hearty laughter.

"My God, my God!" Hanley's voice was little more than a whisper. "But who, who could have done it?"

Marsh raised a quizzical eyebrow. "That's why we still need your help. We can make guesses. We can presume, but we need to know more."

"Know more about what?"

Marsh gave a frustrated sigh. "Anything, anything that might help, any scrap of information . . ."

Hanley listened and then tapped the stem of his pipe against the intricate fluting on the wooden pillar. He recalled the panic in Kingsland's voice, the haunted look in his eyes that night he had visited him in Chelsea. And then he remembered the hysterical phone conversation he had just had with Rupert's homosexual friend.

"There is something, maybe. I got a call this morning, before the launching. Someone, an acquaintance of Rupert's." He lingered over the word "acquaintance" as though it was something distasteful, then passed on. "I believe it was the person who lent him the flat in Chelsea."

"I see. What did he want?"

Hanley stared at Marsh blankly and then raised his eyebrows in a gesture of puzzlement. "He said that he wanted to give me something. A package that Rupert had left with him."

Marsh's eyes narrowed, there was a renewed excitement in his voice. "Well, what's the problem?"

"There's no problem, except that I asked him to mail it to me and he insisted that I collect it."

"Then collect it." Marsh spat the words out like an order.

Hanley knocked the pipestem rhythmically against the wooden pillar and stared out across the garden towards the trees at the back wall. The last time he had been here Kingsland had been alive. He took a deep breath. "All right, I'll do it, when I get the time."

"I'll go with you, and I'd prefer we do it tonight."

Hanley did not "prefer tonight", but he knew that Marsh would not take no for an answer. "All right." He stepped on to the lawn and took a deep breath. "Murder. But who?" He turned and glared at Marsh.

Marsh stood for a while under the verandah, as if he was mulling the question over in his mind. Then he stared at the rear wall of the garden and the sail-loft beyond and said quietly, "Death by strangulation is a trademark of the *Sicherheitsdienst*, the intelligence organisation of Hitler's SS. Many of their

operatives move in and out of Britain in other guises –
businessmen, embassy officials – but there's nothing we can do
about it, without evidence."

Hanley swung round. "You know that the Germans did
this?"

Marsh took another long drag of his cigarette and then
rubbed his thumb along the deep crease between his eyebrows.
"You haven't been listening. We cannot prove it; we simply
know that it follows a pattern."

Hanley paused, absorbing it all. "And yet," he said thinking
of Weichert, "we still invite them to our launchings."

20

The rain slowed the traffic around Soho. It was something that
did not improve Hanley's humour. They caught the tail end of
the theatre crowd around Piccadilly Circus and along Shaftesbury Avenue. Hanley used the time to look up at the theatre
awnings. Yvonne Arnaud and Ronald Squire in *Laughter in the
Court* at the Shaftesbury, Jack Buchanan in *This'll Make You
Whistle* at the Palace. As the car crawled along, Hanley thought
how long it was since he had been to the theatre. It was one of
Eunice's long-standing complaints.

He tapped the stem of his unlit pipe agitatedly against the
palm of his hand and thought how strange Eunice had seemed
at the reception. He had expected her to spit out some bitter
jibe when he told her he had to go to London, but she had
simply smiled rather coldly. "I hadn't really expected the
leopard to change his spots."

Later he had seen Eunice standing by the fireplace talking to
Weichert again. It was a long time since he had seen such a look
of relaxation on her face. The easy laugh, the sparkling eyes. He

recalled Marsh's comment as he followed Hanley's gaze. "A dangerous man, Weichert. Of all the staff in their embassy he has a lot to answer for."

Marsh slammed the steering wheel and cursed the crowds hurrying between the cars. Then he leaned forward and wiped the steam off the windscreen with his handkerchief. "What is the address again?"

"Frith Street, something called the Unicorn Club."

"I believe it's back here somewhere." Marsh turned left off Shaftesbury Avenue and into a dark maze of streets. He gave a satisfied chortle. "In my younger days I used to know all the clubs around Ham Yard. The Hambone, Mother Hubbard's, the Morgue, the Pavilion."

Hanley listened and nodded politely. It did not sound like Marsh, and he wondered if the man wasn't trying to make himself sound more human.

"There, that looks like it."

Hanley glanced out at where Marsh was pointing, and saw a faded sign with a unicorn painted on it. It was surrounded by a string of lightbulbs, a third of which were dark. Marsh pulled to a halt about twenty yards away and prepared to get out.

Hanley laid a hand on his arm. "I think I should go in alone. This Ronnie chap seemed a bit on the nervous side."

Marsh nodded and pulled a revolver from the pocket of his overcoat. "You should take this . . ."

Hanley had just opened the car door. He pushed the gun away and got out, then glanced back and gave a bitter smile. "It didn't help much the last time, did it?" He turned, quickly crossed to the sign hanging over the goulash-smelling dustbins, and made his way down the steps.

The foyer with its air of faded decadence disturbed him. It was seedy and that was the word that had come most often to his mind while he was following the trail of Rupert's life from London to Cambridge to Oxford. The seediness of the homosexual world.

"Yes, can I help you?"

The ginger-haired cloakroom attendant stifled a theatrical yawn as Hanley crossed to him.

"Yes, I'm looking for a, a performer called Ronnie."

The young man pursed his lips in a mocking smile. "Performer, eh? I suppose you could say that." From inside there was the sound of a piano crashing into life. He glanced down at his wristwatch and then leaned to the side of the counter and pulled back a heavy velvet curtain with a tattered gold fringe. "About time, lazy sod."

Hanley caught a glimpse of the nightclub beyond the curtain. It was not a large room and there was a small stage at the front. The stage lights were just flickering on, and a performer, dressed as a flamenco dancer, walked into the bright spot. At that point the young man let the curtain fall. "Juanita's not for everyone."

Hanley's eyes showed a flicker of distaste. "Is Ronnie here?"

The young man flashed his petulant little half-smile again. "He'll be on in twenty minues, so don't get him too excited, will you?" He pointed to a doorway in the opposite wall.

Backstage, Hanley saw a door open and the bright lights around a dressing-room mirror. A man was sitting at a table crammed with make-up and wigs, gazing into the mirror. Hanley was struck by how ludicrous he looked. He was a round-faced man with a small curved nose and heavy eyebrows. He had applied an almost white make-up in a large oval, leaving his pink skin uncovered all around.

"I'm looking for Ronnie."

The man swung round, a startled look in his eyes. "Oh! And what do you want him for? Who are you?"

Hanley recognised the rasping Yorkshire accent from the telephone call. He stepped inside and the other man recoiled. "My name's Hanley, you phoned me."

A look of relief flooded the man's face. "Christ but you gave me a fright." He gave a shuddering sigh and then reached into the back of an open drawer and pulled out a half-bottle of whisky. "I didn't know who you were standing there." He took a swig and then offered it. "I wasn't made for all this secret stuff."

Hanley waved the bottle away and felt a pang of doubt and

142

anxiety. He pulled the door closed and then sank down on the edge of the make-up table. "What do you mean, secret?"

Ronnie took another swig from the whisky bottle. "Oh, hiding envelopes . . . seeing poor Rupert shitting himself with fear . . . and then afterwards, you know, hearing how he died suspicious-like."

"Hardly suspicious, he hanged himself."

Ronnie turned from the mirror and stared at him, a wide-eyed look of disbelief on his face. "So they say. Yes . . ."

"I found him . . . in the cottage." Hanley laid stress on the "I" as if to say, I dare you to challenge my integrity.

Ronnie nodded slowly. "Oh I see. I see." He fumbled around amongst the make-up and then picked up a cigarette. "Well I'm sorry. I, well, I'm sorry. I know you were a good friend." There was a silence. Outside the pace of the music had hotted up and shrieks of laughter mixed with the quickening Latin rhythms. Ronnie lit the cigarette and took a deep drag, leaving an incongruously bright red smear at the end. "Look, I'm sorry to bring you here. I was afraid of anyone seeing you come to my place or seeing me go to the yards. I mean I know it's bloody stupid but after a while he got me scared. You know he stayed in my place for a while, it was the least I could do."

"Yes, I do know. I had to meet him there."

Ronnie sucked on his cigarette again and then stared off into the depths of the mirror. "Oh God but he was afraid of prison. He kept talking about it. I said to him, they've chucked you out because you were a queer, they're not gonna go and stick you in prison as well. Unless of course he'd run off with the petty cash." Ronnie gave a chortle and then turned and fixed him with a questioning look. But Hanley gave away nothing. He simply stared at him blankly until Ronnie started babbling on again. "But I know he was scared of something, scared shitless at times. I'd hear him kind of sobbing in the next room. I felt helpless."

"You said you wanted to give me something, an envelope, a package."

Ronnie took another drag at his cigarette and then laid it carefully down on top of a jar of Bovril. "Yes of course, can't

143

keep you nattering here and I've got to get on soon 'n' all. Can't have Miss Brazil screeching her lungs out all night." Ronnie chortled to himself as he reached up and took down one of a number of battered hatboxes from a shelf. "I told him I'd hide it away. He was real keen on me keeping it safe." He pulled out a bright red wig, took something from underneath and handed it over to Hanley.

It was a heavy brown manila envelope, the kind they used in the offices at the dockyard. Hanley stared at it then turned it over in his hands and slipped it into his coat pocket. "Thank you. I must go."

Ronnie nodded, picked up his cigarette and returned to his seat in front of the mirror. "Well, at least I got it safely into your hands whatever it is."

Yes, whatever it is, thought Hanley. He stood for a moment at the door, wondering if he should make one final remark about Kingsland, then decided against it. "Thanks."

Outside, Marsh had contented himself with watching the prostitutes strolling up and down. He was scrutinising a plump, young brunette on the other side of the street and didn't notice Hanley until he opened the car door.

"Ah, there you are." Marsh watched as Hanley settled into his seat and then continued, "Was there anything?"

Hanley pulled out the manila envelope.

Marsh reached up and clicked on the inside light. "Ah, good. Did he touch you for anything?"

Hanley looked up from the envelope somewhat puzzled. "What?"

"Money? Did he ask for any money?"

"No, no." Hanley untied the clasp at the top and pulled out a bundle of papers. There was a letter on top addressed to him. He glanced over at Marsh. "I'd just like to read over it first."

"Yes of course." Marsh turned aside and looked out the window again. The young brunette was just starting off down the road with a well-dressed, middle-aged man wearing a bowler hat.

"Good Lord!"

Marsh glanced back. Hanley had a pile of papers spread out across his lap, lists, line-drawings, calculations.

"What is it?"

Hanley bit his lower lip and then looked up at the rain-spotted windscreen. "It's a list of everything he passed on to the Germans."

"What!" Marsh held out his hand and Hanley passed a bundle of the papers across to him. He quickly scanned it, flicking from one page to the other. "I'm not a technical man, Hanley, what is this? I mean it's not the whole goddam submarine, is it?"

When Hanley spoke his voice was full of bitterness. "No, but it's a copy of just about every major innovation we made on the *Graplin*."

"Everything? I mean, what does he say in the letter?" Marsh suddenly sounded desperate.

Hanley picked up the letter and started reading it again. "I didn't finish it, I got to this list of drawings . . ."

Marsh broke in, impatiently. "Well, read, read on!"

Hanley could see that Marsh was after something else. But what? He was scanning the rest of the letter when, in a flash, it all became obvious. He stopped reading and looked angrily at Marsh. "Is this what you're after?" He turned back to the letter and read, " 'They pushed me to get information on Grainger's project, but I know nothing about it, and I'm glad I don't . . .' " Hanley glanced up again and saw Marsh's face almost instantly relax. "What does this mean, Marsh?"

Marsh gave a shrug of relief. "It means that it's better than we thought, they don't know about . . ." Marsh stopped and glanced out of the rain-spotted window again.

When Hanley spoke, his voice had a biting sarcastic edge to it. "I know nothing about it either."

Marsh nodded slowly. "Yes, yes."

There was another pause. A gust of wind splattered rain on the roof of the car. "Marsh, it's time I was told what's going on. I didn't ask to be dragged into the middle of this, and I don't appreciate being used, like a puppet."

Marsh cleared his throat. "I wish I could, Hanley, but this

145

clearance can only come from the top. I promise you, you'll be brought on board soon."

Hanley glanced back at the letter then held it up to the window to finish reading it so as to catch more light. When he turned to Marsh, his face was tense and drawn. He tossed the letter into Marsh's lap. "I think you'd better make that sooner rather than later."

"What?" Marsh raised a puzzled eyebrow. Hanley nodded towards the letter and Marsh picked it up and scanned through it. " 'They pushed me to get information on Grainger's project, but I know nothing about it, and I'm glad I don't, I don't believe I could have withstood their pressures,' " he read aloud. " 'But if for some reason I am not around, I must ask you to warn the Admiralty. It's my belief that they have someone else in the yards, someone who they are hoping will give them the information they are looking for about this project . . .' "

Marsh laid the letter aside and slowly banged his open palm against the rim of the steering wheel. He stared out of the window into the night. "Aaah God, just what we need, just what we need."

21

Kitty gave a superior smile as she strutted past the couples outside the Empire Cinema. They were lining up for the first night of Gracie Fields in her new picture, *The Queen of Hearts*. Well, they could have her! Kitty was sick of broad northern accents, she'd started a new life down here in the south.

And things weren't going too badly, all things considered. She had the job at Johnsons', the newsagents, and through Tom she had managed to land some weekend work at the Parrot, helping at the bar and in the cloakroom.

She glanced up at the large clock in front of Webber's, the jewellers. Quarter to eight. She quickened her pace, the last thing she wanted was to have Eddie Brent see her come in late.

The newspaper-seller outside the fish and chip shop was still doing a roaring trade selling the latest, special edition of the papers. Kitty pushed through the crowd who stood around reading and arguing as they munched their chips. She had had enough of the King and his problems. For the last week her hands had been constantly blackened with newspaper ink. Nobody at Johnsons' could seem to get enough of Edward VIII and Mrs Simpson.

Inside the Parrot, Elsie the cloakroom attendant was leaning on her counter, reading through a copy of the *Daily Mirror*. "Oh I think this is all terrible, don't you, Kitty?"

Kitty flicked her hair back out of her eyes. "If you're talking about the abdication, I couldn't give a damn." Then she pulled a small mirror and a tube of lipstick from her handbag.

Elsie looked somewhat startled, but only somewhat, since there was a bovine quality about her that seemed to defy real animation. "Oh I can't believe you mean that, Kitty. I mean King Edward seemed to care about the ordinary feller. I mean look at him crying when he went to see the Welsh miners."

Kitty raised a cynical eyebrow and carefully finished her lipstick. "Look, Elsie, I've heard enough about him in the last week to do me a lifetime. I just know he'll never have to go to bed hungry, neither will she, so why should I worry about them, all right?" With that Kitty marched across to the exotically panelled glass doors and slipped inside.

The club was almost empty. It didn't usually fill up until after ten on a Friday night. Kitty glanced up towards the small stage at the front where Susie Popham, her friend from the Anchor, was filling in and playing a medley of cinema tunes.

Susie looked up from the piano and nodded towards Kitty, inviting her to come up and join her. As Kitty made her way past the empty tables, she marvelled how Susie could play and talk at the same time. When she reached the piano she stood for a moment and watched her soft white hands gliding over the

147

keys. Susie turned and gave her a bemused wink. "Did you put any money on your brother tonight?"

Kitty's face fell, she had forgotten about Tom's fight in London. Susie laughed. "My God, Kitty, you're something else. Your brother's gonna be in the ring risking his handsome looks in about half an hour and you've forgotten."

"Oh and since when've you found him handsome? I thought you had your eyes on that pain-in-my-arse Ernie."

"You're really too hard on Ernie, you know."

Kitty grimaced and then saw something resembling a blush creeping up along Susie's neck. She was about to continue her half-humorous taunting when she heard the clatter of pots out in the back-room-cum-kitchen. "What's going on? Is Eddie trying to make himself a cup of coffee?"

Susie laughed. "No, get on with you, Eddie's up in London with Tom."

Kitty nodded. She'd been through all that with Tom in the last few weeks. Whether he should sign up with Eddie Brent or not. She was bored sick with it. It was obvious to her. If Eddie could make him more money, Tom *had* to sign with him. What did it matter what Danny Brockway thought? All right, Danny was a nice man, but in Kitty's book nice wasn't money, and money was the only thing that really mattered.

There was the clattering sound of another pan hitting the ground and then the sound of someone shouting. Susie lifted her eyes to the ceiling. "That must be Jimmy Lee with one of his 'guests'."

Kitty looked puzzled. Jimmy Lee was half-Chinese and ran one of Eddie's businesses, a small laundry that had a number of contracts with various parts of the shipyards. The front of the premises was on Sudbury Street, one street away, and the building backed on to the rear yard of the Parrot. Kitty had seen Jimmy Lee around the Parrot a number of times, slipping out and in like a shadow. "What do you mean one of his guests?"

Susie gave another laugh. "You know, over in his Shangri-la." She turned and saw the blank look in Kitty's eyes, then continued, "No you don't, well, it doesn't matter."

Kitty was irritated. "What are you rambling on about?" But Susie just shrugged and turned back to her piano. "Oh nothing, nothing!"

Kitty gave a disgusted look, then strutted to the rear door, flung it open and walked into the back room. It was long and narrow with a door that led out on to the yard. Along one side there were two gas cookers and a cupboard with a large coffee urn on it. At the far end Jimmy Lee was holding a sailor over the sink. She watched in increasing disgust as the man heaved up in a series of dry retches. When he seemed exhausted, Jimmy dragged the sailor under the tap and turned it on full force. The sailor groaned and tried half-heartedly to struggle free. But Jimmy kept him firmly in place for about half a minute, then suddenly pulled him out from under the gushing water and tried to stand him upright. The sailor was a good foot taller than Jimmy, but he looked like a limp rag doll in his arms. His dark hair was plastered to his forehead and the water continued to run down his head on to his uniform.

"You. Wake up, wake up." Jimmy Lee's eyes had a cold, hard gleam to them.

The sailor's head lolled backwards and forwards on his shoulders. His eyelids drooped and his eyes seemed glazed and unfocused like a drunk. "No, no. Sleep, sleeeeep . . ."

"No, you go. You go now." Jimmy Lee slapped him quickly around the face, then turned and marched him towards the coffee urn. It was then that he saw Kitty for the first time. He paused then flashed her a broad, cardboard smile. "Miss, maybe you help, you give me cup of coffee. I go outside, walk him in the air."

"Yes, yes." Kitty was so engrossed in the strange scene that she barely mumbled her assent. She picked up a cup, turned the tap on the urn and watched the steaming black coffee gurgling into it.

The sailor swayed as he watched her, then gave a moronic smile and turned to Jimmy again. "Jus' 'nother lil' pipe Jimmy, jus' 'nother."

Jimmy Lee snatched the cup of coffee from Kitty's hand and

quickly pulled the sailor towards the back door. "Shut up!" He kicked it open and disappeared into the darkness.

Kitty stood for a moment watching the last drops of coffee dripping on to the white-painted surface of the cupboard. Then she followed them to the door and pushed it open.

The yard was wide. The rear of the laundry was on the other side, opposite the back door of the club, a two-storey building with small-paned windows. In the light that spilled out Kitty saw Jimmy Lee dragging the sailor into the alleyway that led out to Sudbury Street.

She was wondering what to make of it all when she heard laughter echoing around the yard. A laundry van was parked over to the left. Kitty recognised Ernie's laugh and walked forward a few steps. Just behind the van, a number of beer barrels were stacked beside a mound of wooden crates. Ernie was sitting there with Benny Peters, the drummer, sharing a bottle of beer.

"Hey Ernie."

Ernie slowly turned and flashed her a blandly happy smile. "Hello Sis, what can I do you for?" Then he and Benny started giggling again.

Kitty was disgusted at his schoolboy manner, but she knew there was no use saying anything to him. Now that he'd got this weekend job at the club he thought the sun shone out of his arse.

"Did you see that Jimmy Lee dragging the sailor across the yard?" Kitty noticed the strangely perfumed smoke for the first time and then saw Benny passing a lighted, hand-rolled cigarette across to Ernie.

"No." Ernie shook his head and took a deep drag at the cigarette. "But don't worry about Jimmy." Ernie gave another inane giggle. Benny gave a stuttering little laugh, too, then glanced at his wristwatch, stood up and stretched, "'s time we were going in."

Kitty started back across the yard. "That sounds like a good idea, before poor Susie wears her fingers to the bone."

In the darkness behind her she heard Ernie giggling again. "Yeah, we can get back to this later."

150

Whatever he was up to now it didn't sound as if it boded well. Then Kitty shrugged. Well, if it wasn't gambling it was bound to be something. In her mind Ernie was doomed for the rubbish-tip.

22

Hanley gripped the railing around the bridge and gazed out over the dark sea. He took a deep breath, smelling the combination of salt air and oil. He loved the feel of a ship at night, the low throb of its engines, the sound of men's voices. There was somehow a unity of purpose on a ship that was missing on land and at such moments Hanley came closest to feeling nostalgic.

Hanley looked along the decks to the prow of the ship gently rising and falling with the waves. The *Cumbria* was the first of the old C-class cruisers to have the new four-inch-high angle anti-aircraft guns fitted. He stared at them absent-mindedly as they gleamed dully in the ship's lights and then made a vague mental note that they did not have their canvas covers.

He filled his pipe, lit it, and continued gazing out to sea. Here and there beams of moonlight shone through the clouds and caught the waves in glittering silver streaks. He took another deep breath of the bracing air and then rubbed his hand along the cold metal rail, feeling the raindrops, slick on his palm.

It was just two days ago that he had received the call from Marsh. "I've got the clearance for you to see this new technology. This will put everything into focus . . . everything."

Hanley puffed on his pipe and gave a cynical laugh. "Everything into focus . . ." He very much doubted that. At this point in time, his whole life seemed to be spiralling out of focus.

"So what do you think of Grainger and his friends?" Hanley quickly turned and saw Marsh silhouetted in the open door.

"I'll tell you that when I know what they're doing."

"It won't be long." Marsh crossed to the rail, took out a cigarette and rolled it between his finger and thumb. "Got a light?" As Hanley pulled out his matches, Marsh looked at his watch and glanced up at the sky to the east.

Hanley tossed him the box. "A wild and beautiful night."

"Hmm?" Marsh looked distracted. He glanced at his watch again, then struck a match and lit his cigarette.

Suddenly the warning siren blared and the whole ship exploded into action. Marsh tossed his cigarette on to the metal deck and ground it out, then tugged the sleeve of Hanley's jacket and shouted, "Down here!" He clattered down the steps to the upper gundeck with Hanley following close behind.

All round them the gunners were running to their positions at the anti-aircraft batteries. Hanley and Marsh pressed themselves back against the wall of the one remaining six-inch battery, allowing the men to pass, then quickly followed them. Across all the upper decks the gun platforms were being readied.

A young officer, close to Hanley, picked up a headset and listened intently. He scribbled furiously on his clipboard and then barked orders to the men. The gundeck turned to his precise instructions and the barrel moved skywards as if to seek out some invisible enemy.

"There they are!"

Hanley stepped back in amazement when he heard the shout. He glanced up into the sky just in time to see the three aircraft breaking out of the silver-ribboned clouds. With a thunderous roar they dived straight towards the guns.

Hanley was stunned. It was as if the frenetic activity on the ship had somehow attracted the planes. They had appeared, suddenly, magically, like wasps buzzing round a jam-jar. Hanley leaned back against the cold metal wall behind him. The officer shouted his orders, the new anti-aircraft guns barked as they shot off their blanks. Another officer sat by the sights assessing the accuracy of the test.

152

Within minutes it was over. Then followed a few seconds of silence, complete silence, except for the drone of the now distant planes. The men at the gun battery slumped back in a communal sigh of relief. The throbbing noise of the ship's engines returned. There was a respite, a moment with just the sound of wind and waves. Then a spontaneous cheer resounded around the decks.

Marsh took out another cigarette, lit it and handed the matches back to Hanley. "Yours, I believe." He gave a boyish smile, and took a deep drag.

Hanley felt dazed. "I presume you're eventually going to explain all this."

Marsh took another long drag on his cigarette and Hanley could see the deep relief in his eyes, masked behind the cocky smile. "Yes, but it's a bloody marvel, isn't it? This is the first time I've ever seen it in action, a bloody marvel."

"Marsh, how the hell did they know when those planes would appear? Do you have fighters up there, dirigibles?"

"No, this is all the work of Grainger and his friends. Come on, let's go and see."

Marsh turned and went inside. Hanley followed. Halfway up the narrow metal steps he heard the high-pitched screech of electrical equipment, followed by the crackling noise of voices over a radio receiver. At the top, equipment was stacked all along the passageway. Two storerooms and a cabin had been cleared and they were packed with a variety of strange gadgets. Thick black cables were running everywhere.

There was a darkened room at the end of the passageway. A lanky young man in his mid-twenties was leaning over a desk. Another man sat beside him wearing a pair of headphones. They were both bathed in a green light that flickered rhythmically across their faces.

When the young man turned round Hanley saw it was Grainger.

"Ah gentlemen, not a bad night's work, eh!" Grainger stepped forward into the light and gave a boyish smile, then ran his hands through his already tousled dark hair. He dodged forward through the mess of cables and machinery. "Welcome

153

to the magic cave. And apologies to you, Captain Hanley. I feel like an interloper in your yards. I would have had you round for a cup of tea a long time ago but the Admiralty have strict rules about fraternisation with the locals." Grainger gave a guffawing laugh and then scratched the top of his head, leaving his hair in an even greater state of disarray. "Anyway, now you're here let me show you round." He stepped back into the darkened room again. "Basically this is all very simple, we're using radio waves to find the position and distance of objects within our radius. We call it radio detection and ranging, radar for short."

They were now standing beside the operator. Hanley had seen nothing like it before. In front of them was a screen, with a greenish line of light sweeping round it, like a large seconds hand on a clock. At the top of the screen a wraithlike line snaked across from one side to the other, illuminated by the passing "seconds hand". After a couple of sweeps Hanley recognised it as the outline of the Isle of Wight and the Solent. He found himself catching his breath with excitement. It was night-time and yet here was this machine peering into the darkness, seeing what no man could possibly see. As he stared at the strange, spectral screen, he noticed three small blips appearing approximately halfway between the phantom coastline and the centrepoint of the sweeping radius.

Hanley leaned forward and pointed to them. "These wouldn't be our air force friends would they?"

"Yes, yes," Grainger seemed genuinely pleased, like a teacher who had found an unlikely star pupil. "Well done, Captain, that's your bandits precisely. I think they're turning to give us one more flyover."

"My God. That's marvellous, bloody marvellous." Hanley's mind was thrown into a state near confusion as he conjured up all the possibilities. He watched the three blips moving towards the centre of the circle. Then he heard a radio in the next room crackling into life. "Delta beta three six; delta beta three six; flying over for damage report."

Grainger gave a satisfied laugh and gestured towards the screen. "We already know what you're doing."

Hanley watched, entranced, as the three little blips jumped forward again. "Dr Grainger, I, eh, in layman's terms, how does it work?"

Grainger gestured towards the door and they followed him into the passageway. "In simple terms, we transmit radio waves." He took a pencil stub from his pocket and drew a small narrow triangle on the wall. "Then we have a receiver." Just beside the triangle he drew a small arc. "The radio waves will bounce off any object in their path and that is what we pick up on the receiver. We then translate those signals into direction and distance."

Hanley stared at the simplistic line-drawing on the wall, the circle with its two strange hieroglyphs in the centre, and shook his head. He gave a long chuckling laugh as if he had just been handed an unexpected gift and tapped the wall with his forefinger. "It's so simple. It's, eh, it's pure genius."

Grainger flipped the pencil stub into the air and stared deep into Hanley's eyes, flashing a boyish smile. "You seem duly impressed, Captain. I hope you remember this when I keep pestering you for your assistance in the months ahead."

"Captain Marsh." A young radio officer stepped out of one of the doors along the passageway.

"Yes."

"Message from Captain Stewart, sir. He requests that you, Captain Hanley and Dr Grainger join him and the rear admiral in his quarters."

Marsh nodded and then gestured towards the stairwell. "We'd better go, gentlemen. We can't keep the rear admiral waiting."

Grainger started along the passageway then turned to Hanley and raised an eyebrow. "Indeed!" There was a twinkle in his eye as though he regarded them both as schoolboys forced to do their teacher's bidding. Hanley suppressed a smile. He liked this young man.

As Hanley started down the steps after Grainger, he realised that Marsh was not behind them. He glanced back and saw him standing by the wall, carefully rubbing at the pencil drawing with his hand. "Where else are you working on this, apart from here and the dockyards?"

Grainger half turned and gave him a sly smile. "You've guessed right, Captain, I'm only part of a rather large team. Some of my other colleagues are trying to adapt this equipment to be carried on aeroplanes, but most of them are in the middle of establishing a chain of land stations, along the Thames Estuary and the southern approaches, in fact, that work's almost completed."

Hanley's face again registered surprise. "I didn't realise it had gone so far."

"I suppose that means that Captain Marsh and his friends must be doing something right," he glanced over Hanley's shoulder, "wherever he is."

To the right of them a small corridor led to the captain's quarters. The door was open and the sound of voices drifted out. Hanley pulled Grainger by the sleeve. "What precisely are you doing in Chatham?"

Grainger turned and stared at Hanley for a moment, then slumped back against the wall furiously scratching his hair. "Precisely, hm? I wish the word could apply. Land stations are fine. That's because you have as much room as you want. But my problem is to get all that equipment into a small space."

Hanley's eyes narrowed. "How small?"

Grainger sighed. "Well, I think you've maybe guessed. We're planning to experiment with it on the *Graplin*."

Hanley was at once both excited and incredulous. "You are going to use it underwater?"

Grainger gave a snorting laugh. "I wish to God we *could* use it underwater. No, it would have to be used at periscope depth but even then think of what it could do, think of the increased warning range you could have both against ships and aircraft."

Hanley did think, and for a moment was overwhelmed with the possibilities. It would open up a new era in submarine warfare. The limits were no longer as far as the eye could see. This new radio eye would allow them to reach beyond the horizon. Then the cold reality of his engineer's mind swept over

156

him. "But the *Graplin* hasn't been constructed to accommodate this."

Grainger shrugged his shoulders. "No, no it hasn't. But we have the whole of the fitting-out period to make the changes. Anyway I suppose we'd better get inside." He quickly started along the passageway, as if trying to avoid further conversation.

Hanley did not move, but stared down at his pipe, smacking the bowl rhythmically against the palm of his hand. He felt a strange mixture of anger and exhilaration. The *Graplin* was supposed to be fitted out by the summer of 1937. That gave them about six months.

"Well, Hanley, what do you think?"

Hanley turned as Marsh approached him. "I, eh, I'm impressed."

Marsh nodded, gave a smile at Hanley's understatement, then continued, "I think you can now understand my fears about Kingsland, and what else he might have passed on."

"Yes, yes of course." Hanley pressed his thumb into the dark ash of the pipe-bowl.

Marsh watched him closely then asked, "What is it?"

Hanley looked up and glanced along towards the open door. "From everything I hear, this programme is going to be accelerated. But what about Kingsland's letter, his warning about the other possible leak in the yards?"

In the dim light, Marsh looked tired. "We've been trying to develop a plan ever since we got hold of Kingsland's letter. Of course there's no proof that we still have a spy in the yards, but with all of this, we can't leave anything to chance." Marsh took out another cigarette and absent-mindedly tapped its end against the silver case. His grey-blue eyes seemed focused somewhere else. "We need your help again, we need a red herring." He slipped the case into his pocket and slowly twirled the cigarette between his fingers.

"What exactly do you mean?"

"The Germans know nothing about radar, we're certain of that. We can keep a tight control over the land stations, but now that we're beginning to adapt it to ships and planes and hopefully submarines, a larger and larger number of men will come into contact with some part of this project. We can make sure each group will only work within a very limited area so that very few people actually know the overall picture. However, we think we also need a diversion."

Marsh lit his cigarette, drew on it deeply and then glanced towards Stewart's quarters to check that they were still alone. "A diversion will kill two birds with the one stone. If the information starts turning up in Germany, we will know that we do indeed have a spy and, most important, it will also mean that radar is still safe from discovery."

"And are we supposed to come up with this 'red herring'?" Hanley's voice betrayed his irritation.

"First of all you've got to realise there is no 'we' in this. Grainger, you, and Rear Admiral Walker will know, and that's all."

"I see. And everyone else is suspect, hm?" Hanley raised his eyebrow in disgust.

Marsh stared at him, his eyes were cold. "Yes, everyone."

Hanley nodded slowly. He was obviously not happy with his brief, but he knew it was necessary. "And the 'red herring'?"

"We've just closed down two years of research on a combined acoustic-magnetic torpedo. The material we worked on was a failure. That can be the front for Grainger's work."

"So if any of the research turns up in Kiel, we'll know where it comes from."

"Yes."

"You seem to have everything sewn up, Marsh."

Marsh stared at Hanley. He did not appreciate the bitter tone in his voice. "Nothing's sewn up in this business, Hanley . . . I simply know that we have to catch our man before he catches us."

They stood facing each other. Then Hanley took out his matches, lit his pipe and nodded towards the open door. "We should join them inside." He started walking down the passageway.

"We can depend on your help then, Hanley?"

Hanley turned and gave a cynical smile. "I didn't know I had a choice."

23

Eunice was late. She swung into the long, elm-lined driveway of Brampton Hall scattering the gravel across the gateposts and sped towards the high-arched entrance hall. She quickly parked amongst the other cars at the edge of the wide circular front drive and then gazed at herself in the mirror. As she did so, she heard the raucous sound of jazz music jigging incongruously across the manicured lawn. She brushed her hair back and glanced towards the lighted windows in the west wing. The party had started, she must hurry!

A young maid answered the bell, took her coat and then led her along the dimly lit corridor to the music room. On either side Brampton family portraits lined the walls. As she approached the other end, she saw light flooding out of the open double-doors to her right. Olivia suddenly rushed out and threw her arms around Eunice. "Darling, you made it." Olivia looked a bit like an Arab harem girl, wearing a pair of loose-fitting slacks that did not exactly flatter her plump figure. She steered Eunice into the room, then pulled her over towards the bar and lifted a bottle of whisky. "This do?"

Eunice nodded and glanced around. There were about twenty people scattered about but the room was so big that it seemed almost empty. A number of them had gathered around a long, marble coffee table on which a wireless was precariously perched.

". . . and there will follow a programme of traditional

Scottish music up until ten o'clock, when King Edward will give his farewell address to the nation . . ."

"Farewell address! My God, but Baldwin has a lot to answer for, the smug little pig farmer." Olivia spat the words out as she thrust the whisky and soda into Eunice's hand. The liquor slopped over the sides and dribbled through Eunice's fingers on to the glass surface of the bar. "Ooops, sorry darling. It's just that I get so bloody angry. It's typical of this country. All this constitutional hoo-ha has nothing to do with morals. He's being kicked out because he wants to change things, wants to drag us into the twentieth century."

Eunice had only been half listening to her friend. After all, she had heard most of it before, last night when Olivia had phoned her. As Olivia rambled on, attacking "the dwarf mind, Baldwin" and "the Archbishop of Cant", Eunice peered over the top of her whisky and gazed around the room. She recognised a few people from Olivia's London soirée, but not all.

Along the outer wall a number of French windows opened out on to a conservatory. This too was lit, and Eunice could see couples sitting amongst the palms and vines. She noticed the young Italian Count Andrezzino leaning against the outside wall, smoking, and could not help suppressing a smile of admiration for Olivia's sheer gall. She denied herself none of the sybarite pleasures, even when she was at home.

Unaware of her friend's musings, Olivia had been pouring herself a large glass of white wine, still talking away. But when she glanced up she saw Eunice looking towards the conservatory. "Oh sorry, darling, there I go again, I must be boring the arse off you poor old dear when you've just driven across half of England to see me."

Eunice grinned. "Hardly half of England, Olivia. Although I have to say it is a pain driving up through all the . . ." Eunice stopped short in the middle of her sentence. Hans Weichert had just walked in through the French doors. He was wearing a tweed sports jacket and a pair of cavalry twills and looked at the same time both terribly English and strangely foreign. He could have passed for a stockbroker down from the City for the weekend, but there was something about the way he held himself, something assertive, almost strutting, in his manner.

He was talking to a small, handsome, dark-haired woman wearing glasses. He gestured to the radio, obviously making some point about the evening's events, then caught sight of Eunice out of the corner of his eye. He gave a half wave, half salute, and smiled. It was a strange smile, as if for a few moments he had found himself unguarded and let the boyish, joyful side of him shine through.

"Oh yes, Commander Weichert." There was a wickedly disconcerting tone in Olivia's voice. "I do apologise, Eunice, I have to confess to being a little Machiavellian. I met up with him at one of Ribbentrop's dinner parties at the German Embassy earlier this week and he very casually asked about you." She stopped, and gave Eunice a knowing wink.

"Oh, come on, Olivia, you're acting as though we're in the fifth form again." Eunice laughed dismissively.

But Olivia was not about to let her friend off the hook so easily. "Don't act the innocent with me, Eunice, fifth form or not, my antennae are rarely wrong."

Eunice put her drink down on the glass top of the bar and clicked the side of it with her fingernail. "I see." She was not sure how she felt about being manipulated by Olivia. "And that's why he's invited here the same weekend as me?"

Olivia leaned back and pulled a black cigarette box towards her. She opened it, took one out. "Oh, that and," she gave a grin and lit the cigarette. "Well, to tell the truth, my American friend Ruthie there is a writer for a New York magazine. She wanted to talk to him."

Eunice gave a good-natured laugh. "You really are a horse's arse sometimes, Olivia."

"Ah, wait." She held Eunice fixed with that dreamy sensual look of hers. "I still believe that he's got his eye on you."

"I am married you know, Olivia."

Olivia cast her eyes towards the ceiling. "Oh, come on, darling, don't feed me that horse manure. It's me, you know! Look sweetie, I'm not trying to make Hanley out to be a

161

monster, any more than Brampton is, but I just want you to consider how much he actually deserves your fidelity."

Eunice bit into her lower lip. She felt resentment and a slight anger. "Can't we talk about something else?"

Olivia was quick to see she had pushed it too far. She gripped Eunice's arm and pulled her friend towards her.

"I did hear something this week that nearly blew my head off." Olivia took a gulp of white wine and then peered around Eunice as if to ensure that they could not be overheard. Eunice smiled at her friend's theatrics, but appreciated her finesse at so quickly changing the subject.

"It was at Ribbentrop's shindig and I met up with one of Brampton's old school chums Johnny, well, perhaps I'd better not say. Anyway he's one of the top men in Intelligence. Well, apparently Baldwin's damned government had the King – Edward! – followed."

Eunice looked puzzled. "I don't understand."

Olivia leaned even closer. "The government believed that information was being leaked from the King's dispatch boxes."

Eunice shook her head, still not clear what was being said. "Leaked to whom?"

Olivia raised her eyebrows like a teacher with a slow child. "To the Germans, my dear."

Eunice was stunned. "They thought that the King . . .?"

Olivia held up a hand to silence her. "They weren't willing to say who they thought was doing it, but they suspected everyone, the staff at Belvedere, Mrs Simpson, and if truth be told, even the King, or else why were they following him?" Olivia suddenly gave a grunt of disgust. "God, I can't even believe I'm saying it. Imagine, spying on the King!" She banged her drink on the glass and groaned. "Oh God, what would it matter if he was passing them information anyway! The Germans are our friends. Edward was smart enough to see that. I don't know if he was even passing them the time of day, but I know that he agrees with Hitler's objectives."

Eunice stared past her friend at the bottles lining the back of the bar. Listening to all this was a long call from the conversations she had heard in Chatham. Almost everyone there, including Hanley, regarded the Germans as their potential enemy.

"Anyway," Olivia continued, "I see you've had enough of my garbled politics. Come over with me and talk to our American musical genius. I know he's a bore but we might just be able to persuade him to write a song about me."

Olivia was just about to cross the room when the King's radio address started so she quickly walked over to the sofa by the marble coffee table and plonked herself down on it.

Eunice stood for a moment and listened.

". . . I have now decided to renounce the Throne to which I succeeded on the death of my father, and I am now communicating this, my final and irrevocable decision . . ."

Eunice's mind started to drift. She wondered if anything was ever really "final and irrevocable". Certainly the vows between her and Hanley did not seem to be. And if they weren't, where was she drifting to? She glanced over and saw Weichert still deep in conversation with the American woman. She felt a flush of confusion, lifted her glass and walked through the French windows into the conservatory.

She stopped beside a large rattan palm and ran her fingers along the sharp edge of one of the leaves. She felt like a moping schoolgirl. Why did it bother her that Weichert was in there paying attention to that silly American? She pressed her forefinger into the spiky point of the plant and wondered, were pain and pleasure always so close together?

"Aaah. It is the earnestness of Americans that I find most difficult. I can take their innocence. But they are so earnest."

Eunice swung around. Weichert was standing beside her. He was smiling, but his eyes had that entrancingly dangerous quality that had so moved her before. For a moment she drank in his intensity. She felt a chill, a strange sweet chill, flowing through her as though a drop of iced water had slowly and sensuously dribbled down her back. Then she gave a vague flicker of a smile and turned to stare into the darkness beyond the glass. "I had always thought Germans earnest."

Weichert leaned forward, placing his hands on the mouth of a large red earthenware urn. He glanced out towards the

163

moonlit lake in the distance and for a moment caught her gazing at his reflection in the glass. "Ah, yes, but I hope we are not earnest over trivial matters."

Eunice took a deep breath and inhaled the damp, earthy smell that lingered amongst the compost and leaves and flowerpots. "You're very tough on your lady friend."

Weichert gave a hard-edged laugh. "I would hardly call her a friend, she simply wants information on the new order in Germany."

Eunice turned and once more caught his eyes in the darkened glass. "I thought I saw much more than desire for information in her eyes."

They stared at one another and she realised with more than a little trepidation that she had just betrayed her deep interest in him. She found herself catching her breath in confusion. She hated the fact that she could feel this strong attraction and yet not feel free enough to express it.

"Maybe," he paused, gave a playful smile, and then continued. "But I have to say I wasn't really looking at her." There was just enough stress on the last word to make Eunice wonder. She nervously adjusted a strand of hair behind her ear. Then she turned and focused on the gaunt, bare trees, silhouetted in the moonlight beyond the glass.

"And what do you think of our present constitutional turmoil, Commander?" Eunice could feel herself building a barricade around her emotions. It was all too close, too raw, too dangerous. Even though she now avoided looking at his reflection, she could sense him standing beside her, hear his gently relaxed breathing.

She noticed a movement out of the corner of her eye as he leaned forward again and placed his elbows on the rim of the tall earthenware urn. Then he folded his arms in an engagingly relaxed posture. "I believe that most Germans would support King Edward. He has chosen the road of high romance. Germans have always admired men of deep passion."

Eunice turned from the glass and flashed him a sceptical look. "I must say I had always thought of the Germans as being cold, logical, precise people."

164

"Ah, of course you would think that." Weichert gave a good-natured chuckle, unfolded his arms and gently drummed his fingers along the rim of the urn. "That is the English view," he continued. "They want to see themselves reflected in others, they are the ones who are cold and dispassionate. But, they forget that *we* are the children of Beethoven and Heine, Nietzsche and Wagner, that we take romance beyond the superficial and the ephemeral into the realm of sublime passion." He stopped and turned towards her, raising a cynical eyebrow. "I am sorry, you must find this little rampage of mine rather boring."

She fixed him with an intense, almost petulant look. "Do you *really* think that I do?"

He stared back at her as if taking her measure and then gave a bare flicker of a smile. "No, I suppose I don't."

Eunice took a step towards the window and one of the long, stringy leaves of the rattan palm flicked up against her face. Before she could move, he had quickly reached forward and, with a dry rustling sound, pushed the stray leaf away. For a moment his hand lingered. She gazed at him and had a peculiar feeling of time suspended. She saw a long shapely hand like that of an artist, delicate and caring. It curved in towards her, almost disembodied, as though he was about to stroke her cheek, cup her chin in his palm.

The King's speech was over and all around them they heard the noises of the party; the rollicking sounds of the jazz and the dancers; the clinking and clattering of the cutlery as the servants set up for dinner in the next room. Yet somehow, they were suspended in their delicate cocoon of silence.

Finally Weichert glanced away from her towards the dark glass. "I was to return to London this evening but I," he paused for a second as though considering and then continued, "I was wondering if you were staying overnight."

"I don't know, Olivia's asked me, but I haven't decided yet."

He stared at her, straight and uncompromising. "I wish you would stay, it would give me an excuse not to face that long journey tonight."

Eunice felt a rush of blood to her head. It had been said. It

165

was out in the open now. She stared into those clear blue eyes and knew instantly what she would do. But as to whether she had decided or whether it had been decided for her, she could not tell. She only knew that for the first time in years she was being swept along by the joy and passion of the moment, and it felt good.

24

The atmosphere in the admiral's office was icy. Hanley had every sympathy for the yard managers, but now he also understood the importance of the Grainger project and why it needed to be pushed forward with all haste.

A large table had been set up in the middle of the room and the admiral's desk had been pushed to one side. To Hanley's presently cynical cast of mind, that in itself showed the importance of the occasion. A set of the *Graplin*'s blueprints had been placed on the table, and Grainger was just finishing his explanation of the changes he needed.

". . . this device will need to be placed above the bridge, I don't believe it can be made retractable at this time. Of course, at this stage it's still all experimental."

There was silence for a few seconds. Finally Rear Admiral Walker stepped forward and tapped the end of a pencil rhythmically against a tight roll of blueprints.

"Gentlemen, this is of course difficult but it isn't a matter of choice. This is all part of a quickening pace of rearmament and we should be glad of it." Walker paused and cast a quick sideways glance at Hanley, then he continued, "I know this puts tremendous pressure on all of us, but the end result will be worth it."

Lieutenant Commander Crowe stepped forward and cleared

his throat. As captain of the *Graplin*, Crowe was the man who would take it through all the problems of its fitting-out and trials. "Gentlemen, I have had a lot of trouble with this. The *Graplin* was not originally an experimental boat and in my opinion it's a very dubious proposition for it to become that at so late a stage."

Walker tapped the roll of blueprints again but this time Hanley could see just a slight flicker of uncertainty in his eyes. Grainger, too, looked decidedly ill at ease. Hanley saw him turning his head towards the window, as his long fingers absent-mindedly twisted around his dark curls. He knew that Grainger was not happy with the "red herring" that Marsh had invented. Marsh had spent a long time constructing an intricate plan to use the acoustic-magnetic torpedo as a front for Grainger's radar work at the yards, even though Grainger had declared at earlier meetings that he would not waste his time pretending to work on "this dodo". Marsh did not appreciate having his efforts described so scathingly.

Hanley rapped the edge of the table with his pipe. "Gentlemen, as Captain Marsh explained, this experimental work on the torpedo has gone as far as it can go. This could be one of our most important weapons against the new U-boats. So, if we need to adapt the *Graplin* to monitor the tests, then by God we'll do it and we'll do it in good time."

Hanley saw that his speech had had an effect. He noticed that Marsh had a self-satisfied grin on his face, as though his favourite pupil had just won a prize. But Hanley had his own doubts about the intricacy of Marsh's plan and he wondered how long they could keep up the pretence that the top-secret radar was only a monitoring device for the acoustic-magnetic torpedo.

As the others went back to the various blueprints, Hanley noticed Gillings standing by the window, staring into the cold December night. He watched him for a moment, wondering what was on his mind. Suddenly Gillings spun round and caught Hanley's eye. "These electricians that are needed, how they're going to be chosen. Is that to be left up to engineering?"

Hanley had hoped the question would not come up until he had spoken to Gillings in private. "I believe that Dr Grainger has prepared a list, but apparently Captain Marsh has problems of security clearance with some of the names."

Grainger stepped towards them and flashed a cocky smile. "I, however, have no problems. If a man is bright enough I can use his skills. I left my list next door with the secretary to make copies . . ." Grainger walked out trailing his words behind him.

"Mr Gillings." Hanley started towards the secretary's office and indicated that Gillings should follow him.

The outer office was in shadow. There was a small lamp over the desk and one of the streetlamps threw a stream of dull yellow light on to a line of heavy oak filing cabinets. Grainger stood by the desk reading through a manila folder. He turned as Hanley entered, pulled a list from the folder and waved it.

"Here we are. Ah, Mr Gillings."

Hanley looked round. Gillings had just walked in behind him.

"Cast your eye over this now, if you like," Grainger continued, "I'm sure the admiral's secretary'll have copies for us all tomorrow." Grainger held out the paper.

Gillings walked over to the desk, took the list and glanced at it under the lamp. He quickly raised an eyebrow. "You've got some fifty names here."

"Ah, yes, but we only need twenty-two, that's to give us some choice, although there are some I'd really like to have." Grainger leaned over and scanned the list. "Dickson, Peters, Fenwick, I believe they've done some of the innovative work on small electric motors and we have some bright apprentices too. I believe Terry Gillings is your son, he's top of his class, I hear."

"Yes, eh yes." Gillings was obviously pleased to hear about Terry. Then he glanced down at the list again. "Captain Marsh said something about a problem with some of these men."

"Yes, a problem with security." Hanley turned and saw that Marsh had walked in behind him. He strolled over to join them at the desk, then slipped a small notepad out of his pocket and opened it. "We have five communists on that list . . ."

Grainger gave a grunt of disgust and threw up his arms. "Oh come on, man, you aren't really going to push this, are you? I

168

don't give a damn who's a communist or even a Tory for that matter, though few of them have the brains for the kind of work we do."

Marsh glared at Grainger. "Communists are security risks because they owe allegiance to another country."

Grainger gave another groan. "Oh bollocks, Marsh, that's the same palaver they used to give out about Catholics. If a man's got the brains let's use him."

Hanley could see Marsh flinching. He was not used to anyone speaking back. For a moment Hanley thought he was going to strike the young scientist.

When Marsh did speak his voice had a decidedly frosty edge to it. "Perhaps the decision isn't yours, Grainger."

"And perhaps it is. Just remember, my brief is to get this project done, and quickly."

There was something about Grainger's youthful arrogance that amused Hanley, but he quickly stepped forward and raised his hands. "I think we can do without an argument at this time."

Marsh's eyes flickered to the side and took in Gillings. "Yes, you're quite right."

Grainger shut the manila folder and dropped it back on to the desk. "Whatever you say, gentlemen, I have work to do." He started towards the door and then glanced back over his shoulder. "Although I should tell you, I intend to choose from the whole of that list."

Marsh was obviously not happy. He closed his notebook and looked as though he was about to slip it back into his pocket.

Gillings looked a little lost. "Wouldn't it be best if I knew about these men? I mean I could give some opinions. I heard Dickson's name there, I do know that he's a bit of a troublemaker but . . ."

"Mr Gillings," Hanley cut across the other man. "I read Captain Marsh's list this afternoon." He paused for a moment and seemed almost reluctant to continue. "The thing is, I, eh, I don't know if you're aware of this already but your son's name is on it."

There was a moment of silence. Somewhere outside, along

169

the dark river, a tugboat sounded a long mournful siren. Then Gillings sucked in his breath. "Pardon?" His voice was barely audible and he seemed genuinely puzzled. He glared at Hanley, wide-eyed. "I don't understand."

Hanley gave a quick glance at Marsh as if looking for help. Marsh tapped the edge of the notepad against his palm and then said brusquely, "My sources tell me that he's a newly joined member of the Communist Party."

Gillings looked stunned and then slowly shook his head from side to side as if he was just seeing the flaw in an argument. "No, no, there must be some mistake. We've, eh, no, that's impossible . . ."

Hanley saw first the doubt, and then the pain of the new knowledge reflected in the man's face. Suddenly he felt an overpowering wave of sympathy. He thought of Nigel and Elizabeth and how quickly they had seemed to grow away from him.

As he watched Gillings he saw him visibly sag. Gillings slowly brought his hand up and distractedly tugged at his ear. He looked as if he was still trying to make sense of what had been said.

Marsh looked uncomfortable with the silence. He cleared his throat, then slapped his notepad against his palm and slipped it back into his jacket pocket. "I believe my sources are accurate. We have someone working inside King Street, the Communist Party Headquarters in London, and they have access to their membership files so we can be . . ."

"It's all right, Marsh," Hanley's tone was impatient and dismissive. He had the sneaking suspicion that Marsh enjoyed twisting the knife. "We understand. I think we can leave it at that for now."

Marsh nodded and strode purposefully back into the admiral's office. Gillings' head drooped forward. He stared first at the desk and then slowly raised his eyes to look out of the window into the night beyond.

Hanley felt ill at ease. He did not know whether to go or stay. He could hear the voices in the other room, the rustling of paper, the sound of Crowe's nervous laugh. Finally, trying to sound as matter-of-fact as possible, he said, "I presume then that you didn't know about your son. Did you?"

"No, I," Gillings' voice petered out. He took a deep breath and with the surge of energy he felt the first stirrings of anger. "No. I should have known though." Gillings thought of the day in the factory when he had first seen Dickson and Terry together. He felt another tremor of anger. Then he said between clenched teeth, "I should've seen the signs."

"Well. It's not the end of the world. I'm in agreement with Grainger on this one. They need good men working down in his place. The best, whatever their politics. I'm quite sure that Grainger'll have him working on the project."

"Yes . . . yes . . ." Gillings shook his head in an attempt to look as if he was in agreement, but he was obviously distracted. The truth was that he did not care whether Terry joined Grainger's research team or not. He only cared that Terry had deceived him, that his son had done the very opposite of what he had asked.

"I must get back to this meeting. You'll join us in a few minutes, will you?"

"Yes, of course."

Hanley walked to the door, then glanced back at the shadowed room. Gillings had crossed to the window and was staring out at the line of streetlamps leading out to Thunderbolt Pier. Hanley wanted to offer some words of comfort but he felt like an intruder.

"Hanley!" Rear Admiral Walker's sharp clear voice cut through the conversation in the next office. Hanley turned and went out, leaving Gillings standing alone in the dark.

25

Eunice got out of a cab at the corner of Berners Street and struggled against the gusts of icy rain towards the hotel. She was burdened down with the last of her Christmas shopping and relieved to finally struggle in under the shelter of the front portico.

"Let me help you, ma'am."

The doorman walked forward, took the umbrella from her, then quickly shook it out and folded it. Eunice arranged her Christmas parcels and brushed rain from her hat and long brown and orange tweed overcoat as she stared through the glass doors into the busy foyer beyond.

"Ma'am." The doorman swung open the doors as he returned her umbrella. Eunice thanked him and strode inside. She was immediately engulfed in a welcoming warmth. The place seemed full of seasonal smells. The dining room was off to the right and the rich aroma of roast turkey and the sharper, spicy smell of Christmas puddings drifted out. Over to the left the foyer opened into a large area furnished with comfortable armchairs and sofas grouped around a number of elegant coffee tables. At the back, dominating everything, there was a gigantic open fireplace containing a blazing log fire.

Every seat was full and every table was laden either with drinks, or trays with pots of tea or coffee and plates of sandwiches and hot-buttered crumpets. The sweet spirituous smell of brandy seemed inextricably interwoven with the heavy smell of tobacco smoke and the whole place hummed with the festive good cheer of the season.

Eunice's eyes eagerly searched through the crowd. Over by the fire a group of middle-aged businessmen stood jostling one another like public school boys on an outing, clinking their brandy glasses and making loud seasonal toasts. Their self-satisfied laughter rolled out loudly across the intervening crowd. Eunice leaned to the right in order to look past them, and suddenly felt a strong hand under her arm.

"Oh." She spun round and saw Weichert standing beside her. He flashed her a polite, restrained smile as if he was all too aware of their lack of privacy. Then he took off his wide-brimmed fedora and shook spots of rain on to the red-carpeted floor. As he did so he leaned forward and said in a soft low voice, "I'm glad you could make it."

"Excuse me, sir." A small, pear-shaped waiter pushed past them, sweating under the weight of a trayload of drinks. In order to get out of his way they edged along towards the end of a nearby sofa. There seemed to be an office group seated beside them and they were loudly trumpeting the fact that they had managed to get seats for *Night Must Fall* at the Cambridge Theatre.

"I had to make it. It's almost two weeks since I've seen you." She moved in close in order to be heard and caught a whiff of his distinctive cologne. Memories of that other night at Brampton Hall flooded in. She looked up at his smooth skin, his handsome chiselled looks, and she wanted to stretch out and touch him. Yet at the same time she felt an almost tremulous sense of shyness.

He gave her a warm, reassuring smile. "I know, I felt the same about you but I couldn't see you before this. I had to fly to Berlin." As he spoke, he shook the last drops of rain off his hat and pulled it across between them so that it shaded her hands from the surrounding crowd. Suddenly she felt his fingers brushing along the back of her hand and searching for her palm. He rubbed the soft skin and then squeezed hard. She felt like a girl again, consumed by a sweet warm pain, a deep throbbing sense of desire that excluded everything else.

She shook herself and drew in a deep breath. "We, eh, we should sit, and have a drink."

"I've taken a room. I took my bag up earlier." He nodded towards the lifts behind the reception desk.

173

She looked surprised and raised a quizzical eyebrow. "A room? I don't understand."

"Here. For us. If I've misunderstood . . ."

"No, no." She grasped his hand behind the hat and squeezed it hard. Then she gave a flickering smile of relief, almost a half-laugh. "I just didn't expect . . . I thought we were meeting for a drink."

"That's all it need be, a drink. But we must be alone and I thought it would be more discreet than going to my flat, just in case. You understand what I mean?"

She shook her head in agreement. Yes, of course she understood. She raised an eyebrow and whispered, "We should go then, now."

All the way up to the room she felt as if she were suspended in some kind of dream. She was sure that the lift operator must have sensed what was going on between them. But in fact he was engrossed in his football pools and only looked up long enough to let them out at the third floor.

The hallway was empty and had that particular hotel smell of bedclothes and lavender, and the dry, dusty smell of carpet. They said nothing as they walked along, but Weichert's very closeness made Eunice feel as though something was tugging at her breath.

As the door swung open she saw that there was a light on inside. He gestured for her to enter and she walked in ahead of him. The curtains were open and the lights from Oxford Street cast a speckled pattern of whites and reds and blues across the wall. There was a writing-desk at the window with a briefcase sitting on it and an open suitcase on the bed.

Eunice crossed to the bed and ran her finger along the hard edge of the leather case. Then she gave a gentle laugh as she noticed the shirts, ties and socks stuffed inside. "You look as though you're about to move in."

She heard the door being firmly closed behind her, and then the lock being turned. They were alone now.

"I'm travelling to Northern Ireland tomorrow. I've been invited to spend Christmas with Lord Londonderry at his estate in County Down." As he spoke he crossed to the window.

He glanced down into the street then slipped off his overcoat and tossed it on to the chair by the writing-desk.

She stood watching as the dappled lights from outside played on his handsome features. "I wish I could come with you. It always sounds so idyllic. County Down is such a gentle name." As she continued to speak, he walked slowly round the bed towards her. She began to feel as if her words were a meaningless smokescreen to keep her passions at bay. "I conjure up visions of soft, rolling green hills and woods."

He placed his finger on her lips. "I'd ask you to come but we both know that that's impossible." She stared deep into his eyes and was shaken by his intensity. Here was someone who wanted her. After years of officers' wives, bridge parties and hospital visits, here was a man who *wanted* her, wanted her in bed, wanted to touch her, wanted her in all the intense, sweaty, physical ways she had longed for. For one strange, awful moment she thought she was going to cry. She felt the tears welling up in her eyes, then bit into her cheek, and firmly suppressed them.

He smiled again and let his forefinger gently glide along her lip. "But tonight, I hope tonight isn't impossible. I want you to stay here with me."

She pressed her lips hard against his finger and said softly, "Yes, I've already thought of that. I told my housekeeper I'd be staying at Olivia's in Bedford Square."

Weichert raised a questioning eyebrow and Eunice smiled. "It's all right, Olivia and I are old friends."

Weichert stared at her for a moment as if pondering something, and then asked, "You said your housekeeper, but your husband, what about him?"

She pulled back from him and glanced towards the window. "We've hardly spoken in the last few weeks. I doubt if he'd notice if I was there or not, he seems to spend all of his time at the yards."

Weichert gave a short, brittle laugh. "They must be busy, building up their fleet to fight the new German menace."

She suddenly swung round on him. "I really don't want to hear about the Navy, you understand. I have enough of it with

175

Hanley and his . . ." She stopped in mid-sentence as he reached out and grabbed her by the forearm. His grip was tight, demanding. She gazed up at his eyes and saw that cold intensity again. That sharp-hued blue, like the edge of deep cracked ice.

"I can assure you I haven't brought you here to talk about ships." His voice had a dark edge to it, something that oscillated between anger and passion. He slowly pulled her towards him, so close that she could feel his breath warm on her face. "*Ich will dich . . . Ich will deinen Körper. Ich will mit dir schlafen.*"

She was shaken by the intensity in his voice. "What?"

He lifted his other hand and gently but firmly stroked it along her cheek. Then he cupped her chin, and angled it upwards. "I said I want you."

He bent forward and slipped his hands behind her neck, burying them in her thick dark hair. At the same time he pulled her towards him and kissed her on the lips, gently at first but then with increasing passion. She felt that throbbing slowly grow in her loins. She wanted to consume him, wanted to have him deep inside her. She could feel him slowly pushing her backwards towards the bed but she did not want it that way. She wanted to lead as well as follow.

She pulled her mouth away, and stared up at him with fiery eyes. When she spoke her voice was low and strained. "And I want you, Herr Weichert, my God I want you."

Before he could stop her, she had swung round and toppled him on to the bed, grabbing him by the collar of his jacket and pulling him close so that their lips were barely touching. For a moment they just lay there, still, feeling each other's warm breaths. Then he leaned forward and delicately ran the tip of his tongue along the inside of her upper lip. She gave a gentle moan, rolled on to her back and gave a laugh. "God, I'm still dressed for the rain." She sat up and started to undo the buttons on her long tweed overcoat.

Weichert lurched forward again and slipped his hand under the open flap of the coat. Eunice looked at him somewhat bemused and then drew her leg up on to the bed. She was

176

wearing a black crepe skirt. Slowly it slipped up her leg, giving a tantalising glimpse of her long elegant thigh. He glanced down at her shapely legs and then pulled himself closer to her.

She watched him undo the buttons on her blouse and then felt him slowly and sensuously starting to rub her stomach. She caught her breath as she waited for him to reach up and touch her breasts. Then she stretched out and ran her fingers through his blond hair.

He gave another of those boyish smiles, then suddenly pulled back and stood up. She flinched with surprise. "If you're staying then," he continued, "I would like to take you out to dinner first. Somewhere quiet, private."

"First?" Eunice burst out with an infectious trilling laugh. "Well, at least I have the promise of pleasures to come. But why not first and last, we could have dinner in the middle, so to speak."

Weichert looked down and thought how beautiful she looked with her rich dark hair carelessly tumbling across her shoulders, her coat lying open showing her long elegant legs. He gave a quick smile and then crossed to the window.

"Doesn't that appeal to you?"

"Very much." He reached over and pulled the curtain closed, shutting out the gently playing pattern of lights from the street below. Then he turned and looked at her. "But we should never forget that there are prying eyes everywhere."

She had started to undo the rest of the buttons on her blouse but as he spoke she glanced up. There was something chilling in his voice. Something that seemed beyond concerns with adultery. But then he smiled at her again, that warm boyish smile, and the thought went from her head. She wanted him, that was all she knew at that moment. She wanted a salve for all the years of loneliness and neglect and here he was, alive and wanting her, her alone.

As he pushed her back on the bed he slipped his hands up inside her blouse and on to her breasts. Then he pushed his thumbs firmly against her nipples. She closed her eyes and felt herself slowly falling away.

26

"Another one, Lizzie." Gillings pushed the empty glass across the bar. The landlady took it and then glanced over at him as she poured out the whisky. "Don't see too much of you this weather, Mr Gillings."

He looked at her blankly. "No, no."

She brought the whisky back, quickly rubbed the dark scarred surface of the bar and placed it in front of him. "In for a bit of Christmas cheer are you, then?"

Gillings nodded, attempting a smile. "Yes, yes I suppose."

The landlady was a plumpish woman, with a mane of brownish-red hair, striking but not handsome. She was the widow of a first mate who had died in a ship's fire in Alexandria. After his death she had managed to buy herself the Spinnaker, the local pub in Old Brompton, with the compensation money. She regarded her customers as neighbours, and indeed most of them were.

Gillings slowly swirled the amber liquor around the glass, and stared hard at the viscous residue. With his furrowed brow and dark look he obviously had problems on his mind. For a few seconds she stood there considering whether she should try to draw him out. Then she decided against it. He was always a quiet man but tonight in particular he looked as though he wanted to be left alone.

"Well, give my regards to Mrs Gillings."

Gillings nodded. She gave the counter another wipe and then walked down the bar to organise the draw for the Christmas turkey.

Albert Gillings rarely drank on his own, in fact he rarely drank at all. But when he did have the occasional pint of bitter or "short 'un" of whisky, he usually came up here to the

Spinnaker. He lifted his glass, walked over to a seat by the coal fire and sat staring into the flickering flames.

He had left Irene at home presiding over a kitchen full of baking bowls and flour. Thankfully, she was so caught up in the preparations for the holidays that she did not hear the bitter edge in his voice when he asked for Terry.

"Terry, no, he's not in. He scoffed his dinner in about five minutes and said he was going to meet a few friends. Get us the eggs out of the pantry, love." It was obvious that Irene knew no more than that, knew nothing about his political activities.

Gillings gave a shudder, then sipped his whisky and stared deep into the coals. "Meet a few friends." It was a phrase that they had heard a lot during the last few months, but now, in the light of what he had just heard from Marsh, it had an ominous ring to it. He pulled the crumpled piece of paper from his pocket, and spread it over his knee. "Resist the Fascists in Spain. Grand meeting. Tailors' Hall. 8 p.m. Wednesday 23rd December 1936."

He drew in his breath between clenched teeth, and then gave out a shuddering sigh. He was seething. Half of him wanted to go down to the hall and confront Terry there and then. But no. He would wait until the boy came home. He tightened his hand around the glass and muttered, "Damn him, damn him."

The small Tailors' Hall was crowded. All the seats were taken and there was a crowd standing at the back, under the tiny balcony. Terry stood at the door holding a pile of pamphlets. The place was boiling hot and all the windows had misted over. Everyone seemed to be smoking and a thick, grey-blue mist hung suspended in the bright lights just above the speaker's head.

". . . We must send money to our Republican allies; we must send medicine, *and* we must send volunteers to fight." The crowd erupted in cheers. The woman speaker had been introduced as Dorothy Fielding, a research biologist from Cambridge. She looked like a scientist to Terry. She was tall, with a thin plain face framed by straight, dark brown hair. This plainness was not helped by her long aquiline nose and thin mouth. And yet her eyes conveyed her passion. They had a radiant quality, almost a beauty.

". . . I know that a lot of you have come here because of politics, but I came because I wanted to tell you about one brave woman: Felicia Browne. She was a friend of mine, a painter, a talented artist. She found herself in Spain when Franco started his rebellion against the government and she felt that she could not stand idly by and see a people lose their freedom. So she stopped her work and joined one of the militias."

The speaker stopped and looked around the crowd. A moment of tense quiet descended. Even from the back of the hall, Terry could see her eyes glistening. She seemed to swallow hard and then continued. "She was killed by Franco's forces during the advance on Aragon in August. She's three months dead and I think of her every day. This is from her last letter." The speaker slipped on a pair of wire-rimmed glasses and read from a well-worn notebook. " 'I know it can be dangerous here. Last week three women were shot by Franco's forces in a small mountain village up near Villafranca. I am scared, but whatever happens to me, I feel exhilarated now, knowing that I fought for the right side, proud of the fact that I am fighting for the side of justice.' "

The speaker paused for a moment and then gazed out over the audience again. "Remember those words, comrades, and in a year's time let us all ask ourselves how proud we are! Next month I'm going out to join Dr Reginald Saxton as a dresser in his medical team. Three weeks ago we raised over two thousand pounds in just over half an hour at the rally at the Royal Albert Hall . . ." The crowd erupted in cheers. She lifted her hand and shouted above them, "Let's see what we can raise here tonight!" Once again the crowd broke into cheers and here and there small groups chanted their slogans. As the applause continued, party workers started pushing up through the crowded aisles with their collection boxes.

One of the men on the stage stepped forward. He was Wally Sayers, a fitter from the Maidstone & District Bus Company, and he was known for his loud "street orator's" voice. He raised his arms and yelled out, "Comrades, tonight we're all going to march down to the war memorial . . ." There was another roar from the crowd. Terry felt someone tapping him on the shoulder and turned to see Reggie Dickson. Reggie pulled him aside.

The crowd were now chanting, "Support the republic. Down with fascism. Support the republic. Down with fascism . . ."

Reggie shouted in his ear, "Take a dickie outside, would you Terry, and see how many police there are. We've got a permit so they should be about. At least they'll keep away the drunks when we get to the Brook."

"Right." Terry quickly crossed the black-and-white chequered floor. He turned at the door and gave a grin. "I thought we were supposed to be saving the lumpen proletariat, not setting the police on them."

Reggie laughed and shouted, "Today Spain, tomorrow the Brook."

Terry pushed open the heavy wooden door and stepped into the cold air. As he stood on the hall steps slipping on his gloves he glanced up and down Rodney Street. Inside, Wally Sayers was shouting at the top of his voice. "No matter who thinks they're gonna stand in our way tonight, we're gonna march down there and lay a wreath!"

There were cheers again. Terry gave a smile and as he started up the road towards the Red Lion pub he could hear the speech continuing behind him. ". . . a wreath in memory of Felicia Browne and all the other comrades who have fallen and are falling in the face of fascist bullets . . ." Finally both the speech and the cheers were buffeted away in the bitter breeze.

Terry walked quickly towards the corner. The wind was whirling a stinging sleet into his face and forcing him to keep his head down. As he got closer to the Red Lion he noticed a group of men standing near the corner. Some instinct made him stop and as he did so, the men pulled back into the shadows. He felt an immediate sense of foreboding and stepped to the side, into an alleyway. He glanced behind him and noticed that it led through to Hood Street.

"In for a penny . . ." He pulled his jacket tightly round him and started jogging up the dark alley.

"Where the fucking 'ell are you going, Jack?"

He had collided with the man before he saw him. He was a big, burly fellow, with dark curly hair and the look of someone who'd been in one too many brawls.

Terry was shaken. He had run out of the alley into Hood Street and found himself in the middle of a large, unpleasant-looking bunch of toughs. As he glanced down towards Barfleur Street he saw a couple of buses and vans pulling in to park. Men poured out of them. Even in the dull light of the streetlamp he noticed the unmistakable black shirts under their jackets and coats.

As he stepped back, a skinny runt of a youth with a bitter, guttersnipe's face, grabbed him by the arm and spun him round. "Well you 'eard the man, 'oo are you, a fucking commie?" The youth's eyes glittered with malice and with his thin moustache and pointed face, it made him look like a rat.

Terry felt angry. All he wanted to do was lift his fist and smash it into the youth's ugly, venomous face. But he took a quick look around and knew that that was insane.

"A what? What're you talking about?"

He glanced up towards Barfleur Street again and saw a number of men pulling large placards out of the back of the lorry. The slogans on them dispelled any doubts he might have had. "Mosley supports Franco" . . . "Franco fights Communist Atheism". He saw some of them pulling out clubs and hiding them under their coats whilst others around him were smacking blackjacks rhythmically against their palms. He felt a surge of panic. He had to get back and warn the marchers.

He glared at the rat-faced youth and shook his arm free. "I was looking for the Nelson Street chapel, youth club, that is if you don't mind."

The big man with the dark curly hair stepped forward and pulled the youth by the sleeve of his jacket. "Let him go, Joey, for Chrissake, it's the fuckin' communists we're 'ere to get . . .

182

we're not after soddin' Christians, the coppers 'ear that and we'll get done."

Terry turned on his heel and started walking slowly back down the alleyway towards Tailors' Hall. When he had got about a quarter of the way into the shadows, he took off at a sprint.

In Rodney Street the crowd was already pouring out of Tailors' Hall. They had unfurled a number of banners, and a piper and two drummers were warming up at the front.

Terry sprinted towards them looking for Reggie. People were filing out, laughing, joking, pulling out placards, getting into orderly lines. He wanted to yell out and tell them, but he remembered his training. He was in the Party, there was a system, a chain of command. You did not cause panic.

Finally he saw Reggie walking out of the hall with Wally Sayers. "Reggie, here! Wait, wait!" Terry pushed through the crowd and pulled Reggie aside.

Reggie gave a laugh. "Here, what's got into you? You seen a ghost?"

Terry caught his breath and gasped out, "There's no police and there's a couple of busloads of Mosley's crowd – waiting round the corner – up along Barfleur and Hood . . ."

"What!" Reggie looked stunned. He glanced along the dark street towards the Red Lion, as though that would in some way affirm what Terry had said. But of course the street and the corner were empty.

Terry grabbed his arm again and squeezed hard. As he did he caught his breath and almost shouted, "No, not here, they're waiting, round the corner."

Reggie suddenly seemed to understand. He grabbed Terry and quickly dragged him across the crowded pavement towards Wally Sayers. "Wally, you gotta listen to this! I asked Terry here to go and have a shufti for the coppers. He says there's frig all to be seen and there's busloads of Mosley's crew waiting for us, along Barfleur and Hood Streets."

Sayers took the information calmly and then glanced down at his hands as if trying to work something out. "Coppers!

183

They've done this before. You give them the gen on a march and the next thing you know, just by accident like, Mosley's friggin' lot are down from London looking for a punch-up. Well! Now that we know, we can do something about it!"

"Listen, Wally, we've gotta march whatever we do." Reggie smacked his fist into his other open palm and Terry could see that his eyes were glittering with the excitement of the moment. "We've got a reporter from the *Mirror* and a young lad from *The Times* down here to cover Professor Fielding. A good rough-and-tumble like this could be just what we need to get the lads off their arses and joining the Party."

Sayers gave a grunt, and glanced up. He looked worried but resolved. "All right, Reg, you get up there and give them your best Agincourt speech. I'll talk to the reporter lads and phone up my pal Eric on the *Chatham Observer*. Go on, get going!"

Reggie quickly pushed his way towards the front of the crowd. Sayers clapped Terry on the shoulder. "Well done, young'un, just remember to keep your head down tonight." Terry nodded and Sayers then made his way back into the hall.

"Hey, hey, quiet. Let the man speak!"

Terry swung round. Reggie was standing on the pedestal of one of the streetlamps. He had gripped the post with one hand and had his other arm raised for silence. Throughout the crowd, people were calling for silence. The bagpipes droned down to a shrill whine and then stopped. Reggie shouted out in a strong, loud voice,

"Comrades, we've just heard that the fascists are waiting for us along the march route, hiding up the side streets, like the cowards they are." He said the words as though they were contaminated and then stopped as if inviting the crowd to react. They erupted with an explosion of catcalls and jeers.

Terry watched with a growing sense of trepidation. He admired the way Reggie teased the crowd along, the way he waited for their anger to crest, but something about crowd manipulation made him uneasy.

Reggie raised his hand again. "Comrades! I don't know

about you, but I don't think we should allow this to stop us marching." There were deafening shouts of "No, no." Reggie continued to talk through the noise. "We've got some reporters here with us, I know they'll be fair and tell it how it is. Comrades, we're not fascists, we're not scum, we're not troublemakers. But I want to warn you. Mosley's crew are a pack of thugs and some of us might get hurt . . . ."

"So what! In Spain our comrades are getting shot! We're 'ere to show we support them." Terry recognised the shaggy white mane of Billy Pringle, one of the shop stewards from Short's Aviation.

Reggie took the cue. He pointed to Billy, clenched his own fist and shouted out, "Right, brother, right! Let's show our Spanish brothers we're behind them and let's show the fascists what international brotherhood really means! Come on, *let's march!*"

The crowd roared its approval. Terry found himself swept up with everyone else. Only after the bagpipes had started up again did he start to analyse Reggie's oratorical skills. It was not so much what Reggie had said, but the rhythm and the passion of his speech. He had fired them up like men about to march into battle. It was just what Wally Sayers had asked for.

Terry walked back to where a group of dockyard workers were parading behind their own banner: "Blockade Italian help to Franco". It fluttered in the chill breeze, smacking against the support poles. The two drummers with the piper struck up and sent a shiver through him. It was as if they were indeed about to march into battle.

"So 'elp me if one of those blackshirts comes close, I'll put him in the morgue." Terry looked over and saw that the speaker was Danny Powers, a carpenter from the yards. As he watched Danny, he saw him slipping a piece of a spar, about a foot long, under his jacket. Some of the men had obviously come prepared.

Terry gazed at the smooth, thick, wooden pole disappearing under the jacket and felt a little queasy. This was exactly what he had seen the blackshirt thugs doing, round the corner. He remembered his mother's diatribes against violence and he felt a pang of guilt. Were these men any better than Mosley's thugs? Surely violence was violence, no matter who wielded the weapons.

> Arise ye starvelings from your slumbers,
> Arise ye criminals of want.
> For reason in revolt now slumbers . . .

All around him the men were picking up the words of the International and singing out at the tops of their voices. Terry found himself being sucked in by the power of the words and he remembered one of Reggie's sayings: "We're not perfect but at least we're on the side of the angels." That was it! That was all he had to remember! All across Europe people were fleeing from fascist murder squads and he was learning that his place was in the front line fighting them. He drew back his shoulders and started to sing the last few lines. No, there was no mistake, he was certain which side *he* was on.

> Then comrades come rally,
> And the last fight let us face . . .

He sang to the end of the verse, his mind dizzy with emotion. At the end of the song, the drums played a long stirring roll and he heard Reggie at the front giving a loud, clear shout. "Comrades, let's maaaarch!"

Terry took a deep breath and stepped forward. He could feel the fear gnawing in the pit of his stomach but he also felt a great comfort in the camaraderie of his fellow marchers.

They got to the Red Lion with still no sign of the Mosleyites. Terry could sense an electric shiver of expectation surging around him. The front of the column turned right into Barfleur Street and within seconds an ungodly barrage of shouting and jeers erupted into the cold night air. The forward movement of the marchers seemed to waver, then it found its resolve again and surged forward.

As Terry turned the corner he was staggered to see the rows of black-shirted fascists barricading the road. They also spread along the pavements towards the marchers, in a massive pincer.

"Nary a fucking copper to be seen!" Billy Pringle shook his mane of white hair in disgust.

The Blackshirts now started a rolling chant, alternating "Mussolini" and "Franco". It was a chilling sound, something that Terry had only heard before on newsreels showing Hitler's Germany.

The column stopped again. Reggie swung round, held up his arms and shouted, "Comrades, we're gonna walk through with heads up. They've no bloody right to block the street. On!" He turned to the front and boldly stepped forward. Within a few steps a bottle whizzed through the air and hit him smack on the forehead. He staggered back trying to keep his footing and as he did so he spun round. In the split second before Reggie fell, Terry saw the blood oozing from the open cut and gasped in horror.

He was not the only one to see it. The front few ranks of marchers at first recoiled then seemed to find their courage. With a roar they charged forward, fists raised. All along the line, vicious fights were breaking out and stones, bottles and sticks were hurling through the air.

When Terry finally managed to struggle through to Reggie he found him groggily trying to struggle to his feet. Wally Sayers was kneeling beside him. "Terry, get him off to the side, I've got to try and get us through this madness."

Reggie gave a groaning laugh as Terry helped him up. "God, Terry, maybe this wasn't such a good idea."

Terry kept them both bent over as he half dragged his friend back towards the corner of the Red Lion. He was just under the streetlamp when he heard the welcome sound of a Black Maria and shouts of "Coppers! Coppers!" He glanced up and saw that a number of Blackshirts had broken through and were running past along the pavement. For a split second he came face to face with the runt of a youth who had confronted him earlier. There was a moment of recognition and then the other boy lunged forward and swiped him across the side of the head. Terry saw the squat ugly shape of the blackjack as it travelled

187

close to his eye. He felt a sharp stab of pain, then a sense of falling. And blackness.

Gillings gave a long hissing sigh through his clenched teeth and then turned back to the window again. The icy wind was shaking the gaunt, bare branches of the cherry tree in the corner of the front garden and he thought of Terry "helping" him plant it, almost fifteen years ago. He saw him toddling around the lawn, tripping over the spade, falling into the hole, his little sailor's suit covered in mud.

Gillings clenched his fists, squeezing them rhythmically as though that would somehow crush the memory. He felt like smashing them into the window, but he stopped himself. He knew that would do no good. There was no other way, he would just have to wait and confront Terry when he came in.

He glanced out beyond the hedge and noticed the first flakes of snow swirling round the streetlamps. Then he felt a jolt as he saw Terry walking past the cherry tree. He had his head bent over against the wind, and his jacket pulled tightly round him. Gillings watched him open the front gate and start down the path. He stepped away from the lace curtain, pulled back into the shadows of the front room and waited.

The key slipped into the lock and then clicked as it turned and opened. Terry gave a long, painful groan. A moment later, Gillings saw him walking down the hall past the open door.

"Terry!"

Terry stopped. "Dad?" He looked puzzled and glanced up the stairs. "Where are you?" He was obviously confused because the front room was in darkness.

"In here. In the front room. I want to talk to you." No matter how hard he tried he could not keep the anger out of his voice. Terry instantly knew that something was wrong.

"I'm really fagged out, Dad. I'd just like to go up to bed if that's all right. Maybe we could talk in the morning."

"Now, Terry. Come in now!"

Terry gave a sigh and walked to the door. "What is it? What are you sitting in here for, in the dark?"

"I'm waiting for you. You can turn the light on now."

Terry bristled at the thought of his father sitting in the dark, waiting to pounce as he came through the door. "No! I can see this is gonna be one of those stupid bloody arguments and I'm going to go to bed!" Terry turned on his heel and started towards the stairs.

That was it! The end of a long day and a longer night. Gillings ran across the darkened sitting room and into the hall. Terry was caught in mid-step, stunned by his father's swift movement. He tried to turn his face towards the wall but Gillings grabbed him by the arm and spun him round.

Gillings stopped in his tracks as if he was stricken. One side of Terry's face was grimy and sweat-stained, as though he had fallen into the dirt. Just above his right eyebrow there was a small cut and tiny drops of blood slowly trickled from it down his temple. Terry saw his father staring at him and stepped back as he quickly wiped the blood away with his sleeve. But he was not quick enough.

"Terry, what happened to you?"

"Nothing. I'm . . . I'm all right." Terry pulled a blood-stained handkerchief from his pocket and began dabbing the cut. Then he gave a shrugging gesture as if to suggest that he had broken no bones.

"I said, what happened?" Gillings was trying to keep his voice low but the strain was beginning to tell.

"A couple of drunks coming out of a pub. I was with some of my mates and I . . ."

"You're lying! You're lying, aren't you?!" Gillings' jaw was set and the words crackled out like jagged pieces of glass.

Terry went ashen. Then he took a deep breath, knowing that he had to face it out. "What the hell do you mean?"

Gillings rammed his hands into his pockets as if searching for something. "Keep your voice down, I don't want your mother to hear this. And watch your language too. I'm warning you, I've had it. There!" Gillings found what he was looking for and yanked the piece of paper out of his right trouser pocket. He thrust it forward like a weapon.

"That's where you were, you liar you, that's where you were, wasn't it?" Gillings waved the paper under his son's eyes. Even

189

as it was whisked past him, Terry caught sight of the words, "Resist the Fascists in Spain." He bit his lip and shrugged.

"Well, so what!" He was beginning to raise his voice, then he gave a long groan. "Look Dad, this is stupid! Let's just talk in the morning."

Gillings grabbed his son by the forearm and gave him a push towards the front room.

Terry wrenched his arm away. "Don't push me. Don't push me!" He was beginning to shout again.

Gillings glared at him but his voice was icily steady. "Get in the front room. I told you I don't want your mother hearing this."

Terry could feel himself starting to shake and a knot of nerves tightening in his stomach. He was tired and angry, but like Gillings he did not want to bring his mother down the stairs and into the middle of this furore. He answered his father in a low throaty whisper. "And I told *you*, I don't want to talk about it tonight."

"Well mister, I'm shittin' well sick up to here with what *you* want!" Gillings jabbed Terry on the shoulder. "Go on, get in!"

Terry knocked his father's hand away. "Don't push me! I told you, don't push me!"

Gillings gave a bitter, angry grin and placed his hands on his hips. Then he slowly nodded his head. "Don't push you, eh? Is that it? Is that what you really said? Don't push you? And what about me then? Haven't I been pushed enough, eh? Don't you think I've been pushed enough tonight?"

Terry stared at him and for a moment wondered if his father had been drinking. He had never seen him so angry. His lips were quivering and Terry was beginning to feel a deep panic. He sensed that the situation was getting out of control, way beyond the ordinary arguments that peppered their lives.

"Look, Dad, I'm sorry." He took a deep breath and tried to calm himself down. "I don't know what you're talking about . . . if we could just leave it until . . ."

Terry had started edging towards the stairs again. But there was no escape. Gillings leapt forward and grabbed him by the collar. "You what! You lying little cunt. You fucking bastard!"

190

Terry flung his arms up and smashed his father's grip. He tried to step back but Gillings lunged and grabbed him again. As his father caught him by the neck, Terry fell back against the coat rack.

Gillings shouted close to his ear, "You listen to me, you shithawk, you listen to me! You know what I had to go through tonight? I was in the admiral's office." Gillings paused to catch his breath.

"Dad, please." Terry tried to struggle out of his father's vice-like grip but only found himself buried deeper in the folds of the coats. He could smell the whisky on Gillings' breath, but he knew that it was not drink that fired the wild rage in his eyes.

"Please my arse! You'll listen! I was there to talk with Grainger, he had a list of candidates for his project and your name came up." Gillings' mouth widened to a grimace as he sucked in a deep breath and continued. "It came up . . . and then there was an objection! You know what it was, hmm? You know what it was?" Gillings pushed himself back a few inches and glared into Terry's eyes. "He's a communist, Mr Gillings. Sorry Mr Gillings, you didn't know? He's a communist, a fucking communist!" He shook Terry violently and a coat fell down from the rack covering his son's head and face.

Gillings ripped it off and then stood back about a foot and glared. "Can you explain that, eh? I mean, would it be too much for you to fucking enlighten me? Just tell me it's not true. That's what I'd really like to hear. Just for once I'd love to hear that my son had listened to me."

Terry wrenched himself free and pushed past his father. As he did, he swung round so that his back was against the front door. "For Chrissake! All right I said we should wait till the morning. You wanna hear? You wanna hear?" He rubbed his neck as he tried to catch his breath. "Yes, it's true, I joined the Communist Party, but you never listened to me, that's why I didn't tell you. I joined because I believe in everything they say. If we don't do something we're gonna be overrun by Hitler and Mussolini and . . ."

"Shut up!" Gillings' screaming shout echoed through the

191

house. There was a split second of bitter silence. Then he continued, spitting his words out like poison. "I won't have your bloody street-corner rhetoric here, don't you bloody dare. Christ Almighty!" he yelled out in despair and then slammed his fist into the front-room door. It rattled back and crashed into the piano sounding out a loud clang.

They both jumped, then Gillings swayed forward with his fist clenched and his forefinger pointing. "You'll quit, do you hear that? You'll get out of that Party, you'll strike your name off their bloody lists and you won't go near any of those bastards ever again. Or by Christ you'll get out of this house!"

"Why, Dad, but why?" Terry ran his hands through his hair in despair, looking as if he would pull it out by the roots. "They're only working to make sure . . ."

"There are no more whys, do you understand me? I'm fed up fucking talking to you. Fed up fucking talking to a brainless brick wall . . ."

"Albert! What is it? Heavens above, what is it? What's wrong with you both, are you crazy?"

They both glanced up the stairs and saw Irene standing halfway down, hastily wrapping Gillings' old dressing-gown around her.

"Go back to bed, Irene, go back to bed please, this is between him and me. It should bloody well have happened a long time ago."

"Albert! Albert! Whatever he's done, can't it wait until the morning?"

Terry made use of the diversion to edge his way towards the stairs. "That's what I said, nothing'll come of . . ."

Gillings swung round and slammed his forearm across Terry's chest, pinning him against the wall. He was furious that Irene had got involved. "Don't you dare drag your mother into this."

"Albert, let him go!"

"Do you hear that? Are you proud of yourself, coming between her and me now? You cunt!"

Irene was scared. She had never heard Albert use language

192

like that in the house. She watched in horror as he slid his hand up and grabbed Terry by the shirt collar. "You'll leave that crew, you won't wreck my life and your own."

Terry was beginning to choke as his father's strong hand tightened around his neck again. Irene saw the colour draining from his face and ran down the stairs, terrified. "Albert! For God's sake! Albert!" She grabbed Gillings by the arm and he turned on her.

"Leave us, Irene. I said leave us!" He was virtually spitting in her face.

Terry was beside himself with anger. He felt humiliated, confused and scared. He did not know what to do, but he feared staying in the same house with his father overnight. When Gillings turned to Irene, he suddenly used the moment to wrench himself free. Then he lunged forward, grabbed his father by the jacket and with all his strength threw him across the hall. Gillings slammed against the front-room doorpost and buckled over, winded.

Irene gave a scream and ran into the hall between them, screaming, "Stop it! Stop it!"

Terry rushed past her up the stairs.

"I'm leaving. I'm leaving tonight . . . you're a lunatic . . ."

Gillings staggered forward holding the small of his back. "Leave and you never come back. Never. You'll come down and apologise or you'll be a bastard to me for ever."

But Terry was already gone and they could hear the sound of banging in his room.

Gillings started up the stairs after him. "He's not getting away with this, he's not hiding in his room . . ."

"No! No, Albert, please. I've never seen you like this." Irene put her arms around him and pulled him back.

Gillings growled, but sank back a step. "You? As well? You don't know the half of it, Irene. He's gone and joined the communists behind our back. Ruined his bloody life . . . ruined our bloody lives . . ."

Suddenly Terry was clattering down the stairs, with an old suitcase under his arm. He stopped in front of Gillings who looked up and glared at him. "Oh, the big bluff eh. Well, you

193

apologise now or by God there'll be no bluff. I'll toss you out myself."

Terry's eyes were blazing with anger and the sweat was pouring down his face. He took a deep shuddering breath and pushed past his father towards the front door. "You've no need to! I'll leave! And it's the last time you'll call me a bastard or tell me what to do with my life. I'll live on my own."

Terry slammed the front door open so that it banged against the wall and shuddered. He ran out of the hall and into the night. "Terry, Terry." Irene rushed forward. She could hardly believe it. She stopped in the porch and yelled again, "Terry please." But he continued on, half walking, half running into the swirling snowflakes. She stood for a while shaking with anguish and disbelief. Finally, only the bitter wind and the stinging cold of the snowflakes convinced her that it was not a nightmare.

27

Kitty dragged Susie into the back room of the club and slammed the door. Then she dramatically flung her coat open and displayed her torn blouse.

"Look! The dirty old bugger almost ripped my blouse off."

Susie stifled a gasp. "Who did that?"

"What do you mean, who? Johnson, that greasy old psalm-singing fart, that's who. He got me in the back room of his shaggin' little shop. Giving me a brooch for Christmas, he says. And, like, he has to put it on." Kitty illustrated by clamping her hand over her exposed brassiere.

Susie winced. "Oooh dirty old bugger!"

Kitty shuddered as if remembering the clammy touch of his hand. Then she shook her hair back and strutted to the sink.

"Well he got his comeuppance. The old dragon herself walked in all unexpected and caught him, like, with his hands full."

Susie stared at Kitty blank-faced, biting her tongue. Then the farcical side of the situation hit her and she burst into hysterical laughter.

Kitty pursed her lips. "I don't think it's funny."

Susie gulped some air and calmed down. "Yes, you do."

"I lost my job, you know."

"I'd bloody well hope you'd leave. You hated it anyway."

The two girls stood facing one another for a second and then broke into uncontrollable giggles. Suddenly Kitty stopped.

"Oh God, Nigel's to pick me up in half an hour. I can't go out like this."

Susie laughed and pulled her long fair hair back behind her ears. "True enough you and Mr Hoity-Toity Nigel couldn't shimmy at the Palais with your boobs hanging out . . ." They started giggling again and Susie pointed across the yard. "Listen, I've got two dresses over in Jimmy's being cleaned for the holidays. He says they're ready, so just tell him I said you could take one."

Kitty glanced out of the window into the darkness. "Yeah but is he still working?"

Susie nodded. "Jimmy Lee's always working." Then she leaned back languorously against the edge of the door and gave her best Mae West imitation. "Well I'd better get in, I can't keep my public waiting, dahling. Anyway . . ." she said, relapsing into her normal voice, ". . . Eddie, Mr Brent's just gone over there. I'd tell 'im your troubles. Bet he takes you on full-time. He might even send out one of his gorillas to kick old Johnson in the balls."

"Hey Susie, thanks."

Susie gave a cheeky wink and disappeared into the noise and smoke of the club beyond.

As Kitty crossed the yard she could see the light spilling through the frosted glass at the back of Jimmy Lee's laundry. To one side of the door the steam pipe was blowing a long, grey-white plume out into the cold air.

For a moment she hesitated, the place looked desolate. Then the cold started getting to her and she tried the doorhandle. It opened easily and she stepped inside. There were only a couple of dim lights strung down the centre of the room. In the gloom she could see lines of large, industrial washing machines. Some were still working, and she could hear water slurping down the drains. The whole place had an eerie feel to it.

Kitty jumped as the snippet of a song burst inexplicably across the dingy room. She quickly crossed to the inside doorway, past the shuddering machines, and glanced down the dark corridor.

Halfway along, a stairway went into the basement. As she looked, two men came up into the shadows. She saw the white flash of a sailor's hat and then recognised the smaller man when he spoke. It was Eddie Brent.

"Look I ain't really interested in how you feel, I'm just a bleeding messenger, you know." As they talked they turned away from Kitty and walked towards the Sudbury Street end of the building.

Eddie continued, his voice sounding irritated, impatient, "This is the way they want to do this, through me, and all I'm telling you is, they're willing to give you a lot of bread just to find out about this . . . whatever his name is . . ."

"Dr Philip Grainger . . ." the other man interjected.

"Yeah. Anyway, you tell me you've got these bills, and I'm telling you they'll be happy to pay them for you if . . ."

The naval man gave a groan and slammed his fist hard against the wall.

There was a long pause, and then Brent said quietly, "I'll tell them you're in the running then, will I?"

The other man shuffled down the corridor, stopped, then cleared his throat and mumbled, "Yes, yes, I'll do my best. But I want money and soon." With that he stepped through the curtain into the front shop and Eddie quickly followed.

Kitty hadn't understood what had gone on but she did realise that it wouldn't have been too smart to interrupt. She waited until they had disappeared then quietly made her way

196

back along the corridor to the top of the stairs. Once again she heard the muffled sound of a song on a phonogram.

> Not much money, oh but honey,
> Ain't we got fun?

She took a few steps down the bare wooden staircase. In the shadows she caught that same strange mixed sweet smell wafting up towards her. Then the door at the bottom suddenly opened and the full tinny sound of the music boomed out.

In the room beyond, Kitty just managed to catch a glimpse of couches and sofas, curtains, low lights, a slow almost dreamlike world, a place full of sleepers. But it was just a glimpse. The door slammed shut again leaving Kitty with her disjointed images.

"Yes missy?"

Jimmy Lee was standing on the step below her, holding her eye with a cold steady gaze.

"Sounds like a party?" she said nodding to the door.

He stared at her with a tight unyielding smile. "Ah yes, party, private Christmas party." He then started up the stairs, making it obvious that he meant her to go ahead of him. "How can I help you?"

"Oh, I'm sorry to come so late, Jimmy, but Susie said I could pick up her two dresses. She said I could borrow one."

"Aah." Jimmy Lee was obviously uninterested in their arrangements, he simply wanted her out of his establishment. "Yes, I have Miss Popham's dresses, they are in the shop, up here, come with me." He started quickly along the shadowed corridor towards the front of the building.

"'ello 'ello, late-night business, nice to see you working so hard, Jimmy." Eddie Brent gave a laugh as he strode out from behind the curtain that led into the shop. "And who's your customer but the charming Miss Cullen?"

"Miss Cullen came in the back way to pick up Susie's dresses." There was an overcareful tone in Jimmy's voice as if he was making certain that Eddie understood how she had entered the building.

"Well, you get her her dresses and I'll escort her back to the

197

Parrot." Eddie turned into a small office and flicked on the light. He nodded for Kitty to follow him inside and then crossed to one of the filing cabinets. He took an envelope out of his jacket pocket and carefully placed it inside.

He flashed her one of his cocky half-grins. "You're not on duty tonight, so you must be out gallivanting, eh?"

Kitty attempted a bright smile. "Yes, kind of way."

Brent instantly picked up the tone in her voice and swung round. "You look a bit ragged round the edges, you all right then?"

Kitty nodded and instinctively gripped the collar of her coat. "Oh yeah, sure."

Brent stepped towards her and gently flicked back a lock of dark hair that had fallen over her eyes. He looked at her carefully. "You've been through the wars, ain't you, what is it?"

The errant hair fell forward again and Kitty released her grip on the collar of her coat and pushed back the dark locks. As she did, the coat fell open and revealed the torn blouse with her cleavage and brassiere showing. She saw a strange look in Brent's eye and clutched at her coat as if to close it. He gently knocked her hand aside and glanced down at her bosom.

"Come on gal, what's happened to you?" His tone was warm and sympathetic.

"It's, it's nothing really, my boss tried it on, that's all."

Brent cleared his throat as if he was about to spit. "Greasy bastard. He needs a quick kick in the balls."

"Well, it's all right though, no harm done." She gave a nervous giggle. "I'd love to see what his wife does to him, she caught him trying to paw me."

"Oh I see." Brent gave a rattling laugh but his eyes stayed firmly on her, assessing. "I reckon you won't be working there much longer eh?"

Kitty nodded. As usual he had hit the nail on the head. "No, I, in fact I was going to ask . . . you . . ." Kitty was not normally shy but somehow the combined events of the evening had robbed her of her usual bravado.

Brent cut in. "I never seen you at a loss for words but if you're asking for full-time work at the Parrot, well I could use you."

Kitty suddenly brightened. "You could, really?"

Brent slowly nodded. "Yeah, I need someone who's got their head screwed on *and* can keep their mouth shut." He stared deep into her eyes. "I think you fit that bill, don't you?"

After a moment she nodded slowly. "Yes . . ."

Brent gave a smile and pulled over the flap of her coat, covering her breast again. "I thought so. You're a smart girl. I've got a lot of interests in London. I need someone to travel up and down for me, delivering like. That wouldn't be too bad eh? Up and down to London. All expenses paid."

Kitty gave a good-natured laugh. "Sounds good to me."

"Miss Popham's dresses are here." She turned and saw Jimmy Lee standing at the door with two clean dresses over his arm.

Brent walked over and took them. "We'll be going now, Jimmy, so you can, er, let your party out whenever you like." Kitty saw that look pass between them again, a moment of shared understanding. Then Jimmy left the room and Brent turned to her with a grin. "Looks like you're overstocked there, eh."

"Susie said I could have my pick."

"Come on, let's go back to the Parrot, you can do your changing there."

He walked her quickly outside and firmly closed the rear door behind them. Then he turned to her and flashed a cheeky grin. "So who's the lucky young lad tonight? The young toff, is it?"

Kitty was surprised that Brent had noticed Nigel. She nodded shyly. "Maybe."

Brent laughed, then grabbed her gently by the arm as he steered her towards the Parrot. "Well, you make sure he treats you right, you hear me." Kitty caught that strange look in his eye again, but only for a moment and then it was gone. A fleeting second later the cocky smile returned. "I mean Tom'd never fight for me again, if I didn't keep an eye out for his little sister."

Kitty felt the pressure of his arm on hers and thought how nice it was to have someone thinking about "keeping an eye out for her".

Nigel stood near the front door of the Parrot stamping his feet to distract himself from the sleet that periodically lashed his back. Now and again the door of the nightclub opened and he glanced up, hoping it was Kitty. He still could not believe that he had summoned up the nerve to ask her out that first time. She was so different to all the other girls he knew. He had hardly ever spoken to any girl outside his own circle, except when they served him in a shop. But after he started going out with Kitty he had to admit that they had always held a fascination for him. The girls he knew had their lives laid out for them, neatly, in tidy boxes. There was horse-riding, and ballet dancing and music. There were tennis clubs and badminton clubs and country weekends. He had always felt that they were boring, but Kitty, Kitty didn't bore him. There was something wild in her, something that challenged life, bit into it. She made him feel excited and alive.

"Sorry I'm late, I was getting changed." Kitty stepped up beside him. There was a mischievous twinkle in her eyes. As he glanced at her he could feel that tightening in his throat. The sheen of her skin, the shape of her face, the way she tossed her dark hair back out of her eyes; she was very beautiful.

He shifted uneasily from foot to foot, feeling awkward. "You didn't need to get changed just to go to the cinema."

Kitty gave a cynical laugh. "Oh yes I did but I'll tell you all about that later when we get out of this cold."

"Kitty?" They both swung round. Terry Gillings was standing beside them carrying a case. He looked distracted as he absent-mindedly flicked the glistening sleet out of his hair.

"Terry, what're you doing here?" Kitty's tone was surprised but also concerned. She quickly took in the suitcase and then glanced up and saw the troubled look in his eyes. "What's wrong? What's happened?"

Terry nodded at Nigel, "Hello again!" Then he glanced back at his cousin. "If I could just talk to you for a minute."

Terry stepped back towards the wall and Kitty followed him. He dropped his suitcase on to the pavement and then stared at it as if gathering his thoughts.

"Terry! What is it?" Kitty was beginning to get worried. She prodded him on the chest with her forefinger.

"I've left home, been chucked out, whatever you call it."

"What!" Kitty was stunned. She had only ever allowed herself to see the Gillings as the "perfect family", partly out of resentment of their "happiness" as she saw it, and partly out of a need to believe that there could be such a thing as a perfect family.

"My dad and I had a terrible row about politics . . ."

"Oh God, Terry. What about your mum? I mean didn't she . . ."

"Please Kitty, I don't want to talk about it." Terry ran his fingers through his hair in a wrenching gesture of despair. "I just wanted to know if Tom was here. I need somewhere to stay and I know he's got a lot of pals so I thought – it would only be until tomorrow – my friend Reggie Dickson'll be able to help me then. He lives in digs and I'm sure he knows somewhere . . ."

"Terry, stop, I hear you."

She pulled at the lapel of his dark overcoat and gave him a reassuring smile. "Listen, Tom's up in London training for some fight he's got after Christmas."

Terry slumped back against the wall and blew out a long misty breath. "Oh God. Ah well, it was just a chance."

"Terry! What's wrong with you, I mean why can't you stay with us? Kip down with Ernie . . . I bet my mum . . ."

Terry shook his head vigorously. "No, no. I don't want that! I don't want to start a whole round of family arguments. My dad'd be really pissed and I don't want your mum . . ."

"For God's sake!" Kitty raised her voice and grabbed his sleeve again. "What the hell does it matter about your dad, I'm not going to let you sleep on the streets tonight."

Terry pulled away and then quickly swooped down and lifted his suitcase. "It's all right, Kitty, honest, I can get a place in the Sally Ann, I'm sure."

201

"Is everything all right?" Nigel had crossed over to them as Terry was turning aside. He had gathered from the tones of their muted conversation that everything was *not* all right.

Terry turned round and gave a forced, cheery grin. "Of course, yeah, I'm just heading off."

Nigel grabbed Terry by the arm. "Terry, I couldn't help overhearing but you know if you need somewhere for the night you can stay with us. I often have friends over."

Terry shook his head. "No, no, it's all right."

"For Chrissake, Terry, it's not all right, you're being a bloody fool." Kitty exploded and then turned towards Nigel. "Could he stay with you, Nigel?"

"Of course." Nigel smiled. "It'd only be a just reward for helping me out with the motorbike."

Nigel saw the turmoil on Terry's face and somehow sensed that he wanted to keep this whole episode quiet. When Nigel spoke his voice was warm and reassuring yet authoritative, like an older brother talking to a younger. "Terry, nobody needs to know you're staying, nobody. My dad doesn't care and neither does my mother . . ." Nigel could not help the passing note of bitterness but it was lost on both Kitty and Terry. "No one cares. I have friends to stay all the time."

At that moment the wind whipped round the corner splattering their faces with icy cold sleet. Kitty shivered and pulled her coat tightly around her neck. "Terry, for Chrissake make up your mind before I turn into a bleedin' blue-arsed brass monkey."

The boys burst out laughing and Terry felt a surge of relief. He looked over at Nigel and gave him a wistful smile. "Yeah well, Kitty's right as usual. If it's all right with you I'll take you up on your offer."

Nigel nodded, "Yes of course, of course it's all right." Then he turned to Kitty, "Though oh . . ."

Kitty gave another shudder as she stamped her feet. "Yeah, I know, that's the end of *Mr Deeds Goes to Town*."

"Look I don't mean to break up your, well, your evening. I could meet you after . . ."

Nigel brushed his objections aside. "Come on, that's enough, we've gone through all that." He turned from Terry and stared deep into Kitty's eyes. "If Kitty likes, she could come back to my house, listen to some records, have a drink."

"Come back to my house." The words rang in her mind. Now all the Daphnes and Priscillas and Dorotheas could go spin on their fat navels. Suddenly Kitty Cullen was respectable, she was being invited in by the front door.

28

The house sounded quiet, too quiet. Hanley closed the door behind him and for a moment sagged against the wall. Then he remembered that his overcoat was covered with melting sleet and snow. As he took it off and hung it up on the coatstand he noticed a pile of Christmas mail tucked behind the phone and beside it a notepad with a message written in Olwen's neat script. "I'll be staying with Olivia in Bedford Square, overnight, last of the Christmas shopping. Eunice."

Hanley read it twice and then slowly dropped it back on to the table. He looked up and gazed into the mirror as if trying to read something in his own eyes. But all he saw was a profound tiredness. At this very moment he did not have the energy to try and sort out the tangled mess that was his marriage.

"I made a stew tonight, sir, so it's ready any time you are."

Hanley turned and saw Olwen at the end of the hallway. She was rubbing her eyes and stifling a yawn. It was obvious that she had nodded off in her chair, beside the kitchen fire.

"Olwen, you look tired, why don't you take yourself off to bed. Are Nigel and Elizabeth in?"

"Master Nigel's out on that motorbike again."

Hanley noted the disapproval in her voice.

"And Miss Elizabeth's upstairs reading," she continued.

"*Was* upstairs reading . . ."

Hanley felt a flood of warm feelings as he heard Elizabeth's voice. Here at least was one bright spot in his day. He glanced up and saw his daughter leaning over the banister. Every time he looked at her he kept seeing his own sister, Mandy. Elizabeth had that same tomboy quality, that same straightforward, outgoing energy. Everything about her had a utilitarian quality, from her straight fringe to her hockey captain's voice and her almost boyish strut. It was as if she was saying, here am I, take it or leave it. He missed her when she was at boarding school, for he felt that they were both cut from the same tree.

She skipped down the stairs and plonked herself beside him, like a midshipman reporting for duty. She was only sixteen and yet she was already taller than Eunice. She leaned close, gave him a squeeze and then a quick peck on the cheek. "Olwen forced us to wait for you, or Mummy, to open the cards . . ." Hanley did not miss the rather cold throwaway reference to "Mummy" but he decided to ignore it. The relationship between Eunice and Elizabeth seemed to deteriorate by the month.

Olwen gave a snort as she turned back towards the kitchen. "Quite right too. You can only open an envelope once. Well, if you don't need me then, sir, I will go to bed." Olwen's bedroom was on the ground floor at the back of the house, next to Hanley's study, and she quickly made her way towards it like a woman bent on sleep.

Hanley picked up the mail and handed it to Elizabeth. "Here you are, you can open them."

"Oh wonderful!" She snatched the pile from him and quickly flicked through them.

Hanley grabbed his briefcase and started down the hall towards his study. He felt exhausted, it had been a long and tiring day. He almost felt like going to bed without eating but he knew that was stupid. He dropped the briefcase just inside the study door and went back towards the kitchen.

Elizabeth followed close behind, ripping open one of the

envelopes. "We've got one from Uncle Bertie and Aunt Maeve. It's all the way from Singapore."

Hanley walked into the kitchen and looked around. Everything was spick-and-span. The gleaming iron and copper cooking pots were hanging from their hooks and the white dishcloths were drying on a rack by the fire. A large saucepan was gently steaming on top of the stove. All seemed neat and ordered and homely. Hanley stood for a moment and felt a shudder of anger coursing through him. The words from the telephone message echoed in his mind. ". . . staying with Olivia . . . overnight . . . last of the Christmas shopping." It all rang so hollow. Eunice had no right to treat the whole family in such a cavalier fashion. He picked up a ladle and a soup bowl and laid them on the counter beside the stove. He had just taken the lid off the simmering pot when he heard a revving sound outside. They both turned to the kitchen window as the headlight from the motorbike flashed by.

"Nigel's back early. I thought he was going to the cinema in Gillingham. You'd better eat your stew, Daddy, or he'll be after seconds, no, I think it's thirds."

"Hmm." Hanley raised an eyebrow as he ladled the steaming hot stew into his bowl. It was true Nigel had the appetite of a drayhorse. Hanley replaced the lid on the saucepan and was sprinkling some pepper on his stew when he heard voices outside.

"Nigel must have some friends with him, I think I'll take this into my study." Then he fixed her with a humorous eye. "Leave the stage clear for the younger generation . . . does that sound better, Elizabeth?"

"Sounds good, but I think you just want to eat your meal in peace and quiet."

After cutting a slice of bread, Hanley plonked it on top of the stew and flashed her a boyish smile. "Could be!" He quickly crossed the kitchen and walked into the hallway. He could hear the back door opening behind him, voices, introductions, but he made his way to his study and closed the door behind him. Elizabeth was right, he really needed to be alone.

He switched on the green-shaded lamp and settled himself

behind his desk, savouring Olwen's stew. As he chewed the meat, the events of the evening rumbled around in his mind. Somehow his life seemed to be racing out of control and he felt it a struggle to keep the pieces in order. Grainger and his experiments; Marsh and his web of espionage – and now Eunice and . . .

He tossed his spoon aside with a clatter, picked up the receiver and put through a call to Olivia Brampton's London house.

As he waited, he absent-mindedly tore his bread into tiny pieces. He was surprised when Olivia answered. He had expected a maid. "Olivia?"

"Yes."

"This is Hanley, James Kerr Hanley."

"Oh, hello James." Her voice sounded languid, almost sleepy. But then that was vintage Olivia, and something that always grated on him. It was a cultivated ennui, signalling that she found him ever so slightly tedious.

"I got a phone message saying that Eunice was staying overnight at your place."

"Well, your message was right, James. How can I help you?"

Hanley crushed the remaining piece of bread in his fist and then tossed the squashed ball into his bowl. God but she could be an irritating bitch!

He took a moment to steady his breathing and then said in a soft, almost whimsical tone, "Well, if it's not too inconvenient, I wouldn't mind talking to her."

"Oh no, not at all." There it was again, that irritating ability to crush all subtlety underfoot by merely ignoring it. Hanley jabbed at the bread again as she continued, "However, she is asleep. The poor darling went to bed with a headache about an hour ago. Damned Christmas shopping gets worse every year. If you just hold on I'll wake her up, if it's important."

"If it's important," the phrase was tagged on almost carelessly. But Hanley knew there was nothing careless about the cold-eyed Olivia. She was telling him that if he was such a bastard as to want to wake his "sick" wife, she would carry out his orders. Hanley tried to rein in his swelling anger. He wanted

206

to let loose with a stream of belowdecks language; order her to wake Eunice immediately. He hated feeling manipulated. But instead he took another deep breath and once more crushed the pulplike bread in his fist.

"Oh no, no, that's all right, Olivia," he was pleased to hear his voice sounded cool and calm and ever so genteel. "Just tell Eunice that I called and I hope she feels better."

"Oh yes, of course I will. We'll pack her on to the train tomorrow, Christmas shopping and all. And maybe we'll see you soon, though I hear the Navy keeps you chained to your desk most of the time, you poor darling."

"Oh yes, that would be lovely, to get together some time, lovely." Hanley's irritation leaked out sideways. "Well, I mustn't keep you, Olivia, nice talking to you and, eh, have a good Christmas."

"Oh, same to you, James, and my love to the children."

Hanley put down the phone and then sharply banged his fist on the desk, rattling both his bowl and the receiver. "Chained to your desk." She had such a way with words, there was a barb in every sentence. Without actually saying it she had told him that Eunice and she had been talking about him, and about the troubles in their marriage.

He stared at the brass stem on the top of the green-shaded lamp as he tried to contain his anger. Then he suddenly glanced at his watch. There was a party in the wardroom at Pembroke Barracks tonight. Lieutenant Commander Crowe, the *Graplin*'s captain, had invited him. He usually avoided such occasions, there was too much rum and gin and general bonhomie for his taste. But just now it felt like a good idea, a very good idea. Just a few drinks, a bit of shoptalk; it would help close out the dark anger that was eating away at the back of his mind.

There was a peremptory knock at the door. "Dad, it's Nigel, may I come in."

"Yes, yes of course." He glanced up as the door opened and saw Nigel silhouetted against the light from the hall.

He looked awkward and it was obvious that he was about to ask a favour. Hanley tapped his fingers on the desk. "All right,

207

Nigel, what is it? Do you need some extra money for the bike or something?"

"Oh no, no. It's just that a friend of mine's stuck for the night. He missed his last bus and I wondered if it was all right to put him up."

"Of course, of course, you didn't need to ask." Hanley swept the crumbs into a pile with his hand and then brushed them on to his plate. "I think the spare bedrooms are ready. But if they aren't don't wake Olwen, just do it yourselves. She's just gone to bed; she looked exhausted."

"Oh right, of course we can do it, thanks Dad."

Nigel turned and started for the door. "And Nigel, I, I'm going out." Nigel turned again and Hanley saw the look of surprise on his face. He continued, "I know it's late but there's a gathering at the wardroom and I ought to put in an appearance for an hour or so." He gave a muted laugh, "So don't wait up, eh?"

"No, no, we won't."

Nigel was confused, his father was rarely so chatty or confidential. He backed into the hall, followed by Hanley carrying his empty bowl. "Shall I take that for you, Dad?"

"Hmm, well, yes why not." Hanley gave him the bowl and then turned left towards the front door. He lifted his overcoat from the coatstand and slipped it on, slowly, as if his mind was elsewhere. As he was buttoning it, he turned to Nigel who was still standing by the study door. "I'll . . . I'll just go on now. So as not to be too late. Say hello to your friends for me then."

"Yes, yes I will."

Nigel watched his father close the front door behind him and heard his footsteps crunching on the gravel driveway outside. After a few seconds he heard the car engine kicking into life. It was strange. He had never seen him like that. He seemed totally distracted, almost fragile.

"Nigel!"

Nigel turned and walked back into the kitchen. Kitty and Terry were sitting over by the fire and Elizabeth was peering out of the kitchen window. She turned to him as he entered and said in a low voice, "Is that Daddy's car?"

"Yes. He says he's going down to Pembroke Barracks, the wardroom. Says there's some kind of a 'do' on that he has to go to."

Elizabeth looked surprised. "You mean he just left?"

Nigel raised an eyebrow and gave a shrug. "Yeah, I don't know, he seems in a funny mood."

Elizabeth slipped past him into the hallway. Nigel glanced after her and heard her going into the front room. Then he crossed to Terry and Kitty who were leaning forward staring at the fire, cradling cups of tea in their hands.

"Terry can stay, no problem." Terry's face visibly relaxed and Nigel gave him a friendly pat on the shoulder. "Come on, we'll take you up now. You look exhausted." Then he gave a wry smile as he tapped Kitty on the shoulder. "And you can help."

Kitty followed Terry and Nigel into the hallway. She stared around her wide-eyed, taking everything in: the polished floors, the rugs, the grand sweep of the stairs. Her mother had once skivvied in a rich doctor's house in Liverpool, and that was as close as she had ever got to the "nobs". And yet here she was, a guest in a house that was even bigger! No, not just a guest, something more.

As they started up the stairs, she shook her head and took a deep breath. She couldn't tell exactly what that "something more" was, but at least she had been invited into the Hanley house, at least now she was on an equal footing with all the airy-fairy weeping daffodils who floated in and out of Nigel's tennis club.

She glanced up at Nigel as they climbed to the first landing. She had been watching him carefully and was seeing a new side to him. There was something about the relaxed way he took charge that impressed her. No, he didn't have that guttersnipe cock-of-the-walk swagger that Johnny McIvor had, but there was an easy, subtle confidence about him. Something almost graceful that made her think of Leslie Howard. That was it, the easy commanding presence of a gentleman.

"In here, Terry." Kitty snapped out of her daydreaming.

209

They were on the top floor of the house. Kitty stared around her and noticed how the edges of the ceiling sloped down. Just above them there was a large skylight and she could see the mix of snow and sleet spitting against the dark glass. In front of them, just at the top of the stairs, there was a bathroom and on either side a bedroom.

Nigel walked into the room on the right and flicked on the light. He dropped Terry's case on to the bed and crossed to the window and closed the curtains. "Well, there you are, that should be all right, what d'you say?"

"Yeah it's great, thanks."

Nigel gave a dismissive wave. "Oh no thanks, I just wanted to know if it was all right."

Terry nodded awkwardly and gave another shy grunt. Meanwhile Kitty gazed around the room in envy. It was plain and simple, but she would have given anything for it to be hers. Instead she had to sleep in that rat hole of a living-room-cum-bedroom in Chichester Street, with its paint peeling off the walls and the smell of meat and bones drifting up from Brindley's butcher's shop below.

"Looks like it's made up, too." Nigel had pulled back the blankets and was looking at the starched white sheets underneath.

"Great, I'm really fagged out." Terry slowly exhaled as he sank down on to the edge of the bed. He stared at his hands for a moment and then cleared his throat. "Look Nigel I really do want to thank you, and your dad."

Nigel edged towards the doorway where Kitty was standing. "Think nothing of it." His voice was cheery as if he was trying to raise the other boy's spirits. "Do you want to come down and talk?"

Terry glanced up at both of them. He had a cut above one eyebrow as though he had been in a fight. His face was white and drawn, and he sat slumped on the edge of the bed like someone who had not slept for a week.

"Well, if it's all right, I think I'd rather just go to bed."

"Of course. You can unpack your stuff in those drawers if you want, and the bathroom's next door."

Kitty walked forward and ruffled Terry's hair. "It'll be all right, Terry. It will."

"Yeah, I know, thanks Kitty."

Halfway down the stairs, Kitty stopped on the landing and stepped across to the large window. It looked out over the front lawn and she gazed down into the mess of swirling snowflakes caught in the lights from the house. "Looks like that's the end of *Mr Deeds Goes to Town*," she said with a rueful grin.

"Well, just for tonight. Do you, do you want me to take you home now or . . ." He walked close to her so that she felt his arm lightly brush against hers. She kept her eyes fixed determinedly on the dancing flakes beyond the window. When he continued she could hear a tremulous note of hesitation in his voice. "Or would you like to listen to some music, have a drink?"

Kitty slowly turned and gave him one of her maddening smiles. Half innocent, half vixen. "Yes, why not. I'd like that."

"Well, first step, why don't we go down and take your coat off and get it dry?"

"Did you get that boy a towel?"

Elizabeth marched up the stairs past them and flashed Nigel her self-satisfied prefect's smile.

Nigel gave a grunt. "No."

"It's all right, I'll do it. You go and entertain your guest. I know where they are in the airing cupboard." For a moment Nigel wondered if he had heard an undue stress on the word "entertain", but then Elizabeth turned away and he decided to let it drop.

"Do you play, Kitty?" Nigel had brought her into the music room and was pointing to the baby grand.

"No, I, I can't."

Her face was a strange mix of confusion and awe, like a child startled awake in the middle of a dream.

"Come on, let me take your coat."

Slowly she unbuttoned and slipped it off. As she did, she continued to gaze around her. There were dark, rich, velvet curtains, a deep pile carpet, paintings on the wall. But the piano, it was the piano that almost took her breath away.

"I've never ever seen one like this, except in a film, like you know one of those Hollywood musicals, with the big white steps and all those girls." She handed him the coat and then let her fingers glide along the edge of the keyboard.

"Kitty . . ."

"Yeah."

"You look . . . beautiful."

She did. Susie Popham's dress was an almost perfect fit. The material had a silk sheen and an elegant neckline that opened down to almost mid-bosom. Nigel was entranced, his eye continually tracing down along the snow-white skin on her neck, past the swelling curve of her breasts to the small black velvet bow at the bottom of the V-shape.

She turned and gave him a full but rather awkward smile. "But it's just the dress. And I have to thank Susie for that."

Nigel knew it was the person not the dress. He wanted to slip his arm around her waist, pull her to him, hold her tight so that her bosom pressed against his chest. He took a deep breath in an attempt to recover his composure.

"I'll just hang this up, let it dry."

Nigel turned away and walked quickly into the hallway. Kitty watched him for a moment. She was so distracted by her surroundings that she scarcely noticed the effect she was having on him. She glanced around her again. Towards the back of the room behind the piano, she saw a couple of bookcases. They stretched from floor to ceiling and were packed with books. Beside them there was a large gramophone with a polished walnut finish. They had things here that she had only ever seen in magazines or the cinema.

"Kitty," Nigel was standing at the door. "Would you like a drink? Dad's out, I can mix you a cocktail if you like."

"A cocktail." She had an immediate image of men in top hats and tails swirling debutantes and film stars across glittering dance-floors. But then she thought in panic, was a gin and tonic a cocktail? Well, what the hell! "I'll have a gin and tonic."

"I'll be back in a jiffy. Why don't you pick out a couple of records, we've got some good band stuff." He pointed over to

212

the gleaming majesty of the gramophone and then disappeared out into the hall.

Kitty sauntered over to the gramophone cabinet, enjoying every moment. She took the band records and set them on top, Roy Fox, Ray Noble and Lew Stone. Then she leaned back and looked around the room again. God, here she was in this nobby house, waiting for a gin and tonic, about to hear Ray Noble and his orchestra. She felt a comforting warmth suffusing her body.

Yes, she liked this. No! More than that, she deserved it!

Terry opened his case, took out his few clothes and then carefully laid his books on the bed beside him. As he sat there scanning the covers, a determination slowly crystallised. He would not go back, he would get Reggie Dickson to find him digs! His principles were important, communism was important! He gave a cynical smile as his finger drifted over the cover of Huxley's *Brave New World*, wondering if all new worlds had to start with such turmoil. At least he wouldn't have to hide his books in the wardrobe any more. He picked up the *Handbook of Marxism* and gave a grunting laugh. It still had an orangey red stain on the cover where he had smuggled it in with a pound of tomatoes.

There was a knock at the door, followed by a girl's voice. "Hello."

"Come in."

Elizabeth stepped into the room. "I think my brother forgot to leave you towels." She carried them over to the chest of drawers and laid them on top.

"Oh yes, thanks."

She gestured towards the books on the bed and gave a broad smile. "You look like a book salesman, with your wares spread all around."

Terry felt awkward. "Yeah, I suppose. I need my books. They're important."

Elizabeth stepped over and glanced down at them. As she did so, she imperiously flicked back her long straight fair hair. He saw this and felt his hackles rising. There was something about the pampered smoothness of her skin, the firm set of her jaw and confidence of her stance that grated on him. He had a sudden image of her as a lady bountiful come to see that the lower classes were "settling in".

"These look interesting."

"What did you expect, penny comics?"

She turned and glared at him, straight, honest and with a brittle edge. "And *why* . . . would I think that?"

Embarrassed, he turned away towards the window. There was something unsettling about her straightforwardness. Perhaps he had misjudged her. "Sorry, I've just had a long night."

She leaned over and picked up a paperback copy of *Capitalism, Communism and the Transition* by Emile Burns. As she came close to him he could see strands of her fair hair slipping slowly across her rose-coloured sweater. They looked like threads of golden silk and he felt like stretching out and curling them around his fingers. Then she stood up and flashed him an amused, whimsical smile.

"Not light reading, is it?" She arched an eyebrow and then flicked through the first few pages of the book.

"I don't know what I'm expected to say to that."

"Pardon?" She glanced up from the book and fixed him with that clear, searching gaze of hers. "Are you a communist?"

He was so startled by her directness that he burst out laughing. Christ, there was no beating about the bush with her. She gazed at him, puzzled. "What's wrong? What did I say?"

"Oh I dunno. It's just you get straight to the point, don't you? No pussyfooting around."

She gave a slightly puzzled smile. "I suppose. But are you?"

For some reason Terry felt reluctant to answer. Perhaps it was because it had caused him too much pain already that night. "Yes . . . yes I am, but why are you interested?"

"Because I've never met one and I keep hearing about Abyssinia and Spain and wondering what the communists are doing."

Terry saw a firmness and intelligence there that reminded him of Reggie Dickson. But yet there was still something about

214

her cool assurance that rankled. "Do they not teach you all that in your posh school then?"

She stared at him for a long time. Then she carefully placed the book on the bed and stood back. "You really do have a chip on your shoulder, don't you." She started towards the door.

Without thinking he jumped up and grabbed her arm. "I'm sorry. Look, I don't have a chip. I, it's just that I'm . . ." He let go of her arm then took a deep breath and suddenly blurted it out. "I didn't miss my bus, or whatever your brother said, my dad threw me out of the house because, well, because he just found out that I'd joined the Communist Party."

She stared at him and slowly nodded her head. There was a look of sympathy in her eyes but also something else, something akin to admiration. "I see. At least you had the guts to stand up for what you believe in."

"Well, I'd rather it hadn't happened. Oh not about the Party, I believe in that, but the other . . . the bust-up with my dad." Then he seemed to summon up his energy and gave a gentle laugh. "But about what the Party are doing for Spain – the Young Communist League have got a campaign on now to send a food ship – it's gonna be leaving from Southampton tomorrow, Christmas Eve. Isn't that doing something?"

Her eyes sparkled with interest. "Yes. Yes. That's doing something."

Terry tried to stifle a yawn. He felt a tremendous fatigue washing over him. No matter how much he was beginning to like this girl, he just did not have the energy to stay up and talk.

She gave a smile. "I'd better leave before you fall over."

"Yeah I'm sorry, but here, take this." He picked up Emile Burns' book and handed it to her. "It'll tell you a lot."

She took the book and slowly turned it over in her hands as if it was an object of value. "Oh, well, thank you. But how will I get it back to you?"

Terry laughed. "I'll drop you a note and tell you where I end up, maybe under the Luton Arches."

"Don't say that."

"It's all right, I'm not that pessimistic. But I'll send you my address and you can post it on to me, or . . ."

There was a pause then Elizabeth gave a quick businesslike smile as she nervously flicked her hand through her fringe and said quietly, "Or maybe we could meet, and talk it over."

Terry nodded. "Yes, yes I'd like that."

"I get home from school a couple of weekends in the term."

"Right, right, I'll drop you a line when I know where I am."

There was an awkward moment during which they looked everywhere but at each other. Then Elizabeth seemed to recover her prefect's manners. Good beginnings and good endings! She patted the book as if she were dismissing a class and gave a curt nod.

"Well, I must let you get to bed. Goodnight Terry, it was good talking with you."

She turned abruptly and walked quickly out of the room closing the door behind her. Terry stared at the door for a moment and then sank down on to the bed. He gave a wry smile. What a night, it was impossible to know what to make of it all!

Kitty walked forward and stretched her hands towards the glowing coal fire. As she did so, she glanced up at the mantelpiece. There was an elaborately carved wooden clock in the centre and on either side family photos. One in particular caught her eye. The woman was darkly handsome. Kitty stared at her, intrigued.

Nigel turned down the music and quietly came up behind her. He tentatively slipped his arm around her waist again and she briefly felt his wrist brushing against the bottom of her breasts. It sent a gentle tremor through her, unlike the crude gropings of Johnny McIvor.

"That's my mother."

"I thought it was. She's very . . . attractive."

"Come on, let's dance while we've still got a band."

A romantic Al Boley number was playing. Kitty allowed herself to move in close and she could feel Nigel's firm muscles as he slipped both arms around and encompassed her. He pulled her close and they stood there for a while, slowly swaying with the music. She could feel him moving from side to side, squeezing against the full softness of her breasts with his chest. She had the sense of being in a dream. She glanced past his shoulder at the fire gently flickering in the grate.

Al Boley faded away and another record dropped. This time it was a fast-moving swing number. Kitty felt a sudden surge of happiness. She stepped back and grabbed Nigel's left hand, forcing him to lead. "Come on, let's try and do a foxtrot."

"Aaah yes, well," he gave a playful grimace. "I'm impressed, Kitty, but I don't think it's for me."

She poked him in the ribs. "Come on, give it a try." When he did not move she swung him round and steered them both down the centre of the room. Side by side, he could just keep his balance but when she started to swing him into the turn, he was gone. His right foot seemed glued to the carpet and when he tried to find his footing with his left he caught the edge of the cherrywood coffee table and tumbled backwards on to the sofa. He still had his arm around Kitty and she fell down beside him.

"You need to go to classes, mister."

For a moment they lay back against the white crocheted cushions, catching their breath. Then she sat forward and gave a mischievous smile. "Come on then, one more time."

He gave another groan and held up his hands. "No, please, have pity, let's just listen for a minute."

She leaned forward and wagged an admonishing finger in his face. "Up, mister, music's for dancing."

He did not answer but just sat there gazing into her eyes. They were beautiful, dark brown, yet with flecks of greenish blue. Kitty watched him staring at her and she could scarcely catch her breath. She felt a pleasurable numbing warmth deep in her stomach, felt as if she was drifting off into that dream again.

"Kitty."

His voice was gentle, almost like a boy appealing for comfort. And when she stared at him that was what she saw in his eyes, the gentleness and shyness. She waited for him to talk and then raised a questioning eyebrow. "What?"

"Can I kiss you?"

217

She gave a smile. Johnny McIvor – of the cold clammy hands and bad breath – would never have asked her that. He would just have presumed and pushed ahead, fumbling for his quick grope. Kitty slid sideways and then lay back against the white cushion. As she did, she smelled the lavender. Oh God but it was a world away from the Roxy dance-hall at the dockside end of Bridge Street, and all those shuffling, coughing, beer-smelling scousers.

Nigel leaned forward and stroked her cheek. Then he let his finger gently trace across her top lip.

Oh God, yes, a world away from the sweaty back seat of Johnny McIvor's battered Austin Seven and the pungent smell of Lifebuoy toilet soap!

She moved towards him and they kissed. It was gentle at first, like the trusting kiss of a child. Then they slowly clasped one another and fell into a long passionate embrace. It seemed to take them both by surprise. Kitty felt her whole body flooding towards him. She was rushing to that gate again, that point of letting go, that point of decision and fear. And yet she wanted to feel him close to her, wanted to keep on touching him. Her fingers played around his neck and ran up behind his ear, curling his hair and gently stroking his ear.

"Kitty, Kitty," she could barely hear him as he mumbled her name. She could feel his body stirring against hers. But she couldn't stop, no more than he could. She felt his hands fluttering indecisively along her body, skimming along the side of her thighs, touching her hips, squeezing her waist. She trembled as his hand brushed across her nipples, then pulled her head back and closed her eyes as she felt his hands cupping her full breasts.

"Oh Nigel, Nigel."

She fell forward again and found his mouth with hers. As they kissed she felt his fingers seeking out the cloth-covered buttons at the back of her dress. Her head was reeling, she wanted it all and yet something was still holding her back. A voice, a small streetwise voice was nagging in her mind. She pulled away with a wrench and stared at him, trying to regain her breath.

"Do you love me, Nigel?" Her voice was quiet and for the first time there was almost something plaintive in it.

Nigel drew back. The question had startled him. He looked at her for a long time. "Yes, Kitty, I do. I've never met anyone like you. I want, I . . ." He faded out in confusion.

Kitty tentatively took his hand and placed it over her breast. They sat like that for a long while, then Nigel leaned forward and nuzzled his lips against her cleavage. Very slowly he ran the tip of his tongue along her exposed skin until he stopped at the velvet bow.

Kitty's head was swirling. She wanted him, that was all she could think. She wanted him to kiss her all over like that. She suddenly grabbed his head between her hands. "I want you, Nigel, I want you like you want me, but I don't want to get pregnant, do you understand? I don't want to get pregnant."

Nigel spluttered, "Oh, I wasn't going to do that to you, I wasn't going to . . ."

"You're not listening. I said I don't want to get pregnant. We should wait until we can do it safely."

Nigel looked like a rabbit caught in headlights. He stared at her vacantly. He had never heard a girl, never heard anyone speak so straightforwardly.

Kitty laughed. "You look like you're gonna be shot."

"No, I just, I just don't know what to say."

She kissed him again. At first gently and then with more and more passion. Then she put her hands behind her back and deftly undid the top buttons on her dress. It slipped down, allowing her breasts to fall forward so that their fullness bulged against the whiteness of her brassiere.

Nigel lifted his hand and gently stroked them. Then he slipped his fingers under the straps, pushed them off her shoulders and watched as her breasts fell full and pendulous from the cups. He had never seen a girl naked before. He gazed in wonder, then leaned forward and kissed them.

Kitty gave another soft, almost inaudible groan, and fell back against the cushions. Nigel followed her and hungrily found her mouth. His hands slipped over her breasts again and

219

this time his fingers found her nipples and gently caressed them.

She had never known such a feeling before. She closed her eyes and once more drifted off into that Hollywood dream. White stairs, elegant women in long white dresses, and music, music, music.

29

Gillings walked to the edge of the dock and peered down at the chain, straining and slackening with the motion of the tide. The *Graplin* sat low in the waters of the basin looking sleek and dark and dangerous. After a moment admiring its lines he glanced up at the sky. Light grey clouds were drifting in from the south-east and the wind was rising. He cleared his throat and spat out into the dark, choppy water. "Damn!" It was the end of March, Easter Sunday was just five days away. Surely it wasn't too much to hope for spring weather. March was supposed to go out like a lamb, he only hoped it would keep its promise.

Up above him there was a grinding of gears and the whine of an engine as the crane swung the massive "closer" plate towards the gaping hole in the stern section of the boat. The engines had been carefully inched onboard during the previous weeks and now it was time to close the *Graplin* from the elements.

There was an echoing clang. Gillings glanced down at the *Graplin* again and saw that the plate had swung in too low and hit the side of the boat. The gang of shipwrights rushed to the edge of the *Graplin*'s deck to steady it. They carefully pushed it out from the hull of the boat and held it there as the crane driver inched it up again.

Gillings started down the gangplank on to the deck and noticed Lieutenant Commander Crowe striding towards him around the bridge. "I see we're going to be sealed in soon, Mr Gillings, thank God."

"Yes sir, if this weather holds up. Do you know if Dr Grainger's on board?"

"I wish to hell Grainger and his crew would keep out of our way, we have enough going on without adding to the circus."

Gillings knew that Grainger and his "crew" weren't really in the way. The boat was crawling with almost a hundred shipwrights, carpenters, fitters, electricians, plumbers and painters, and Grainger had only a dozen men at the most. But Gillings also knew that was not really the point of contention. What really annoyed Lieutenant Commander Crowe and the others, was the secrecy that surrounded Grainger's work.

"And keeping this quiet from all the men isn't pukka," continued Crowe, "damn foolish actually. In the end they're the ones who're going to have to work with the bloody thing."

A screech ripped through the air. At first Gillings thought it was a seagull but it was quickly followed by an ungodly roar. Gillings spun round. The shipwrights were sprinting along the deck towards the stern, squeezing along the narrow edges at the side of the engine hole. It was only the clattering of their heavy boots on the metal deck that drowned the terrified screeching. Gillings could make nothing of the confusion. The closer plate was like a wall cutting off sight of everything behind it.

In the midst of this mayhem, a squat, bald-headed man rushed from behind the plate, pushing the men aside, and yelled up at the crane driver with a voice like a foghorn, "Up! Chrissake . . . take the fuckin' thing up! Up! Up!"

Gillings recognised him as the chargehand, Billy Potts. He rushed forward with Crowe close behind, and grabbed Potts by the arm. "What the hell's going on?"

Above them they heard the grinding whine of the gears. Potts spun round, ignoring Gillings, and yelled at the men beyond, "Going up! Stand clear of the fuckin' plate! Stand clear!" Then he turned to Gillings and Crowe, his eyes blazing, his face chalk-white, drained of blood. "It's Brisley, young Brisley. Got his foot caught under the edge. It's bad . . ."

There was another terrified scream from the prow of the boat. Potts suddenly pushed past them, and made his way forward as quickly as he could. At the same time the massive metal plate swung up and out from the *Graplin*'s deck. As it came parallel, Gillings saw a telltale splash of red at the bottom left-hand corner. He felt a shudder of revulsion.

"My God!" He stepped towards the crowd at the other end of the gaping engine hole and then glanced back at Crowe. From the prow, the bridge, and the midship workhatch, other workmen and members of the *Graplin* crew were rushing forward. Crowe stood staring at the bloodstained corner of the plate. Gillings quickly took in his eyes and for a flicker of a second saw something dangerously indecisive in them.

"Lieutenant Commander."

Crowe suddenly seemed to come back to the present.

"Yes, I, I'll get the infirmary . . ."

"No, we'll need the naval hospital. I'll bring him up to the dock."

Gillings turned back, made his way along the narrow rim by the side of the hole and then pushed through the growing crowd. "All right, clear the deck . . . we need room to get him off."

The young shipwright was lying on his back tossing from side to side like someone possessed. Gillings recognised him as the one who had been tossing bread to the seagulls just a few carefree minutes ago. Two of his workmates were struggling to hold him down as the chargehand Potts ripped open the right leg of the injured man's boilersuit with a penknife. Below that, Gillings could see, it was an oozing bloody mess.

The workmen were still pushing forward and, with the constricted space beyond the hole, the situation at the prow of the boat was becoming chaotic. Gillings saw what was happening and yelled out, "For Chrissake get back . . . clear this! . . . we've got to get this man on to the dock." Then he pointed to two sailors at the back. "You and you. Stretcher now." As the men ran off towards the midships hatch, Gillings

222

caught his first fleeting glimpse of Terry, running aft with Grainger. But Gillings had no time to register any personal feelings. The injured man gave another scream of pain and he quickly turned back to him.

Meanwhile Potts, the chargehand, had ripped away the bloody leg of the boilersuit and was cutting through what remained of the laces on the boot. "Jesus, this is where it chopped him. Oh God!"

With the boot open, the full extent of the damage was obvious. The edge of the plate had dropped on the ankle like an axe, cutting through the muscle and flesh at the front and shattering the bone into grey-white fragments. Potts moved the leg and as he did the foot fell back, dangling like a useless object, joined to the rest of the leg only by a thin flap of tendons and skin. As the foot fell, the blood gushed out as if it had been held back only by the tightness of the boot.

"Holy Christ!" Potts recoiled in anguish.

"For God's sake shut up man." Gillings mumbled his words through gritted teeth. "Give me the knife." Potts handed him the penknife and Gillings quickly made another long cut in the boilersuit, slicing off a length of cloth.

The blood was now everywhere, pumping out of the raw, tattered flesh of the stump and pouring on to the deck. It spread out across the dark grey metal like a puddle of crimson paint, and began to drip into the engine hole. Gillings could feel it seeping into his trousers as he knelt down and looped the strip of cloth tightly around the leg. With each turn of the cloth his hands became more and more bloodied.

Behind him, the two sailors clattered along the deck bringing the stretcher, and in the distance he could hear the bell of the naval hospital ambulance crossing the causeway between the basins. It was just in time. The young shipwright had slumped back, obviously fainting from the loss of blood. Gillings continued to tighten the makeshift bandage. He had managed to reduce the flow but it was still bleeding too much. He glanced up at the two sailors. "Here, put it down."

The sailors quickly moved forward and slipped the stretcher in beside the unconscious man. Then they stepped back as the two shipwrights carefully lifted their workmate on to it. All the time Gillings kept his fist tightly clenched around the knot of the makeshift bandage, and yet still the blood leaked out, dribbling over his hand and down the inside of his sleeve.

"Here!" A long screwdriver was thrust forward. "For a tourniquet!"

Gillings quickly glanced round and saw Terry standing just behind him. It was hardly for a second that their eyes met, but it was long enough for something to pass between them. An understanding, a respect for intelligence and competence. Then the moment was gone.

Gillings turned back to the bandage and inserted the screwdriver between the cloth and the first knot. He gave it a few quick turns and almost immediately the leakage of blood ceased.

Above them, on the dock, the ambulance screeched to a halt, and its clanging bell instantly stopped.

"Up! Up! And take it careful along the sides!"

The walk back along the edges of the engine hole was precarious. One slip and they could all have gone over. Gillings went ahead and then met the stretcher at the other end. The blood was beginning to leak out again and he quickly tightened the makeshift tourniquet before they started up the gangplank towards the open doors of the ambulance.

At the top, Gillings saw that the blood was beginning to seep through the bandage again. He grabbed the screwdriver, twisted hard and then followed beside the stretcher, holding on tight. At the door of the ambulance the medical orderlies took the stretcher. "You going with him, sir?"

Gillings stared at them and then realised that his bloody hand was still clutching the tourniquet. "Eh yes, yes, I suppose I am." He let go and they skilfully slid the stretcher inside. Gillings turned and saw the chargehand Potts wiping the sweat off his brow and neck. Behind him, the other shipwrights were slowly walking up on to the dock from the *Graplin*. Gillings instantly saw the day's work dragging to a halt, the tight schedule collapsing. He glared over at the chargehand.

"It's over, Mr Potts, get your men back to work. That

closer plate's gotta be in place by the end of the day." Gillings clambered into the ambulance and swung round in the doorway. No one had moved. He leaned forward, pushing one of the doors back, and shouted in a loud voice, "I mean now!"

Potts quickly turned to the men and waved his arms. "Come on, you heard it. Move!" Gillings could see the look of hostility on the shipwrights' faces, but he did not care. He had long ago accepted the lonely burden of authority. The ambulance kicked into life and the orderly slammed the door. As it was closing, Gillings caught a brief glimpse of Terry standing at the top of the gangplank. Their paths had scarcely crossed since that fateful day just before Christmas. Terry worked in the rarefied atmosphere of "The Garden Shed" on the new guidance systems for the torpedoes. Gillings had also heard that he had become Grainger's blue-eyed boy and in a strange way that had made him feel proud. Confused but proud. Now Terry was staring at him, just staring. Gillings could not read what his son was thinking. Well, what did it matter? They were virtual strangers now anyway.

The door slammed shut with a final click and Gillings gave a throaty sigh. His hand reached out and automatically found the tourniquet. As he twisted it he glanced down at the gruesome, bloody stump.

Yes, there was more than one kind of pain.

Hanley carefully parked his car in the narrow roadway between Medway House and the admiral's offices, and switched off the lights. In the darkness he leaned forward and slumped over the wheel. He had had a headache all afternoon and it seemed to show no signs of relenting.

"Aaah!" He pulled himself out of the car and slammed the door behind him. As he walked to the front of the office building the wind gusted again and rain started to splatter all around him.

Inside, the building seemed empty, and he could hear his footsteps echoing as he climbed the stairs. In that strange stillness he thought once more of the young workman. He saw his face as the doctor told him that he had lost his foot. The look of shock, almost terror, giving way to tears. God but life could be a bastard!

Below him he could hear the wind rattling the front doors. Because of the wind and choppy water, the shipwrights hadn't managed to get the closer plate secured. That meant they were behind schedule again. And they had to do the trim dives and finish the mine tests in the basin next week! Since they couldn't work on Good Friday, he would have to spend tomorrow trying to persuade them to come in on Saturday and maybe even on Easter Sunday.

As Hanley opened the door of his office he simultaneously heard another door clicking shut. He glanced across the darkened room and noticed a light under Warrant Officer Campbell's door.

"Mr Campbell?"

He heard the rattling slam of filing-cabinet drawers and the clattering noise of something falling. He quickly crossed to the door and opened it. Campbell was kneeling in the middle of the floor scooping up papers and charts and files. He glanced round, and Hanley saw that his hair was tousled and his uniform unbuttoned. But what struck Hanley most was the momentary look of panic in Campbell's eyes.

"Just looking for a few files in your office, sir."

"Oh, yes. Yes, of course." For a moment Hanley wondered why Campbell was overexplaining. Then he glanced across towards the warrant officer's desk and saw the bottle of gin and the glass. God, but he'd been drinking again!

"I'll, I'll just get this cleared away." Campbell dragged all the papers into a loose bundle and staggered to his feet. He swayed unsteadily, then stepped across to a filing cabinet by the window and dumped the whole lot on top.

"Not a particularly good day, sir, eh?"

"Eh, no, no, and it doesn't seem as if it's over yet." Hanley walked over to the desk and picked up the half-empty bottle of gin.

"You object to me having a nip, sir?" Campbell pulled himself to his full height and Hanley noticed that dangerous alcoholic glint of anger in his eye.

226

Hanley plonked the bottle back on to the desk while still keeping his eyes steadily fixed on Campbell. Then he said with measured coolness, "I object to it interfering with work."

"And begging your pardon, sir, that's what you're saying is happening to me?"

They stared at each other and for the first time since they had worked together, an icy silence settled between them. When Hanley finally spoke, his voice was softer, more conciliatory.

"What is it, Mr Campbell?"

Campbell slowly shook his head and glanced out of the window. There was a weary bitterness in his voice. "Nothing, sir, nothing that need bother the Navy."

"It's your wife again."

Campbell visibly flinched. "She's taken a turn for the worse really . . . completely in a world of her own."

There was another pause. All was silent except for the sound of the rain being blown against the windows. Hanley wanted to say something warm and comforting, but he felt awkward, constricted by rank and his own innate reserve.

"Still you've done everything you can for her. You've got her in the best place you could."

Campbell gave a bitter laugh. "Yes, and the most expensive! Sometimes I think I'd be better off dead. I mean *she* would anyway. My insurance'd take care of her, and the pension . . ." Campbell's speech drifted to a halt and he slammed his fist down on top of the filing cabinet. "Ah fuck it!" His head slowly sagged forward and he gazed at the floor. "I, I'm sorry, sir. Sorry for the language. No excuse."

Hanley gave a dry laugh. "It's all right, Campbell, I've heard a few of those before. Even used a few myself. Listen, get back to your billets now. And take some time off . . . until next week."

"But the extra work with this closer plate and trim dives . . ."

Hanley cut across him. "We can handle it. Go down and visit her, or whatever you want. Maybe just go away and relax somewhere."

Campbell stared at him as if he wanted to say something else;

needed to say something else. Then he seemed to think better of it, turned aside and glanced at the rain splattering against the windowpanes. "Maybe I will, sir, maybe I will."

"No maybe, you'll do it. Now! You can leave all this behind, get away for a few days."

Campbell nodded again. "Thank you, sir. Thank you. I will."

Campbell knew that the conversation was over and yet for another few seconds he lingered, as if something had been left unsaid. Then he suddenly took a deep breath and picked up his hat and overcoat from the coatstand.

Hanley turned back to the door and walked into his office. He crossed to the desk, switched on the light and picked up the file of schedules on the trim and buoyancy tests.

"Goodbye, sir," Campbell called from the doorway.

"Yes, yes . . ." Hanley continued to skim the schedules and worksheets as he heard the outer door of the other office closing. Then he glanced up and looked out of the window towards the lamps on Thunderbolt Pier. "Leave all this behind". He wished to God he could have done it himself.

He stared for a long time at the dark shimmering surface of the river, reflected in the light from the pier. Somehow the darkness echoed his mood. He felt sombre, almost depressed, something he had rarely experienced in his life. He had always regarded depression as a luxury for which he had no time. He had always had a sustaining faith in country and flag, and in his service to the fleet and his family. But now, all that began to seem hollow. He felt drained, tired, constantly swamped by the mounting pressures of work.

And then there was Eunice. There were so many nights she had stayed away in London, so many weekends she had spent at country parties. Even when she was at home the strain was enormous. Arguments blew up over nothing, and when they were not arguing, they rarely spoke.

Hanley took out his pipe then walked behind his desk, opened the top drawer and pulled out a box of matches. He took out a match and slowly twirled it between his forefinger and thumb. This coming weekend, over Easter, he had hoped to be able to sit down with her, declare his hope for a new beginning. But now there was another crisis in the yards and he would probably be spending much of the next few days here, especially now that he had to cover Campbell's work as well.

"I was told you'd still be here."

Hanley spun round and saw Marsh silhouetted in the doorway to Campbell's office.

"I knocked but you obviously didn't hear."

"No. My mind's off somewhere else."

Marsh crossed to Hanley's desk and pulled up a chair. The room was dark except for the green-shaded desklamp and it was only when Marsh leaned forward that Hanley saw the rain glistening on his navy blue overcoat.

While Marsh undid his briefcase, Hanley lit his pipe and pulled a file out of one of his drawers. "We're a couple of days behind and we have the trim and buoyancy tests next week. This wind hasn't helped. It's pretty choppy in the basin and we've had trouble with the closer plate being . . ."

"Yes, I heard." Marsh's interruption was hard-edged and dismissive. "I've just spoken to Rear Admiral Walker."

Hanley nodded and watched Marsh's cold grey-blue eyes. There was a single-minded intensity in his look today. This obviously wasn't one of Marsh's fortnightly "catching-up" visits.

"Just yesterday," Marsh continued, "we got word back from our sources in Germany; reliable word. Apparently they believe that we are working on a new acoustic-magnetic torpedo and a device to track it."

Hanley felt winded. He sank back into his chair.

Marsh kept his cold eyes fixed on him and then gave a thin, bitter smile. "We should be happy, Hanley, they're on the wrong trail. And the longer we keep them on it, the better off for Grainger and his radio directional project."

"Yes, yes, of course." Hanley swung round in his seat and glanced towards the window and into the darkness beyond. He was distracted, and focused on trying to put the pieces together. "How much do they know?"

"They seem to be a month behind our . . ." Marsh allowed

229

himself a mirthless laugh and then continued, "our paper-trail."

Hanley propelled himself out of his seat and marched to the window. He gave a long exasperated groan. "Oh God, that's all we need, isn't it. Proof of another spy in the yards."

"Not proof. Remember, we don't know who it is yet."

Hanley turned and raised a sceptical eyebrow. "And even if you did know, you wouldn't do anything about it, would you? You'd want to use him, the way you used Kingsland."

"Exactly."

Hanley felt a wave of anger. He recalled the first time he had met Marsh in the admiral's garden. He had disliked the man then and he still disliked him. Of course Kingsland was a traitor, but there was something almost joyfully predatory in the way Marsh had pursued him.

Hanley absent-mindedly drummed the stem of his pipe between his forefinger and thumb. What he felt about Marsh was irrelevant, this proof of another spy in the yard was the final straw in a long dark year. He sank back against the side of the window and pressed the palm of his hand across his brow. When he spoke it was almost in a whisper. "Who could it be, I mean there are only so many people in the yards who could know."

"Don't presume it's in the yards, Hanley."

"What do you mean?"

"Every one of those people who are privy to our activities have friends, wives, lovers, mistresses, perhaps even a homosexual lover. Who knows?"

Hanley turned round. From where he was standing the green-shaded lamp cast a sickly pallor over Marsh's face and gave a strange gleam to his eyes. He was enjoying all this! The bastard was enjoying it!

Hanley gave an involuntary shiver. Marsh's world was bizarre and distasteful, and at that moment Hanley would have given anything to be a thousand miles away from it.

30

Kitty heard the motorbike engine only seconds before Nigel honked the horn. Then she spun round, her heart throbbing, and crossed the pavement to where he was sitting astride the bike. Though she was pleased to see him she was also angry.

"I've been phoning since last Thursday."

"It's only Tuesday, Kitty." There was something too airily dismissive in the way he spoke.

She pursed her lips in anger. "It was Easter. I thought we might go somewhere."

Nigel suddenly seemed to repent and she saw again that hesitant boy she had first known. "I'm sorry, Kitty. I kept getting your messages, but when I wasn't taken up with the Easter hols and the family . . . I was out . . ."

Kitty pursed her lips again. She was still reluctant to get on the pillion seat. "And what kept you 'out' so much?"

Nigel gently revved the bike, obviously impatient to go. "It's kind of boring. I've been studying with a friend, Jeremy Duckworth, for, well, examinations for Lincoln . . ." Then he added, "College, Oxford."

"Oxford? You mean you're going to go to Oxford University?"

"Well, if I get through my history and all of Marlborough's battles . . ."

Kitty soaked it all in. Nigel going to Oxford. One of the élite. The thought raced through her mind, exciting her and depressing her at the same time.

Nigel gunned his motorbike again, unaware of the effect his scholastic ambitions had had on her. "Well, are you coming then or do we talk here all night?"

She flashed him a coy, engaging smile and settled herself on the pillion. "What'll we do then, Miss Cullen? Go for a drive along the Sheppey road?" There was a suggestive tone in his voice and Kitty knew what he meant. On a number of occasions they had driven out to one of the deserted sheds used by the hop-pickers. There they had made love. In the beginning there had been a quiet passionate tenderness between them. But slowly and almost imperceptibly Nigel had changed until now Kitty began to feel as if she was being used.

She buttoned her coat up to her neck. "No, why don't we go back to your house, just have a cup of Ovaltine or something."

She could tell by the way Nigel suddenly turned his head that he was not happy with the idea. It confirmed a knowledge that had been growing in her.

He gave an awkward laugh. "Well, it's, it's not too exciting."

She wasn't going to let him worm his way out of it. She gave him a simple smile and squeezed him round the waist. "But I'd like to, you know, just do something comfortable."

"Well, why not, I suppose."

She couldn't miss the edge in his voice. He revved the engine again, kicked it into gear and pulled off into the traffic.

Kitty was angry. She had been trying to speak to Nigel for over a week. On Easter Sunday morning her mother had finally cornered her in the kitchen and given her a long tongue-lashing over the dregs of breakfast.

"Kitty, you've been moping around like a broody hen, and I know why. I tell you, I don't like you going around with that lad. I've never seen that kind of thing turn out right, except in the pictures." Kitty squirmed under the assault and Mary, seeing that she was getting somewhere, leaned forward and wagged the toast like a blackboard pointer. "You're both from different ends of the street. I've told you before there's no Cinderella stories for the likes of us."

Kitty was caught halfway between anger and tears, and only the sneaking doubt that what was being said might be true kept her from storming out. Mary had then reached across the table and grabbed her daughter by the wrist. "Kitty, I'm only going to say this because you mean everything to me, and I don't want to see you making the mistakes I did . . ." Mary stopped and Kitty could see the tears in her eyes ". . . but neither do I want to see you making a fool of yourself with the nobs. Take heed of what I've said, love. Take heed, please."

Kitty thought about that all the way back to the Hanleys'. She could still feel her mother's hand closed tightly round her wrist. And the warnings rang in her mind.

Nigel pulled the motorbike into the driveway and rode around the back towards the garage. As they dismounted she glanced up at the rear of the large house and felt a strange and sudden shyness. Was her mother right? Perhaps she did not really belong here. She knew that her mother saw shades of the servant girl at the Hall. But that wasn't true! It wasn't true! With an act of will Kitty tried to close her mind to the doubts.

Nigel pushed the bike into the back of the open garage as Kitty turned and stared out at the long garden. In the moonlight she could see the lawn with the two apple trees and behind that the greenhouse with the moon glittering silver on the glass. She felt a twinge of envy. All they had was a poky little yard filled with dustbins full of butcher's bones and rotten meat.

"Do you want to see our greenhouse?" Nigel had walked up behind and slipped his hand around her waist. She could feel his breath softly on her ear and for a moment her doubts and scepticism melted away. Perhaps he did care about her, care about her enough to love her and marry her and take her into this world of houses and gardens. She leaned back and nuzzled her head against his neck. He kissed her cheek and then quickly passed his hand over her full breast. For a moment she responded to his touch, then she flinched, straightened up and moved away towards the lawn.

"I, I would like to see it."

Nigel glanced back towards the house and then stepped close to her and took her hand.

"It's Mother's pride and joy. We inherited a grapevine."

They walked across the lawn past the rosebushes into the vegetable garden. A grapevine. Kitty had never seen one before but she didn't want to say so. As Nigel pulled open the wood-framed door and with a cavalier bow invited her to enter, a waft of warm damp air enveloped them.

She stepped inside on to the slatted wooden walkway and almost immediately noticed that very individual greenhouse smell of moist earth and heat and burning paraffin. She sniffed.

"It's the heater."

Nigel closed the door behind her and pointed to a large tray of small pots. "Tomatoes, that's why we've got the heat on."

"Oh." Kitty turned away from him and glanced around. In the dim moonlight, she noticed what looked like the thick trunk of a gnarled tree growing against the wall at the far end.

"Is that the vine?"

"Yes, haven't you seen one before?"

"Yes, of course, I just couldn't see it properly in the dark."

Nigel was now standing behind her. He slipped his arm around her waist and then slowly let his hand slide down over her stomach to the outside of her thighs. At the same time he nuzzled into her neck and gently kissed behind her ear.

Kitty wanted to turn round and melt into him. She wanted to believe all her dreams. He was going to go to Oxford. She would visit him there and be introduced as his girlfriend . . . He slipped his hands under her blouse and she could feel his fingers probing along the edges of her brassiere, pressing against the fullness of her flesh.

She turned, and he slowly pushed her back against the edge of a workbench filled with young plants. She felt his hand sliding up and unsnapping the back of her brassiere, and then her breasts falling free from their cups.

She was trembling, wanting him. Yet, at the same time, she could feel the hard edge of the bench along her back and somehow the discomfort brought back all the nagging doubts. Her mind swirled with images of all kinds, and echoed with desires and warnings. She had once overheard Johnny McIvor talking to one of his scuzzy friends in a bar in Liverpool. He was giving his definition of good girls and bad girls, and it had made her sick. "Good girls" you took out and treated to the flicks and after you had seen them safely home you went off and picked up one of the "slags" and took them under the arches.

Nigel now brushed his hands lightly across her breasts, hanging loosely under the unsnapped brassiere. Kitty felt a

234

surge of desire followed by a tremor of fear. Had she now become one of the "slags"? The bad girls. Oh, she knew there wasn't anything bad about them, they were just fools, and had just sold themselves cheaply.

He caught one of her nipples between his forefinger and thumb and firmly pressed. It felt so sweet, so sensual that she caught her breath, threw back her head and let out a tiny groan of pleasure. Nigel stepped forward and leaned down just far enough to pull up the bottom of her skirt. As he inched it up, his fingers teased along the back of her thighs, gliding along her new silk stockings. She could feel him quivering as he came to her suspender belt and allowed his palm to run across the smooth nakedness of her inner thigh.

She felt as if her body was on fire and yet her mind was beginning to pound with warnings. Was this what she wanted? Surely not. Surely she wasn't going to be anybody's fool. She wanted more out of life. She wanted Oxford, the big house, the car . . . She wasn't going to be played with like poor Maggie Harris, with her three bastards. She wasn't going to end up with her mother saying I told you so!

"I've got one in my pocket, Kitty, we could just lie down and do it here, here . . ."

She could hear him panting and the thought suddenly came to her that this was not the shy Nigel she had first known. More and more when they were together, he wanted an edge to their lovemaking, a twist, something novel. Closer to the road, or near a path where somebody might walk by. And now here, tonight, he wanted to make love to her within sight of the house! All she had wanted was to be brought home again, brought home even though she knew his mother didn't approve. His mother! Her anger swelled. Who the hell was she to talk?

Nigel suddenly slipped his fingers under the elastic of her underwear. She felt him tantalisingly stroking her moist warmth, brushing against the intense point of her pleasure. In a last-moment resolve she pushed him back.

"No," she mumbled. "No, Nigel, not here."

He looked at her, startled. Then a wild gleam came into his eye and he leaned forward again.

235

"Why, Kitty? It's safe. It'll be fun here, we can just lie down on the floor . . ."

He reached up with his left hand and caught her breast again, pressing the nipple hard between his fingers. It shocked her with a jolt of pain and pleasure.

"No, Nigel. Stop, please. Stop!"

She pushed him back and once again she saw that look. There was something wayward there, almost dangerous. He pressed forward and she felt his other hand tugging at her underpants, his fingers probing in an attempt at forceful persuasion.

In an instant the whole greenhouse filled with light. There was a brilliant glare, as if they were caught in the inside of an electric bulb. Nigel jerked backwards and stared out over the potted plants. Then, as quickly as it came, the light disappeared and they heard the sound of a car going into the garage.

"Father must be home. I . . ." Before Nigel could finish his sentence, Kitty had slipped past him and strode towards the door. She stood there for a moment tightly gripping the doorhandle and tried to catch her breath.

"Kitty, what're you doing? Come on, come back. Nobody's seen us." His voice was soft and cajoling, a complete antithesis to his actions of a few minutes before.

Kitty spun round and glared at him. "Oh yes, mister, that'd please you down to the ground, wouldn't it! Nobody ever seeing us, that'd be great in your book."

"What do you mean?" He was genuinely startled and confused by her anger.

"What do I mean?" She took a step towards him as if daring him to say something. "You know damn well what I mean. You've got what you want now, so you never take me out. All you think I am is your little scouse tart, the one you slip it to, up the lane and when you need . . ." She faded out with a sob, ashamed that she had let the tears come, but smart enough to realise that they could be useful.

Nigel was shaken. He walked towards her and laid a comforting hand on her shoulder. "Kitty, that's not true, it's not true. I've never met anyone like you . . ." She glanced up again and her eyes flashed. He caught the look and threw up his hands in a gesture of despair. "I don't mean just, you know, like that. You're special! But I can't see you all the time, I've got to study. I've got to . . ."

She ploughed on over his feeble excuses. "You never invite me to your fancy dances, you don't bring me home any more . . ."

"I'm taking you home now. I mean you are home . . ."

Kitty suddenly flung open the door, rattling the glass, and stormed down the path towards the driveway. "Sod you, Nigel! You're a lying mealy-mouthed arsehole!"

Her voice echoed around the open garage and the back of the house. Nigel sprinted after her and grabbed her by the arm.

"Let me go!" She struggled to free herself, stumbled forward a few more yards and finally fell back against the open garage door.

Nigel caught up with her again and gently but firmly took her hand. "Please, Kitty, stop shouting, there's no need to shout. My mother's room's just up there."

Kitty glanced up at the house again then turned and stared at him, slowly nodding her head. There was venom in her eyes. "Oh I see. I see."

Nigel suddenly realised he had said the wrong thing. "What do you mean?"

"It's your mum, isn't it."

"Please leave it, Kitty."

Kitty bashed her fist against the garage door behind her and then ducked out under Nigel's arm. "Oh I'll leave it all right," she shouted. "I'll leave it. I mean who am I? Just some scouse guttersnipe! And we wouldn't want to upset your mother, would we?"

"Kitty, please." Nigel saw the light go on in the back of the kitchen and someone pass the window.

Kitty turned away. She felt wounded, hurt. In her eyes Eunice Hanley was to blame and she would make her pay for it. "Oh you think your mother's so bloody high and mighty, don't you. Well, I've been trying to see you since last week to

237

tell you something. I saw her in London with a man. Going into a flat *with* a man. Arm in arm. What do you think of that?"

Nigel was incensed. He reached forward and grabbed Kitty by the shoulders and shook her. "You bitch, what a thing to say!"

"Bitch is it now? Bitch!" She twisted out of his grasp and slammed her open hand across his face.

"Nigel, for God's sake." They both spun round, shocked. Elizabeth had come out of the back door. "Kitty, what's wrong?" For all their differences in class the two girls liked one another. Elizabeth saw a spark in Kitty, a raw vitality that she preferred to the apathetic country club attitudes at her boarding school. For a brief second Kitty glanced at her then stepped away towards the darkness of the garage.

"Isn't anyone going to tell me what's going on?"

"Nothing, Elizabeth. We just had an argument." Nigel was angrily dismissive.

"What did I hear about my mother."

"Just some nasty little piece of gossip."

Kitty glared at him. She was furious. "Gossip!" She had stewed for days over what to tell Nigel, ever since last week when she had been up in London delivering the usual packages for Eddie Brent. She wasn't supposed to know that they were full of money but she would have been dumb to have missed it! Why else would she have to visit every sleazy bookie in Soho? But on this particular day Eddie had asked her to deliver one of those other letters to the flat behind the Albert Hall. The building was in Queen's Gate Gardens. The front door was open as usual, and so she stepped into the small hall. There was an inside door of elegantly decorated glass and to the right, a small table. Above that, four bell-buttons with names and numbers of flats written beside them. The number on the envelope was four and she noted that the name opposite bell number four was Commander Hans Weichert. She had left the envelope as usual and was starting down the street when a big car pulled up behind her. She heard the driver ask, "And when should I pick you up, Commander?" She quickly glanced round and was stunned to see Eunice Hanley arm in arm with a blond, handsome stranger.

Elizabeth suddenly interrupted her thoughts. "Come on, Kitty, what is it?" She gently touched her on the arm and then turned on the light over the workbench.

Nigel shuffled in to the garage and slumped back against the car. "Elizabeth, leave it, Kitty and I just had an argument, and I'm sorry."

Kitty stared at him. She did not want to continue but knew that she could not leave it there. "Nigel, I didn't say that just to annoy you. I did see your mother going into that house with a man."

"What?" Elizabeth was all ears. "What did you say?"

Kitty took a deep breath and told her story. At the end Nigel seemed stunned and upset, but Elizabeth looked coldly angry. She shook her head, her eyes gleaming. "But who was it, I would love to know who the man was."

Kitty nervously cleared her throat. She did not want to admit that she was delivering a letter to Weichert. Something told her to keep that to herself. "I, I overheard the driver. It was a foreign name, Weichert." She was not prepared for the reaction.

Elizabeth gave a whoop of horror. "My God, Nigel. My God, that's the German chap, the German naval attaché who was at the launching." Elizabeth shook her head, flicking back her blonde hair. "God! Now I remember. And last week, I took a message for her, some man with a foreign accent rang up and said something about tickets to be collected for the Albert Hall that afternoon." She bit down on her lip and then spat out angrily. "Bastard, bloody bastard, using me to do his dirty work."

"Elizabeth, stop it!" Nigel gave a long tired sigh and crossed to the bench. "Listen, it could all just be innocent."

"Innocent be damned. You don't believe that!"

"I don't think we should argue – here."

The "here" referred to Kitty but she did not register it. Her mind was elsewhere, trying to make sense of something that Elizabeth had just said. "The German naval attaché". Images and thoughts chased one another. What was in the envelopes she delivered to him from Eddie? Who was the British naval man she had glimpsed that night at Jimmy Lee's?

"Kitty."

No, no, she wouldn't think about that. It wasn't her business.

"Kitty." Nigel was gently persistent. "I think I'd better take you home." He sounded crushed, tired, and she began to feel guilty about what she had told him.

Kitty nodded. "All right."

"Elizabeth, just wait for me, all right? Don't talk to Mother, promise?"

Elizabeth merely nodded in response. Meanwhile Kitty walked to the door of the garage and stopped. "Elizabeth, I'm sorry, maybe I shouldn't have . . ."

Elizabeth looked up from the floor and gave her a broad smile. "It's all right Kitty, it's not your fault. It's not *your* fault!"

Eunice sat in the music room, sipping a glass of brandy and listening to *Carmen* on the gramophone. As she gazed out of the front window into the night beyond she felt a heavy sadness. Weichert had flown to Paris just a few hours ago, on his way to Rome for meetings. He would be gone for three weeks, he had said. She was missing him already. She had wanted to stay with him over the Easter weekend and had only been dissuaded by Olivia Bramley's cynical advice, "Darling, I never fornicate on holy days, holidays and family feasts . . . it's just asking to be pilloried."

So! She had stayed at home all through Easter although she might just as well have been in Tibet for all the difference it made to Hanley.

The sound of Nigel's motorbike rattling back out along the driveway brought her to her feet. She stared out of the window and saw a young woman sitting on the back. She was just taking another sip of brandy when a movement drew her eye to the hall door.

"Elizabeth!" She almost dropped the glass in fright. Elizabeth was standing stony-faced, silent. "What in God's name are you doing lurking in the hall, you frightened me to death." Eunice stepped towards the coffee table and pulled a cigarette out of

240

the silver box with a shaking hand. "I see Nigel invited his little shopgirl home again."

"Do you object?" Elizabeth's voice had a sharp, cold edge to it.

Eunice took a drag of the cigarette and then fixed Elizabeth with a steely glance. "Yes miss, I do object. I don't like the girl. I think she's cheap." Eunice finished off the brandy, and then plonked the empty glass down on the coffee table with a clatter. "And while we're at it, I don't like the kind of people you've taken to associating with – that bolshy young Terry – "

"*You* don't like!" Elizabeth stepped into the light of the room and for the first time Eunice noticed the strange glitter in her eyes. "Is that what you said? *You* don't like!" She walked slowly behind Eunice's chair and up towards the gramophone, all the time keeping brittle eye-contact with her mother. "Did you say *you* object to my friends?"

Eunice took a deep drag from her cigarette and then nervously flicked the end of it with her thumb. "I don't *like* your tone, young lady, and you'd better watch yourself, or I tell you I'll . . ."

Elizabeth pounced. Her voice was shaking with anger. "I'd better watch *myself*! You were with a man in London. I took the sleazy message for you! I feel like a fool. Tickets for the Albert Hall! You've been having an affair. All these months you've been having an affair!"

Eunice was at first stunned and then incensed. She strode across the room and planted herself in front of her daughter. "Stop! Do you hear me? Stop!"

"No I won't stop. Why should I stop? It's the truth? Isn't it? Isn't it?"

Eunice snarled, "You lying little cow!" She stepped back and then swung at Elizabeth, intending to slap her full across the face. But Elizabeth anticipated the blow and grabbed her mother by the forearm. Eunice staggered sideways as hand and forearm slammed together. Then she winced at Elizabeth's iron grip clamped around her wrist.

"Lying? I'm not lying!" Elizabeth's mouth was now a grim slit of anger and her breath came in short hot bursts. Eunice

241

tried to wrench her arm free but Elizabeth lunged forward and tightened her grip again.

Eunice shouted out in pain. "Let me go this instant or I shall call your . . ." She stopped before she said it.

Elizabeth gave a bitter laugh. "Father? Father?" Angry white flecks of spittle edged around her quivering lips, and she pulled her voice back to a deep whisper. "Why don't you call Mr Weichert, your German boyfriend, Herr Weichert . . ."

"Stop!" Eunice's reply was half screech, half shout. There was a split second of raw-edged silence. Then Hanley's voice ripped across the room.

"What in the name of God is going on?"

Eunice spun round. She suddenly felt like a naughty schoolgirl caught breaking the rules. All she could see in his face was the rigid inflexibility of the stern authoritarian and she felt trapped.

"You, you put her up to this! You couldn't face it yourself. Couldn't accuse me yourself." She strode behind the sofa and gripping the back, leaned over as if it was a lectern. "I don't give a damn, you understand. I don't give a fiddler's damn."

Hanley shook his head in disbelief. "Are you insane? Good God, keep your voice down! You've been drinking again, haven't you, haven't you?"

She burst out with a semihysterical laugh, "Oh yes, drinking! There must be some fault in me, some other reason. It couldn't be you. It couldn't be us."

"Eunice!" He barked at her as if she was some insubordinate midshipman. "I beg you! Whatever this is, not in front of Elizabeth!"

Eunice threw up her hands in a gesture of amazement. She had caught the unrealistic fatherly image of the innocent daughter in his comment. "Oh yes, our *little* Elizabeth! The one who's just accused me of having an affair!"

Eunice's head was reeling. She felt consumed with anger and fear and sorrow. And yet through it all a clear clean line of thought emerged. She should finish it all here and now. Finish with the past. Finish with all the subterfuge and lies.

"Well damn you. It's true, I am having an affair."

"What?" The word came out as a breathy mumble.

Eunice was trembling but trying for all the world to keep a tight rein on her tears. "I'm sorry, but that's it, with Hans Weichert . . ."

Hanley flinched as if someone had just struck him a blow in the stomach. "Commander Weichert? At the German Embassy?" He looked at her aghast.

Eunice sank her nails into the brown velvet fabric of the sofa, as if holding on to her sanity. "Oh yes, damn you! That's the important thing, isn't it – that he's the competition, the enemy – not that your coldness has finally driven me away. Not that I love someone else . . ."

Her nails made a tearing sound along the fabric of the sofa as she wrenched her hands free. "I'm going. I've had enough." She quickly brushed the tears away. "I've had enough of pretence . . ." Eunice strode past him towards the door. "I'm leaving tonight. I'll be staying with Olivia."

She disappeared into the hall. Apart from her footsteps on the stairs all was silence.

"I'm sorry, Daddy, I didn't . . ."

Hanley held up his hand and she stopped. He didn't want anything said. After all, what was there to say? He turned from his daughter and glanced towards the hall. He felt as if a hurricane had just passed by, and he was left looking at the wreckage. But there was nothing that he could do, nothing that could be fixed.

Weichert. He would have to tell Marsh. He lifted his hand and pressed his thumb and fingers into his temples. The very thought pained him, but it would have to be done.

31

"Kitty, here quickly."

Susie had grabbed Kitty as soon as she stepped into the foyer of the Parrot and dragged her across the crowded dance-floor towards the back of the bandstand.

"He's in here." Susie pushed open the kitchen door and Kitty gave a gasp of fright. Ernie was lying on the table, his knees pulled up and his hands clutching at his stomach, groaning. Tom and Eddie stood beside him and Jimmy Lee hovered near the door.

Kitty pushed past them and grabbed Ernie's arm. He looked up at her, his mouth slack, his eyes vacant, the pupils dilated like black inkspots.

"Holy Jesus, what's wrong with him?"

"He's all right. It's all right. He'll be okay – isn't that right, Jimmy?"

Jimmy nodded slowly. "Yes, I have seen before. He will be all right now." He stepped back from the light and retreated into the shadows at the rear of the kitchen.

Ernie made another guttural sound like someone about to throw up. Kitty fell to her knees beside him. "Ernie, for Chrissake lar, what is it?" He continued to stare at her with unseeing eyes then his head rolled back on the hard surface of the table.

"Here, this is what I went for." Susie pushed a bottle of smelling salts under his nose, and he started a wheezing coughing.

"Lemme sleep. Lemme sleep . . ."

Kitty edged in beside Susie again and gently rubbed her hand over his forehead. It felt cold and damp with sweat.

"He'll be all right when he sleeps it off." Brent's voice was tense, as if he was about to explode at any minute.

"Well he can't bloody well sleep on top of the table." Tom was indignant.

"Listen my old sparrow, I wasn't intending to leave him lying here like a loaf of bread. We can take him over to Jimmy's place."

"Excuse me!" Kitty glared at them. "But don't you think you should be taking him to a doctor or something, I mean what the hell's wrong with him?" Kitty's tone was raspingly sarcastic.

There was silence. Brent took measure of the situation and then flashed her an easy, confident smile. "He's, he's just taken something, Kitty, that's all. He'll be all right."

"Poison?" Kitty stared at him wide-eyed, uncomprehending.

"Fucking poison all right," Tom mumbled as he averted his face.

"Oh my God, what?"

Brent glared at Tom and there was a dangerous gleam in his eyes. "Kitty, it's drugs . . . he got some bad drugs."

"Drugs?" Kitty's face registered complete confusion. It was almost a foreign word to her. "I, I don't understand . . ."

Tom shrugged as if he didn't understand it himself. "He took this stuff called heroin – too much or something . . ."

Brent smacked his hand against the table. "Listen, he'll be all right, but it's the last bloody time he does it here. He's fired. I'm not having drugs in my club. I've always said that, so there's no big surprise." A look passed between him and Jimmy Lee, then he continued, "Come on, Tom, help Jimmy over with him."

"It's okay, I can carry him myself."

Kitty was still angry. "We should take him home."

"Oh yes, and let Ma see this . . . for Chrissake, Kitty, let's get him sober first."

Tom slid his hands under Ernie's shoulders and legs and then picked him up. As Kitty watched she had a flash of memory from childhood. Tom acting as father, carrying an injured Ernie up the long dark flights of stairs to that slum in Liverpool. Things hadn't changed, Ernie was still a child, still getting into trouble, still needing someone to look after him.

"Are you going over with them, Kitty?" She shook her head and Brent closed the door.

"Are you really going to fire him?"

Brent saw the icy look in her eye. She may have been just a kid but she was already a woman to be reckoned with. He returned her strong look and then glanced at the empty table. "Yeah, I'm going to fire him. He's history. He's a loser, Kitty – this was a great little number for him."

He expected her to say something but she simply lowered her eyes and stared at the bottom of the door.

"Kitty, I wouldn't want to lose you." He paused again, but she still said nothing. After a moment he crossed to the door leading back into the club and opened it. The music of the band poured in. They were playing "Is It True What They Say About Dixie" and its lively beat seemed peculiarly incongruous. "I'll be in my office if you want to talk."

Ten minutes later, Brent heard a sharp rap on his door.

"Yeah?" He cleared away a pile of letters and invoices as Kitty walked in.

She had only been into his office twice before. It was strange, but for all his pretended bonhomie, Brent was a very private man.

"Close the door, Kitty, I can't hear myself think."

Kitty shut out the noise of the band, and walked over to his desk. Just behind him on the wall she noticed a large photograph of an old lady surrounded by flowers. She stared at it as she sat down. Brent glanced over his shoulder then quickly turned back and pinned her with a narrow gaze. "That's my old duchess. I just put it up there last week."

Kitty looked at him quizzically. "Your mam?"

"Yeah, I've got a house for her out on the Maidstone road . . . loves fuchsias and orchids – grows them for a hobby . . ." Brent watched her constantly as he spoke. It was as if he was looking for a smile or the slightest sign of contempt, like some wary animal revealing a weakness and waiting for the blow.

246

But Kitty could only feel an increased curiosity at seeing this new side of him. She gave a gentle smile. "She looks great. I wish I could do that for my mam."

Brent nodded absent-mindedly. "Listen, Kitty, I'm sorry about Ernie . . ."

Kitty sat forward on the edge of the chair and fixed him with a penetrating gaze. "He got the stuff here, at Jimmy Lee's. Didn't he?"

"I didn't want Ernie over there. I don't want anyone who works for me dabbling with that shit. I warned him . . ."

"Stop, Eddie, you don't have to say any more. I just wanted to know what happened. I know Ernie's a dead beat – Christ knows I've got him out of enough scrapes before – "

She left the "before" hanging and Brent picked up on it. He gave a smile. "He'll be all right. I'll talk to a few of the lads with clubs in London. Don't you worry your head about it any more, he won't be short of a few, I can tell you." Brent got up and walked to a small cabinet along the back wall. "Now, what about a drink?"

Kitty watched him pouring her a gin and tonic and suddenly she felt a tremble of excitement. In a flash she understood that she had nothing to lose. She was either going to spend her life like her brothers, taking orders from others, being a victim like Ernie, or she was going to grab the moment by the balls. She smiled. The image appealed to her. That was what she needed to do, grab LIFE by the balls!

She took a deep breath. "I never told you, but when I was in London the other day, I saw something kinda strange." Now she had started she began to enjoy it. She slowed down. Patience! Wasn't that what her Uncle Wally said you needed to catch a fish? Patience! "Nigel's my friend you know and I, well, I saw his mother going into that house. You know, the one where I deliver those envelopes. She was going in with a man called Commander Weichert."

Brent suddenly spun round, his eyes gleaming dangerously. Everything else had passed over his head, except "Weichert". "How did you find out his name?"

Kitty stared at him, looking as wide-eyed and innocent as she could manage. "It was on the bell for his flat, behind the door. I'd never looked before, but I was so shocked to see her there with him that I . . ."

"Yeah, yeah, I see. I see . . ." Brent started to drum his fingers along the brown leather back of the chair.

Kitty continued with her story but Brent was obviously distracted. Finally he interrupted her. "Nigel. That's Captain Hanley's kid then?" He lingered over the word "captain" just long enough to show his concern.

"Yes." She sensed his unease and decided to go for the big one. There was a certain thrill in facing out his anger like this. "You know, the thing that really seemed to upset Nigel was, well, he said that this man Weichert was in the German Embassy."

Brent visibly flinched. "Did he want to know why you were there?" Brent tried to make the question as casual as possible, but Kitty could hear the strain in his voice.

"Yes . . ." She lingered for a moment, enjoying her power as she watched the tense expectation in his face. "Yes, he did want to know, but I – I dunno why – I just thought I shouldn't tell him, you know, the truth. So I said that I was just delivering something in the neighbourhood and had like, you know, walked up the street by accident."

"So he doesn't know about . . ." He stopped in mid-sentence as the realisation sank in, then allowed himself a smile of relief and sank back into the armchair.

Kitty pounced. She flashed him a bright innocent smile. "No that's right, he doesn't know about me delivering packages from you to Commander Weichert . . ."

There was an icy silence. Brent stared at her. The smile was still there but he also noticed that hard gleam in her eye. She held his look and then continued, "And of course he'll *never* know, not from me." Her voice was quiet, but steady and firm as a rock, as if to say, "Test me".

Brent continued to stare at her, biting his lip, deep in thought. Then his face slowly relaxed and he gave a dry chortle.

"I believe that, Miss Cullen . . . I really do."

He brought the drinks over to her. "Cheers!" They clinked

glasses and drank. He watched her as she lowered the glass and noticed the liquor glistening on the full curve of her lips.

Kitty saw the spark in his eyes and she knew that she had started to climb another step away from the tenements. It was no surprise when his hand came up and gently stroked her face, instead the gesture was reassuring. She had not gauged him wrong.

His hand lingered on her cheek then playfully tapped her chin. "I know you've been thinking about it, Miss Cullen, but perhaps now's the time you should think of taking a place of your own."

"What?"

"You 'eard me. I got a nice property on the top of Brompton Hill . . . a nice flat at the top."

"You know I couldn't afford that."

"No! I don't know that. I'd be your landlord remember. You'd just move in." Brent crossed to his desk and picked up a set of keys.

"Eddie, I . . ." It was one of the rare occasions when Kitty found herself fumbling for words. She knew that this was an important moment of choice. She could escape the squalor of Chichester Street, but what would she have to give in return? She stared down at the bubbles in her drink. "I eh . . . What do you expect for this, Eddie?"

There was a long silence in the room. Outside, the band was playing but it seemed to belong to a different world. Brent jangled the keys in his hand and took a deep breath. She could tell that he had not taken her question well.

"I expect nothing, Kitty. I've never expected nothing outta life. I've fuckin' always taken it."

At that precise moment she thought he was going to spring at her. He seemed poised on the edge, like an animal about to pounce. His eyes had an almost feral gleam and every small movement seemed charged. She waited. He took another deep breath. Then the tension around his mouth gave way to a smile. "And it isn't what you think. With you, Kitty, I'm gonna wait till you come to me."

He turned and dropped the keys into a glass bowl on his desk then slowly walked to the door and opened it. The raucous sounds of the crowded club swept around them.

"Eddie!"

He stopped, but still continued staring at the smoky dance-floor beyond.

"Eddie, come back."

He turned and gazed at her, lightly stroking his finger over his moustache. "I want you to know, Miss Cullen, that I've never walked back for any woman before."

"If I did take this place, it wouldn't mean I'd belong to you, or anything like that?"

Eddie gave a grunting laugh. "I reckoned you'd never belong to anyone, that's why I like you, 'cause you're like me."

Kitty stared into his eyes and in a flash understood how alike they really were. With that awareness came a flood of sympathetic feelings. Very purposefully she walked across to the door and slipped her arms around his neck. He was not handsome in the wild and sensual way that Nigel was, but he had that directed energy, that strength and will to survive.

She drew him back into the room and closed the door. They needed to be alone.

32

The most difficult part of Eunice's revelation was the fact that it forced Hanley to tell Marsh. Even the thought of that set his teeth on edge. Eunice left the house the same night as the argument, and first thing the following morning Hanley phoned the Admiralty and left a message for Marsh.

Marsh did not return his call. But the next evening, Friday, Hanley returned to his office to find him standing by the window, gazing out towards the Medway.

"Hope you don't mind, I let myself in."

"No, not at all."

Hanley crossed to his desk, flicked on the green-shaded lamp and unconsciously scrutinised his files to see if they had been disturbed in any way. When he looked up, Marsh was staring at him with those intense grey-blue eyes.

"Your secretaries seem to have melted into the weekend already." As he was talking he moved away from the window and circled around to the other side of Hanley's desk. ". . . And Warrant Officer Campbell didn't seem to be here."

Marsh had an annoying habit of delivering sentences that were neither full statements nor full questions. Hanley, however, felt obliged to explain. "Yes, I eh . . . he needed some time off. He should be back next week."

"Ah I see." Marsh sat down and pulled out his cigarette case. Then he took out a cigarette and slowly turned it, alternately tapping each end on the metal. "You wanted to see me?"

"I wanted to give you some information. I didn't mean to drag you down here. I'm sorry about that. I think a phone conversation would have been sufficient."

"Perhaps, we'll see."

Hanley peered at Marsh over the top of the green shade and wondered what exactly that meant. For a few moments he watched the blue smoke curling up from Marsh's cigarette and drifting into the broad cone of light cast by the lamp. He felt thoroughly awkward.

"My wife and I have separated. I believe she's gone to the house of an old friend in London," Hanley paused and Marsh simply stared at him, with unemotional eyes. As he watched Marsh he felt a cold sweat breaking out around his neck and down along his back. Why, of all people, should he be forced to expose his private life to Marsh?

"You may think this is a personal matter but I . . ." He found his throat drying and quickly stepped across to the window as he cleared it. He glanced out, unseeing, into the evening and then turned back to the still silent Marsh. "The thing is, she tells me that she's been having an affair

251

with, well, with Weichert, the naval attaché at the German Embassy."

Hanley spoke in a clear, calm voice but in fact he felt consumed with anger. He slid his hands into his pockets so that Marsh would not notice his clenched fists, then quickly pulled them out again and walked back to his desk. Marsh's silence had completely unnerved him and he felt obliged to continue. "So I'm telling you, because it is possible, in the light of our previous conversation, that she has been, well, used. I mean I do bring, and have brought, papers home."

Hanley felt sick as he spoke these words. He looked over at the other man and raised his eyebrow, indicating that he was waiting for a response.

Marsh simply nodded. He took another deep drag of his cigarette and then sat forward. "Yes, we believe that's a strong possibility."

Hanley's mouth fell open, like a child piecing together an impossible puzzle. "What do you mean 'we believe'? You mean . . ." Hanley fumbled through the words, until his voice finally faded away.

Marsh took a final drag of his cigarette and then stretched across the desk and stubbed it out in the overflowing ashtray. "You see, Hanley, we've known for a long time about Eunice and Weichert. We've actually had them followed."

Hanley felt a sudden flash of cold, bitter anger. He glared at Marsh, "You mean, all this time, I . . ."

Marsh shrugged. "You have to understand that we have a delicate situation with Grainger and the radar. We know that our red herring, our cover story about the acoustic-magnetic torpedo, is being accepted in Germany. We still don't know who is leaking this information. It could be anyone, anyone, you understand. So the most important thing is that we couldn't, and can't, rock the boat."

Marsh spoke in clear, logical terms like a maths teacher trying to hold the attention of his last class of the day. But Hanley was not impressed by such cold reasoning. He felt used, betrayed.

Suddenly his temper snapped. He pushed himself back from the desk, shaking the trays and pens and knocking files off the edge. They fell to the floor, bursting open and scattering papers and drawings everywhere. He stood up, glanced away and then quickly turned back, slicing his finger through the air like a knife.

"I've wanted to say this for a long time, Marsh, you're a bastard, a cold bastard. I have to work with you and I will, work with you. But to have known for all these months what was going on and not to tell me . . ."

Hanley smashed his fist against the back of his chair and sent it hurtling towards the wall behind him. Then he strode around the desk, across the room and stopped at the door. "If you want me I'll be at Pembroke Barracks, in the wardroom. At the bar." He turned away and then instantly swung back. "And you probably will want. I'm sure you have the remainder of my marriage carefully plotted out as well."

Hanley slammed the door behind him, and then made his way up to the wardroom in HMS *Pembroke*. Marsh joined him an hour and five gins later. By then Hanley's anger had ebbed and he was beginning to feel grimly numb.

But just as Hanley had suspected, Marsh had no words of comfort, only a new batch of orders. "They had to keep the status quo – Eunice could not be 'apprised' of any suspicions – if nothing new turned up in Germany then they could be almost certain it was her, since she no longer had access . . ."

Marsh had then left Hanley alone with his gin. It was an unusual sight in the mess and one that caused many a turned head. Hanley was not a drinker but now, just this once, he was glad of its numbing qualities.

He could not get Eunice out of his mind. He could in some measure understand her anger, her drinking, her arguments, even the affair; all of that. But there was one thing he could neither understand nor believe. The very thought of it screwed him into a black despair. No. Surely Eunice couldn't have taken papers and plans from his study at home? She could not be a traitor. It was an act beyond his comprehension.

That night, for the first time ever he drank alone and drank till the bottle was finished. And the next day he returned to his true salvation. His work. And his duty.

33

A chill, pre-dawn breeze idly flapped the rows of triangular bunting hanging between the dockside lampposts. Underneath, the last of the workmen hurried along the pier towards the *Graplin*'s gangplanks.

Hanley stood midships near the bottom of the conning tower, watching the final stragglers, and then glanced past the flags and the cardboard placards, with their photographs of the new King, George VI, towards the first pink grey glow of dawn.

He heard someone clattering down the steps from the bridge above him. "Lieutenant Commander Crowe thought you might like to glance over the orders, sir." Lieutenant Farnsworth, the young engineering officer, appeared beside him, with a clipboard full of papers. Hanley glanced at him for a moment. He had that full, confident face of the young, that gleaming eye of invulnerability. Hanley took the clipboard and gave a businesslike nod.

"How come they've got you as a messenger boy, Farnsworth? Isn't there enough to do in the engine room?"

Farnsworth gave a cheery laugh. "It's all under control, sir." Then he raised an eyebrow and continued, "I'm just trying to stay abovedecks as long as possible. It's like a tin of sardines down there."

Hanley glanced down at the lading. "*Graplin*. First diving and torpedo equipment trials. Wednesday 19th May 1937." He ran his finger along the passenger list. The *Graplin*'s normal

254

complement was 59, the papers listed 113, that meant 54 extra officers, dockyard workmen and scientists.

"Just par for the course on the first test trial, Farnsworth. Everyone wants to get a first look."

"I suppose so. Anyway I'd better take my last breath of fresh air and get below."

Hanley heard the note of excitement in the young man's voice. The first sea trials of a submarine were always something special. They could test and test all they wanted in the dockyard basins, but for a submariner the only real trial was a sea trial.

As Farnsworth walked briskly for'ard Hanley saw a group of fitters around the torpedo loading-hatch. They were waving newspapers and jeering with each other about the cricket scores and as he listened, he wished he could have shared their enjoyment of the trivial, their ability to live in the moment. But he couldn't, he felt weighted down with responsibilities.

He heard a shout above him and looked up at the mast above the bridge, where a young midshipman was unfurling the white ensign. As he watched the flag flapping out to its full length, he noticed the strangely curved, metal shape of Grainger's radio detection receiver just behind it. Then he saw Grainger himself on the bridge. He was obviously working on the wiring and the connections, bobbing up and down like a curly-haired student let loose among a group of serious-faced, white-capped officers.

Seeing Grainger working at his radar apparatus brought the whole bloody mess about Eunice and Weichert to the forefront of Hanley's mind again.

He gripped the *Graplin*'s guardrail and then squeezed the metal, as if he could somehow wring the whole terrible incident from his memory. But he couldn't. He had lived with the knowledge for almost six weeks now and still there had been no resolution. They would neither clear her name nor charge her.

"Looks like smooth sailing today, sir."

Hanley spun round and saw Campbell standing beside him.

"I love a red sky in the morning, always forget though whether it's a shepherd's delight or a sailor's warning."

Campbell gave a muffled laugh. "Good Lord, I made that rhyme."

Hanley nodded distantly. Campbell seemed in an unusually good mood. "You seem very cheery this morning, Mr Campbell."

Campbell seemed to stiffen. He glanced away for a moment and Hanley noticed him nibbling nervously on the inside of his lip.

Up for'ard the tug hooted as it tightened its line. There was a slight shudder and then the *Graplin* moved gently forward, into the river. Hanley glanced up past the still dripping, green-and-brown-slimed gates and saw groups of workmen above, following the *Graplin*, walking along the top of the dock. They gathered at the end of the Bull Nose and cheered as they saw the submarine passing below them. Behind him, Hanley could hear the sad echo as the sound rang hollowly along the wet dock walls.

Campbell watched them as well and gave a distant smile. "I've made up my mind about a few things during the last few weeks." Then he took a deep breath like a wine connoisseur sipping a rare vintage. As he breathed out he gave a satisfied laugh. "This is going to be my last trip, and by God I'm going to enjoy it."

"Last trip?"

"Yes, sir. I shouldn't really have said that, it's a bit premature." Campbell shook his head and then gave a wry smile like a schoolboy who had spoken out of turn. "I'd like to see you first thing tomorrow morning and talk then, that is if we don't dock too late tonight."

Hanley knew when something should be pursued and when it should be dropped. He simply nodded. "Yes, of course."

"Anyway I must get below. First Lieutenant Pringle and Mr Gillings are starting a stage-by-stage check of the telemotor control valves to the for'ard and aft pumps . . ."

Hanley nodded and watched Campbell walking back towards the bridge. What was Campbell saying? Was he going to ask for a land posting closer to his wife?

Hanley suddenly laughed and turned away towards the open

water. Closeness. He had seen Eunice for a brief meeting in London earlier in the week and she had told him that she was planning to go and live in Germany with Weichert. Closeness. Oh yes, all through those years when he was struggling he had needed someone by his side. He had needed closeness but she was never really there. Oh, she would turn up at all the "right" times and smile and nod, but she had never shared the struggle. The most painful thing for him to admit was that class had come between them. He was the son of a shopkeeper who had proudly scrimped and saved to send him to a minor public school and Eunice had grown up as a young "lady", one of the county set, a woman who expected privilege as a birthright.

No, there had never been closeness and only now was he beginning to accept that as true.

The spray from the bows of the *Graplin* was shooting up over the boat like a fine mist. He breathed in its salty, refreshing coolness and stared out over the water as if hoping that the sea could somehow wipe away the past.

"Port ten, half ahead."

Hanley glanced up towards the bridge above him. Lieutenant Commander Crowe had just shouted down to the coxswain at the upper steering position.

"Port ten, half ahead." Chief Petty Officer Boyle's deep voice rumbled up from just below the bridge.

Almost immediately Hanley could feel the boat listing to port as it ploughed on towards the open sea and the appointed diving position some twenty miles east of Shoeburyness. He glanced out over the opaque water towards the Isle of Sheppey that lay to the south, off their starboard side. The sun shone down through a patchwork of clouds, and cast a dappled palette of greys across the choppy waves. For a moment he felt its mystery flooding over him; a mystery greater than all his personal troubles. No matter how skilled, every sailor knew he was finally unable to get the better of the sea, and unable to fully love her or hate her. She was there to be served.

Hanley stared at the glittering slivers of sunlight as they bounced on the breaking waves and he suddenly felt a deep sense of satisfaction. This was his home, this was his service. There was no betrayal here.

Gillings relished the last of his salmon sandwich then pulled the fob watch from his waistcoat pocket and clicked it open. It was one-fifteen. They would be starting their first dive soon. He flicked his fingernails against the side of the half-empty mug of tea. He felt agitated and wanted to get the day over as quickly as possible.

Terry was somewhere for'ard. He hadn't seen him yet, but he had already spoken with Grainger and later he had seen Reggie Dickson coming out of one of the heads. Gillings kept chewing it over in his mind. Yes, Terry was there, with the rest of the team, up in their "secret" closet. He wrestled with a residual bitterness on one side and a desire to talk to his son again on the other.

"Apple, pear, orange, anyone?"

A young petty officer was passing a large basket of fruit around the wardroom. The tiny area was crowded, but then so was everywhere else on board. Men were stretched out all along the walkways and squeezed into every nook and cranny. It was no wonder, after all, there were fifty-four extra dockyard workers and naval men on board for the trial.

Gillings waved the basket away, then got up and squeezed his way to the end of the table and on out into the passage. He glanced for'ard. All around men were finishing their lunch. The "big eats" as they called it, a special meal provided by the yards on all first sea trials. The men loved it, a bottle of beer, good sandwiches, cake, fruit.

"You 'ad one of these veal pies, Mr Gillings?"

Gillings turned. Len Gates, one of the electrical superintendents, was perched precariously on a red metal junction-box. He held up the half-eaten pie and gave a broad grin, as he wiped the sweat from his bald head. "They've outdone themselves this time."

Gillings nodded and gave a mischievous smile. "Better than a plateful of baby's head anyway."

There was a laugh from the workmen seated around the mess. Gillings carefully picked his way through the diners and walked aft towards the control room. Behind him he heard the beginnings of an argument on the merits of that particular dockyard delicacy, a small meat pudding, steamed in a cloth for hours. Gillings grimaced, it was something that he had never appreciated unless it was doused in HP sauce.

The control room was crowded but less so than the rest of the boat. Gillings walked past the helmsman's station. It took up a half wall looking for'ard. The helmsman's chair, which was towards the outside wall of the boat, was faced by a confusing collection of dials and levers, consisting of rudder indicators, clutch controls and dials indicating the revs of the diesel engines. Lieutenant Farnsworth, the young engineer officer, was standing beside the helmsman checking engine revs on one of the red-rimmed dials.

Gillings squeezed round the massive bulk of the periscope. Lieutenant Caldwell, the torpedo officer, was standing at the aft end of the diving panel, scanning the many pressure dials. "All seem in good order, Lieutenant?"

Caldwell looked round. "Oh yes, yes, Mr Gillings."

"Are we still on time for the first torpedo trials?" Gillings was obviously impatient.

Caldwell glanced at his watch and then looked up, nodding towards the conning tower and the bridge. "Well, we should be if we start diving within the next fifteen minutes, though it looks as though . . ."

As he was speaking he heard Lieutenant Commander Crowe's voice booming out over a megaphone above. "Tug *Merriweather* . . . Tug *Merriweather* . . . take your station one-third of a mile to my starboard quarter. The diving course will be 230 degrees."

Caldwell waved his clipboard. "There we are, right on the button. I'll get back on station."

Up above, the bridge was cleared and the conning-tower hatch closed and locked. Gillings heard the echoing clang of the metal and he felt a nerve jump in his stomach. They were finally sealed off from the outside world.

Caldwell was making his way for'ard, past the helmsman's station, towards the bow torpedo room when Lieutenant

Commander Crowe came clattering down the metal ladder from above. There was a growing tension and excitement in the air as Crowe stepped into the corner and took the telephone. "Chief Watson, radio C-in-C Plymouth, about to dive for four-hour duration. Standing by for torpedo trials and . . . er . . . Garden Shed experiments." It was obvious to everyone in the control room what Crowe thought of Grainger's intrusion on to his ship. "Give exact position."

Gillings watched as Crowe replaced the receiver and quickly stepped back towards the periscope. "Check all valves, sea-cocks, check bowcaps and telemotor controls."

A buzz went through the control room and travelled through the boat. All they awaited was confirmation from Plymouth that their diving position had been received and logged.

Gillings stepped back from the diving panel and glanced aft along the passageway towards the engine room. The diesels had been shut down and the electric motors turned on. He could see Chief Stoker Mitchell leaning back against the door, brushing the sweat from his brow and swigging from a bottle of beer. All around everyone waited. There was a sense of expectation, a gathering hush. No matter how well planned and how well built the *Graplin* was, everyone on board knew that this first sea dive was the true test.

"Excuse me, sir, but Dr Grainger wants to know when the first torpedo'll go."

Gillings immediately recognised his son's voice behind him. For a moment he determinedly stared towards the engine room.

"Tell him in an hour, if that's all right with him." Crowe's irritation was evident in his voice. "Anyway I thought the point of this magic box was . . . He was going to tell me about my torpedoes."

Gillings swung round. He was sympathetic with Terry's position. To say the least, the crew were not overly happy with Grainger and his experiments. Terry suddenly saw his father and caught the look. He glanced back towards Lieutenant Commander Crowe, nodded, and gave a wry smile. "Thank you, sir."

260

Then, as he turned, Terry flashed his father another tentative look. Gillings felt a moment of confusion and then a strange flicker of joy. And yet he could not smile, could not take that first step towards him. Terry turned away and walked for'ard but then stopped in the doorway and glanced back over his shoulder one more time, before he pushed his way up through the crowded passageway.

Gillings took a deep breath and turned towards the blueprints laid out beside him. It was just a diversion, something to do with his hands. Seeing his son again, at such close quarters, had thrown his mind into turmoil. In the weeks following the accident involving the young shipwright, he had thought a great deal about Terry's quick actions and firm resolve. Here was a mature young man, someone with initiative and courage, someone Gillings would normally respect, that is, if he hadn't . . .

"It's Chief Petty Officer Watson, sir. He's just received radio signal – C-in-C Plymouth acknowledge receipt of diving signal."

Gillings looked up from the tightly rolled corner of the blueprint. There was a moment of expectant silence then Crowe said firmly, "All right gentlemen, let's do it. Open up for diving. Slow time."

The whole control room suddenly came alive. Gillings saw Captain Hanley standing over by the helmsman with Warrant Officer Campbell next to him. To his left, the seamen at the diving panel were moving with the dexterity of musicians behind some great mechanical organ, spinning brass wheels and cotter pins, opening depth and pressure gauges and allowing the power of the telemotor to travel to all the control valves.

The first hiss of air immediately turned into a muted roar like the gasp of some gigantic animal preparing for struggle. Gillings felt a surge of adrenalin. He knew that the main ballast tanks were being flooded in pairs and that the *Graplin* was slowly and steadily settling into the sea. Gillings was a practical man, but there was always something about this moment that stirred him. Now the boat was truly coming to life, truly entering into its intended element.

261

Up above, the men on the tug *Merriweather* watched as the slate-grey waters washed across the *Graplin*'s decks. Next the railings disappeared, followed by the gun. Inch by inch the conning tower and bridge and mast slipped under the waves. Then, with a final swirl of white foam, the last evidence of the *Graplin* disappeared. It had successfully passed its first trial.

34

After the *Graplin* resurfaced, the hatches were opened and sweet, cool, tangy air percolated into the control room. The first dive had been perfect. Hanley took a few deep breaths, and then walked for'ard to try and find Grainger.

The small radar room was in fact no bigger than a cupboard and was locked from the inside. Hanley knocked.

Grainger opened the door looking wilder than ever, with his dark curly hair sticking out in jagged points. "I tell you, Hanley, I'm sick of this bloody Bulldog Drummond espionage rubbish!"

Hanley glanced past him at the screen. "Is everything functioning, Dr Grainger?"

"Seems to be now. We'll see what happens when we get down to periscope depth . . . which I hope will be within the next half-hour if they're going to shoot those torpedoes."

"What I don't understand is how you are going to track torpedoes when they're in the water?"

Grainger gave a grunt of disgust. "I'm pretty certain we can't, but Intelligence, Marsh that is, insist that we go through with their little charade," he gave a laugh "and we might surprise ourselves and actually come up with positive results. Anyway, the plane's due over at four o'clock and that's our real target."

"Prepare to dive. Periscope depth. Torpedo test . . ." The captain's voice crackled out over the speaker behind them.

"I'd better get back to the control room again, you don't seem to have much room to spare here, Dr Grainger."

"No. And, eh," for a brief moment Grainger looked almost shy. "Wish me luck with this one."

Hanley nodded and then closed the door carefully behind him. As he did, he heard the first whoosh of air into the ballast tanks. The *Graplin* was submerging once again.

"Damn stupid bastards. Apologies, Mr Gillings, I just wish I could get my hands on the man who did this."

Lieutenant Caldwell, the torpedo officer, was in the tube compartment of the bow torpedo room, leaning into the space between the tubes and pointing forward. Albert Gillings stepped over the coaming of the portside door and knelt beside him.

"One of my men just spotted that the bowcap indicators are numbered wrong."

Gillings gave an exasperated sigh as he took out his torch and shone it into the shadow of the tubes. "Bloody hell!" They were indeed numbered wrongly, one to four in sequence and five and six reversed.

Gillings turned awkwardly in the confined space. "Tell them to power the bowcaps to five and six in sequence and we can see what happens."

Caldwell shouted the order to the petty officer at the telephone position just beyond the tube compartment door. Petty Officer Edmunds was the TGM, the torpedo gunner's mate. He was a tall, fair-haired, athletically built young man in his mid-twenties and though he looked confident it was in fact his first posting as a TGM.

Caldwell squatted down beside Gillings and listened. Within a minute they heard the whirring sound of the telemotor in action.

Petty Officer Edmunds shouted from the telephone position, "Number five powered, sir."

Gillings held the torch steady and watched the indicator on six moving.

After about thirty seconds Edmunds shouted again. "Number six powered, sir."

Gillings and Caldwell saw the indicator on five moving. Gillings wiggled out from the space and gave a grunt. "Great! It's like reading Chinese, all arse about face."

Caldwell laughed as he slapped his hand against the edge of the oval-shaped steel door. "I'd better tell the captain . . . I think we can proceed though, now that we know the problem."

While Caldwell stepped over to the phone station Gillings glanced back at the massive steel tubes and experienced a feeling of uneasiness. He was about to say something when he heard Caldwell shouting, "All right, they're closing the caps, then we're going to blow the tubes. Let's prepare to load tube five." Then Caldwell added with a twinkle in his eye, "Or is that six?"

The torpedo stowage compartment was suddenly all activity. The torpedoes were stored along each wall of the compartment, in metal cradles. Hinged metal straps held them in place, fastened at the top by butterfly bolts. Now the sailors spun the bolts as they prepared to carefully roll out the first torpedo.

Caldwell stepped through the port door, in behind number-five tube. "Dawson!" A short, muscular seaman with cropped black hair joined him in the torpedo room. Caldwell pointed up front. "Check the bowcap manual indicators."

Dawson squatted down and Gillings noted with amusement the bosomy girl stretching voluptuously on his flexed bicep. He moved back to give Dawson room and then decided it was time to get out of the way. As he stepped back through the starboard door into the stowage compartment he kept close to the hull, away from the men struggling with the last of the torpedo straps.

Petty Officer Edmunds yelled forward from the phone position, "Caps closed, sir."

Caldwell glanced at his watch. "Dawson, what do the indicators say?"

"Both caps closed, sir."

Caldwell paused for a moment as if he was undecided, then said, "All right, blow tubes five and six."

264

Gillings heard the hissing explosion of air as the tubes cleared of water. But then he heard something more, a distant clunking sound. He looked over at Caldwell, but the lieutenant was busy checking the test cock lever in the middle of the torpedo tube door.

Caldwell shouted, "Tube clear of water." Then he turned and caught Gillings' eye, caught that glitter of doubt. After a second he added thoughtfully, "Hold on though . . . I think I'll recheck . . . we'll open up the drain valve."

Caldwell turned back and was leaning down to twist open the brass cock when the phone rang again. He stopped, with his hand on the gleaming wheel, and glanced up.

"It's the captain, sir, he says we're running out of time."

Caldwell glared at Edmunds as if it was his fault, then gave a hissing sigh. "All right, line up the torpedo, it's fine, I'm opening up the tube."

Gillings was stepping forward to tell him to wait, when he saw Terry walking into the compartment. Terry was carrying a stopwatch and a pad. He quickly took in the activity for'ard, then leaned back against the doorway in the second water-tight bulkhead. As he did so, he glanced over and saw his father.

Gillings felt that sheet of ice slicing between them. He wanted to take the few steps across the metal deck and say hello. But he couldn't. Those few steps were a chasm. Instead he turned away and focused on the men working in the bow.

He had barely turned when there was a roaring sound followed immediately by a shattering clang. For an instant Gillings' mind went blank, then the pieces of the puzzle fell together. The test cock in the rear door of the torpedo tube must have been faulty. It had shown dry but in fact the tube was flooded and the bowcap open to the sea.

Through the first valuable seconds everyone stood stunned. Then a shock wave of increased air pressure hit their ears and shook them into action. The *Graplin* shuddered and the first water licked over the edge of the coaming and into the stowage compartment. The sight of the frothing brine catapulted Gillings forward.

Caldwell was already shouting frantically, "The doors, the doors."

Gillings jumped in through the starboard door. Caldwell and Dawson already had the port door unlatched and were swinging it back to lock it. Number-five tube was wide open, just in front of the door and the water was gushing in mercilessly, a grey, icy stream of potential death. When the port door was swung halfway over the force of the water caught the back of it and slammed it shut.

Petty Officer Edmunds and another seaman immediately bolted the eighteen butterfly clips around its edge and for a moment the water leaking over the nine-inch-high coaming was halted. But it was only for a moment. Soon the water began to pour over the starboard door.

Caldwell had found himself on the wrong side of the roaring flood. He could not pass through its violent, thrusting flow so he tried to clamber over the top, taking footholds on the pipes and valves surrounding the tubes. As the brawny Dawson was reaching out to help him, the *Graplin* took a lurch in its slow descent downwards. Dawson was slammed forward against one of the tubes, smashing his chest on the rear doorhandles. He let out a muffled groan of pain. Caldwell struggled to keep his grip but finally fell backwards into the roaring explosion of water and slammed viciously against the bulkhead.

Gillings lunged forward and grabbed his collar, then he dragged him through the water, back towards the safety of the open door. Caldwell's forehead was gashed open. He was groaning but barely conscious. Gillings heaved him up to hoist him over the coaming.

"Here, here . . . Mr Gillings . . . get Dawson!"

The petty officer, Edmunds, had grabbed Caldwell under the arms and was dragging him back into the temporary safety of the stowage compartment. As he did, water sluiced across the floor, spilling into cracks and crevices.

Gillings was breathless. "Take him aft quick . . . I'll get Dawson . . ."

Dawson had slipped down into the water and was trembling with the cold. He was attempting to pull himself along the floor

266

whilst at the same time clutching his stomach and ribcage. Gillings waded through the flood and grabbed him under the arms. The water was bone-chilling and Gillings' lower legs were beginning to feel numb. He stumbled, then caught one of the drainage pipes to get his balance and wrenched the stocky young sailor up on to his feet. "Come on, Dawson, get the bloody hell out of here!"

Gillings half dragged him, half carried him to the door. Leading Seaman Smith saw them, left his end of the torpedo and ran over. But then there was another lurch forward as the angle of descent increased. Smith was a thin angular man and he tottered in mid-deck, flailing his arms like a drunken marionette. All round him, tools, loose pieces of pipe, beer bottles, sandwich boxes and clothing tumbled towards the bow but he staggered on.

"Here, here, I'm here."

With a massive effort Gillings pushed the injured Dawson out of the door and Smith pulled him up the deck and towards the second watertight bulkhead. The others strained to help, keeping their balance by holding on to the metal torpedo straps and even the torpedoes themselves.

All the time the water was pouring in. A relentless, frigid flow, swirling and foaming amongst the tubes and pipes and seacocks as if in mockery of the builders' efforts. What good was all the planning now? The sea was inside not out.

Gillings had staggered back towards the bow. He got behind the other door, released it and let it fall forward. Now all he had to do was to drag it "uphill" and then secure it from the stowage side. He glanced down and saw that the water was pouring over the coaming and aft into the stowage compartment. Since the angle of descent was in fact working against this, he knew that the bow must be filling up at a frightening rate.

Gillings started pulling the door uphill, then suddenly there was an ugly fizzing sound, followed by a strange gurgling hiss. Gillings experienced a moment of terror as he realised that the electrical circuits were fusing. He looked up. The lights blinked, came back again and then finally died.

The bow torpedo room and the stowage compartment were

267

both plunged into darkness and silence. Gillings gripped the metal edge of the door and squeezed hard, as if to reassure himself. Aft of him, beyond the door, pandemonium broke out. Seamen yelled out as they fought to keep their balance in the dark.

Edmunds shouted, "Who's for'ard?"

"I am . . . Gillings." Gillings stopped for breath and then shouted over the chaos again, "I'm closing this starboard door . . ."

In the blackness Gillings heard someone splashing beside him. He reached out. "Here, my hand." The other man took the hand, and pulled himself for'ard as he stepped over the coaming. "It's me, Dad."

There was a gaping silence filled only by the deadly roar of the sea. Gillings felt swamped by conflicting emotions. Then he slowly squeezed his boy's hand and could feel the pressure of love exerted in return.

"Good bloody lad. Come on, feel here . . ." He guided Terry's hand down to the edge of the door where he had maintained an iron grip. "There was a handle there. Let's pull together."

They strained and sweated until finally they got it within a foot of closing.

Behind them at the other end of the pitch-black stowage compartment they heard Edmunds yelling out, "Gillings, the captain says evacuate, evacuate. We're to close the second bulkhead door."

Gillings knew why. The water was quickly rising up the floor of the stowage compartment and if it lapped over the coaming into the next compartment aft, it would seep under the floor and into the batteries underneath. If the water hit those batteries the resulting chemical reaction would produce clouds of poisonous greenish-yellow chlorine fumes. That would mean a painful, suffocating death for all on board.

"Come on, Terry, we can do it!"

Terry could hear the grit in his father's voice and he gave a grim smile. They made another tremendous heave and then felt a surge of joy as they heard the clang.

Gillings immediately stretched up and flicked over the

topmost clip. The door was secure! As he tried for another, Edmunds' voice rang through the darkness again. "For Chrissake come out now!"

Gillings immediately grabbed Terry by the arm and they staggered over to the port side where they started clawing their way up the sloping deck, aft towards the second bulkhead. They were using any handholds they could get: torpedo straps, piping, valves. As they got closer they saw a light from beyond the bulkhead and realised, with relief, that it was just the electrics in the two for'ard compartments that had fused.

Suddenly there was a shuddering jolt that shook the whole boat from bow to stern. This was followed by a series of reverberations and then another jolt. The bow of the *Graplin* had obviously hit the sea-bed. Furniture flew, pipes broke, men crashed forward, tumbling against walls and doors and bunks. Gillings was caught completely unawares. One moment Terry felt his father just behind him, the next moment, Gillings was tumbling backwards into the darkness.

"Dad, Dad! I'm coming back."

"No. No!"

But Terry heard the agony in his father's voice and he shouted with full authority, "Yes. I'm coming back!" The boat was rocking and shuddering at the same time like a gigantic vibrating tube.

"Terry, watch out! A torpedo strap. It's loose." Gillings was breathless and his voice sounded weak.

Terry felt ahead of him with his hand. Two-thirds of the way along the top torpedo he found the sharp edge of the metal strap. He slammed it up out of his way and staggered on down the deck into the waist-high water.

"Dad?"

"Here, here . . ."

Terry bent forward, fumbling blindly, and finally found his father lying crumpled against the bow bulkhead. He knelt down in the freezing water, slipped his arm around his father's back and lifted him to his feet. Gillings groaned in pain and his legs went from under him.

"Dad, what is it?"

269

"The metal strap . . . slashed my chest . . . my arm . . ."

Terry waited to hear no more. He leaned over and slung his father across his shoulder, in a fireman's lift. Then he started back up the swaying deck, staggering under the weight. The icy water surged around him and tugged at his legs, so that each step was a hazard. It was an impossible task but somehow he found the strength.

Back at the second bulkhead they had recovered from the jarring crash and were starting to pull the door closed again.

Edmunds stepped forward into the pitch-black stowage compartment and saw vague shapes moving towards him. "Here, here," he extended his arm and Terry clasped it. Then Edmunds steadied himself and hauled the boy and his father up past him.

Terry staggered on, and the men at the door pulled both of them through. He made it to the side and then, exhausted, collapsed on to the deck. Behind them, the last back-breaking effort was made to pull the door closed. There was a satisfying clang as the metal lever was dropped into position and the bulkhead secured. It was just in time.

Terry caught his breath and then dragged his father back from the crush of men milling around the door. He laid him down on one of the beds in the seamen's mess, just aft of the bulkhead. In the brighter light he saw that his father's face was tight with pain and his right hand was clutching at the left side of his chest and his upper arm.

Terry tried to catch his breath. "Dad, how is it?"

Gillings grimaced and gave a guttural groan. He pointed towards his coat and Terry saw a spreading patch of darkness where his father's blood was seeping into the cloth.

"Oh God!" Terry pulled back the ripped coat and saw that the shirt was also torn. Beneath it there was a gash across his father's chest and he thought he could discern the grey-white of his ribs. He winced and turned aside.

Gillings saw the look and attempted a laugh. "Not too good, eh?"

Terry shook his head. "No, it's all right, but we just need the MO. You need to be bandaged."

Terry walked quickly into the passage and grabbed Edmunds. "Call the medic. He needs bandaging."

Edmunds looked dazed. His hair was plastered to his forehead and his uniform and face were smeared with grease and dirt. But hearing the word medic, he immediately crossed to the telephone station and phoned back to the control room.

Terry went straight back into the seamen's mess. "What the hell are you doing?"

Gillings was trying to pull himself up on the bunk. His face was white with pain and his jaw tightly clenched. Terry took him firmly by the shoulders and steered him back down on to the bed.

"Lie back, Dad, you'll be fine."

Edmunds leaned in through the open door. "MO's on his way. Listen, bloody good job you did. We just shone a torch through the window in the escape hatch. Looks like that starboard door might hold for a while . . ."

One of the seamen shouted from outside, "Petty Officer, it's Lieutenant Commander Crowe on the phone . . ." Edmunds backed out into the passageway and then crossed to the phone station near the second bulkhead door.

Terry turned to his father again. "D'you hear that? The other door into the bow torpedo room's held."

Gillings attempted a smile and then slowly shook his head. "We only got one of eighteen clips . . . we'll be lucky if it holds for an hour." He took another deep, painful breath and continued. "Still we did our best . . ." He stared up into Terry's eyes. "The both of us . . . that's something."

Terry looked at him for a long time, then gave a shy flicker of a smile, and turned his head away. There was nothing more to be said.

Outside, in the passageway, he heard Edmunds shouting out to his men. "The captain says we're cutting engines . . . prepare for the stern to sink until she levels off on the bottom."

Gillings pressed his head back against the pillow, in preparation for the impact. But it was not that that worried him. He was not the only man on board to feel a cold tremor when they heard the word "bottom".

271

35

Irene Gillings woke suddenly and sat up on the sofa. She was drenched in sweat and her heart was racing. She had had a frightening nightmare. She was standing beside the crumbling wall of the bitumen factory at the end of Agnew Street looking out over the Mersey. An old barge was berthed about twenty feet out from the dock of the factory. The river was calm, like a mirror, but Irene's mood was tense and expectant. Then, with an agonised screech, two people shot to the surface. She rushed forward and this time she saw that it was Terry and Albert. Both covered in blood, both wild eyed and desperate, screeching out for her help. "Irene . . ." "Mum . . ." "Irene . . ." "Mum . . ." Their calls interlaced one another as if in competition and yet she knew she was helpless to do anything for either of them.

She went into the kitchen, filled the kettle and put it on the stove. But when she tried to light the gas, her hand trembled so violently that she broke three matches in a row. Finally one lit and the gas ignited with a pop.

She tottered over to the kitchen table and collapsed into one of the chairs. What was wrong with her? She let her head sink into her hands and found herself starting to cry.

Then she slammed the table with her clenched fist. She wouldn't do that! She had had enough of tears. When Albert came home tonight, she would give him an ultimatum. Either he and Terry made it up or . . .

She glanced up at the kitchen clock. Four. Maybe they'd be forced to talk on the *Graplin*. They were both out on it today.

Slowly the full meaning of that hit her and her dream took on a more horrible aspect. It wasn't the struggle between Albert and Terry, it was the submarine, the submarine. She buried her head in her hands. "Oh God!" She felt as if she was going crazy. She'd soon be certifiable if she stayed cooped up in this kitchen any more.

She sat up straight and took a deep breath. She was being silly. She had the dinner to make. She had to go to the greengrocer's. As she stretched across the table for her purse, she heard the front door bell ring. She quickly took off her apron and made her way through the living room and down the hall, smoothing out her olive green skirt as she went.

Mary Cullen stood at the door, looking tired and somewhat bedraggled in an old overcoat with an incongruously bright silk scarf tied around her hair.

"Mary!"

Mary raised her eyebrows, looking like a little girl who had stolen an apple. Then she gave a wisplike smile and shrugged her shoulders as if to say, Here I am. "I'm sorry, Irene, if I'm in your way tell me to buzz off home. But it's just that Tom has this big fight in London tonight and, well, you know that Kitty's gone and left home now and she's living in some flat . . ."

Mary stopped in mid-stream. All through her barrage she had noticed Irene's eyes slowly widen. Then suddenly Irene burst into tears and stumbled over the threshold, throwing her arms around her cousin.

"Oh Mary, Mary, I'm delighted to see you. Come in. Come in."

36

The *Graplin* had finally settled on the sea-bed at three fifty-five. The final jarring shudders had snapped the one clip on the starboard door of the bow compartment. The effort by Gillings and Terry to secure number-one bulkhead had been in vain. Both of the for'ard compartments were now open to the sea.

There were two escape chambers on the boat. The for'ard chamber was built into the second bulkhead. It opened three ways, for'ard into the flooded torpedo stowage compartment, aft into the seamen's mess, and above through the escape hatch into the sea,

Hanley had just been inside the box-shaped chamber with Lieutenant Commander Crowe, peering through the glass scuttle with a torch. What they saw had been chilling. The two front compartments were now almost completely flooded.

They had said nothing to each other until they crawled back out through the circular entrance hatch at the bottom of the chamber. Then Crowe had turned and Hanley saw the panic in his eyes. "My God, we, I don't know . . ."

Hanley saw the glistening beads of sweat trickling down the other man's temples. He led him over to the portside hull of the boat and then waited for the seamen securing the entrance hatch to step away. When he spoke his voice was quiet but firm. "You will order the indicator buoy released, then fire a smoke candle from one of the guns that will give our position to the tug."

Crowe looked round at Hanley and slowly his eyes began to focus again as though he was managing to calm his initial panic.

Hanley went on, "We're lying at one hundred and sixty feet. Few, if any, could withstand the pressure of escaping at that depth. I would suggest that we slowly raise the stern so that the aft escape hatch is closer to the surface." Hanley paused and glanced around him to see that no one was close, then continued quietly, "That way we might just avoid a catas-trophe."

That word seemed to shake Crowe. He glanced back towards the escape chamber, then took a deep breath and drew himself up as if he was determined to reclaim his authority. "We could also attempt to close that rear door on number-five tube and pump the two for'ard compartments dry."

274

Hanley raised an eyebrow. "How?"

"We send a couple of men for'ard by the escape hatch and they can make their way through the stowage compartment and into the bow torpedo room."

"I don't believe that anyone can function long enough with the pressure at one hundred and sixty feet."

Crowe's eyes flashed. "Captain Hanley, if no one wants to do it, I'll do it myself."

Hanley was perturbed. There was something too emotional in Crowe's response.

"Lieutenant Commander Crowe, you will do no such thing." Hanley's voice was sharp-edged and tough. "I'll go before you. You're the captain of this boat until the very end."

Crowe glanced down and nervously tugged at the cuff of his jacket, running his thumb along the lowest ring of gold braid. "Yes, yes . . ." He nodded slowly. "Of course, you're right. But I have decided that we are going to try this."

Within half an hour they were making their preparations to go through into the flooded for'ard compartments. Hanley was doubtful of the outcome but he also knew that it was important to be doing something, in order to keep up the men's spirits. Meanwhile he had convinced Lieutenant Commander Crowe to start preparations for the attempt to raise the stern. This would not be a simple matter. They would have to pump out ten tons of fresh water and, after that, over fifty tons of fuel. Complete pumping systems would have to be adapted. It would take time and, meanwhile, the hopes of all on board could be focused on this expedition for'ard through the escape chamber.

There had been a number of volunteers. Hanley however had insisted that he should be one of the two men to attempt it. The other man was Petty Officer Edmunds. This made perfect sense since he was the torpedo gunner's mate and knew every inch of the two for'ard compartments.

Warrant Officer Campbell had brought Hanley a handful of bolts to help weight them down against the effects of the water. Edmunds was fitting on a Davis Submarine Escape Apparatus, and he laughed as he watched the bolts disappearing into Hanley's pockets. "Be nice if it was gold bars, eh sir?"

Hanley gave a wry smile. "Nowhere to spend it, Petty Officer, that's the trouble."

"I wish you would reconsider, sir. Let me go in your place." Campbell's voice was almost a whisper, but all the more forceful because of that. He continued, "You have family responsibilities."

Hanley slipped the last bolt into his jacket pocket and pulled on a pair of gloves. "So do you, Mr Campbell."

Campbell had picked up a DSEA and was holding it out for Hanley. There was a peculiar glint in his eye. "It just might serve us all best if I took the risks, sir."

Campbell had been acting strangely all day, like a man who was in a dream, and his talk had been full of such "meaningful" statements. But Hanley had no time now to think about Campbell. He simply avoided the whole matter by taking the DSEA set and strapping it on.

"Gentlemen." Lieutenant Commander Crowe came for'ard, glancing at his watch. It was already five o'clock. "Let's do it, when you're ready."

Leading Seaman Smith, one of Edmunds' torpedo crew, swung open the circular hatch at the bottom of the escape chamber. As he did, a welter of shouted good wishes came from the group standing around.

Hanley picked up the rope that would keep Edmunds and him tied together. As he straightened up he took one last look around and noticed the intensity of hope written on every face. Then he ducked down and crawled into the chamber. A moment later Edmunds followed him.

There was a ringing clang as the hatch was slammed, then a moment of absolute silence. Hanley handed one end of the rope to Edmunds and tied the other end around his waist. "Petty Officer, I've been through the diving school, some ten years ago I should add. But don't push yourself, only about twenty per cent of their intake can endure close to two hundred feet. If you feel dizziness, ear pains, chest pains, signal and we stop."

276

Edmunds nodded. "Yes, sir." Then he took a deep breath like a man making his resolve. "I'm ready."

They both put on the nose-clips and clamped their mouth-pieces between their teeth. Hanley looked towards the glass scuttle where he could see Crowe peering in and gave the thumbs-up sign.

They waited for about thirty seconds and then the first of the water began to flood in. It was grey and frigid, and as it swirled around his legs, Hanley shuddered with the first icy impact. Soon the water was up to their chests and Hanley could feel the pressure. It tugged and stretched at his clothes, binding them tightly to his skin, like bands of elastic.

The throaty click-click of the oxygen valve was a monotonous comfort. He was further reassured by the acid-tangy taste of his purified exhalations coming back through the container of soda-lime crystals. It all meant that his DSEA was working.

The water swirled above his head, tugging at his hair, and the pressure built in his ears. He blew against the nosepiece and, bit by bit, his ears popped and cleared. Hanley felt good. He focused his thoughts and went through each part of the journey for'ard, through the stowage compartment, up to the bow compartment door . . .

Suddenly he felt a desperate tugging on his arm. He turned as fast as the water would let him, and saw that Edmunds was sinking down the side of the chamber. His eyes were wide open and white with fear. He was pointing to his ears and grimacing so intently that the oxygen was bubbling thickly from his mouth. Hanley was reaching out to grab him when he heard the sound of the pumps being reversed. They must have seen Edmunds' plight.

It seemed like an age, but the escape chamber was finally drained to just below the level of the coaming. Edmunds was dragged out. He was groaning in pain and mumbling, "I'm sorry, sorry . . ." Crowe had him quickly taken aft to be tended by the MO.

As Hanley caught his breath he was offered a cup of cocoa. He gulped down a mouthful of the hot, sweet beverage and then

277

noticed that the engineering officer Lieutenant Farnsworth and Leading Seaman Smith were each strapping on a DSEA.

Lieutenant Commander Crowe motioned him aside. "We have two more volunteers."

Hanley shook his head frantically as he steadied his breathing. "No, just one. I'll go again."

"Excuse me, sir, but this isn't a time for heroics."

Hanley gave a choked laugh. "And you won't get any. It's a matter of statistics. At the very most about one in five of these men can take that water pressure. We know I'm one of them, let's hope one of these is another."

Crowe stared at Hanley for a brief second and then quickly turned away. "Farnsworth, you step down. Captain Hanley's going to try again. Good luck, Smith."

Smith nodded. "Thanks, sir." He glanced around, gave his mates a cheery grin and then crawled for'ard through the hatch. Hanley scrambled in after him. The contact with the air had brought on a wave of shivering and he wanted the renewed shock of cold water to be over as quickly as possible.

The hatch clanged shut, closing them into their own world. As Smith tied the wet rope around his waist Hanley scrutinised him. He was an athletic-looking young man, and looked as though he would be up to it. But Hanley knew that looks were no guarantee. The ability to withstand pressure was simply the luck of the draw.

There was a rapping signal on the glass scuttle and again the water started flooding in. Hanley felt it creeping up his legs like a tight rubber band unfurling over his skin. "Remember, Smith, just stop if it's too much. Same for me."

Smith nodded. Hanley checked his end of the rope. Then he lifted the torch from the jacket pocket of his uniform and shone it through the for'ard scuttle. The water in the torpedo stowage compartment looked dark and foreboding.

Inside the escape chamber it had risen up to chest level and he could already feel the pressure on his lower ribcage. He glanced over at Smith and the young man still seemed to be all right. Perhaps they would manage it this time. He knelt a bit lower into the rising water and felt for the lever of the for'ard

278

opening hatch. Yes, there it was! He quickly straightened up and bit into the end of the oxygen tube. As he took his first breaths, the water rose up over his face and he ducked down. After the initial shock he opened his eyes and looked over at Smith. At first he thought the seaman was waving at him. Then, as his eyes adjusted to the gloom, he saw that Smith was gesturing wildly and slowly like a spastic figure in a dream.

Hanley signalled to him and the young man pointed to his throat and then started to sag downwards. Hanley lunged forward, grabbed him by the shoulders and tried to keep him upright. As he did, Smith jerked backwards like an elastic band snapping shut and clutched at his chest. That was it! Hanley stretched out and rapped on the glass scuttle.

Smith had fainted away. His mouthpiece had fallen out and was bubbling oxygen freely. Hanley lifted the pipe, forced it back between his teeth, then hauled the other man up as high as he could. After a few minutes they broke the surface of the retreating water and the chamber began to ring with Smith's choking coughs.

When the water had fallen far enough, the aft hatch was slammed opened. Smith was curled up clutching his chest and they had difficulty pulling him through the restricted opening.

By the time Hanley hauled himself out they had already taken him away to a bunk. There was still chaos in the small area behind the escape chamber and for a moment he remained on all fours, trying to get his breath. Then he felt a strong arm under his elbow. It was Campbell pulling him to his feet. "Come on, sir, we'll get you into some dry clothes right now."

Hanley held Campbell at arm's length and then took a deep breath as he tried to steady his breathing. "No, no, we should try again."

Hanley was trembling with the heat loss, and his lungs felt as if a hundred hot needles were shooting through them. But all that did not matter to him. His mind had narrowed to one crystal clear idea. He would go back into that chamber and face the water again. That was his duty.

He reached out and steadied himself against the metal bulkhead behind him.

"Sir."

Hanley looked up and saw that Crowe had edged between him and Campbell. Hanley pulled himself up straight, willing himself to attention. "Is there another man ready to go with me?"

Crowe shook his head. "No. I've decided against it. You were obviously right about the pressure."

Hanley clenched his teeth. He wanted to argue for another attempt. Now that he had started, he wanted to go through to the end. But Lieutenant Commander Crowe was the captain of the *Graplin*. There was nothing else to be said.

Crowe continued, "We're going ahead with your original plan. We're going to put all our efforts into raising the stern and then use the aft escape chamber. I'd like to talk to you in the wardroom after you've dried and changed."

Hanley nodded. He watched Crowe making his way aft and then felt a sickening wave of tiredness sweep over him. For a moment his knees sagged and he felt the acid taste of bile in his mouth.

"Come on, sir, you've got to get out of those bloody clothes. We've got enough problems without you catching pneumonia."

"Enough problems." The bleakness of their situation hit him and for the first time he allowed himself to think of home, the children and, of course, Eunice. Surely it could not end like this. Surely death would not close over him, before he knew about Eunice, and Weichert, and the charges of espionage . . .

Campbell's brawny hand closed around Hanley's forearm and gently tugged him away from the bulkhead. Hanley glanced around and saw the men carefully draining the remaining water from the escape chamber. It was a lesson. There was only the moment, the task at hand. With a steel-like effort he closed out the burgeoning panic.

37

Olivia swirled the dark red wine around her glass and then stared at the serrated residue of alcohol as it trickled down the side.

"It's a Montepulciano. I adore it. Brampton and I went crazy over it when we visited Florence. I can see however that it doesn't seem to speak to you in the same way."

Eunice stared at her blankly across the remains of the spaghetti dinner and raised an eyebrow. She had felt a black depression growing ever since she had visited Elizabeth at school that afternoon. "I'm sorry, Olivia. I, it was just so terrible with Elizabeth. I thought she might have understood a little or had a little time to think but she seemed so unforgiving, as though I was to blame, completely."

"Ah, children! It's so easy to be full of righteous indignation at thirteen."

"She's sixteen. And a formidable young lady."

Eunice gave a sigh, then got up and walked over to the window. Sixteen, she thought. What age would she be when they next met? Especially since Elizabeth had refused to come and visit her in Germany.

"Eunice, you're strangling your napkin."

Eunice glanced down and saw that she had screwed the linen napkin into a tight ball. "Yes, oh yes. Sorry."

"Oh for God's sake. I don't care about the damned napkin, I care about you."

Olivia got up and crossed to the window, then plonked herself down on the well-padded arm of a settee. She was wearing a pair of baggy black pants and pulled one knee up under her chin like a thoughtful genii. "It's obvious to me. You've been smothered for years and now that you've tried to

281

take control of your life, you feel guilty." She reached over and gently ran her fingers along the back of her friend's hand. "Hey missy, I'm talking to you." Eunice turned and gave a sad flicker of a smile. Olivia continued, "And you act as though it's the end of the world. You're only going to Germany. You can come back and forwards as much as you want. You can use this, as a home away from home."

Eunice grabbed her friend's fingers and squeezed them. "Thanks Olivia, thanks."

"And where's Mr Weichert in all this?"

Eunice shrugged. "I don't know. I told him I'd be going on down to Chatham after I saw Elizabeth but I couldn't face James and Nigel as well as . . ."

Eunice stopped in mid-sentence and Olivia could see the strain in her friend's face. "Come on, let's do something wild and plebeian," she gave a forced laugh as she walked over to the coffee table and picked up the newspaper. "Ah yes, here we are, *Wings of the Morning*, Henry Fonda, Leslie Banks. No, forget that one. What about *Seventh Heaven*, James Stewart. No! Sounds a little sappy, doesn't it?"

Eunice pursed her lips. "Yes, maybe we should both get drunk and go to the motorcycle racing at Crystal Palace. Isn't that a *Daily Mirror* thing to do?"

Olivia gave a slightly forced giggle. "Well, at least we can start on the drinking end of it."

As she crossed to the bar they heard the sound of the bell ringing downstairs. Olivia picked up a bottle of brandy from behind the counter. "Oh God, if that's Chloë and Rachel again I shall put my head in the gas oven. Vapid, silly flappers!"

She poured two glasses and handed one to Eunice. They clinked, and were taking their first sip when the maid came in. "Excuse me, ma'am, it's Mr Weichert."

Eunice quickly placed her glass on the counter. "Yes, I, I'll go down." She looked confused.

Weichert was just starting up the stairs when he saw her. "Hello? I just dropped by to see if Olivia knew where you were."

She gave him a light kiss on the lips. "I didn't have a good time with Elizabeth. I've just got back. I was going to phone you later." She gave a winsome smile. "But I was trying not to unload my depression on you."

He gave her a strange, appraising look and for the first time she felt a coolness, a distance between them.

"What's wrong? Have I done something . . ."

"No, no." He held up a hand. "Can we go in here?" He gestured towards an open door along the hall.

Eunice walked inside and Weichert followed. She pulled him towards her and gave him a passionate kiss, then sensed his coldness and quickly let go. Please God, surely he wasn't going to tell her it was all over. It couldn't be! But as she looked at his stern face she knew that something was wrong.

"Please, Hans. If you've something to tell me, for God's sake do it."

"I can only presume that you haven't heard anything."

She stared at him, puzzled. "Heard anything about what?"

Weichert brushed his hand through his blond hair and then distractedly smacked his gloves against his hand. "Apparently the *Graplin*, the submarine that your husband was on today, went down and hasn't surfaced since three this afternoon."

Eunice was thrown into confusion. At first she had a pure sense of relief that Weichert's message to her was not his goodbye. But almost immediately she felt a wave of fear and guilt.

"You mean he's dead. They're dead?"

She was visibly shaking. He stepped forward and grabbed both her arms. "No. It does not mean that. No one knows. Many a submarine has gone down and the whole crew survived. There may just be some problem that can be fixed."

Eunice slowly pulled away from him and sat down on the hard arm of the sofa. She felt drained.

After a few seconds other thoughts flooded into her mind. "But I just phoned Olwen. Why didn't she tell me?"

Weichert stared at her for a long time, then turned aside, looked back and flashed her a fleeting, cold smile.

"She didn't know. As far as I'm aware, the information hasn't been released yet."

283

"But then how do you . . ."

Weichert held up his hand and flashed the smile again. It slowly widened into a tight-lipped grimace. "Eunice, I don't ever want to speak of this again but obviously we monitor all of the Naval radio signals that we can and . . ." he paused as if he was carefully choosing his words. "Eunice, you know that you have to keep my name out of this."

"Yes, yes, of course." Eunice stared straight ahead of her at the gleaming brass fender around the fireplace. This couldn't be true. Couldn't. "I should tell Nigel and Elizabeth."

Weichert looked annoyed. "Why don't you go to Chatham first, then see if the news has broken through regular channels."

Eunice nodded. Yes, that sounded sensible. She glanced up at Hans and understood then that she had to think of him, too. She quickly got up from the arm of the sofa and pulled him towards her, squeezing him hard. She felt an overwhelming sadness as if it was a leavetaking. "What'll happen? I mean, it all seems to be falling apart. What'll . . ."

He placed his forefinger on her lips and pressed firmly. "Stop. Do what you have to do. Everything will work itself out." Then he slid his fingers away and kissed her long and hard.

For a moment everything seemed all right again. But only for a moment.

Hanley glanced at his watch under the table. It was ten-thirty. He took a deep, unsatisfying breath and looked around at the other men in the wardroom: Lieutenant Commander Crowe, Jackson the portly Admiralty inspector, Lieutenant Farnsworth the young engineering officer, Grainger and Warrant Officer Campbell. They all looked tired, and each of their faces had a waxy sheen. He noticed that, for all of them, breathing took both concentration and effort. The *Graplin* had been underwater for seven hours and already the air was beginning to thicken.

Hanley looked at the scribbles on the pad in front of him. By his rough calculations the air would be deadly with carbon dioxide by mid to late afternoon next day. He tossed his pencil on to the paper. His calculations had given them all cause to

284

think and there had been a good minute's silence. "Well, gentlemen, that's it . . . at least we know how fast we have to work."

"Yes . . . yes." Lieutenant Commander Crowe drummed his fingers on the table and then flicked the edge of his logbook. As he did so, the curtain was pulled back.

"Gentlemen." It was Gillings, looking fitter than he had done earlier that evening, though he still felt an aching pain from the wound in his chest.

"Come in, Mr Gillings . . . we've just started."

Gillings settled himself in the corner beside Campbell. Campbell offered him a tot of rum from a tin mug, but Gillings shook his head. His mind was fogged enough with the growing lack of oxygen.

Crowe continued in a quiet, almost resigned voice. "As you can probably all tell, we are now at an angle of about thirteen degrees. That's from offloading the drinking water. If we go on and offload the fuel . . ." he paused and looked over at Gillings, "and the stern rises to the surface, we can expect to be at an angle from the horizontal of about thirty-three degrees."

There were a few grunts around the table. Then Farnsworth leaned forward and wiped the sweat from his brow. "It's steep but it's not impossible."

Hanley simply looked at his papers. Not steep for a young man like Farnsworth, he thought, but there were a lot of older men on board. Still, that was a problem for later.

Lieutenant Commander Crowe nervously drummed his pencil on the table as if he too had thought the same thing. Then he looked over at Gillings. "And how are we progressing, Mr Gillings?"

Gillings sat forward. He looked pleased. "Well, it's been difficult but I think we should be ready to start pumping the fuel in about an hour or so . . . I *think* . . . but the work's slow because the men tire very easily . . . we should be ready to start by about midnight."

Hanley glanced over at Gillings and saw a look of satisfaction in his eyes. Hanley knew that he had every right to be pleased. It had been a nightmare of replanning and rerouting to prepare

285

for the fuel being pumped out. Many other systems in the boat had had to be cannibalised, pipes removed, connections reshaped, and all with the limited tools they had on board. All over the boat the small gangs of fitters were working under Gillings' personal supervision. Hanley had nothing but admiration for the man.

"Good, well done, Mr Gillings." Crowe, too, sounded pleased.

"I'd better get back to it." Gillings got up and pushed his way through the curtain.

Hanley sat back for a moment. Now all that was left was to wait. Wait for the fitters to finish, wait for the pumps, wait for the morning.

Kitty watched the tiny line of bubbles streaming to the top of the champagne. They ought to be here by now. She tapped her bright red fingernails on the rim of the glass and then glanced at her new wristwatch, a gift from Eddie Brent. It was eleven fifteen. Tom's fight should have been finished an hour ago.

She dipped her forefinger into the champagne, then lifted a drop and placed it on the tip of her tongue. She loved being up in London, loved all the nightclubs squeezed in behind Piccadilly Circus and Shaftesbury Avenue. She especially enjoyed this place.

She glanced around at the large posters of the movie gangsters on the walls. James Cagney, Edward G. Robinson, George Raft. The Chicago nightclub tried to recreate the ambience of an American speakeasy and it specialised in the latest American swing music. Because of the music Kitty had set about trying to persuade Eddie Brent to get her brother Ernie a job there. In the end he agreed. He had friends he said. It wouldn't be a problem.

She heard the saxophone weaving in and out of the melody and looked towards the stage. Ernie had stepped forward into the spotlight and she could tell by the look in his eyes that he was loving every moment. He seemed to be directing his playing at a table over to his right. When he stepped back out of the light and let the trumpeter take over, a blonde-haired

286

woman in a long black dress stepped up and slipped a note into his jacket.

Kitty looked back again at her glass and thought of her own situation. Perhaps she shouldn't have taken the flat that Eddie had offered her. But then she had loved it from the first moment she'd seen it. Oh, the "flat" was really just a bed-sitting-room with its own bathroom and kitchen, but it was hers, a space of her own.

Kitty clinked the champagne glass and stirred her nail gently through the bubbling liquid. Her mother had been almost hysterical when Kitty had told her that she was moving in. Phrases like "kept woman" and "decent people" had been tossed about the kitchen. But in the end Kitty had stormed out. It didn't matter what her mother thought, she knew that she had no choice. She wasn't born to live in the slums all her life. She was meant for higher things.

Kitty was taking a sip of her champagne when Eddie slipped into the chair beside her. " 'allo Miss Cullen, graduated from a gin and tonic, 'ave we?"

Kitty glanced up at him, large liquid eyes, half schoolgirl, half vixen, and gave him a broad smile. "You told me to order what I wanted . . ."

Eddie gave a dismissive wave, " 'ave a bloody case if you want."

Kitty saw Tom sidling up beside him and grinned. "A case? Did you win then?"

Tom slumped into the chair opposite, and gave a sidelong glance at his sister as he tried to focus his eyes on the table. "No, no . . . I made a big mistake in the third round."

"What?" Kitty sniffed her disapproval. "I thought you were the favourite. Everyone was betting on you."

"Yeah. You said it." Tom turned and glared at Eddie, who casually took an envelope from his inside pocket and handed it to Tom. "I think we've said enough about this, Tom."

Tom looked angry. He quickly snatched the envelope and hid it under the table. But he was not quick enough for Kitty. The flap was open and she noticed the wad of notes inside.

"What's that? How come you're so rich if you lost the . . ."

She stopped in mid-sentence as she saw the guilty look on her brother's face, and understood immediately. "Tom, you didn't . . ."

"Leave it alone, Kitty, just leave it alone!" Tom's face was contorted and he seemed caught between anger and tears. Then he spun round and glared at Eddie. "Why'd you have to do it in front of her? I'll be bloody ruined if it gets out . . ."

Eddie looked at him coldly. "There's no secrets between Kitty and me. Kitty's my right-hand man. Isn't that right, Kitty?"

She was about to say something when a waitress came over. "Mr Brent, there's a telephone call for you at the bar."

Eddie raised his eyebrows. "Great! Can't even get a quiet friggin' minute for a drink."

Eddie quickly got up and walked to the bar. Kitty just sat there staring unhappily at her glass.

"Kitty, I just want to say that I had to . . ."

"Oh shut up!" She looked up and glared at him angrily. "You're a bloody wanker. Just like all the other Cullen men. Piss artists, good-for-nothings . . ."

"Hey, wait a minute!"

"No I'll wait a minute nothing. I don't want to talk and that's it."

Tom jumped up. "All right, well sod you, I'm off to my friends." He turned and stomped his way through the crowded tables towards the exit.

Kitty watched him. She was angry and disgusted. Tom had obviously thrown away the fight. And he had done so because of money that he owed Eddie. Yet at another level Kitty felt a deep confusion. Eddie had let her see all this and he was obviously pulling her even more tightly into his enterprises.

Before she realised it, Eddie had slipped into the chair beside her and was gently touching her on the arm. She turned to him, slowly emerging from her own conflicting thoughts.

"Kitty, I just had a call from Chatham. I got some bad news. One of their submarines, the *Graplin*'s gone down . . ."

"Oh God!" He did not finish the sentence. She knew that

Terry and her Uncle Albert were on it, and she knew what she had to do. "I've got to go down there, Eddie, I've got to go to my Aunt Irene . . ."

38

A chill was settling over the submarine. All the vital systems had slowly closed down and the cold was creeping up from the dark depths of the sea, up from the flooded for'ard compartments, and through the double hulls. Finally the men began to feel it burrowing into their very bones.

It was in that still, dead period of early morning that the men found time to sit and think. It was not a time they would have chosen to ponder on their fate, for it was that time of night when fears creep unhindered from the back of the mind; that time when men begin to examine their souls and reassess their memories.

Terry had worked for hours with a gang of fitters, rerouting a section of fuel piping in the narrow spacing under the engine room. The conditions were unbelievably cramped and he had continually poured with sweat as he beat a flange into shape and then assembled the connection.

He was tired now, very tired and cold. He had finally found himself a comfortable niche at the for'ard end of the starboard diesel engine. There he settled in against the piping, drew his coat loosely around his chest and shoulders and pulled out his paperback copy of Emile Burns' book *Capitalism, Communism and the Transition*. Elizabeth had returned it to him only last week and now he had the added pleasure of reading her notes to him in the margins. But tiredness and the lack of air made it almost impossible to concentrate, and very slowly the book slipped out of his hands, and his eyes closed.

He saw Elizabeth, waiting for him at the bandstand in the park in Gillingham. She was dressed in a blazer and a grey skirt and had her blonde hair loosely tied back with a blue velvet band. She sat on the steps and pointed to the open book before her. "I have a number of problems with Burns' view of history . . ."

Terry found himself gazing into her pure blue eyes, then pushing back the errant strands of golden hair that fell across her jacket. He wanted to kiss her, pull her to him, but he couldn't get past the book and every time he tried to, it got bigger and bigger, until it was like a massive door between them.

Terry felt the jacket being pulled up around his shoulders. He opened his eyes and saw his father kneeling beside him.

"Sorry, Terry, I didn't mean to waken you."

Terry pulled himself up and leaned back against the fuel pumps as he tried to shake himself awake. "Why don't you pull up a pew and stay a while?"

Gillings laughed. "Your grandmother used to say that."

"Yeah I remember . . . and then she'd laugh and shake like a jelly . . . till the tears ran down her face."

"We had some good times during those holidays up in Birkenhead, I didn't know you remembered that far back."

Terry nodded and there was an awkward pause. Finally he patted the deck beside him. "Join me . . . please . . ."

Gillings glanced at his watch. It was three in the morning. He could sit for an hour or so, then he would have to get back to the final part of the pumping operation in the control room. But in the meantime, he could talk to his son.

His son. Once more he could relish the word.

The rattling of the teacups startled Eunice awake. She glanced around her for a moment, confused, then slowly got her bearings. Chatham. An office . . .

"Sorry, ma'am, we thought you might like a cup of tea." The young seaman was setting a tray on the desk in front of her.

Eunice shook her head. She felt very groggy. "Tea. Ah, yes

that would be very nice, thank you." She pulled her hair away from her face and then pinned it back tightly.

As he poured her a cup she glanced up at the clock behind him. It was four fifteen in the morning.

"There's no news, I suppose?"

He turned and looked at her with big sympathetic eyes and she saw that he really wasn't much more than a schoolboy. And then the thought occurred to her, how many other young men like him were down there, on the *Graplin*?

"No, ma'am, not yet. Except they have ships coming in from everywhere and the tug stayed by their marker buoy all night. Milk? Sugar?"

"Hmm? Oh, yes please. I think a lot of sugar."

He grinned. "Yeah, it's the only thing that makes this dockyard tea drinkable. Here." He offered her the bag with the teaspoon sticking out of it and she stirred three heapings into her cup.

"Are they still next door?"

The seaman lifted the tray and laughed. "They're all over the place by now. I should 'ave a trolley."

Eunice watched him as he walked next door into the admiral's office. She took a delicate sip of the tea. It tasted good.

She had been waiting in the dockyards now for almost five hours. Olivia had driven her down from London and then gone to stay at the house. On the way Eunice had decided not to tell Nigel until the morning, reasoning that it would do him no good to suffer through the watches of the night.

The phone rang in the next office and she crossed to the door and looked inside. Rear Admiral Walker was leaning against his desk, thoughtfully stroking his beard and staring at a large map. He was surrounded by a group of younger officers, most of whom Eunice knew from the wardroom and dinner parties.

He cleared his throat. "What's the latest weather?"

The phone rang again and one of the men answered it. Another group were gathered around a crackling radio, set up on a trestle table by the wall, taking messages from various ships. Eunice suddenly felt very much an outsider. She stepped back out of the light, into the shadows of the secretary's office, feeling confused and ill at ease. She took another drink of the tea and then a deep shuddering breath. Yes, that was what she needed, some fresh air, a chance to collect her thoughts.

She quickly walked along the corridor, through the elegant, marble-floored vestibule and out through the front doors. There was a fresh pre-dawn chill in the air and as she walked towards the river, a half-moon slowly emerged from behind a large black cloud hovering over Rochester. At first it rimmed the cloud with silver and then as it edged out further it seemed to spatter the water with glittering daubs of light. Her mind flooded with memories. She and Hanley; Portsmouth and the promise of all those years ago; those blissful holiday weeks on the island of Sark . . .

"It's a long night, isn't it?"

Eunice swung round at the sound of the voice. A man in captain's uniform stood along the railing from her, peering out at the river. For a moment the profile reminded her of Hanley but the figure quickly turned and the moment was gone. As he walked towards her into the hazy blue light from one of the pier lamps, she was struck by his look of intensity, those sharp grey-blue eyes and thin face. There was something almost predatory there.

"Sorry. You look startled. We've met before, I don't know if you remember. Captain Marsh." He held out his hand and she took it. A firm, warm handshake but still the eyes held her in a cold gaze. It was then that she remembered. It was at the party after the launching of the *Graplin*.

"Oh yes – Captain Marsh – it was at a reception in Medway House."

Marsh nodded, pulled out his silver cigarette case, opened it and offered her one.

"Oh yes, yes I will."

He struck a match and as she puffed the cigarette into life, she noticed his steady unwavering eyes.

"You made it down from London in good time, I hear."

"Yes." Eunice inhaled the cigarette, then turned towards the pier and blew the smoke up towards the lamplight. What in the

292

name of hell did he mean by "in good time"? She took another quick drag and looked away from him, upriver towards Rochester. Perhaps she was being oversensitive because she had heard the news from Hans. But what was so wrong about that?

"Is there any news yet?"

He shook his head. "No, not really." Then he glanced up into the eastern sky. The first dull glow of dawn was beginning to wash across the heavens. "But I'd say if they're going to make any movement in the *Graplin*, we'll hear about it soon."

"Yes . . . yes, I suppose so." She took another lingering drag of the cigarette. "What brings you down here, Captain Marsh? I thought you were based in London."

Marsh gave a thin-lipped smile. "Oh I'm based all over the place." Until then he had been playing with his cigarette; now he lit it and in the wavering light she once more noticed the cold hard look in his eyes.

He flicked the lighted match out into the river and continued, "But I, we, have a new device on board, something that interests us. Captain Hanley may have mentioned it."

She gave a dismissive shrug. "He may have, I haven't really been paying much attention recently." A cold breeze rippled over the dark river and sent a shiver through her. She drew up the lapel of her suit jacket.

Marsh held his arm up to the lamplight and glanced at his wristwatch. "I must get back in. Don't stay out here too long. You might catch a chill."

Eunice nodded and then watched him as he marched smartly back to the offices. Why was it that everything he said seemed to have a resonance to it? "Chill." It was an apt word for him to use.

293

39

Hanley felt painfully tired. Each step up the steep angle of the deck was like a mile walk in itself. There was, however, one deeply satisfying thought that sustained him. The boat now lay at about thirty-three degrees to the horizontal and that meant that the stern was either at the surface or very close to it.

All around him men were lying in any space they could find. Some were asleep, wrapped in Navy blankets, others leaned back against the engine blocks, reading yesterday's well-crumpled newspapers, playing cards or just talking.

Hanley paused about halfway through the engine room and leaned against one of the sets of silent piston rods that lined the sides of the Sulzer diesel engines. The lack of oxygen was beginning to dull his faculties and his only thought was for air, pure, sweet, clean, cool air.

"What's the time, sir?"

Hanley glanced down and saw a dark-haired young workman looking up at him from behind a paperback. The young man's face was smudged with oil but Hanley still recognised "the young Gillings lad". He stared at him for a while, his mind sluggish, and then a memory stirred, an argument with Eunice some months back. She had told him that their daughter Elizabeth was seeing too much of some "bolshy young chap" from the yards. The incident had slipped between the slats of their wrecked marriage but this chance encounter brought it vividly back to him.

"You all right, sir?"

"Eh yes . . . yes . . . concentration's going with this air . . . time . . . it's almost eight o'clock."

"Thank you, sir."

Terry returned to his book. For a while Hanley stared at him.

He was a handsome young man and, for all the fatigue, there was a look of determination and strength on his face.

"Captain Hanley."

Hanley looked up along the steeply sloping deck and saw Lieutenant Commander Crowe standing by the aft escape chamber. He took another deep breath and pulled himself up the deck towards him, picking his way between the groups of waiting men.

" 'ere sir, see if you can get us up before that MCC test match on Saturday."

"Bugger the MCC, mate. I'm dying to see if they've gone and got us on the newsreels."

Hanley laughed as he stepped over a bunch of young engine fitters playing poker. He was glad to see they had not lost their sense of humour. They would need it.

The aft escape chamber was built into the fifth watertight bulkhead. It opened three ways, aft and uphill into the stokers' mess, for'ard and downhill into the motor room, and up and out into the sea. If everything had gone according to calculations, it would now be opening close to the surface of the water.

Hanley took the last few difficult steps from the engine room and through into the motor room. Crowe had positioned himself over by the massive electrical switches on the port side, out of earshot of the group standing around the bulkhead.

"We're ready . . . Mr Gillings just informed us that the last of the fuel's been pumped out. We should be able to start sending them up now."

Hanley pulled a sheet of paper from his pocket and handed it to Crowe. "I've made the list, Crowe, but eh . . ." Hanley shrugged as Crowe scanned it. "You can change whatever you want. I've put Grainger and some of his men at the top of the list . . . and then workmen with families after that . . . I thought I'd leave it at the first fifty . . . for now."

Crowe glanced up from the list and nodded. "Right . . . it's fine." Crowe did not need to hear the rationale behind that last remark. If they did not get help from above, the air would run out before they needed to make another list!

Crowe turned away and looked aft towards the escape

chamber. "All right lads. I've got a list of the lucky blighters who get to take a bath first."

There was a murmur of excitement. Hanley made his way through the bulkhead door and pulled himself towards the stokers' mess beyond. It was empty except for Warrant Officer Campbell. He was squeezed in behind a table, seated on one of the lower bunks.

"Sounds pretty busy out there, sir."

"Yes, we're just about to send the first pair up." Hanley perched on the edge of a small shelf by the door, then loosened his collar and wiped the sweat from around his neck.

Campbell lifted a tin mug. "Care for a tot, sir, I've got a flask on me and there's a couple of clean mugs over there." Campbell pointed to the small sink to the side of the doorway.

"No . . . no thanks I'm fine . . . it's . . . a cup of coffee I could do with, Mr Campbell." Hanley gave him a tired smile, but Campbell stared back stony-faced.

"I was hoping we could have a talk, sir . . ."

"Captain Hanley, could I see you out here for a moment?"

Hanley threw up his hands in mock despair. "I'll be back in a moment."

Hanley pushed back the curtain and stepped into the passageway. Grainger was standing in the doorway of one of the heads. He was slumped against the doorpost like a scolded schoolboy.

Lieutenant Commander Crowe was standing on the other side of the passageway holding on to one of the fuel pipes. "We seem to have a problem, sir, and I think you can help us solve it . . . Dr Grainger?"

Crowe glanced over at Grainger who nervously ran his hand through his tangle of black curls. When he looked up, Hanley could see that his face was ashen. As he turned to Hanley he took off his glasses and rubbed them on the tail of his shirt.

"I can't go up . . . I don't think I should be the first to get out . . . I'd feel very bad about that . . . very bad . . ."

Hanley glanced over at Crowe, looking for some kind of lead. Crowe shrugged in an almost petulant manner. "I explained

296

that you carried sealed orders about what he had to do under certain circumstances . . ."

Hanley stared into Crowe's eyes and felt a twinge of anger. There was no place for weakness in authority. You forced the decision through when it was made, forced it through whatever the consequences. "Leave it with me for a moment, Crowe." Hanley's voice was terse, almost dismissive.

Crowe turned and walked back through the bulkhead door into the motor room. Hanley stepped over to Grainger and said in a quiet voice, "You have to go up, you know the orders as well as I do."

"I know . . . I know but I still feel that me being selected first . . . it's unfair . . . privilege . . ."

"That's cockamamie, Dr Grainger . . . it's nothing to do with you as a person . . . it's the knowledge you carry in your head . . . you're just a talking book of theorems to the Admiralty."

Grainger squeezed his fists, cracking the knuckles, and then gave an exasperated sigh. Hanley suddenly sensed Grainger's real problem. He reached over and lightly grasped the young man by the arm. "You're afraid to go up, aren't you?"

Grainger swung round and his eyes flickered with anger. "What do you mean?"

Hanley tightened his grip. "You tell me, mister, and quickly! We have a boatload of lives at stake!"

Grainger visibly sagged, then turned to Hanley and said quietly, "Yes, I hate the water. I've never been able to go under . . . I've always hated pressure on my ears. I . . ."

Grainger was about to continue when Hanley stepped in close and grabbed him by the lapels of his jacket. His voice was a quiet but firm growl. "You do what I tell you, mister . . . you understand. You give me five minutes of your time . . . five minutes, that's all. It's not too much to ask in my books!"

Hanley gritted his teeth and grabbed Grainger by the belt of his trousers. Then he twisted it and pushed against his stomach. "Just tighten your stomach muscles . . . hold hard and don't let go . . . that's all you think about . . . nothing else, not ears, not mouth, not water. Five minutes, hold tight, follow the other man and kick." Hanley leaned in close so that they were almost nose to nose. He knew that the force of anger in his eyes was intimidating. "Five minutes, mister, that's all! Do it!"

As he stood back he saw that animal gleam of violence in the other man's eye and he knew that this was the moment to strike.

"Lieutenant Commander Crowe," Crowe leaned in through the bulkhead door and Hanley continued, "we're ready to go."

Grainger swung round and glared at Hanley. There was anger there, yes, but something else, respect. He nodded and then made his way past Crowe into the motor room.

"Jackson, the Admiralty inspector, was slated to go up with him, wasn't he?"

"Yes . . . he's waiting . . ."

"It's too risky with Grainger. I think we should send up Petty Officer Edmunds."

"Edmunds? But he passed out . . ."

"We're at the surface . . . at the most thirty feet down, not one hundred and sixty. Edmunds'll do it. It'll also show Grainger some Navy grit."

Hanley was right. Edmunds was happy to vindicate himself. Within five minutes both he and Grainger were inside the escape chamber. Crowe gave the signal to Leading Seaman Smith to close the hatch. This was followed by the hissing rush of water as the flood valve was opened. The water quickly rose up and Hanley made his way through the bulkhead door so as to watch them through the aft-facing glass scuttle.

By the time he arrived at the other side of the escape chamber, the water was above their heads. He peered anxiously inside. The light was dim, but he was relieved when he saw Edmunds turn to both scuttles and give the thumbs-up sign.

Hanley found himself catching his breath as the seconds tensely ticked by. Then, miraculously, he saw the chamber fill up with daylight. A joyous shaft of clear, brilliant sunshine. His heart pounded with joy. Next door he heard a shout, followed by a cheer that rumbled along the whole length of the boat, down into its cold, dark, silent depths. Suddenly there was light, suddenly there was hope and life!

Hanley watched the two men's legs disappearing upwards

298

and then the chamber going dark again as the outer hatch was closed to prepare for the next escape.

"They've done it, eh sir?"

"Yes, Mr Campbell . . . they bloody well have."

At the other side of the bulkhead they heard Lieutenant Commander Crowe preparing the next pair for the escape chamber. Hanley turned back to Campbell. "Sorry, Mr Campbell, I was called away . . . you were telling me something."

Campbell pointed back to the empty stokers' mess. "Could we go in there, sir, if you don't mind."

They made their way uphill and sat down at the table. Now that the excitement had passed, Hanley felt exhausted. He leaned forward and let his head sag into his hands. All he wanted to do was sleep but instead he willed himself awake and looked up. He could not help noticing a peculiar, haunted look in Campbell's eyes.

"One way or another, sir, I'm glad I'm finally talking to you. If we were going down I'd want you to know and eh . . . if we make it then I've eh . . . well, made my own little appointment with Fate."

Hanley was puzzled and irritated. He was too tired for all this double talk. Campbell saw the look and gave a nervous smile.

"I'm sorry, I know I'm going on, I should just get to the point. I . . . I'm glad Dr Grainger got away . . . Captain Marsh should be pleased too."

Campbell paused and took a sip from his cup. Hanley watched him and as he did so he had a sinking feeling in his stomach. An unexplainable intuition.

Campbell took a deep breath and laid the cup on the table. "The thing is, sir, I needed money to keep my wife in the sanatorium . . . I was broke and I was approached by someone . . ."

Hanley gave a shuddering sigh. "For God's sake, man, what are you trying to say? Just spit it out."

"For the past year, I've been selling . . . selling documents to the Germans."

40

One after another they went up. Propelled by their own
buoyancy they shot through the hatch and into the cold grey
water. Once up, they seemed to bounce to the surface where
they bobbed like so many corks. There were two other ships
close by, apart from the tug, *Merriweather*, and virtually within
seconds they were picked up out of the waves.

Soon after the first two men were lifted from the water, the
information was relayed back to Chatham. Within half an hour
the good news had travelled from the admiral's offices through
the covered slips where the shipwrights were working on the
new submarine; on to the fitters in the factory and the
electricians working in the dry docks along the basins. Thank
God their workmates would be saved! Now it was just a matter
of time!

At the northern end of the sand-coloured sail-loft, groups of
women sat quietly on the steps or leaned against the black iron
railings. Rear Admiral Walker had opened up one of the rooms
inside the building as a waiting area and allowed them to come
into the yards. None of them knew that this was the same room
that had been used for Lieutenant Commander Kingsland's
court martial. And the irony, if irony it was, was happily lost. In
its own tragic way the *Graplin* had touched so many lives!

Inside, Irene Gillings held the large brown teapot under the
boiler and watched the hot water gushing out of the tap. She
had scarcely slept a wink and yet still felt as if she was in the
middle of a nightmare. Surely this could not be happening to
her. Surely Albert and Terry couldn't both be caught up in this
tragedy.

"Irene, wake up, I've turned it off." Mary had taken the
teapot from her and was replacing the lid.

"Oh yes, yes, my mind was gone. I'll take it over to the table next to the cups."

Irene walked over to the trestle table and put down the pot. All through the room, women huddled around tables or sat quietly against the walls, all dealing with their worry in different ways. Irene was keeping herself sane by doing things. Setting up the tables, finding chairs, organising the hot water, the tea, the milk, the biscuits. She almost felt that if she could keep working, somehow the sea would give up her menfolk, release them into the world of the living again.

She did not say these things to Mary Cullen, but then she did not have to. Mary suffered along with her and knew that the best thing she could do was just to be there, and occasionally try to divert her.

"Well, Tom lost his first fight."

"Hmm."

"Kitty says they all met up in one of those clubs afterwards last night."

"Why didn't you go up?"

Mary pursed her lips in distaste. "I don't like London and I don't like those clubs. And to tell you the truth I dread to think what Ernie's up to these days. My God, but I reared a brood, didn't I?"

Irene laughed. "They're fine, Mary. There's no family I know escapes without some kind of rumpus." A couple of women had come forward and Irene started pouring them cups of tea. "I was very touched that Kitty came down."

Mary shrugged, but she was pleased herself. She and Kitty had hardly spoken since the argument over the flat, but she had to admit that the girl had shown real signs of maturity in the way she had come to Irene's side.

Mary grunted. "She looked wrecked though, staying up all bleedin' night in those places. I can't talk to none of them."

Irene laid the teapot down again. "Well, she's a good girl for all that. You've got a good family, they're . . ." Irene's voice faded out. She could feel her eyes filling with tears, but she couldn't allow herself to give in to them.

301

Just at that moment, Kitty ran in bursting to tell the momentous news from the *Graplin*.

"They've come up," she yelled. "Some of the men've come up. I was just down at the offices and they told me. Four already and more coming."

The effect was instantaneous. Chairs and tables were pushed back, one woman caught her by the wrist, others crowded round.

"Who?"

"What are the names?"

"How many, did you say?"

"What time?" Kitty was lost in the babbling group before she could get across to her mother and aunt.

But Irene did not care. She had heard the message and it sent a shudder of relief through her. She quickly turned away and this time could not stop the tears flowing.

"Please God . . ." she said, clasping her hands together in prayer. "Please God keep them safe. Send them home together."

41

Hanley sat alone in the dimly lighted stokers' mess, his forehead resting in his hands, peering intently at the tabletop. After the warrant officer's confession, he had sat like that for a long time, incapable of saying anything. Finally Campbell had left him and slowly made his way down the deck, past the activity around the escape chamber and for'ard to the control room.

Campbell's story had shaken him to the core. He was the last man Hanley would have expected to betray his country. And yet, after he had told everything, it all made perfect sense.

Campbell's despair over not having the money to make proper provision for his wife had eventually led him to hate the Navy. Bitter remarks made in bars had finally brought him to the attention of the Germans. They had obviously been searching for new sources of information about the mysterious Grainger project, following the death of Kingsland.

Hanley did not know the name Eddie Brent when it was mentioned, but he had heard of the nightclub, the Chinese Parrot. So this man was the intermediary with the Germans, well, perhaps Brent had also been the intermediary for Kingsland. Perhaps he had been more than that! Hanley's mind began to spin with the possibilities. Then he deliberately calmed himself down. This was not a time for emotion. He needed to focus his energy on one thing, survival.

He would get out of the *Graplin*. He *had* to get out. Now that he knew the truth he had to tell Marsh, vindicate Eunice. It did not matter about her affair with Weichert, it did not matter about anything now. There was honour at stake, family honour. If the *Graplin* were to go down, and this knowledge with it, the black stain would remain against her name.

He lifted the cup and kept it tilted back until the last dribble of rum fell on to his tongue. No! He couldn't think properly. His mind was awash with disconnected thoughts. And yet somehow, in the midst of the turmoil, he saw something bright and clean and sharp. He would do everything to get back to Eunice, everything to clear her name. But he was now certain that he was not doing it for love! The love, the passion, was gone. It had been gone for years. And he had helped destroy it.

Once again his head slowly sank down into his hands. That knowledge, that sudden knowledge was hard to take. Perhaps it was the lack of oxygen, perhaps it was the gushing of relief, but the tears spilled through his fingers and dribbled down his forearm. He had not loved for years. Perhaps he could no longer love. Perhaps his slavish service to this treacherous wanton, the sea, allowed no room for any other love.

The light grew dimmer but he did not notice. The batteries were gently fading, the precious minutes were ticking by. So many things had happened to him in the last year, so many pieces of his life had fallen asunder, that at this dark moment there seemed nothing left. He shook his head and stared at the tin cup, the table, the bunk. He could feel his spirits sinking, his mind drifting off into sleep. A great sense of loneliness and silence flowed over him, tugging him into darkness.

It was only the shouts of panic that shook him from his dreamlike stupor. He jumped up quickly and staggered into the passageway. As he looked downhill and for'ard into the motor-room, he saw the first wisps of whitish blue smoke.

Lieutenant Commander Crowe shouted out in a voice shrill with fear, "Close bulkhead number four . . . contain the smoke . . . put on the escape sets . . ."

Hanley moved with a speed born of years of practice drills. He lunged over to starboard, just opposite the stoker's head, and broke open the white box of DSEAs. He quickly strapped one of them on and jammed the tube into his mouth. Even so he caught the first sickening whiff of the smoke. It had a pungent acid smell and he knew immediately what had happened. The escape chamber had obviously not been adequately drained before it was reopened and seawater had flowed over the coaming and on to the electrical switchboards.

Hanley felt immediately revivified by the oxygen from the DSEA set and though his eyes were stinging from the smoke, he quickly made his way through the door of bulkhead number five into the motor-room.

All around the deck, just outside the escape chamber, seamen and workers were frantically soaking up the seawater, using anything that came to hand, newspapers, clothes, sheets, blankets. Hanley could see, even as he entered, that they had it under control.

After a few minutes watching the bluish smoke disperse Hanley carefully pulled off his nose-clip and breathing tube. If breathing had been difficult before, now it was almost painful. The air had a burning, acrid quality and it seared the throat as it went down.

Crowe quickly followed Hanley's action. He knew that they could not use up the limited supply of oxygen in the DSEAs.

They would have to start sending men up again as quickly as possible and they would need every set they had.

Crowe pulled himself aft towards the escape chamber again. "All right, men . . . masks off . . . off! . . . Open bulkhead four . . . Waugh, warn them for'ard about smoke . . ."

By the time Crowe got up beside Hanley he was wheezing with the effort. He took a moment to calm his breathing then continued, "It's bad . . . we must move faster."

Hanley shrugged. "How many have gone?"

Crowe stared at him blankly for a moment as if his brain was not working, then he shook his head. "Eh . . . ten . . . ten . . . five pairs. I . . . I'm going to send up four next . . . save time . . ."

Hanley looked surprised. "I don't think . . ."

Crowe cut him off. "Sir, we must do it, we have no time."

Hanley sank back against the wall as Crowe shouted out the orders. He sympathised with the man, the strain was enormous. But then that was the burden that came with responsibility.

He watched the four men getting into the escape chamber. There were two seamen from the *Graplin*, Barnes and Anderson, and Jack Wallis the electrical foreman. A young fitter called Denison was the last. He gave a cheery lopsided grin as he crawled through the hatch. "If anybody's got their pools to post, I'll do it for a bob."

The men who waited behind laughed. Gillings edged his way over to Hanley and said quietly, "I hope to God no one panics, or they're all gone." Hanley nodded. He knew what he meant. The space was small enough with just two men. You needed a reserve of nerve and discipline to work it with four.

Leading Seaman Smith opened the flood valve and the chamber quickly flooded. As the seawater was gushing in, Crowe ordered more men aft from the control room and the other areas for'ard.

Meanwhile Hanley noticed Smith's growing agitation and made his way across to the chamber. "What is it, seaman?"

Smith gave a shrug, then turned and said in a low voice, "Well . . . maybe nothing but it's still dark in there . . . I don't think they've opened the hatch."

Hanley glanced at his watch. They had been inside for ten minutes. God! How had the time drifted away! He shook his head and tried to focus. All around him men were moving slowly as if they were in each other's dreams. It was the air! The damned poisoned air!

See! He must see! He slipped his torch from his pocket and shone it through the scuttle. The water was dark grey, almost khaki-coloured. He moved the fuzzy beam around and suddenly a face appeared, terrorstricken, eyes glaring. Then fingers clawed across the glass. Hanley pulled back and shouted, "Empty the chamber."

For a moment nothing happened, then he shouted again, "Drain down . . . now!"

It took almost twenty minutes. Every second seemed interminable and every man around the chamber felt as if he was in there with them, enduring the agony of suffocation.

When the water was almost down to the bottom of the hatch a fitter leaned over to unclip it. Hanley grabbed his arm. "No! Wait till it's under the coaming. It'll kill us all!"

The man looked as if he would rip his arm away and continue, but Hanley's eyes were overpowering. "Move away! Now!" Hanley turned and watched the water level. When he saw it was safe he quickly unclipped the door and pulled the lever.

"Holy Christ!" Smith instinctively jumped back as the young fitter Denison slumped out on to the coaming. Hanley stepped over and pulled him out across the floor, Gillings dragged out another man. Within seconds all four men were strewn across the deck like sodden scarecrows. But it was too late, all were dead except for Denison and he was dying. As Hanley held the young man in his arms, he pulled out his tube and tried to shake him into consciousness.

Denison's eyelids fluttered and he gurgled out a mouthful of water. "The hatch . . . couldn't open . . . stuck about six inches . . ." His voice was a searing rasp that lasted for only a moment and then once more faded away with him into his last sleep.

Hanley laid him down on the deck beside the others, then straightened up and looked around. Everyone was deeply shaken. Gillings had crouched down beside his son, his head in his hands. Crowe had slumped back against the hull of the boat and his eyes were staring vacantly at the empty escape chamber. There was a chilling silence. As though somehow the certainty of defeat and death had finally been accepted.

Hanley drew in a number of shuddering breaths and stepped across to Crowe. His fists were clenched, his fingernails biting into his palms. No! Not this way! You did not meet death this way, lying back waiting for it to come. You charged at it, fighting every step.

"Crowe . . . we must try again . . ."

Crowe barely lifted his eyes. When he spoke it was in clipped phrases, between snatched breaths. "The hatch . . . closed . . . more'll die . . . we can wait . . . the ships above'll rescue . . ."

Hanley shook his head furiously. "No, we must try again . . . we can't be sure . . . must try and open the hatch . . . carry a message about number-five torpedo tube . . . send a diver down . . . close it . . . then we can blow the two for'ard compartments."

Hanley felt as if they were talking in exchanged telegrams, but he couldn't stop. It was as if some giant hand was pressing down on his chest and his breath was unable to support more than a phrase at a time.

Crowe seemed to think for ages, then slowly shook his head. "No, no. If the men don't get out . . . how'd the message get out?"

Even now Hanley saw the humour. The time it took to formulate even such a simple thought and then the time to voice it. But it was tragic too. Time was leaking away. Time! Time! They needed to move quickly! Hanley could sense his own fuzzy thought processes grinding away their response. The men inside the chamber. The message. Hatch only opens six inches. Then the idea came to him.

"We must do it . . . write out the message . . . float it up through the gap in the hatch!"

A pause, then Crowe asked, "Who'll volunteer?"

Hanley listened, thought, responded. "I will . . ." He glanced around him. His eyes lit on the two Gillings and he noted the boy's strong shoulders. "But I need someone else."

307

As Hanley made his way across the deck, Crowe shouted out, "All right, we're going again." The men responded in confusion and then sullen amazement. Four men had died in there.

As Hanley knelt beside Terry the latter flashed him a wry smile. "If you're looking for volunteers, sir . . . I'll go."

All around them, throughout the motor and engine rooms, they could hear the grumbling, fearful accusations of the other men.

"Fucking crazy . . ."

"Bloody murder . . ."

"Should wait for above . . ."

But Crowe cut across them. "That's enough . . . we're going to do it again." He glanced over at Hanley and saw him nodding his assent as he pointed to Terry. Crowe continued, "We have two volunteers."

The grumbles turned to whispers of admiration, and then shame, that others would be risking their lives for them.

Hanley knew that if they were to do this they should do it fast. If they could make the hatch work again then others could follow. He sent a seaman in search of a hammer and crowbar, then took a new DSEA and handed one to Terry Gillings.

"Here, I'll strap it on, Terry."

Hanley glanced at Albert Gillings' arm in the sling and knew that it would be awkward. But he also knew that such moments were important. He simply nodded and walked over to Crowe to collect the waterproof message and float.

At first neither father nor son said anything. Gillings methodically wrapped the straps of the breathing apparatus around Terry and then tied them. Finally, when it was finished, they stood facing each other. A tense silence. Terry bit into his lip, then grasped his father by the arm and said in a voice choked with emotion, "Dad, I want to tell you that I love . . ."

Gillings shook his head furiously, as he tried to keep the tears from spilling down his cheeks. "I know!" He laid his hand over Terry's and squeezed it. There was too much to say and yet at the same time nothing, because he *did* know. They both did. They knew about the competition, the frustrations, the arguments. But finally and most important they knew about the

308

love, for that had survived the tempers and tempests. That deep love of father and son.

Gillings took a steadying breath. "When we get out of this ... you can come home or stay in digs ... whatever you want ..." He squeezed Terry's hand hard. "But you're a man, Terry ... a bloody Gillings ... whatever you do, do it well!" Then he wrenched himself away and gazed fixedly at the line of diesel engines behind him.

All around they were making the final preparations for their attempt, checking the hatch-clips, flood valves, drain valves and vents. Hanley was kneeling by the open hatch looking up into the escape chamber when someone handed him the hammer and crowbar.

"Thanks." He glanced round and saw Warrant Officer Campbell squatting beside him. The two men stared at each other for what seemed like an age, then Campbell offered his hand. "Whatever happens, sir, I'm ... sorry ... just sorry ... I never meant to harm anyone, sir ... especially you ... never meant to harm anyone ... I hope you'll take my hand."

Hanley looked down for a moment and paused, reluctant to make that final gesture. It was difficult for him, but in another way he realised that it was a relief. For it meant that Eunice was now cleared of all suspicion. He stretched out and firmly clasped the other man's hand. "Wish me luck, Campbell."

"I do, sir ... always." Campbell stood up quickly and stepped away, then made his way down the deck for'ard through the engine room.

"Ready, sir?" Smith was standing with his hand on the flood valve.

Hanley nodded and then glanced over at Terry. "All right, Mr Gillings, are you ready?"

Terry nodded awkwardly. There was something almost ominous about being addressed as Mr Gillings with his father beside him. But he shook off the feeling, laid his hand on his father's shoulder and squeezed hard. Gillings nodded and Terry quickly moved across the deck and ducked down into the chamber. He saw that Hanley had already placed the hammer

309

and crowbar inside and had the watertight wallet containing the message and float tied around his waist.

The hatch clanged shut behind them. A ringing, ominous sound. Hanley flashed Terry a grim smile. "You say you can swim underwater?" Terry nodded and then glanced down as the water started flooding in around their feet. Hanley saw the tension in the lines of the boy's face. But he saw something else, the determination to survive. He was a good choice. Hanley gave him a playful punch on the arm. "It'll be all right . . . do what I do . . . and don't panic. If the upper hatch sticks, we use the hammer and the crowbar. If it still doesn't budge we send up this pouch . . . and get them to flood down again."

The water was now up to their waists and swirling in a relentless flood. "No bloody heroics, right . . . let's just do the job . . . okay?" The water pressed in on their diaphragms, tugging at their already unsteady breathing. They quickly put on their nose-clips and inserted their mouthpieces as the water tumbled and frothed against the walls and finally submerged them.

Hanley knelt down and picked up the hammer and crowbar, then kicked himself up towards the outside hatch. He could see Terry beside him in the murky water and handed him the crowbar. Then he undid the clip and pushed the hatch. It did not move!

He pushed again, harder and harder, levering himself by lodging his feet against the side of the chamber, but still to no avail. He paused for breath and then swung back the hammer and delivered a number of slow but steady blows to the metal. The resistance of the water was infuriating. His movements had the liquid smoothness of a dream. Elegant but futile. He paused again and then in one last, wild, angry gesture struck another blow. Unbelievably the hatch opened! The light flooded in and he felt a glorious surge of joy. He kicked himself further up the chamber and pushed it again, but once more it had stuck. This time, at about five inches.

Hanley sank down for a moment. He was thinking better now that he had the oxygen from the DSEA. Whether they got out or not, he should let loose the waterproof packet now. He unstrapped it from his waist and immediately felt the buoyancy of the cork float, wrapped inside. He reached up and squeezed it through the narrow opening, sending it on its way to the surface.

Terry was already beside him and had slid one end of the crowbar towards the narrowest wedge of the hatch opening. Then he leaned back and tugged on the other end of it. It moved barely an inch. He quickly swung the crowbar round to the wedge at the other side of the hatch and once more heaved down on it. For a second or two nothing happened, then the hatch suddenly gave under the pressure and slammed open. Terry fell backwards into the chamber and the crowbar tumbled down behind him.

Hanley could scarcely believe it, they were free. There was the surface of the water rippling in sunlight, just twenty odd feet above them. He signalled to Terry and was about to kick himself out of the hatch when he looked back. The boy was lying motionless at the bottom of the chamber with the crowbar beside his head. Blood was gently drifting upwards from him in a thin, mistlike, red stain.

Hanley hauled himself backwards to the bottom. The tube had fallen from Terry's mouth and Hanley quickly jammed it back in between his teeth. The boy seemed to choke and groggily opened his eyes. Hanley grabbed him under the arms and hauled him upwards.

At the top of the chamber, he got beneath Terry and started to push him through the hatch. As he did, he could see that Terry was helping as well as he could, gripping the rim of the hatch and pulling. Finally, with both of their efforts, Terry made it through and Hanley quickly followed.

Outside, Terry floated near the hull, disoriented, his hand clutching the wound on his head. But Hanley had seen the daylight above and it gave him the will and strength to act for both of them. He edged over towards the boy, grabbed him around the chest and kicked hard, driving both of them towards the surface and the sun.

Back inside the *Graplin*, the mood was once more optimistic and they were already preparing for the next pair to go. The escape

311

chamber was closed and drained as quickly and as safely as possible. In the meantime Lieutenant Commander Crowe sent Lieutenant Farnsworth and Chief Petty Officer Boyle back to the control room to make all the preparations necessary to pump air back into the flooded for'ard compartments. This was of course all contingent on a diver closing the outside cover of number-five torpedo tube. But surely, they all thought, that would be soon, now that Hanley had made it up to the top!

Chief Stoker Mitchell and a young electrician called Greene were next. Gillings lay back against the edge of number-five bulkhead door and watched. He noticed that the young man looked distracted, almost desperate, his hands clasping and unclasping like dry pumps. For a moment Gillings thought of stepping forward and suggesting that Greene wait for a while, perhaps move back a place until he had calmed down. But even as he formed the thought a great sense of lethargy swept over him and it seemed more important to lie still and husband every breath.

The hatch closed and within seconds he heard the gurgling hiss of the water as the flood valve was opened. He felt a deep sense of joy now that Terry was safely gone. He knew that he himself was about tenth down the list. Another five openings and he would be speeding up to the surface. Or maybe by then a diver would have come down. He slowly went over the options in his mind, like someone recounting the day's events just before sleep. They could attach a hose to the whistle connection on the bridge and pump high-pressure air on board . . . they could . . .

A strange noise shook him out of his reverie. It sounded as if the aft hatch was being opened, the one that led into the stokers' mess. Gillings catapulted to his feet and staggered over the coaming of the bulkhead door towards the aft-facing entrance of the escape chamber. For a moment he had to close his eyes as he felt a hammerlike pulse, thumping at the back of his neck. His head was reeling with an excruciating pain. A headache brought on by the carbon dioxide poisoning. He grabbed for the pipes along the wall and tried to steady himself. The grinding noise continued and now he knew for certain that the wheel of the hatch mechanism was being spun to the open position from inside the escape chamber.

In the few remaining seconds the frightening explanation formed in his mind. The outside hatch had jammed again . . . someone in the chamber had panicked . . . desperate, they wanted to get back into the boat . . .

Gillings staggered towards the hatch lever and had barely slipped his fingers round it, when it was suddenly wrenched away. An angry wall of frothing grey water exploded in his face and flung him backwards towards the stokers' mess. The flood valve was still open and the sea poured in unobstructed. Within seconds the dark, surging tide had swirled across the deck and was cascading downhill, over the coaming of the bulkhead, carrying all before it.

In a last desperate effort Gillings attempted to stagger against the raging water and slam back the hatch. After a few steps, the body of young Greene sluiced out of the chamber and hit Gillings head on. His legs buckled under the blow and with a final gasp of air he collapsed into the icy torrent.

Gillings' last thought was the kitchen at home, a teapot steaming, the smell of toast. Walking up behind Irene, slipping his arms around her and squeezing her. Tight . . . tight!

He felt his throat closing with the pressure and then there was darkness.

42

Hanley wandered slowly away from the front door of the dockyard chapel towards the gaudily painted ship's figurehead at the end of the path. On either side, the crowd gently nudged their way past him until he finally realised he was in the way, stepped back on to the grass and stood under one of the trees.

He stared at the grief-stricken faces of the crowd as they passed. They were the families of the dockyard workers and submariners, lives ruined for ever by miscalculations and bad luck and human weakness.

Hanley stiffened. No. He couldn't travel down that route again. He had to stop, place the tragedy behind him. There was nothing more that could be done now.

Back through the crowd, towards the door of the church, he saw Eunice standing with Nigel. He could see her awkwardness as she addressed the officers and wives who passed her, and he felt sorry for her. She was obviously an alien in these yards, an alien in this Navy, in his life. She looked up, sought him out in the crowd and then started towards him.

"Daddy."

Elizabeth was standing beside the path with Terry Gillings. Terry looked tired and shaken. He had a bandage around his forehead and bruises around his eye, yet he managed a half-smile and a nod. Hanley nodded his response, but a wealth of shared understanding went with it. There was a bond there that two humans rarely shared. A bond sealed on the edges of life and death.

Then Hanley noticed Irene Gillings on the path behind Terry. Her shoulders sagged and she was holding on to Kitty's arm. She glanced at him and Hanley was staggered to see the change in her. He had met Irene Gillings at a number of ship's launchings, but this was another woman, a shadow of that person.

He immediately walked over to her and took her hand. The deadness in her eyes did not lift, but there was a glimmer of recognition.

"I'm so sorry, Mrs Gillings. So sorry . . ."

Irene nodded her head and then replied in a flat unemotional voice, "Thank you. Thank you."

Hanley sucked in a deep breath and searched his mind but he knew that there were no words to help her.

"I think we should move on, sir, go home." Terry stepped forward and firmly took his mother's other arm.

Hanley nodded and watched the sad party making its way through the crowd, up towards the dockyard gates.

"I'd like to go with them, Dad. Terry would like it."

"Of course . . ."

Elizabeth stretched up and kissed him warmly on the cheek. As she did, he could see the tears welling in her eyes. He pulled her back and whispered in her ear, "I'm proud of you."

She nodded as if to say, I know. And that certainty of his love made him feel somehow whole.

He watched as Elizabeth walked down the path past the ship's figurehead and joined the Gillings. It was the ending of a chapter and the beginning of another, not one he could ever have predicted.

"James?"

Eunice was standing just beside him, and Nigel was tactfully lingering a few steps behind both of them. She flashed him a nervous flicker of a smile and continued, "I thought I'd say goodbye."

"Yes, yes."

She extended her hand. He took it, and for a brief moment they once again sensed the pulse of each other's bodies. It was perhaps the last time and they both knew it. Finally Eunice stood back. "I'll go to London. I'll leave from there tomorrow." She paused and caught her breath. "Let's write and be . . . well friendly."

"Of course."

Eunice quickly turned and walked away. Hanley watched her and then heard Nigel's footsteps behind him.

"I'll, eh, I'll be home later, Dad."

"Yes."

Nigel nodded and walked away. Soon both of them were lost in the crowd. Hanley stood there for a while and felt a great sense of depression sweeping over him.

Then he stirred himself. He must do something, something. He stepped forward. Home. No, he couldn't go home, not yet. After all, what was there? He walked to the end of the path and then took a sharp right turn by the side of the church. He would go to his office, absorb himself in work. The whole mess of

315

Grainger and the radar had to be confronted. Now they would try it on the new T-class submarine they had in number-seven covered slip.

A car honked its horn beside him and he glanced over. Captain Marsh had pulled up in a black Wolseley and rolled down the window. Hanley stopped.

"Sorry, Hanley, I seem to have missed the service. Come on, get in and I'll drive you down to the office."

Though he disliked Marsh intensely, he was relieved to see him. Marsh at least provided the possibility of some real diversion, some relief from his depression.

As they drove down the hill, Marsh said quietly, "By the way, your story about Warrant Officer Campbell checks out. It's tragic but it does clear your wife."

"Did you ever doubt that it wouldn't 'check out'?"

Marsh didn't answer but he gave one of his thin-lipped smiles.

Hanley could feel his anger building. But then he shrugged. What was the point? The man would never change. "And what are you going to do about that Eddie Brent person?"

Marsh pulled the car over into a parking place just opposite the admiral's private offices and turned off the engine.

"Nothing."

"Pardon?" Hanley almost choked on the word.

"Nothing." Marsh turned and stared at Hanley, a cold, penetrating look. "He's useful, he's always been useful."

"What the hell does that mean?"

"It means the file's closed. It stays with Naval Intelligence."

Marsh turned in his seat and opened the car door. He was just about to get out when Hanley grabbed him by the arm.

"You don't brush me off like that, Marsh, not after what I've been through." Hanley's face was rigid, his jaw clenched.

Marsh slowly sank back into the seat. "It's simple, Hanley. If it wasn't Brent it would be somebody else. When we know he's the pipeline, it's easier to spot the slime that crawls towards him."

Hanley let go of his arm and Marsh got out of the car. "You coming in then?"

316

Hanley shook his head and said slowly, "I'll be over in a while. I need some fresh air."

He watched Marsh walking around the side of the building and then got out of the car himself. It was Sunday. The yards were quite empty. He would walk. Just walk. That was it. It was one way of clearing the taste of Marsh out of his mouth.

Kitty stood by the window of her flat and looked down across the dockyards to the Medway. She could scarcely believe that her Uncle Albert was dead. She knew that the service was to mourn him and all of the others, but it still made no sense.

She glanced at her watch. She would have to go round to the Gillings soon. She had only called in at home to get some money for her mother. Kitty opened the drawer in the table beside the bed and pulled out two ten-shilling notes. Then she sank down on the bed and gave a sigh. Even if she did not understand this catastrophe, she knew that she could be of use to the Gillings family. She didn't hear the first knock at the door, but then she heard Nigel calling her name.

"Hello." He was standing in the hall, looking shy and disconsolate.

"Hello . . . I saw you at the church with your mother. Come in."

He walked inside and gazed around awkwardly. "It looks like a nice place."

"How did you know I lived here?"

"I made some enquiries at the Parrot."

"Oh."

They stood facing each other in an uncomfortable silence. Then Kitty pointed into her bed-sitting-room. "I suppose you'd better come in."

They walked inside and she pulled a chair over to the table. Then she drew back the curtain across her kitchenette. "I can make you a cup of tea if you like."

Nigel hesitated in the middle of the room. He ran his hand nervously through his dark hair and then smiled at her. "Look, it's all right Kitty . . . I just want to talk."

He stepped forward and gripped the back of one of the chairs,

317

squeezing and unsqueezing it in an uncharacteristic display of nerves. "I came to say I'm sorry, Kitty. I miss you."

She felt her heart skip a beat as he said it. "I miss you too. But it's too late, this place belongs to Eddie Brent, you understand."

Nigel nodded. He had already heard about her and Eddie Brent.

"And anyway," she continued, "what's the use? Your mother'd only stop you again."

"My mother's leaving. She's going to Germany."

"Oh. Is that why you're here then?"

"Maybe. I don't know, I don't know." He slid down into the chair and cupped his head in his hands. "I shouldn't have come. I'm sorry."

Kitty stood for a while running her hands along the edge of the cold sink. Nigel looked beaten, like a little boy who was lost and had for a moment found a warm refuge. She stared at him for a long time and then slowly, almost imperceptibly, drifted over towards him. What did it matter about Eddie? There was no reason that she could not have two men in her life. Especially when she was in control.

She ran her hands through Nigel's dark hair and drew him towards her breasts. He turned, surprised, and then pressed his cheek against the smooth roundness of her blouse. She could see the tears glistening in his eyes and she knew that she was right. She was mistress of her own fate now. Damn what others thought!

Hanley walked towards Thunderbolt Pier and then stood staring out at the river. He felt angry, tired, empty. Everything seemed to be in vain. Everything he had worked for, everything he had hoped for in his family. All in vain.

He took out his pipe and lit it, then watched the blue smoke drift lazily upwards, undisturbed by any wind. As he glanced along the skyline he noticed a gleam way down to his right. He watched as it got larger and larger until he finally recognised it as a Gloster Gladiator. It zoomed down low over the basins and even this far away he could hear the siren on the C-class cruiser as it whirred into action.

The noise echoed past the dry docks and the factory, over the boilermaker's shop and the mast ponds and on through the massive covered slips. The whole yard seemed filled with the ominous sound and it sent a chill through him. It was just a trial, a test of the new systems, but somehow it said everything he needed to hear. He was there to be on guard, to wait, to prepare for attack. That was his job, no, more, his duty. There was no room for depression, no room for personal displays of anguish. For him there could be no failure, only unending service.

He looked out over the river and took a deep breath of the sweet, salt air.